THE THREE KINGS

Doris Davidson is a retired primary school teacher living in Aberdeen. She has been writing novels since 1984, although *The Brow of the Gallowgate* was the first to be published – in 1990. Her married daughter is a civil servant and lives in Surrey, but her son, an art teacher, also lives in Aberdeen, and presented her with a grandson in 1987.

DORIS DAVIDSON

The Three Kings

HarperCollins*Publishers*

HarperCollins*Publishers*
77–85 Fulham Palace Road,
Hammersmith, London w6 8jb

A Paperback Original 1996
1 3 5 7 9 8 6 4 2

A catalogue record for this book is
available from the British Library

Set in Sabon by Rowland Phototypesetting Limited
Bury St Edmunds, Suffolk

Printed in Great Britain

For Lillias and Ted,
who brought the Three Kings back to my memory
and sparked off the idea for this book.

My thanks to Alex Thomson and his aunt
for their help.

1907

She was thankful that the moon was obscured by clouds. She had waited until well after midnight before setting off on the most agonizing errand she had ever undertaken in all her seventeen years, but there was little more than an hour between sunset and sunrise on the Moray Firth at this time of year.

Her furtive glances behind would have made any observer think that she was up to no good – no decent lassie would be abroad at ten to one in the morning – but he or she would have been very much mistaken. Although she was anxious not to be seen, she had no evil purpose in mind. Coming to the end of her mile-long journey, she set her burden on the step of the house she had vowed never to enter again, but at the stopping of the motion, a weedy mew issued from the basket.

'Hush, my bairnie,' she whispered, alarmed that someone might hear, but she could not stop the soft moan that was wrung out of her. 'Oh, littl'un, I hope you'll forgi'e your mother some day.'

First making sure that the note was still pinned to the shawl, she whipped round and ran back up the hill, her heart tight with grief, her eyes stinging with unshed tears.

PART ONE

Chapter One

✤✤

1922

'I could kill her for this!'

Having said the words fairly loudly, Katie Mair took a guilty glance around her, and was thankful that no one else was in sight. It was only April, of course; too early for the summer visitors who came to Cullen every year. Though she would be fifteen years old in two months, she was so used to talking aloud to the Three Kings that she sometimes forgot they were only rocks. 'But not ordinary rocks,' she assured them, hastily, to avoid giving offence.

Nobody could argue with that, she thought, sitting down on the ground to admire them: two rearing out of the shingle but below the high-tide mark and the third surrounded by grass. Granda had once told her that their name had evolved from the legendary three kings of Cologne, and that long, long ago, some local wit had referred to them as the Three Kings of Cullen and the name had stuck. But she had always thought of them as the three kings from the Bible – the wise men – which was why she had come to them with her troubles ever since she was very young.

They towered over her now, yet when she saw them from the harbour wall, they reminded her of three hunched men who had run out of the sea shedding small pieces of themselves in their hurry to reach dry land before being surrounded by the incoming tide. When the water was swirling gently, she could imagine that they had emerged from a peaceful bathe and left a trail of rocky footprints in their wake. She knew it was silly, but when the waves were churning and frothing in a frenzy, she believed that her 'friends' were foaming at the

5

mouth, that they were as angry as she was at something her grandmother had said. The best time of all was when the sea was mirror-still and she could feel a calmness stealing over her, too, as if they were soothing away her troubles.

Only an occasional ripple stirred the water tonight, and the three outlines stood out starkly against the last feeble rays of the sun, fast disappearing beneath the horizon, so she felt that they shared her sorrow.

'I didn't really mean I'd kill Grandma.' She spoke softly, apologetically, now, 'but I get so mad at her. She's never wanted me, and she only took me in because there was nobody else to have me. You'd think she'd be sorry for me being an orphan from birth, but she doesn't care tuppence. She could hardly wait till I was fourteen and she could put me into service.'

A small sob escaped her, and it was a few moments before she could carry on. 'It wasn't so bad when I was with the doctor's wife. Mrs Fleming's always been very nice to me, and I could get home every night, but now I'm being sent miles and miles away, and I'll maybe never see you again.'

Dashing a tear away with her fingers, Katie got to her feet and stood with head bowed as the darkness closed in on her, and when she looked up all she could see were three uneven shadows. With a shiver, she turned to walk home.

She was hardly inside the house when her grandmother said, 'I suppose you've been along the shore again?' Her voice was so sharp it sounded as if she were accusing the girl of some wicked sin, and William John winked sympathetically at his young grand-daughter. 'It's her last night,' he reminded his wife, 'so she's likely been saying goodbye to the sea.'

Tutting testily, the elderly woman snapped, 'Goodbye to the sea! You're as bad as her wi' your nonsense! Drink that milk, Katie, as long as it's hot, and then get through to your bed, for you've to be up early in the morning.'

As she lifted the cup, Katie watched Mary Ann taking the teapot off the hob at the fireside and going to empty it down the drain in the back yard, her black skirt showing less than an inch of her gun-metal lisle stockings. Her hair, a yellowing white, was dragged into a knot behind her head, her back was as straight as the pole the leary used for lighting the street lamps in the town, her bosom seemed to run in a great curve from her neck right to the top of her legs, with no waistline to break it up. She could have been a model for Lewis Carroll's Red Queen, except that the effect was spoiled by the loud squeak that accompanied each step she took.

'Her stays are creaking better,' William John whispered, and, as he had hoped, Katie's mouth broke into an unwilling smile. 'You'll be fine,' he went on, 'dinna worry. She . . .' here he inclined his head to the door through which his wife had vanished, '. . . was in service when I ken't her first, and if you turn out as good a housewife as her, you'll do fine.' His eyes twinkled again. 'As long as you dinna end up with her tongue.'

Katie was forced to giggle at this. 'And I hope I don't end up with a mouthful of gums like her, either.'

About to say something about his wife's toothlessness, William John heard her coming back and changed his mind. 'Come on, then, Katie lass, off to bed wi' you. Tomorrow'll be here afore we ken where we are.'

Katie wished them both goodnight and went into her own room. The box containing her clothes was on the floor behind the door – in the morning, her grandfather would lift it on to the cart he was hiring from Rennie, the carrier, to take her to the Howe of Fenty – and the sight of it reminded her that there would be nothing of her left here. Grandma would throw out the old clothes she was wearing today – after they had been washed, of course.

Surprisingly, she slept well, and woke resigned to her fate. She was not the only one who had to work away from home. Only a few of the girls she had known at school had found employment locally; some had taken to following the herring fleet, but some, like herself, had been sent into service in another place, and they seemed happy enough any time she

7

saw them. It was just . . . from what she had gathered, the Howe of Fenty was an awful long way away.

Lifting her spoon, she stole a glance at her grandfather. His hair, silver-white, was curling over the tips of his ears and Grandma would likely be nagging at him soon to have it cut. Katie, however, preferred it the way it was now, for it suited him better. His cheeks were ruddy from working out in the yard in all weathers, and when he turned suddenly and caught her looking at him, the compassion in his fading blue eyes made her heart swell with love for him.

Her last spoonful of porridge was hardly into her mouth when William John said, 'Are you ready, then, Katie lass?'

Being only six o'clock on an April morning, it was still quite dark when she climbed up on the cart and waited for him to load her 'kist' of clothes. There was no sorrow in her as she bade goodbye to her grandmother, who grunted, caustically, 'Mind and do everything you're told, now.'

It was not a fond farewell, but Katie was too intent on storing the familiar features of the house in her memory to notice. A one-storeyed building with an attic, like most of those in Seatown – the part of Cullen where the fisherfolk lived – its gable end was towards the sea, raised pointing picking out the shapes of the stones with which it was built, and white-painted cement blocks ornamenting the edges of the door and the two front windows. She would keep it all in her mind and take it out if she felt homesick, which would be every day, more than likely. She heaved a shivery sigh as her grandfather sat down beside her.

'I'll be back some time the morrow,' he told his wife, then clicked his tongue to the horse.

Katie turned back to look at the gaping arches of the long railway viaduct spanning the Burn of Cullen. They didn't look so friendly in the early morning as they did when the sun was shining, so she let her eyes move to the right, but she caught only a glimpse of her three beloved rocks before they were hidden from her view.

The horse plodded up the narrow alley between the houses, and they turned left when they reached the main road, on up the steep hill of Seafield Street, passing under one of the arches of the other viaduct, which separated the huddle of small cottages from the rest of Cullen. It was a long haul for the poor mare, but William John let her take it easy, and it did not take long to reach the open countryside, with the sea on their left, though she could only see it when the moon broke through the clouds. They had not gone far before they turned right into a side road and were leaving Cullen Bay and the Moray Firth behind. She was glad that her grandfather kept silent, for her heart was too full for her to hold a conversation. She did not know exactly where their destination lay, but they were going farther and farther inland, and she would never be able to walk to the sea on her times off. She would never smell the tangle on the shore again, never sit on the harbour wall with her feet dangling over the water splashing against it.

They were well over half an hour into their journey before William John spoke, having obviously given her time to get over her sadness at leaving home. 'I'm sure the Gunns'll be decent folk, Katie lass, if Mrs Cunn's anything like her sister. There's nae a finer woman in the whole parish than Mrs Taylor.'

Katie was not inclined to be charitable at that moment. 'Sisters aren't always the same, and Mrs Taylor's got to be nice when she's married to a minister. Do you know what Mr Gunn does for a living?'

'He's got his own shop and it must be doing well if he can afford to pay for a maidservant for his wife. I think you're the first she's had, so she'll likely feel a bit strange wi' you, but as long as you do what she tells you, she'll have nae reason to get angry at you.'

'Grandma gets angry at me for nothing,' Katie pouted.

'It's just the way she's made. She's nae the kind to show affection, but it's there.'

9

'No it's not. She doesn't like me.'

'Nay, lass, you're wrong there.'

'She's sending me away, isn't she? Why couldn't she have left me at the doctor's? I was happy there.'

'She thought it would do you good to get away from Cullen, and she didna want you having anything to do with the fish.'

'I didn't fancy going to the fish myself. I wanted to stay with Mrs Fleming.'

'Your Grandma wanted you to meet different folk, nae just the fisher folk, and she thought you'd be better wi' a lady like Mrs Gunn.'

Leaning back and letting the mare go ahead in her own time, William John laid his rough hand over the small smooth one. 'I ken it's hard for you to leave us, Katie lass, but we'll aye be thinking on you, and wondering how you're going on. Never forget that.'

'Maybe you will, but Grandma . . .'

'So'll she, I'm telling you. Now, just cheer up so we can enjoy the scenery. I havena been so far from hame since I was a young laddie.'

'Where did you go?'

'Me and some other lads went to Aberdeen, but I wouldna like to bide there, it's ower big for me, and the lassies . . . well, they looked doon their noses at us rough lads.'

'Did you ever have another lass besides Grandma?'

'Not a one. The minute I saw her, I ken't she was the one for me, she was that bonnie.'

This came as a surprise to Katie. It was difficult for her to visualize Mary Ann as a pretty young girl. 'Why did she not get false teeth when she lost her own ones?'

'She wouldna go and see about it.'

'She wouldn't look so bad if she'd teeth.'

William John gave a sheepish laugh. 'I can still picture her like she was . . .'

'Did you love her, Granda?'

'Aye, I did that, and you'll maybe nae believe this, but I

still feel something for her.' He grinned suddenly. 'That's when she's nae going on at me for messing up the place.'

Katie smiled in sympathy. Her grandmother was very house proud, and made sure that no dirt was brought in on feet or on hands. 'When I've got a house of my own, I won't go mad if anybody messes it up.'

'You'll feel different when it's your own place. It'll be a good while yet before you're old enough to get wed, but I hope you'll pick a good man when the time comes.'

'I'll look for somebody like you, Granda.'

'When love strikes you, you'll nae care what he's like – buck teeth, hook nose, cross eyes . . .'

'Oh, I could never love anybody like that.'

'I was only joking, but I'll tell you what I mean. I aye hankered after a wife wi' fair hair and your Grandma had brown hair like you, but her eyes were that blue – just the same as yours – I fell in love wi' her straight away. You canna plan that kind o' thing, you see, nae when Cupid fires his dart at you, and I've never been sorry I wedded her.'

When William John fell silent, Katie pondered over what she would expect in a future husband. He would have to be tall and handsome like Granda, that was one thing, but she wouldn't care what colour his hair or eyes were as long as she loved him and he loved her. She tried to think if any of the boys who had been at school with her would fit the bill, but the only one she had ever liked was George Buchan, and he hadn't been any taller than she was, and not all that handsome, though he'd had something about him . . . Still, she might meet the right person once she was away from Cullen. Maybe that was what Grandma wanted for her. The Gunns might have sons who took their friends home . . .

Katie brought her conjectures to an abrupt stop. If there did happen to be any young Gunns, they certainly wouldn't take any notice of a servant girl like her. 'How far have we to go now?' she asked.

'A fair bit still.'

When he judged it appropriate, William John said, 'We'll stop here and gi'e the mare a wee rest, and we can stretch our legs a bit.'

She jumped nimbly on to the stony road and waited until he made his stiff descent, then she slipped her hand into his as if she were still a little girl and they strolled along together, while the horse nibbled at the grass verge. After about ten minutes, William John let out a long gusty breath. 'We'd best get on, lass.'

When they were back on the cart, he took a paper bag from his pocket and held it out to Katie, who helped herself to one of the thick slices of bread Mary Ann had buttered for them, and one of the chunks of cheese. As he took a share, William John laughed, 'It wouldna do if your belly's rumbling when you meet Mrs Gunn.' Taking a huge mouthful, he picked up the reins with his free hand and gave the horse a gentle flick.

Over the next two hours, he regaled Katie with tales of his youth, which, although she had heard them all before, made her almost forget why they were together on the strange road. Then he stopped again to give a nosebag of oats to the mare and to let them exercise their numb legs. 'It's a good thing it's a dry day,' he observed, squeezing the hand that had slid into his. 'There's nothing worse than going into somebody else's house wi' the water dripping off you.'

Getting no reply, he said, gently, 'Oh, lass, it'll nae be as bad as you think. I'd never have let her put you to the Howe o' Fenty if I thought . . .'

'I'm scared, Granda.'

'Ah, my wee dearie, there's nothing to be scared at. Mrs Gunn canna eat you.' Katie giving a tremulous smile, he went on, 'Once you get the first day in, you'll feel as easy wi' her as you did wi' Mrs Fleming.'

'I suppose so . . . but what if Mr Gunn's not so nice as the doctor?'

'He will be, and any road, you'll nae see much o' him.'

Katie was satisfied with that. She hadn't seen much of

Doctor Fleming, and it would be the same with Mr Gunn, so it wouldn't matter what he was like. 'Is there any bread and cheese left, Granda?'

Her grandfather grinned. 'That's my lass.'

They sat down by the side of the road to eat the last of what Mary Ann had given them, then after removing the mare's nosebag, they climbed aboard the cart again and carried on in companionable silence.

Over an hour and a half passed before William John pointed to a large farm on their right. 'That must be Rennie's cousin's place. He said he aye stops there the night if he's been to Huntly, for it's ower far for the horse to go there and back in the one day. He said I'd recognize it by the crooked lum and the three whitewashed outhouses at one side, and the stables at the other side.'

'Will you be sleeping there tonight, Granda? Is that why you told Grandma you wouldn't see her till tomorrow?'

'It'll be the first night I've ever spent away from her since the day we were made man and wife.'

Only a quarter of an hour later, they saw a signpost to the Howe of Fenty, and Katie's throat tightened as the cart turned into the bumpy track. It was late afternoon now, and the sun was shining brightly, but the thick wood on each side of them gave the place an eerie, unearthly atmosphere, and she hoped that the house itself would be more welcoming.

William John turned to her with a lop-sided smile which told her that he, too, was finding it hard to keep cheerful. 'I'm going to miss you, Katie lass.'

The soft-spoken words were almost her undoing. 'I'll miss you and all, Granda,' she gulped, fighting back her tears, for she couldn't let her new mistress see her weeping.

When the house came into view, a wave of disappointment swept over her. She had pictured a big imposing mansion and there was nothing imposing about this place. It wasn't even all that big – a tall, square, forbidding building with four chimneys, only one of which was smoking – and when they went round the side, she saw that it was built on the bank of a river. Her grandfather drew the horse to a halt outside the back door. 'Write and let us ken how you get on, lass, and mind, say if something's bothering you and you dinna like it, and I'll come as quick as I can to take you hame again.'

'Grandma wouldn't be pleased. She's glad to see the back of me.'

'Nay, lass, she'll miss you as much as me.'

Although she found this impossible to believe, she jumped to the ground without arguing, and her grandfather got off to lift down her box. 'I'll not wait,' he said, gruffly, laying it on the doorstep then spinning round and getting up on the cart. He held his silver head erect while he turned the mare, and kept a smile on his face when he waved to her, but as she watched the cart going back up the track, she saw his shoulders slumping and knew he felt just as miserable as she did.

She was about to knock timidly on the blue door when it was opened. 'You'll be Katie,' Mrs Gunn smiled. 'Was that your grandfather? What a nice-looking man, but he should have waited and I'd have given him something to eat.'

Katie's icy heart warmed to her. 'He's getting lodgings at a farm back the road a bit, and stabling for the horse. Um, where'll I put my kist, Mrs Gunn?'

'Just leave it there and Sammy'll take it up to your room for you.'

Presuming that Sammy was the gardener or the odd-job man, Katie left the box where it was and followed her employer into the kitchen. She seemed a nice woman, though she did look as if a puff of wind would blow her away.

Mrs Gunn gestured for her to be seated. 'I've always done everything myself, but I'm not very strong, and I'm finding it a bit too much. I'll carry on doing the cooking, because my husband's fussy about his food, and I'll do the dusting and maybe some polishing, but I'll leave you to do the heavy cleaning and the washing and ironing. I hope that won't be too much for you?'

'Oh, no, I'll manage that.' As she said it, Katie had a moment's panic, wondering how many rooms there were and how many people she would be expected to wash for.

'My husband and I always eat in the dining room . . .' Mrs Gunn broke off with a nervous giggle. 'Angus likes to make out we're better off than we are, and he speaks about the dining room, but it's really just this end of the parlour. Anyway, you'll serve our meals in there – that'll save me having to shuttle back and forth like I've always done – and you'll take yours in here with Sammy. There are two bedrooms on the middle floor, so that's just four rooms to do, though I'll expect you to keep your own room clean . . . I've put you in one of the garrets. You won't have to bother about the other one, it's never used.'

Mrs Gunn drained her teacup and leaned back. 'You'd better unpack first, then you can do some of the ironing. It's been lying quite a while, because I haven't felt up to tackling it, and I couldn't face washing last week, so you'll have to do it tomorrow. I'll leave you to find your room on your own . . . the stairs take too much out of me . . . it's the second door on the top landing.'

The steps of the first flight were wide and shallow, but those to the garrets were narrow and steep, and, young and fit as she was, Katie was puffing by the time she reached the top. She found that her room was smaller than she had been used to, and had no fireplace, but there was a low chest of drawers and a high single bed with a flowered quilt. At one side of the bed there was a wooden chair, and at the other a small table holding a candlestick and a box of matches. Although the only window was a small skylight in the roof, the sun was streaming in, so she gave a grunt of satisfaction and opened the lid of her box.

As she hung her skirts and blouses in the cupboard in the corner, Katie wondered when Sammy, whatever his position here, had taken her box in, for he hadn't come through the kitchen. He must have taken it in by the front door, which

15

seemed a bit senseless when it meant he had to carry it all the way round. Still, she shouldn't care, as long as it was here. After laying her underclothes and stockings neatly in the drawers, she went down to begin her duties.

Mrs Gunn was preparing vegetables, but told her where to find the iron. 'Angus doesn't come home for dinner until half past six,' she went on, 'so we need not set the table just yet. Now, about your time off, Katie. There's really nothing to do round here, we're so far off the beaten track, and even a half-day wouldn't be long enough for you to walk into Huntly and back and give you time to do anything when you're there. As for going to Cullen . . . well, you won't be able to afford the fare very often, and you'd have to go to Huntly first and change trains at Keith, in any case, and they don't run at very convenient times . . . so . . .'

She eyed the girl a little uncertainly. 'I don't know how you'll feel about this, but I thought . . .' She stopped again with an apologetic smile. 'I believe most ladies give their maids an hour off every week and a Sunday afternoon once a month, but I am offering you a long weekend off every six months. Friday, Saturday and Sunday, and I wouldn't expect you back until the Monday, by the first train you can get. Do you think that is fair?'

Ignorant as she was of how much free time a live-in maid should expect, Katie still felt somewhat cheated – she'd had every Sunday off in her last position – and to make sure that she had not misunderstood, she asked, 'You mean I won't have any time off till October?'

Mrs Gunn seemed slightly uncomfortable. 'It'll be more suitable for both of us. As I explained, you couldn't go home and back in one day. Do you understand?'

Remembering that a servant was in no position to argue or negotiate, Katie gave a bleak nod. 'Yes, thank you.' After all, she thought, some employers would make no allowance for the difficulty she would have in getting home.

The woman beamed in some relief. 'That's settled, then.'

She was much younger than Katie had expected, under forty, by the look of her, though her face was pale and there was a sadness about her eyes at times. Her fair hair, greying and dull, was coiled into earphones which didn't suit her, and she had worry lines on her forehead, yet she seemed quite friendly. Accustomed to the sharp orders and reprimands dished out by her grandmother, Katie had been delighted when her first employer treated her as a person, not as somebody who should jump to her bidding, and her fears that Mrs Gunn would be different had vanished within seconds of meeting the woman, though she had a nerve expecting any maid to work so long without time off.

Satisfied with her arrangements, Mrs Gunn began to chatter again. 'Angus has a business in Huntly.' She gave another of her nervous giggles. 'Well, he calls it his business, but it's just a small clothing shop, though he makes a decent living from it. He used to cycle the five miles every day until he bought the motor car about six months ago. I've never been in it myself, I'm too scared, but he's very proud of it. Not many shopkeepers in Huntly have one yet, and I think it makes him feel . . . superior.'

To Katie, Angus Gunn sounded as though he had ideas above himself, but she didn't like to say so, and Mrs Gunn was asking her a question. 'How long have you lived with your grandparents?'

'Grandma told me my father, her son, was lost at sea not long before I was born, and my mother died giving birth to me. There weren't any other relations, so she took me.'

'Oh, how tragic, but you were lucky that your grandmother was willing to have you, otherwise you could have been sent to an orphanage.'

Katie had never thought of that, but she dismissed the idea and screwed up her nose. 'She only took me because she thought it was her duty.'

'Nonsense! I'm sure she loves you, though it couldn't have been easy for her to cope with an infant at her age.'

17

This was another thought new to Katie, but she had no time to consider it because Mrs Gunn was still prattling on. 'I'm glad I only had one child. Sammy's a bit backward, you see, and he was a lot of work when he was younger. Of course, he's seventeen now, and able to work in the garden and do little jobs about the house. Angus blames me for Sammy's ... handicap, but he can be most unstable himself at times. He always had a quick temper, and he has been much worse since he got the head wound in the war ... shrapnel, you know, and I'm sure they didn't get it all out. He was invalided out of the Scottish Horse and he has never got over the shame. I am sometimes quite afraid of him.' Stopping in embarrassment, she said, 'But you don't want to hear about my troubles.'

Katie had heard enough to make her apprehensive of what went on there, and was glad of the silence that followed. She would get on all right with Mrs Gunn, but how would she fare with Sammy – who had turned out to be the son of the house – and his father? She didn't like the sound of either of them.

At five o'clock, she was told to light the fire in the parlour, and at six she had to set the table in the dining end, her employer saying as she supervised, 'Angus prefers to help himself, so put everything in serving dishes.'

Katie was not impressed with Mr Gunn when she saw him. In direct contrast to his wife's petite fairness, he was tall and dark. Everything about him was dark – skin, hair, eyes and lowering eyebrows – even his suit and tie. Despite his long face having the beginnings of jowls, she thought that he would probably be classed as handsome by some women, but he didn't appeal to her. She felt quite disconcerted when he looked at her with a weird smile, and was extremely thankful when he went out again as soon as he had eaten.

While she did not take such an instant dislike to Sammy, she was uneasy when she sat with him at the kitchen table. He, too, was tall, but it was a gangling tallness, as though his bones had never hardened. His hair was a shade lighter than his father's and grew at several different angles from his head. His round face was fresh-complexioned and still little-boyish, and it was only too evident that he was 'one o' God's bairns', as her grandmother described such poor unfortunates in her better moods. His intent stare unnerved Katie, and when she asked him if he wanted more potatoes, he just wobbled his head from side to side and kept on staring at her, so she was most relieved when he rose from the table and disappeared through the back door.

Utterly exhausted when she finished tidying the kitchen, she went up to her room, reflecting, as she undressed, that she would never come much in contact with Mr Gunn, nor with Sammy, but, even so, she didn't think she would ever feel happy at the Howe of Fenty. And it was miles from anywhere, at the back of beyond. So much for her grandmother's hope that she would meet different people. The three Gunns were the only folk she would ever see, and she could do fine without seeing two of them again.

Wishing that she was in her old bed at home, she pulled the blankets up round her chin and the tears which had been hovering for some time came flooding out.

Chapter Two

When she and Mrs Gunn were putting on clean sheets in the second bedroom the following day, Katie tried to find out something about its occupant. 'Sammy doesn't say much,' she ventured.

Her employer gave a sad smile. 'He's scared of strangers, but he's harmless. My husband is sometimes quite hard on him – he's never got over him being . . . the way he is – so please don't say anything if you see him slapping Sammy. The boy expects to be punished if he does anything wrong.'

Katie could well imagine Mr Gunn taking his displeasure out on his son; he looked the kind of man who would take a delight in hurting others. She was somewhat surprised that Sammy didn't join his mother and her for lunch, and when he did come in, he gobbled his meal at great speed, as if he couldn't wait to go outside again to be away from them.

Dinner was a quiet affair in both kitchen and 'dining room', Mr Gunn apparently having little to say to his wife and she to him, and Sammy once more staring dourly at Katie over the table and giving his head a shake or a nod when she offered him anything. He scampered off as soon as he could, whereas Mr Gunn shifted from the table to a more comfortable chair at the other end of the parlour. He had not spoken once to Katie since she arrived, but she was conscious of him watching her while she cleared the dishes, and didn't let her eyes stray anywhere near him.

As she washed up, she reflected that things shouldn't be too bad; she would see him for half an hour in the mornings and less than an hour every night, so she could put up with that, and she got on very well with Mrs Gunn. After giving the floor a last sweep, she made sure that everything was in order then went upstairs. She would have liked to have had a short rest by the fire, but she felt safer in her own room.

Sammy remained uncommunicative over the next few days; not truculent, more distrustful, and Katie did her best to show him that she wanted to talk to him and would listen if he wanted to tell her anything. By the look of things, his mother and father didn't have much time for him. Still, however sorry she was for him, she felt it might be best not to be over-friendly.

Her pity for him was intensified when Mr Gunn came in by the back door one night and, without a word of warning, gave his son a stinging slap on the cheek. 'You left the spade out,' he thundered.

'I forgot,' Sammy muttered. 'Mother said she needed some logs and I . . .' Another slap brought him to a halt.

'No excuses, boy! You know perfectly well that tools rust if they are left out of doors overnight.'

'I won't do it again.'

'You had better not!' Mr Gunn swept past Katie and went across the hall to the dining room.

Touching the red patch on his cheek, Sammy looked at Katie and said, as if explaining his father's cruelty, 'Sammy was a bad boy.'

'Forgetting to put a spade past isn't all that bad.' She nearly added that his father shouldn't have hit him, but she didn't want to stir up more trouble between them.

She had been at the Howe of Fenty for almost two weeks – Sammy having overcome his shyness with her – when events took an unexpected, and most unwelcome, turn. Laying the tureen of soup at the side of Mr Gunn's plate, she was dismayed when he placed his hand over hers. 'I hope you have settled in, Katie?' he murmured, looking up at her with something in his eyes that spread ribbons of alarm weaving all through her.

'Yes, sir, thank you,' she muttered, not daring to remove her imprisoned member.

'That's good.' He released her then, and, drawing away, she glanced across to see if his wife had noticed, but Mrs Gunn was unconcernedly smoothing her napkin over her knees.

Feeling that she had been sullied in some way, Katie went straight to the sink to wash her hands when she returned to the kitchen, which made Sammy observe, earnestly, 'Did you put your thumb in the soup?'

Wishing now that she had thought of emptying it over Mr Gunn's head, she laughed. 'No, I just wanted to be sure my hands weren't dirty.'

'Mine aren't dirty, for I washed them before I sat down,' he confided, holding up his large paws for her to inspect.

'They're nice and clean,' she smiled.

He seemed pleased at that and watched while she made the next course ready for his parents.

When they finished dinner, Mr Gunn addressed his wife as he stood up. 'You look tired, Marguerite. Why don't you go to bed, and I'll give Katie a hand to clear the table.'

Her smile was a little wan. 'Thank you, Angus, I do feel rather tired.'

Katie's heart had given a jolt at the thought of being alone in the kitchen with him, and she was relieved to find Sammy still there. Ignoring his son, Mr Gunn turned to her when he had set the dishes on the draining board. 'You are a very pretty girl, my dear. Do you know that?'

Feeling as she did about him, she couldn't thank him for the compliment, and he went on, 'You'll have boys after you in a year or two.' His hand snaked out when he passed her, patting her lightly on the hip as he left the room.

She could see by Sammy's deep scowl that he was angry at this, but she thought it wisest not to refer to it, and as she lifted the kettle from the stove to fill the basin, he stood up. 'You're prettier than all the girls that were in my class at school,' he mumbled, his face brick red, and she was glad that he didn't look at her when he loped towards the back door; she was sure that the horror she felt must show in her face. It would be difficult enough to deal with Mr Gunn if he tried to do more than pat her bottom, but would she be able to ward Sammy off if he tried anything?

When she went up to her own room, the rain was making such a din on the sloping skylight window that she knew she wouldn't be able to sleep until it stopped, and to pass the time she took out her writing pad and pencil to write a second letter home. She wouldn't give it to the postie for a few days, though, for it was little more than a week since she first wrote, and she had made up her mind to make it once a fortnight. The writing took some time – it was so difficult to know what to say when every day was the same – and the rain was even worse when she finished. The water had become too much for the guttering, and was cascading to the ground as if a valve in some huge pipe had been opened. Giving up, Katie undressed quickly and got into bed, pulling the covers right up over her head.

Eventually, however, she realized thankfully that the rushing noise had lessened to a steady plop, then an occasional drip, and she was dozing off when she heard a different sound, a more familiar sound, like waves lapping the shore – but Fenty was nowhere near the sea. Puzzled, she stood on her pillow to look out of the skylight and discovered, in the almost dawn, that the river had burst its banks and must have reached the back of the house, though she couldn't see from this angle. On the point of going to warn the Gunns, it occurred to her that this must happen every time there was heavy rain, and she lay down again, wishing she could leave the horrible place. But it would take far more courage to face her grandmother's wrath than to stick it out here.

'I hope the rain didn't keep you awake last night,' Mrs Gunn remarked, after breakfast. 'None of us has ever slept up there, and the rain must make an awful noise on the roof. Angus did offer to go up in case you were afraid, but I thought

23

you'd be more frightened if he came into your room in the middle of the night.'

Katie merely nodded at this. How could she tell his wife that she'd have died of fright if that awful man had walked in on her?

'She's happy enough, that's one good thing.' William John laid Katie's latest letter down with a smile.

'I ken't she would be.' Mary Ann stood up to clear the breakfast table. 'The minister's wife's a genteel body, and when she said her sister was looking for a decent lassie to help her in the house, I was sure she was hinting for Katie. And I ken't the doctor's wife would easy get another maid ... one o' the lassies that left the school at Easter.'

'You should have asked Katie about it first, though, for it come as a shock to her. Still, it looks like she's got ower it, and no harm's been done.'

Mary Ann's shrivelled mouth shrank even more. 'I'd never want to harm her, you should ken that.'

'I ken that, but I'm nae so sure Katie does.' William John stopped there. He wished his wife had shown the girl a bit of love sometimes, but it was best not to rile her by saying so; he'd had the sharp edge of her tongue too often over the forty-odd years they'd been wed. With a sigh, he stood up and went out to the yard.

Taking what he needed from the small lean-to shed by the back door, he sat down on his stool to carry on with the trawl net he had begun two days before. He had originally been a sail-maker, but there were hardly any sailing boats nowadays, so he had turned his hand to making and repairing nets. His rheumaticky fingers were much slower than they used to be, and from force of habit, he drew on the leather pad he had always used to protect his thumb from the end of the curved needle when he was pushing it through the stiff canvas – though he didn't need it to make nets.

His mind was still on his wife as he began weaving knots in the tarry ropes. Mary Ann had been a right bonnie lass when he first met her, her hair as rich a brown as Katie's was now, her wide eyes as dark as new-dug earth, her trim figure setting his blood coursing through him like fire through a forest. He'd lost his heart to her at first sight, though she had never been a loving person, not even to him, and he sometimes wondered why she had married him. His love for her had become a little blunted over the years, the rot setting in at the time their son had brought Lizzie Baxter to the house.

God alone knew why Mary Ann had taken such a dislike to her, and it had started even before she came to see them, when young William John told them about her. As soon as he said she was a Portknockie lass, his mother's mouth had set in a tight line, and it was obvious that she wasn't pleased. When the girl did come – a canty wee thing with a bonnie smile – it had taken Mary Ann all her time to acknowledge her. He could still remember how shocked he was at his wife's manner. He didn't understand what had turned her against the lass, and he'd hoped she would come round, but she never did. Lizzie's very name had been like a red rag to a bull to her for a long time. Even when their son had come to tell her she was a grandmother, and pleaded with her to go to Lizzie because the birth had been very bad, Mary Ann had shaken her head and said she couldn't.

William John's mind skipped the days that had followed, days in which bitter words passed between him and his wife, and picked up his memories a month later, when he had placed the infant in her arms. He would never forget the look in her eyes at that moment, tender and loving as he had never seen them before or since, then it was as if a shutter had come down behind them. He was sure that it was shame at not having gone to Lizzie when she needed her that had prevented her from showing love to the child, for he knew she did love Katie, in spite of her apparent indifference.

Likely it was because the lassie reminded Mary Ann of

Lizzie Baxter – the same russetty glints through the brown hair, the same oval face even to the dimples at the corners of the mouth, and sometimes, looking at Katie, he could see Lizzie's laughing eyes again, with the tawny flecks making them seem as if they were dancing – that was, until she had recognized the animosity in the older woman.

Give Mary Ann her due, she had looked after Katie as well as Lizzie could have done, fed her and clad her, sat up with her when she had the croup, nursed her through the measles and the chickenpox, helped her with her home lessons once she started school, but nothing more than that. There had never been the warmth between them that there should have been, the warmth and love that only he had been willing to supply. And Katie had missed her grandmother's love, that was why she had taken to seeking comfort from the sea when she was unhappy.

He had tried to make it up to the poor lass by reading to her when she was small, by taking her for walks in the summer, by setting her on his knee in the winter and telling her the tales his seafaring father had told him when he was a boy, but it wasn't the same. Many a time, he had wanted to shake Mary Ann, to tell her she would get rid of her shame at how she had treated Lizzie if she showed Lizzie's daughter her true feelings, but he had let it go on for the sake of his own peace, and it was too late now. All he could do was pray that some day Katie would find a man to cherish and cosset her – a man who would love her as she deserved to be loved.

Katie still got upset each time Mr Gunn struck his son, but she could do nothing about it and, in any case, Sammy was obviously afraid of his father and accepted the punishments as natural. He would just look at her sheepishly when they were left alone and then go outside, disappearing into the furthest reaches of the garden. She didn't like to say anything to Mrs Gunn, who also seemed to be afraid of her husband.

She would sit with her head bowed while he ranted on at her about the slightest thing, and Katie had even seen him twisting his wife's arm and accusing her of looking at him in an offensive manner. Not that the poor woman ever let her feelings show, though she had an awful lot to put up with. It must be awful to be married to a man like that.

Katie was always uncomfortable in his presence, and was thankful that he never found fault with anything she did – not yet, anyway – for she didn't think she would be brave enough to answer him back. He might strike her, too. As long as she did everything she was told and kept well clear of him, she would be all right.

With the lengthening of the days, Katie longed to be free of the house if only for half an hour and asked Mrs Gunn if she might be allowed to go for a walk before she went to bed. Being told that the late evening hours were her own, she went to her room to take off her pinafore and put on her jacket, because it was still cold at nights. It was pleasant to be ambling through the trees and to hear the crack of twigs under her feet, but she decided not to go too far in case she couldn't find her way back. She didn't fancy wandering about the woods if it was pitch dark.

She had been out for only about twenty minutes, thinking nostalgically of the walks she used to take along the shore at Cullen and wishing that the Three Kings were there to confide in, when the mist came swirling up from the river, so thick that she could hardly see even a few yards in front of her. She turned quickly to go back, but the trees were menacing now, looming up at her like witches with their scrawny arms stretched out to catch her, and she cried out in terror when something brushed against her shoulder.

'I'll take you home.'

In her relief that it was only Sammy, she was glad of his company, and smiled when he trotted just ahead of her like some huge dog, turning every now and then to make sure that she was still following him. She could laugh at herself now for being afraid of him when she first met him. He wanted to be noticed, that was all, and his mother and father had no time for him. 'Do you often come to the woods at night?' she asked him.

'Every night,' he told her. 'I like the woods.'

'You don't come if it's dark, though, do you?'

'I like the dark. I see things.'

'What kind of things?'

'Just things.'

His mysteriousness amused her, it was so childish. He was just showing off, of course, because he couldn't really see anything if it was dark, but it was best not to argue with him. When he stopped abruptly, she walked into him and he let out a low gurgle of laughter. 'I know your name. It's Katie.'

'That's right.'

'I like you, Katie.'

A pin-prick of fear stabbed her, but she said, 'I'm cold, Sammy. I'd like to get back to the fire.'

'Not far now.' He turned and trotted on, and in a few minutes they had reached the back door of the house.

Holding it open for her, he said, 'You'll not tell my father I was walking with you?'

'I won't tell him, and thank you for showing me the way. If you hadn't, I might have got lost.'

She turned up the lamp in the kitchen, and saw that his face wore a look of deep pleasure at her words. Poor thing, she thought, he never gets any praise, and the only time his father pays him any attention is to slap him. 'Would you like some hot milk before you go to bed?' she asked, lifting a pan from the shelf. 'I'm going to heat some for myself.'

His eyes shining, he gave a sharp nod and sat down at the table, watching her every movement until she laid a cup in front of him. Gripping it with both hands, he drained it quickly, then stood up. 'I'd better get to my bed before my father comes in.'

When he went out into the passage, Katie hurriedly rinsed out the two cups and the little pan. Like Sammy, she wanted to be out of the kitchen before Mr Gunn came in, and she wondered where he had gone, because his motor car was still standing outside.

The next few weeks passed uneventfully, even her birthday in June going unmarked. Katie had not expected a present to be sent from Cullen, but she was a little hurt that not even a card came. Of course, her grandmother was one of the old school, who thought that cards were a waste of money, that a birthday was just another ordinary day, but it would have been nice to think that somebody had remembered she had now turned fifteen.

She had learned from Sammy, when they were having dinner together one evening, that he was not paid for any of the jobs he did around the house, nor for the gardening, and she felt angry that his father took advantage of him, but it was really none of her business. All she could do was to talk to the boy and let him see that she regarded him as a friend.

She was in the habit now of going for a short walk each night if it was dry, and Sammy sometimes joined her, walking alongside her silently through the trees or along the river bank, She felt safe with him, and actually hoped to see him as she sauntered in whatever direction she chose to take. It was good to have company, and he didn't expect much in the way of conversation.

The days were long, the air was warm, and she had stopped thinking so much of home. She liked Mrs Gunn and did not object to having more work to do than when she first came – she could see that the woman wasn't fit and was puffing at the least exertion. It wasn't her place to say anything, but one day, when her employer sat down with a thump, her face pure white, Katie murmured, 'You should see a doctor, Mrs Gunn.'

'Angus says there's nothing wrong with me, and he doesn't believe in doctors.'

This made Katie surer than ever that the man was a callous brute, though she hadn't the courage to say so to his wife. 'But you're not well, anybody can see that.'

'I don't feel well, but Angus says I'll be all right if I take things easy for a while.'

'Let me make tonight's dinner. You can sit down and tell me what to do.'

Having done the preparations and the cooking, as well as all the housework, Katie was so tired that night that she went to bed as soon as she had tidied the kitchen, but she was quite pleased that Mr Gunn seemed to have enjoyed the meal she had made.

After a few days of teaching Katie her way of cooking, Mrs Gunn began to take a rest in the afternoons, and the girl wondered if a pattern was being set. Her body soon got used to the extra work, but the peculiar looks Mr Gunn sometimes gave her were unsettling, frightening. She told herself that she would soon tell him where to get off if he laid a finger on her again, yet deep down inside, she wasn't so sure.

The August day had been very hot, and Katie, tired though she was, felt that she had to get out for a breath of air before she suffocated altogether. She was strolling along slowly, drinking in the smell of the moss and the trees, when Sammy appeared at her side. 'You haven't come out for a long time,' he said, accusingly.

'I've been too tired.'

'I thought you didn't like me any more.'

'Oh, it wasn't that,' she said, sorry that he'd been hurt by her absence. 'It was just by the time I finished all my work, I was ready for my bed.' This satisfied him, and he trotted along happily at her side.

First thing the next morning, Mrs Gunn called Katie to the

bedroom as she passed on her way down to make the breakfast. 'I don't feel able to get up at all today. Will you manage to do everything on your own?'

Having done everything on her own for some days now, Katie had to smile, but she just said, 'I'll manage fine, but I'd better get Sammy to go for the doctor for you.'

At that moment, Mr Gunn emerged from the wooden folding screen where he had been dressing. 'There is no need for the doctor. My wife will be up and about again in a day or two.'

'Yes, sir.' Katie went out wishing that she could tell him what she thought of him.

When he came down, she went through to the dining room apprehensively, laid his plate of porridge in front of him and walked away, but he called her back. 'My wife's illness is just in her mind, you know.'

'She hasn't looked well for a while.' She had to say it.

'She thinks herself ill, actually thinks it on herself. She has done it many times before. Do not look at me like that, Katie, I am not an unfeeling man. In fact, I have got feelings that might surprise you. Now, take a tray up to her, but do not sympathize with her, it will only make her worse. A few days' rest is all she needs.'

'I hope so, sir.' Katie was glad to get away from his dark penetrating eyes. There was something about them lately that hinted at a touch of madness.

When she went through with the teapot and the toast, he said, 'I have been thinking, Katie. My wife being in bed will cause you extra work, so, until she is on her feet again, I will take my meals in the kitchen. That will save you having to set the table in here.'

'It's no bother, sir,' she protested, dutifully, knowing that she would feel safer with him in the kitchen since Sammy would be there, too.

'I do not like eating alone, so we will start tonight.'

She didn't tell Sammy about this arrangement in case he

refused to eat with them, and held her breath when he came in for dinner in the evening. He did look surprised when he saw his father, though he said nothing and kept silent during the entire meal, but at least he was there.

As he did twice a week, Mr Gunn went out after dinner, and Katie was sure that Sammy would join her in her walk if only to find out why his father had dined with them. She had just left the house when he popped out from behind a tree.

'Why was he there?' he demanded. 'Sammy doesn't want him in the kitchen. Sammy likes when it's just me and you.'

'It's only till your mother's better.'

He walked on for a few moments before remarking, 'Sammy's seen him.'

'Your father? I know you've seen him.'

'Far down in the woods.'

The thought that she could have run into Mr Gunn at any time on her solitary walks terrified Katie, but she said, 'I wondered where he went.'

The boy gave a sly smile. 'Sammy knows. Sammy has a place, a special place, secret. Sammy sees things.'

Not heeding his last sentence, Katie said, 'It's nice to have a special place, isn't it?' Her own special place was on the shore at Cullen, which wasn't really a secret place, but it was where she had spilled out all her frustrations and fears, which was maybe what Sammy did, too.

'Do you want to see my special place?'

'Not tonight, Sammy. You can show me some other time.'

Next night, when Mr Gunn came into the kitchen, he looked sternly at his son. 'You did not trim the hedge properly.'

Sammy raised his head abruptly. 'I did. I cut it all.'

Katie stepped back in astonishment as the man took his balled fist with full force against his son's mouth. 'Do not answer me back, boy! I will not have my meals spoiled! Go up to your room this instant and stay there until morning.'

Discretion, and fear, kept Katie from protesting, and she

watched sadly as Sammy trailed out, his shoulders hunched. She was so upset for him that she hardly ate a thing, but Mr Gunn's appetite was not impaired, and she jumped when he said, as if he knew what was going through her mind, 'Do not smuggle anything up to him, Katie. He would get completely out of hand if I did not chastise him.'

When she brought down his wife's tray, Mr Gunn had already cleared the table and was standing by the sink. She was ready with a polite refusal if he offered to dry the dishes, but this was not what he had in mind. His arms clamped round her, and he said, in a strange, hoarse voice, 'I have been waiting weeks for a chance like this.'

'Let go of me!' She struggled against him, straining her head away when his mouth sought hers.

'Come now, Katie,' he coaxed. 'I only want a little kiss.'

Sick at the thought, she slapped his face without thinking of the consequences. 'I'm not paid to kiss you, Mr Gunn, and if you don't stop this minute, I'll tell your wife.'

His beetling brows shot down fiercely, but he let her go and went out. Hardly able to believe that he had taken no for an answer, Katie sagged with relief. She had got off easier than she had feared.

If she had seen the expression on Angus Gunn's face as he settled into his armchair in the parlour, however, she would not have felt so complacent.

Chapter Three

✤✤

More wary than ever of Mr Gunn, Katie hoped that he wouldn't send Sammy to bed early any more, but it happened again only a week later. He had reprimanded his son for not chewing his food properly and the boy had begun, 'I've got good strong teeth, I don't need to . . .' That had been enough and Sammy was banished to his room.

Katie had remained sitting after the meal was finished, thinking that Mr Gunn would get tired of waiting for her to stand up, but when he pushed back his chair, he came and stood behind her. Her heart palpitating, she forced herself to remain perfectly still, but when his hands slid round her neck, she jerked away automatically.

'You little fool,' he muttered, 'I could be a very good friend to you, if you would let me.'

He went out without waiting for an answer, but Katie was trembling when she stood up. Friendship was not what he was after, the dirty old devil, and how much longer would he pester her before he gave up?

When Sammy joined her on her walk the following evening, it occurred to her that he could help her. 'Listen, Sammy,' she began, 'I can't do anything about your father hitting you, but I want you to promise me you won't answer him back again. That's what makes him send you to bed early, and I'm scared he might do something bad to me if there's nobody else in the kitchen.'

Screwing up his face in deep thought, he took some time to reply. 'You want Sammy to be good?'

'Very good.'

His face broke out in a wide smile. 'I promise. I wouldn't want him to do bad things to you.'

'I know you wouldn't.' But she couldn't help thinking that she was wasting her time – his father could send him to bed for nothing if he felt like it.

Fortunately, only the next morning Mrs Gunn announced that she was feeling much better and would come downstairs. She certainly had a little more colour in her cheeks, and after a few days she had regained her previous, rather doubtful, health and was doing more housework than she had done for some weeks prior to her mysterious illness. With his wife back on her feet, Mr Gunn had no option but to sit with her in the dining room again, and it was not only Sammy who was pleased that his father would no longer have his meals in the kitchen.

While Mrs Gunn was in bed, Katie had thought that she would never get the weekend off she had been promised, but her employer had not forgotten. 'You've been here for six months now,' she said, one day in October, 'so I think it's time you went home to see your grandparents. You had better take the opportunity as long as I'm feeling well enough to cope by myself.'

Katie murmured her thanks, and Mrs Gunn went on, 'I'll pay your fare to show my appreciation for the extra work you had to do while I was laid up.'

'There's no need for that, Mrs Gunn, I was glad to do it. I wasn't expecting anything . . .'

'I know you weren't, but it would make me feel we hadn't imposed on you unfairly.'

Very early on Friday morning, therefore, Katie set off in a steady drizzle to walk the five miles to the railway station at Huntly. By the time she boarded the train, her coat was wet, and her brown hair was plastered black against her head, dripping into her eyes, but even that did nothing to spoil her fizzy anticipation of seeing her grandfather again. She waited at Keith impatiently for the other train which would take her to the coast, thinking in amusement, when she saw her reflection in the carriage mirror, that she looked like a drowned rat, and when, at last, she caught sight of the sea, the waves glittering in the sun which had emerged from the dark clouds, her breath caught in her throat. It wasn't long until she spotted the familiar broad outline of the Bin – the hill was a landmark for miles – and she knew that she was almost home.

Her excitement at fever pitch when she came out of Cullen Station, she ran all the way down the hill to Seatown and burst into her grandparents' house. Mary Ann – her sleeves rolled to the elbow, corseted figure erect as ever as she stirred a pan on the hob – turned round startled by the intrusion, and Katie came to a breathless halt, disappointed that her grandmother had shown no pleasure at seeing her.

'You should've let us ken you'd be here the day,' Mary Ann said, brusquely.

This deflated Katie's spirits even more. 'I wanted to give you a surprise,' she mumbled.

'You did that right enough, coming in like a raging lion. Have you forgot your manners since you went to the Howe o' Fenty, or do the Gunns nae bother with suchlike things as knocking on folk's doors?'

'I'm sorry, Grandma.' Katie hadn't thought it necessary to knock since this was her home, and felt like a four-year-old again being reprimanded for the heinous crime of losing her handkerchief.

'Well, you'd best take off your coat now you're here.' A suspicion suddenly forming in her mind, the old woman said, 'You havena lost your job, have you?'

'No, I've got the weekend off, and I haven't to go back till the first train on Monday. Can I hang my coat up by the fire? It got wet when I was walking to Huntly Station.'

'It hasna been raining here.'

At that moment, William John walked in from the back, his eyes lighting up when he saw his grand-daughter. 'Oh, Katie lass, it's good to see you.' He opened his arms and she ran to kiss his leathery cheek. 'How did you get here?' he asked then, hugging her tightly, 'and how long are you biding?'

When he learned that she'd had to walk five miles to catch the train, his smile vanished. 'I thought you said in one of your letters Mr Gunn had a motor car. Did he nae offer to take you to the station when he was going to his shop?'

She toyed with the idea of telling them that she would not have accepted a lift if he had offered, but it would worry them to know she was afraid of the man. 'I like walking.'

Over the fish soup – a delicacy known as Cullen Skink and made with a large smoked haddock, milk, potatoes and onions – it was William John who plied her with questions, frowning when she described Sammy Gunn as being 'a bit simple'.

'A daftie, is he?' Mary Ann observed, dryly.

'Not a real daftie,' Katie protested. 'He went to school, and he knows what's going on, but his father doesn't pay him a penny for doing the garden or all the other jobs he does.'

'The creature likely doesna ken what money is,' the old woman remarked, derisively.

Katie was stung into exclaiming, 'Sammy's not a creature, he's a nice boy and I'm sorry for him. We sometimes go for walks together in the woods at night.'

'Katie Mair!' Mary Ann's eyes blazed. 'You dinna mean to tell us you and him are – he's nae your lad, is he?'

Her scandalized face made the girl smile. 'No, he's not my lad, but his mother and father don't bother with him and he needs a friend.'

William John shook his head. 'Oh, Katie lass, you'll have to watch yourself. You never ken wi' laddies like that. If you get ower friendly wi' him, he could . . .' He trailed off, too embarrassed to say what was in his mind, then ended, a trifle lamely, '. . . He could go for you.'

Katie's laugh was scornful. 'Sammy wouldn't try to kill me. He's kind and gentle.' His father would be more likely to try that, she reflected. She wouldn't put it past Mr Gunn to murder somebody, he was wicked enough.

After supper, she said she was going out. 'Just for a wee while, to get the sea air into my lungs.' Going along the shore, she wondered if she could still confide in the Three Kings, and came to the conclusion that she would have to try. There were things she couldn't tell her grandparents, things they would be angry about though maybe they were just in her imagination.

In the eerie, still darkness, it was easier than she thought. 'I've only been away six months,' she began, when she got near enough, 'but it feels like years, for I don't like the Howe of Fenty very much. Mrs Gunn's all right to work for, though I'd to do everything myself when she was ill. I get on fine with Sammy, he's the son, and he says he's got a special place and all. I think he feels the same about it as I do about coming here. Grandma and Granda say I shouldn't walk in the woods with him, but he's my friend, and he wouldn't hurt a fly.'

Katie paused for a moment, wondering whether to mention Mr Gunn, or if it would bring bad luck. But he was the main reason for her unease at Fenty, she couldn't ignore that. 'Mr Gunn's not a nice man. He hits Sammy for the least little thing, and he wouldn't let his wife get the doctor when she was ill. He only tried to kiss me once, and he's never done it again, but I can't help being scared of him.'

She stopped as if waiting for advice. At first, she'd had a sense of reassurance from the rocks, but now everything had changed. A coldness seemed to be coming from them, seeping right inside her as though they were telling her that she was right to worry, that Mr Gunn wasn't to be trusted. On her way home, she even had the feeling that they were warning her that he was to be the means of changing her life in some way . . . and not for the better.

She went straight to her old bed in the back room when

she returned home, saying nothing of her increased fears. If Granda knew how scared she felt, he'd want to take her away from Fenty, but her grandmother wouldn't let him. She'd just laugh at her for thinking the Three Kings could speak to her. But they had! They'd told her to be on her guard against Mr Gunn because he meant to do her some ill.

In the morning, she shrugged off the alarming thought; her imagination had got the better of her, that was all, likely because she had been too emotional last night at being home again. What could Mr Gunn do to her, after all? As long as she made sure he never got her on her own, she'd be as safe as houses. She had nothing to fear from either him or his son, despite what her grandfather had said about Sammy.

She dressed to the accompaniment of raindrops pattering on the window pane, but she was not downcast because it was too wet to go out. It would be just like old times again, with her grandfather sitting by the fire talking to her.

After breakfast, Mary Ann busied herself making the soup for their mid-day meal, then plied her sweeping brush round her husband and grand-daughter before she took out a duster and made an exaggerated onslaught on the furniture. All the time she was working, she gave the impression that she was paying no heed to their conversation, but Katie knew that she was taking in every word.

The rain had not gone off by afternoon, and Katie offered to make the supper, but her grandmother said, sarcastically, 'And have you spoiling good mince?'

'I've been doing all the cooking for the Gunns for a long time, and none of them ever complained.'

'Aye, well, some folks is easy pleased.'

William John put his oar in now. 'Ach, let the lassie show you what she can do. It's nae often you get the chance o' somebody cooking for you.'

'It's nae often anybody round here does anything for me,' she snapped, glaring at him. 'Some folks would sit on their backsides all day.'

'Sit down on yours for a change, then,' he grinned. 'What can the lassie do to spoil mince?'

His wife continued to glower at him for a moment, then plumped down on the chair Katie had vacated, pursing her lips as she picked up her mending basket from where it was kept next to the wall, and William John winked at Katie.

'Well, now, I'm sure you canna fault that,' he commented some time later, wiping his mouth with the back of his hand.

'No,' Mary Ann conceded, 'I must say the doughballs were near as good as I make myself.'

'Better,' he mouthed to Katie, who had to turn away to hide a smile.

'That was just grand,' he said of the seven-cup pudding, and although his wife had to admit it was good, she took the gilt off the gingerbread by adding, 'Of course, I couldna afford to make something like that every day.'

'I wouldna want it every day,' he laughed, 'but it's been a real treat, hasn't it?'

'Aye,' she said, grudgingly, 'it has that. You'll make a good wife to some man some day, Katie.'

Coming from her grandmother, this was high praise indeed to the girl. 'Not for a long time yet,' she chuckled, to cover the pleasure she felt.

On Sunday afternoon, Katie and William John took a walk to the Bin, the frost-nipped air putting fresh roses into both their cheeks, and the Howe of Fenty was not brought up in their rare spurts of conversation. Man and girl were content to be in each other's company again, free from Mary Ann's disapproval of their closeness, and Katie felt closer to her grandfather now than she had ever done, closer even than to the Three Kings. He was like a rock himself, though his back wasn't quite as straight as it used to be, and she could tell him things she wouldn't tell her grandmother. He hadn't changed much since she was a little girl; he still wore the navy ganzies his wife knitted and covered his silver hair with the same old peaked cap . . . at least, it looked the same one, but maybe it wasn't.

On Monday morning, William John said he would walk to the station with Katie, and Mary Ann, cheeks more hollow than ever, came to the door to see her off. 'Watch yourself,' she cautioned, then muttered, as if it had been dragged out of her, 'I've been real pleased to see you.'

This was so unusual that Katie's eyebrows shot up, but she just said, 'It'll be another six months before I'm back, but I'll keep writing.'

Once Katie was in the carriage, William John reached up and took her hand. 'She really did miss you, Katie lass.'

The train moving slowly forward, he gave her hand a tight squeeze then walked away, but not before she had seen the moisture in his eyes. Sitting down, she blinked her own tears away.

When she arrived at Huntly, she was taken aback to see the gangling figure who loped forward to greet her. 'Sammy! What are you doing here? Did your mother send you?'

He grinned bashfully. 'I heard her saying you'd likely be back on this train.'

Katie's heart swelled with fondness to think that he had wanted to meet her off the train when it was a ten-mile walk there and back. 'You shouldn't have come. It's too far.'

The light went out of his dark eyes. 'Are you angry?'

'No, I'm not angry. It's good of you, but I hope you're not too tired to do your work when you get home.'

It had still been dark when she left Cullen, but the sun was shining now, and with the shambling boy pointing out the different trees they passed, commenting on the colours of the leaves which littered the ground and imitating the calls of the various birds they saw, Katie was amazed at how short the time seemed until they reached the track to Fenty.

Sammy hung back as they neared the house then made for his shed, and gathering that he didn't want his mother to know that he had gone to the station, Katie didn't enlighten her.

Since his wife's recovery, Mr Gunn had not made any more advances to Katie, and although she was beginning to think he had just been testing her before, and that he would not bother her again, her scalp prickled with alarm when she went into the dining room that night and his weird eyes fastened on her. 'Your holiday has done you good, Katie,' he said, his hand touching her leg under the tablecloth. 'You look prettier than ever.'

Unable to move away in case his wife noticed why, Katie mumbled, 'Thank you, sir,' gritting her teeth as she felt her skirts being pulled up.

'Yes,' Mrs Gunn smiled, quite ignorant of what was going on, 'you do look better than you did when you left. It's a pity you can't go home more often.'

When the man's fingers touched the bare skin at the top of her stocking, Katie could stand it no longer. 'I'd better get back to the kitchen before the tatties boil dry.' She pulled to the side, but kept her head up as she went out. She'd be damned if she would let him see how upset she was.

She kept well away from him when she took in the second course, twisting her body awkwardly to set the dishes within his reach, and feeling like hitting him between the eyes when she noticed his sneering smile. She would have to take care not to stand so close to him in future.

It was so unusually mild for November that Katie told Sammy when they were having dinner that she was going out for a walk later. She didn't want to run the risk of meeting Mr Gunn by herself, though the moon was shining as bright as day, for he'd come home in a vile temper and had hit his son for nothing that she could fathom, and he had shouted at his wife for asking what was wrong with him. She had taken only a few steps into the wood when Sammy sprang out from the back of a tree. 'There's a rabbit's hole down there,' he informed her.

'Where? Let me see.'

He pointed out several rabbit holes, showed her a clump of toadstools he had found and a thick knobbly tree he said he sometimes climbed. 'You know everything about this wood,' she said, admiringly. 'I'd never have noticed any of that if I'd been by myself.'

His chest swelled proudly. 'I know what my father does.'

'He's got a shop in Huntly.'

'What he does in the wood.'

His secretive grin made her curious. 'What does he do?'

'With a woman.'

So that's why Mr Gunn went out at nights, Katie thought, but it didn't really surprise her. 'You'd better not let him know you've seen him,' she warned.

'I see him nearly every time. He waits for her if she's not there.' Sammy furrowed his brows, then added, sounding quite puzzled, 'It's not always the same one, but he always does the same thing. The first time I saw him, I thought he was trying to kill her, but she liked it. They all like it.'

Katie tried to change the subject. 'Did you remember to clear up all the mess from your bonfire?'

He was not to be sided-tracked so easily. 'He puts his arms round her first, and kisses . . .'

'Did you clear up the mess?' she repeated.

'Yes.' He turned to face her and when he opened his mouth again, she burst out, 'I don't want to hear what your father does, Sammy. It's his own business, not ours.'

He cowered away and she regretted having been so sharp. 'I'm not angry with you, but don't tell me any more.'

His mouth closed, but his eyes lost their look of dread. 'I can see him from my special place.'

Katie grabbed at the opening this gave her. 'Oh, I nearly forgot about your special place. Show me now.'

This succeeded in taking his mind off what his father got

43

up to, and holding her hand he pulled her forward. 'I found it when I was a little boy, and I never told anybody else, just you, because you're my friend . . . aren't you?'

'Of course I'm your friend. What kind of place is it?'

'Wait and see.' He was almost skipping along in his glee, but he didn't speak again until he drew to a halt, pointing his finger. 'There,' he breathed, reverently.

All she could see was a cluster of bushes in front of a broad, gnarled chestnut tree. 'It's a nice place,' she said, not understanding why he thought it so special.

He dragged her on, pushing aside the bushes until she saw the hollow between the roots of the tree. Releasing her hand, he went down on his knees and crawled in backwards, looking up at her from inside. 'There's just room for me,' he said, sadly.

'Well, it's your place,' she reassured him. 'If there was room for somebody else, it wouldn't just be yours.'

'I often come here. Sometimes, I sing to myself, sometimes I say things. Things I want to say, about Father hitting me, and bad things like that, but I say about you sometimes, all good things.'

'That's nice.' She shook her head when he told her to go in after him. She couldn't help feeling a great pity for this child-man who had no one to confide in except a tree, but hadn't she been the same, telling all her troubles to three rocks?

'I don't know what's wrong with my legs,' Mrs Gunn observed one forenoon some weeks later. 'It's all I can do to walk.'

Having noticed that her employer's gait had been somewhat stiff recently, Katie said, 'Go back to bed, and I'll come and rub some liniment in. If it's rheumatics, that should help you, and a few days' rest, and all.'

'Yes, perhaps that would be best.'

The liniment, however, did not help, nor the days spent in bed, and Katie began to wonder if Mr Gunn had been right. Maybe the illness *was* just in his wife's mind, and she was imagining she was an invalid.

Then came a day when Mrs Gunn said, 'There's something far wrong with me. My legs are absolutely dead this morning.'

The anxiety on her face made Katie say, 'Will I tell Sammy to take the old bike and go and ask the doctor to come?'

'I think you'd better. Angus won't be pleased, but he just doesn't understand how I feel.'

It was late afternoon before Doctor Graham appeared, and his face was grave when he talked to Katie after examining his patient. 'It could be poliomyelitis, what people know as creeping paralysis, or perhaps sclerosis, where the cells of the muscles waste away and the whole body becomes gradually affected, or muscular atrophy, which has similar symptoms. She tells me that she has always been delicate, and that she has had spells of this before and recovered, but she says it is worse this time. Only X-rays would show what it is, but when I said I'd like her to go into hospital for a day, she told me that her husband would never agree, and she grew so agitated I didn't pursue it.'

'Mr Gunn's against doctors of any kind,' Katie ventured.

'I'll go to his shop tomorrow and explain the situation to him, but if he refuses to allow her to go for X-rays, I can do nothing more. She will get progressively worse, until . . .' He stopped, shrugging his shoulders.

When Mr Gunn came home, Katie told him apprehensively that she had sent for the doctor, but he did not take his anger out on her. He stormed upstairs, and she could hear him shouting at his wife, still persisting that her illness was in her mind. It was all Katie could do to stop herself going up to give him a good piece of her mind, but at last the row came to an end. Fearful that in his temper he would turn on Sammy, she had given him his dinner and sent him out, but the man

45

walked straight out at the front, slamming the door behind him.

She was not surprised when he came home next day and told her that he had refused permission for his wife to go into hospital. 'If God means her to die, so be it,' he ended.

She was absolutely appalled. What kind of man was he? How could he be so cruel? But he was smiling again. 'In view of my wife's illness, I am going to move into Sammy's room, so as soon as you have finished in the kitchen after dinner, I want you to change the sheets and make up a bed for him in the other garret. You will be all right there, will you not, boy?'

Casting an appealing glance at Katie, Sammy nodded, and after the meal, when his father had gone out, Katie asked him to help her to move his things. The minute he saw where he was to sleep, his sullen face cleared. 'I'll be next door to you,' he beamed.

She had been thankful that Mr Gunn had not taken this room himself, since there was no lock on her door, yet she didn't like the thought of Sammy being so close. 'You'll be next door,' she said, tartly, 'and that's where you'll stay.'

'But it'll be nice to know you're so near,' he insisted. 'I never had a friend before, and I like you an awful lot.'

With a rush of affection, Katie patted his cheek, and they went down to take up some more of his belongings. There was a whole pile of comics, given to him by the baker's vanman, whose wife had been clearing out their son's bedroom and wanted rid of them. Although they had been in pristine condition when Sammy got them, he had looked at them so often that they were now almost in tatters, yet he still treasured them, so they were shifted to his new room. There was a shoebox full of old fir cones and things he had picked up in the woods, and many other items of the kind a seven-year-old would cherish, and he carried them up as if they were the crown jewels.

The trouble was, as Katie had discovered, that his new

room was much barer than hers, and storage space was limited to one old wooden trunk with an arched lid, so she stowed his clothes at one side and the rest of his things at the other. He would probably jumble them all up by rummaging through them, but it couldn't be helped, and she could tidy it when it got too bad.

He hadn't let her down by answering back, that was one good thing, though it couldn't have been easy for him to be uprooted from his familiar surroundings, and what was more, he had kept sitting stubbornly long after dinner was over so that she wouldn't be left alone with his father, who was now dining with them again.

Nevertheless, as fond as she was of him, her mind was made up. If, as the doctor had seemed to predict, Mrs Gunn should die, Katie Mair would be out of the Howe of Fenty like an arrow from a bow, Sammy or no Sammy.

Chapter Four

✣✣

1923

The winter had been long and hard, Katie having to scrape the frost off her skylight window every morning, and even off the downstairs windows sometimes. The gales had blasted against the panes with such force that it was a wonder to her that they hadn't been blown in, but the only casualty had been the outhouse where Sammy kept his gardening tools. He had gone out one morning to check that everything was as it should be, and had run back in shouting that his shed roof was lying round the side of the house. He had been determined to take out the ladder there and then to fix it on again, and it had taken all Katie's powers of persuasion to convince him that he could just as easily be blown down.

After another night of hurricane-force gales, he had gone to the woods to make sure that his special place had come to no ill, and had come back to say that a lot of trees were lying on the ground, concluding with pride, 'Mine's still standing, though.'

When the blizzards began, usually starting late in the evening and continuing through the night – sometimes all the following day, too – Katie had been astonished by the sheer volume of each fall. With Cullen being on the coast, she had never seen drifts like there were at Fenty, reaching halfway up the ground-floor windows or higher. Every morning for more than a week, Sammy had been ordered to clear the snow from his father's motor car and dig out a way up the track to the road, but more than once it had proved an impossible task. On those occasions, Mr Gunn had stayed upstairs all day and only appeared for meals, his face so sour that Katie was glad when he went back to his room.

On one such day, she heard him yelling at his wife before he even came down for breakfast. 'I swear I'll make you pay one day, Marguerite,' he stormed. 'You have put me through years of hell with your frigidity.'

Not knowing what frigidity meant, Katie strained her ears but she couldn't hear what the woman was saying until she raised her voice in fear-filled entreaty. 'Please, Angus, not again! No, no! I can't stand any more!'

Sure that Mr Gunn was trying to kill the woman, Katie was halfway upstairs when he came out of the bedroom, his face dark with anger until he noticed her and did his best to suppress his heavy breathing. 'My wife will not require any breakfast today, Katie,' he said, his voice trembling and pitched a fraction higher than usual.

'Yes, sir,' she murmured, 'but I'd better go up and see if she needs anything else.'

On the same step now, he gripped her shoulders with both hands. 'Leave her!' he thundered, his long fingers digging into her so deeply that she had to grit her teeth so as not to cry out, 'or I shall . . .' He broke off and flung her from him. 'You are just the same as she is!'

He propelled her downstairs and stood at the front door until she returned to the kitchen. 'You had better watch your step, my girl!' he snarled. 'I am quite capable of dealing with you as well as Marguerite!'

His glittering eyes, cold and hard, were boring into her and it was some minutes after he went out before she stopped shivering. What did he mean – deal with them? Was he going to kill them? He looked mad enough for it when he was angry . . . and which of them would be his first victim?

Thinking that Mrs Gunn would not want her maid to know about her troubles, Katie waited a while before she went to see if the poor woman had suffered any ill effects. It was almost eleven o'clock, therefore, when she carried up a cup of tea, and she had to hold back a cry of dismay when she saw the marks on her employer's face and the ugly bruising coming up on her arms.

Looking up at her as if beseeching her to say nothing, Mrs Gunn muttered, 'Wasn't I silly? I fell out of bed and Angus had to come and lift me back. I hit my head on the table and banged my arms, but they're not so sore now.'

Katie was astonished that the woman was covering up for her husband after what he had done, but if that was what she wanted, it would be best to play along with her. 'Would you like me to rub some ointment on your arms to take the sting out? Or put a cold cloth on your face?'

'No, no, I'm fine. I just got a bit of a shake-up.'

It was that brute of a man who needed the shake-up, Katie thought as she went back to the kitchen. How could he hit a helpless woman? But she could not interfere between husband and wife, not unless Mrs Gunn was prepared to tell the truth about her injuries. If it wasn't that she felt so sorry for the poor creature, she would pack her things and leave the Howe of Fenty right now.

Katie worked off her anger by scrubbing and polishing, but when Mr Gunn came in at lunchtime from wherever he had been – likely trudging through the snow to simmer down – she felt it bubbling up again, and was tempted to throw a pot at him. Not appearing to notice any difference in her manner towards him, he smiled at her when she set down the tureen.

'I think it will not be long until the thaw comes, thank goodness,' he said, with no trace of shame or repentance. 'We will be back to normal in a day or two.'

Back to normal? Katie was amazed that he could be so calm. What did he think was normal? He wasn't normal, that was one thing sure.

That night, Sammy was again at the receiving end of his father's anger – for coming in without knocking the snow off his boots – but took the thump on his ear without a word, although it made his head rock. Biting back what she wanted to shout, Katie was thankful that he had not been sent to bed, and the meal was eaten in total silence.

While the long, cold snap lasted, Katie had tried to keep the fire in Mrs Gunn's room burning twenty-four hours a day, even when it meant that she had to get up in the middle of the night to refuel it. Having no fireplace, her garret room was like an ice-house, but she was young and healthy and survived the hardship with not even a slight cold.

But the snows had gone at last, the gales had died down and suddenly there were snowdrops everywhere, their little white heads bowed as if in grateful prayer that they were hidden no longer. The daffodils and narcissi blossomed, then the tall tulips, red and yellow, swaying in the more gentle breezes. Katie happened to say one day that she loved tulips best of all the spring flowers, so Sammy brought in a huge bunch for the kitchen, and kept renewing it until the plants were exhausted of blooms.

With the advent of spring, life at Fenty returned to its previous normality, as Mr Gunn had predicted, although Katie considered it most abnormal. The atmosphere in the house made her feel uneasy, especially when he was there, even if he had calmed down since the day he attacked his wife. Mrs Gunn was no better, but then again, she was no worse, which was a blessing. Katie had given up any hope of getting her weekend off at Easter, for how could she leave the poor soul with nobody to look after her except a husband capable of anything in his tempers . . . even murder?

After being cooped up inside for so long, Katie was glad to get out for a walk again in the evenings, and Sammy was usually hanging about waiting to join her. He told her one night that he would take her to see something nice, and she exclaimed with delight when he led her to a small clearing carpeted by pale yellow primroses.

'Would you like to see something else nice?' he beamed.

'Oh, they're lovely,' she said, when he took her along the river and showed her some willow trees heavy with dangling, fluffy catkins. 'My Granda used to call them lamb's tails.'

He giggled at this, but she could tell that he was proud to have given her some pleasure; a little friendliness was all he needed to make him happy. During their walks, he named the insects and animals they saw, and the different wild flowers – Nature Study seemed to be the only part of his schooling to have penetrated his dull brain, probably because it had appealed to him – but when he was at home he didn't say much and was withdrawn and unresponsive when his father was in the kitchen with them.

He was sitting by the fire one rainy afternoon, looking lost because he was forced to be indoors, so Katie tried to think of a way to cheer him. 'Why don't you go upstairs and speak to your mother for a while?' she said, at last.

'She doesn't like me,' he growled.

'What a thing to say! Of course she likes you, you're her son. Up you go now, and let me get on with my work.'

He rose to his feet slowly, looking like a dog that had been kicked, and Katie's conscience pricked her. 'Don't go if you don't want to. I just thought it would be something for you to do.'

'If you want me to go, I'll go.'

He was back in less than a minute, his untidy, dark head bowed. 'She said she wanted to be left in peace.'

'You should have said you just wanted to keep her company for a wee while.' Katie suspected that his mother was ill at ease with him, and wished that she hadn't made him go.

'I didn't want to keep her company. I like it best in the kitchen with you.'

She tried now to think of something to occupy him. 'Would you like to pare some tatties for me?'

Pleased to be asked, he set to the chore with alacrity, and when she next went over to the sink, he had filled a large soup pot with peeled potatoes. 'There's enough there to feed an army,' she laughed.

His face fell. 'Has Sammy done too much?'

'It doesn't matter. I'll put what I don't need into cold water, and that'll save me having to do any tomorrow. If you want something else to do, pare some of the carrots you took in yesterday out of your sand box. About six would do.'

When he had carried out this assignment, he said, 'I'm really helping you, amn't I, Katie?'

'Yes, you are, but that's all I need just now, and the rain's off, so you'd better get back to the garden.'

She shook her head sadly when he went out. What on earth would happen to him if she were to leave?

Two days later, Katie had just risen when the row started, and she dressed as quickly as she could, wondering what was going on. Then she heard her employer saying, quite loudly, 'You always managed to get somebody else.'

'I should never have had to go to anyone else,' Mr Gunn roared. 'One of a wife's duties is to satisfy her husband.'

Katie could not quite hear what Mrs Gunn replied, but it sounded like, 'No one woman would ever satisfy you, Angus.'

The man's angry shout of, 'You bitch!' made Katie take her shoes in her hand and run down the stairs in her stockinged feet, but even so, the man heard her when she arrived at the open door. She thought he'd had his hands round his wife's neck before he stepped away from the bed, but his back had been towards her and she couldn't be sure. He didn't seem put out to see her, and walked past her with a smile and went into his own room.

It was Mrs Gunn who was red-faced and flustered. 'You must have wondered what was happening,' she murmured, unable to meet Katie's eyes. 'What a fuss Angus kicked up because he dropped his collar stud when he was in speaking to me and couldn't find it amongst the blankets.'

Her hands had covered her neck, but not before Katie had seen the red marks. 'Are you sure that's all it was?' she asked. 'It sounded more than that to me.'

Still keeping her eyes averted, Mrs Gunn said, 'You should

53

know by now how worked up he gets when anything upsets him.'

Katie knew that, but what she had overheard had not been about a collar stud. However, as long as Mrs Gunn persisted in her unlikely explanation, she could do nothing . . . not that there was anyone to turn to. She fastened on her shoes and went down to the kitchen to make breakfast.

When Mr Gunn came down, he said, 'Marguerite called me in to look at a rash on her neck. It did seem a little red, so perhaps you should rub in a little ointment for her.'

Katie was amazed by his effrontery, but he was staring at her as if daring her to contradict him. 'I'll do it after I've cleared up down here,' she murmured. And little good it would do, she thought, for it certainly wasn't a rash.

The July day had been hot and sultry, and the thunder began about thirty-five minutes after Katie went to bed. She could not think what had wakened her until a garish light flashed briefly into her room. Her grandmother had ridiculed the fear of such storms out of her when she was very young, so she was not scared, just a bit uncomfortable. Thinking that she may as well clip her nails to take her mind off it, she leaned across to the little table to light the candle, then rose to take her scissors out of the chest of drawers. As she went back into bed, there was a low grumbling noise and she was quite relieved that it came from some distance away.

By the time she had finished her manicure, the thunder was much louder but she blew out the candle, hoping that the storm would not bring rain, because she had to wash Mrs Gunn's nightdress and bedding in the morning. She was about to rise to put past her scissors when her door creaked open, and thinking that Mr Gunn had taken advantage of the noise to come to her room, she remained as still as she could. If he thought she was sleeping, he might go away. Hearing no movement, she breathed more freely. She couldn't have shut the door properly and the vibrations had made it swing open by itself.

'Can I come in beside you, Katie?'

It was Sammy's voice, and she knew by its quiver that he was terrified, but she couldn't let him come into her bed. 'Go back to your own room,' she told him, gently. 'Thunder won't hurt you.'

Another, much louder, roll sounded, and he crossed the floor in two huge strides. 'Please, Katie?' he begged.

'No, Sammy, a boy and a girl can't lie in the same bed.'

'Why?'

'Just because.' At the next vivid flash, he bent over with his hands covering his eyes, and she felt a shudder of fear run through her, too. 'Sit down on the edge, then.' She was quite pleased to have someone there with her, although she knew there was nothing to be afraid of.

He had just plumped down when another peal of thunder made the whole room shake, and he jumped up and slid in next to her. 'Sammy's frightened, Katie.'

His teeth were chattering, whether from fear or cold she couldn't tell, so she put her arms round him and held him close. 'My Granda used to tell me to count how long it was between hearing the thunder and seeing the lightning, and that tells you how many miles away the storm is.'

At first, they could count as many as seven, then the interval between lightning and thunder became shorter and shorter, until they were coming simultaneously, and the ferocity of the storm had Katie's teeth chattering, too. 'It must be right above us now,' she told the shaking boy. She was so glad of his company that she scarcely noticed his loud, adenoidal breathing close to her ear.

After what seemed like hours, Sammy whispered, 'I counted to three that time.'

'It's going away, thank goodness.'

She waited until the night was almost silent before she said, 'You can go back to your own room now, Sammy, but don't tell your father you've been in my bed. He wouldn't understand.'

Reluctantly, Sammy swung his legs round. 'I never tell him anything, anyway,' he muttered, his bare feet plopping on the waxcloth as he padded out.

Ashamed now of her own weakness, Katie wished that she hadn't given in to it, and wondered if she could depend on Sammy to keep a secret. Turning to her other side, she was puzzled to find something hard digging into her arm, and smiled when she found it was the scissors she had been using earlier. She laid them on the chair at the side, and then snuggled down to try to get some sleep before rising time.

At breakfast, Mr Gunn raised his eyebrows at her. 'You survived the storm all right, Katie?'

'Yes, thank you.' She was conscious that Sammy was having difficulty in keeping still, but she didn't dare do or say anything to warn him to keep quiet.

Mr Gunn had a somewhat secretive expression, too, but he turned to his son. 'It's time you started work, boy!'

'I haven't . . .' Remembering that he shouldn't answer back, Sammy began again. 'Can I finish my cup of tea first?'

'Do not take too long about it.'

The boy regarded Katie with some entreaty after his father went out. 'Was Sammy good?'

'You were very good,' she assured him. 'If you don't annoy him, he won't get angry with you. But you'd better go and get started now.'

The thunderstorm having cleared the air, the sun, helped by a fresh wind, dried the washing quickly, and after she took up Mrs Gunn's lunch, Katie spent most of the afternoon ironing. By the time she went to bed, she was fit to drop. She was thankful that the wind had died down, for it often howled like a banshee through the ill-fitting skylight and her body was crying out for the sleep she had lost the night before. It crossed her mind that she should prop the chair under the handle of her door in case Sammy came back, but she didn't really think he would, and she was too tired to bother, in any case.

She fell asleep within minutes, but the sound of the latch being lifted had her instantly on the alert and wishing that she had obeyed her earlier instinct to jam the door. 'You're not getting in my bed again, Sammy,' she said, sternly.

There was a swift intake of breath. 'So I was right.'

She realized, with mounting horror, that it was Mr Gunn this time. 'I was certain I heard him coming in here last night,' he said, his voice holding the satisfaction of a man whose suspicions have been proved correct. 'You let me think that you were not a girl like that, and you do not know how pleased I am that you are.'

Even at a month past her sixteenth birthday, Katie was still too innocent to know what he meant, but the memory of how cruel he had been to his wife made her defend herself. 'He came through to me because he was scared of the thunder, that's all.'

'Do not try to pull the wool over my eyes, Katie, I was not born yesterday.'

He was standing at her bedside now, panting heavily, and she shook in terror when he whipped the bedcovers back. She opened her mouth to scream but his lips clamped over hers and only muffled moans came out when he flung himself on her. His teeth grated against hers as his hands slid very slowly, but firmly, round her neck. Her skin shrank from his touch, and her heart almost stopped when she saw how wild his glistening eyes were . . . no, not just wild, unmistakably mad! He was going to strangle her! The same as he would have strangled his wife if she hadn't heard them quarrelling and stopped him.

Fighting for her life now, she writhed in desperation, but her struggles were to no avail; they even seemed to make him worse. His legs held hers firmly, his body imprisoned one of her arms, and she wondered if she should try to scratch him with her free hand, but her nails were too short to make any impression. Then it struck her; her scissors were still on the chair! Very carefully, she edged her hand over, and just as her fingers touched the metal, the man, with his mind on the pleasure he sought, forgot himself so far as to lift his head for a second – long enough for Katie to give a piercing shriek.

His mouth came down again even more fiercely, his hands had slipped and were now gripping her breasts but she had managed to get hold of the scissors. Swinging her arm in a huge arc, she struck at his face, and he jumped back with a scream of agony when the blades tore down his cheek.

'You little bitch!' he shouted, trying to grab hold of the weapon before she struck again, but he had just prised her fingers open when Sammy charged in.

'Leave her be!' he screeched, yanking his father off the bed with a strength doubled by fury, and the scissors went skittering across the floor unnoticed by any of them.

Pulling the blankets up around her, Katie watched the boy landing punch after punch on his father, who was trying to excuse himself by gibbering that he was only doing what Sammy himself had done the previous night, but nothing would stop the onslaught. He was edged back through the door, then the petrified girl heard a hoarse cry and a series of dull thuds. For a short time, all was still, then came the sound of returning feet, and Katie was certain that Mr Gunn had pushed his son downstairs and was coming back to finish her off. Cringing, she closed her eyes and waited, not daring to move a muscle as he reached the landing and came into her room. 'No, no! Please, no,' she whimpered.

'It's only me, Katie.'

'Oh, Sammy,' she breathed, holding her arms out to him and bursting into tears.

This time it was he who comforted her, stroking her cheek with one rough hand while his free arm went round her. 'Oh, Katie, stop crying,' he pleaded. 'Sammy's got you now, so don't be frightened.'

He held her until her hysterical sobs quietened, then she

said, still hiccupping a little, 'Will you light the candle for me, Sammy? It's on the table there with the matches.'

He did as he was bidden, and turned to look at her in the flickering glow. 'Did he hurt you?'

'He'd have killed me if you hadn't come in. Did you push him down the stairs?'

'I didn't know he was on the top step till he fell over. I was going to punch him some more, but he didn't get up again so I just came back to you.'

All Katie wanted now was to be left in peace. 'Go back to your bed, Sammy. I want to sleep'

'He might come back.'

'He won't come back.' Not tonight, any road, she thought. He would have had enough tonight, and she would jam her door every night after this.

She gave a long, juddering sigh when Sammy left her. She wouldn't sleep, but she couldn't cope with him any more, not after what she had just been through. Her mouth felt bruised and unclean, her skin crawled at the memory of the silk-smooth, clammy fingers working like a snake coiling round her neck. She shuddered at the thought of those fingers squeezing the life out of her, which they would have done if she hadn't managed to scream. Sammy may be simple-minded, yet he had run to help her the second he knew she needed him.

Her shock was receding when she wondered how Mr Gunn was feeling. He deserved to be horse-whipped, but at the very least she hoped he was black and blue all over. She could picture him picking himself up off the first-floor landing and hobbling to his room . . . but she hadn't heard a single movement since he fell, except for Sammy coming back. Could he have been severely injured? Had he broken his back?

She had to make sure. She couldn't leave him in pain, no matter how wicked he was. She wouldn't even leave an animal to suffer if she could do anything to help it. Getting up, she lifted the candlestick and crossed to the door. In her agitation, her fingers could barely grip the little lever of the latch, but she eased it up without a sound, praying that the door wouldn't creak as it usually did – she didn't want Sammy to hear her.

Tiptoeing to the top step, she looked down the narrow well of the staircase and nearly dropped the candle when she saw the figure on the landing below, lying as still as the dead. Her faltering feet took her down a few steps, but she halted when she saw the dark ominous pool round his head . . . blood! He really *was* dead!

In panic, she raced back to the boy's room. 'You've killed your father, Sammy!' she gasped. 'You'll have to run away, or they'll hang you for murder!' He sat up abruptly, his mouth gaping. 'Get up, Sammy!' she shouted. 'You'll have to go away from here!'

'Where to?' His voice cracked uncertainly as he pummelled his fists into his eyes to waken himself properly.

'Anywhere away from here!' she told him, urgently. 'Get up and dress yourself!'

His feet hit the bare floorboards with a resounding smack. 'Will you come with me, Katie? Please, Katie?'

Recalling her own attack on Mr Gunn, she knew that she couldn't stay there any longer, either, and Sammy wouldn't manage on his own. 'I'll have to dress, and all.' She was going out when something else occurred to her. 'We'll have to take some clothes with us, just what we can carry.'

After frantically pulling on her skirt and blouse, she put on her coat, slipped her feet into her shoes then wrapped a few things into her shawl and returned to Sammy. Fully dressed, he was standing looking helplessly at what he had set out on his bed. 'I haven't a bag to put them in,' he wailed.

Shaking her head in irritation, she laid the candleholder on the floor, rolled his clothes inside a shirt and tied the sleeves together. 'Carry it by the knot, like me,' she told him, picking up her own bundle with one hand, the candle with the other and creeping downstairs in front of him.

'Don't look,' she ordered, when they reached the landing, but neither of them could take their eyes off the body as they skirted round it. The face was bloodied – which was only to be expected after the battering Sammy had given it, and what she had done – but she could see now that most of the blood had come from somewhere on the side of the head.

Sammy stared incredulously. 'I just punched his face.'

'He must have hit his head on something.' She turned away and her stomach gave another sickening lurch. Mrs Gunn was lying in the doorway of her room, her face a ghastly grey, her eyes turned up to the ceiling, blank and unseeing.

Chapter Five

Transfixed with horror, it was some minutes before Katie's brain started to function again. Mr Gunn had really been insane! He'd even killed his wife before he came upstairs to strangle her, and he'd likely meant to finish Sammy off, as well. Even though she had sometimes wondered which of them would be his first victim, she had always told herself that murders only happened in books and to stop being so fanciful. Glancing at Sammy, still staring down at his dead father in perplexed disbelief, she dragged him away before he could spot his mother. A second shock might make him go berserk, too.

Once they were outside, she threw the candle on the ground and they ran through the woods at breakneck speed, stumbling over branches blown down in past gales. The sky was so black that Katie couldn't see a thing, but Sammy – knowing every inch of the area – guided her through the trees and round stumps and whole trunks until she could run no farther.

'I'll have to . . . stop a minute,' she gasped.

Her chest felt like it was being compressed in a vice and there was a stitch in her side, so she leaned against a tree trunk until she was fit to carry on. Sammy's breathing was rattling like a traction engine, but it didn't seem to bother him as he waited patiently beside her. When her own breathing was easier, she said, 'We'd be quicker going along the river bank. Nobody would see us there.'

'The salmon poachers?' he offered.

'Oh.' She had forgotten the men whose unlawful activities were carried out on moonless nights such as this. 'I suppose we'll have to keep to the woods, it'll be safer.'

They set off silently again, not running but walking as quickly as Katie could manage. At one point, Sammy picked up a long, straight stick and swished at bushes until she felt like screaming, but she knew that he didn't understand the danger they were in. Maybe he was pretending to be a knight in shining armour saving a damsel in distress, and it was best to leave it like that, for his poor brain couldn't cope with more than one thing at a time; her own brain was having difficulty with all the things she had to worry about.

They were far beyond what Sammy thought of as his woods now, which were actually part of a dense, very extensive forest, and when they suddenly emerged into an open field, a narrow strip of light was showing on the horizon. 'The sun's coming up,' Katie said, uncertain of how to proceed. 'We'd better go back in the trees till I think what to do.'

They sat down on a fallen trunk, and Sammy said, with a little giggle, 'It's fun, this.'

She was glad that he could look on their predicament as fun, for her head was spinning with images of the two dead bodies they had left behind. And where could they go with no money, not even a few coppers to buy any food? She had kept the wages Mrs Gunn gave her under a sheet of paper in the bottom of her chest of drawers, but she had forgotten about it in her haste to get away.

'What's wrong, Katie?'

Sammy's gravelly voice made her jump, but she tried to keep her voice light. 'Nothing's wrong. I was thinking about something, that's all.'

Should she go back for her wages? Should she tell Sammy he would have to go on alone? But he couldn't fend for himself. How long would it be before the bodies were found? Nobody ever went to the house . . . except the tradesmen in their vans. The baker came Monday, Wednesday and Friday, and the butcher on Tuesday, Thursday and Saturday, but she was in such a state she couldn't remember . . . 'What day is it, Sammy?'

His brows came down in thought, his eyes darted from side to side searching for inspiration, then he said, 'I hoe the vegies every Thursday and I did them yesterday.'

'This must be Friday, then.'

Would the baker just go away when he got no reply to his knock on the back door? It wasn't likely, Katie thought, for he always got a big order, and he would maybe go in to see where she was. He would be puzzled that she wasn't in the kitchen, but being just a van driver, he surely wouldn't go upstairs? And neither would the butcher tomorrow. She and Sammy should be safe until one of the men got alarmed at getting no answer at the house for days and reported it to the police. It was awful to hope that the corpses would lie undiscovered for maybe a week, but she couldn't help it.

It was herself and Sammy that she had to worry about now, Katie thought. Even if no one came after them, there was still the problem of where they should go, and what they would do when they got there. They would have to find jobs, but who would employ a boy like Sammy? All he knew was flowers and vegetables and grass. Unless ... would a farmer hire him? Farmers always needed strong laddies.

'Would you like to work on a farm, Sammy?'

'Are we going to a farm?'

'Not just yet, in a day or two, maybe.' They would have to get far enough away from Fenty so that nobody would connect them with the deaths when Mr and Mrs Gunn were found.

All day they walked, with only little stops to rest or to eat the wild rasps they found – bramble bushes were more plentiful but the berries were still green – and to slake their thirst with the cool clear water of the burns and springs they came across. Katie was thankful that Sammy had accepted the need to keep going, but she dreaded the time when he would demand some proper food.

They kept to those fields where trees or hedges offered them some cover until Katie felt that she could walk no longer and decided to find somewhere to shelter for the night. Dusk was gathering fast when she saw a barn, well away from the farm to which it belonged and in such a dilapidated condition it had obviously fallen out of use. 'We could sleep there,' she said, pointing, and had to hurry to keep up with Sammy as he sprinted forward with a beaming smile. The door was hanging off its hinges, but they managed to wriggle through the gap. 'There's no beds,' he wailed.

'We can make beds for ourselves,' Katie said, cheerfully.

She scraped together a layer of old straw, expecting him to do the same for himself, and she was too tired to protest when he flopped beside her when she lay down. In fact, she felt comfort rather than anger when he fitted his body to the curve of her back. It did cross her mind fleetingly that they were like the Babes in the Wood, then, exhausted, she fell into a deep sleep.

The novelty of living rough wore off the next day for Sammy. They had not been walking long when he stopped. 'I don't want to go any farther.'

'We can't stop here,' Katie told him, hoping he wasn't going to be difficult. It was bad enough having to keep a sharp lookout for other people without having to force Sammy to do what he was told. 'Come on, before somebody sees us.'

He shut his eyes and shook his head obstinately. 'I want to go home.'

Katie's patience deserted her. 'All right, I'll carry on by myself, and you can go home so the bobbies can catch you and string you up.'

His eyes flew open. 'String me up? Like I string up dead crows to keep the other crows off the garden?'

'Yes, just like that, and you'd be as dead as they were.'

'But why would the bobbies string me up?'

'Have you forgotten you killed your father?'

He didn't answer, but she knew from the dark look on his screwed-up face that he was remembering. Her spurt of anger evaporated. He didn't know his mother was dead, too, which made him an orphan, like her. 'Oh, Sammy,' she said, gently, 'we've got to carry on, we can't go back.'

'How far yet?'

'I don't know. Just till I think we're safe.'

As they trudged forward again, Katie turned to smile at him. 'We'll be all right, don't worry.' But her own mind was far from easy. She had lashed out at Mr Gunn with her nail scissors, and it was just by luck that she hadn't stabbed him to death. If the police ever did find them, they would ask about the cut, and not only would Sammy be charged with murder, she would be charged with attempted murder, and they could end up on the gallows together. Nobody would believe that Mr Gunn had killed his wife, they would think Sammy had done that, as well. Not that it would make much difference to him – they couldn't hang him twice. And maybe it was a good thing Mrs Gunn was dead. She couldn't describe them to anybody. No one would know what they looked like . . . but the doctor knew, and the baker and the butcher knew. They could give descriptions.

She wouldn't be able to relax until they were out of the area of any search, and she would be better not to remind Sammy again about what had happened. He would soon forget and wouldn't be able to tell anybody about it.

They stemmed their hunger that day with a large turnip from a field, Sammy slicing into it with the large gully knife he carried in the pocket of his trousers. The raw vegetable was more substantial than the rasps they had eaten the day before, and lasted them all day. The sun was low in the sky when Katie spotted a big shed that would be an ideal place to sleep. It was in better repair than their last refuge, but it did have several holes in the roof. 'I just hope it doesn't rain,' she sighed, then brightened when she saw the huge heap of hay in the corner. 'It's likely animal fodder,' she told Sammy, as she picked up an armful, 'but we can use it to sleep on and put it all back in the morning.'

Their fragrant bed was so comfortable and warm that Katie was unwilling to move when she awoke. Sammy was still asleep with his arm round her waist, snoring with his mouth open. If they only had something decent to eat, she thought, it would be quite nice to stay here for a day or two.

The crowing of a cockerel made her feel more hungry than ever. Where there was a cockerel there must be hens ... and nobody would miss a couple of eggs. Her thoughts now only on her rumbling stomach, it didn't cross Katie's mind that she had no means of cooking, and removing the imprisoning arm, she got up cautiously and crept outside. There was no sign of a hen run, so she supposed that the birds were just left to scratch around where they pleased. She dropped to the ground to avoid being seen and was crawling through the long grass when Sammy's panic-stricken voice halted her.

'Katie!' he screamed. 'Where are you, Katie?'

All hell broke loose then. Two collies came bounding over, snarling and snapping at her when she stood up; dozens of hens appeared from all around her, flapping their wings and cackling loudly in fear. At that, the cockerel added his contribution to the cacophony, which brought a woman out of the low house at the far side of the yard some way ahead. She ran over to calm the dogs, then looked from Katie to Sammy. 'What's going on?' she demanded.

Red with embarrassment, Katie mumbled, 'I'm sorry. I was looking for eggs ...'

'Oh! You were trying to steal my eggs, were you?'

'I was just going to take two,' Katie defended herself, trying feverishly to think of further explanations.

'It's still stealing.'

Katie had a sudden brainwave. 'Sammy's my brother and our mother's in hospital in Aberdeen, so we're going to see her, but we've no money for food or a bed. That's why we slept in your barn last night, and we're awful hungry.'

A trusting soul, Jeannie Low had no doubts about what she had been told. Why else would a young laddie and lassie be on the road penniless? 'Oh, you poor things,' she exclaimed. 'Come inside and I'll give you some breakfast.'

On the way to the house, she said, 'Have you come far?'

Katie told the truth this time. 'We've been walking for two days already.'

In her small kitchen, Jeannie filled an enamel basin with hot water from the kettle so that they could wash while she scrambled some eggs, and as they gobbled up this feast, she told them she was a crofter's wife and that her man was out in the fields. Katie was relieved that Sammy kept silent – he was so unpredictable that she had been afraid he might come out with their whole terrible story.

Jeannie sent them on their way with some home-made scones, a big lump of crowdie cheese and oatcakes to eat with it, and called after them, 'I hope your mother's a lot better when you get to the hospital.'

Katie felt quite guilty at deceiving this kind woman, and, luckily, they were well out of earshot before Sammy said, in a puzzled yet accusing voice, 'My mother's not in hospital.'

'I had to tell her something,' Katie explained. 'She was wondering why we were wandering about with no money.'

'You said I was your brother. Am I your brother now?'

She was quite proud of having thought that up on the spur of the moment. 'Yes, you're my brother now.' It would save him putting his foot in it if other people asked them any questions.

She rationed the food they had been given, half in the middle of the day, and the rest when she judged it must be suppertime. Sammy dabbed up the last crumbs as they sat by the edge of a burn, hidden from anyone's view by the waving stems of yarrow and couch grass. 'I like this place,' he said, content-edly. 'Can we stay here, Katie?'

'No, we'll have to go a bit farther.' She was beginning to have doubts as to her sense of direction, and wished that she had asked the crofter's wife where they were. They had followed paths through woods, cut across fields and jumped burns, doubled back on their tracks when they came too near habitation of any kind, and now they could be anywhere . . . maybe just a stone's throw from where they had started.

'I'm stopping here.' The boy folded his arms and looked at Katie defiantly when she stood up.

With another unexpected flash of inspiration, she said, 'We're on a walking holiday, and folk on walking holidays keep on walking.'

'A holiday?' The word was familiar to Sammy, but he had to dredge his sieve-like brain to find out why. When it came to him, his look of perplexed concentration cleared. 'I used to get holidays from school, but I didn't have to go walking.'

'Ah, yes, but they were only holidays for children. When grown-up people get holidays, they stop working and go to another place till it's time for them to go back to work.' Searching for another carrot to dangle, she added, 'We'll look for a road now, we'd get on a lot faster.'

He sprang to his feet at once, but when he began to chant, 'A holiday on a road, a holiday on a road,' she put her finger to her lips. 'You can't make a noise, though. We still don't want anybody to see us, it's a secret holiday.'

This was so intriguing that he bounded along at her side with a mesmerized expression until he saw a road to their right. 'That one?' he asked, hopefully.

Smiling and nodding, she wondered if she was being rash, but they would get on much quicker if they kept to the road, wherever it led them. Only once over the next few hours did the distant throb of an engine make them lie down in a dry ditch to escape detection, and the bus passed and was out of sight in seconds. Back on the highway, with his schooldays freshly recalled, Sammy said, 'Hide and seek, Katie?'

'Yes,' she laughed, 'and nobody caught us.'

They were only a little farther on when Sammy gave a shout of delight. 'Strawberries, Katie.'

She was on the point of saying they would be too easily

seen in such an open field, but hunger overrode caution, and he was already heading towards it. The berries, probably being grown for some market, were large and luscious, and when Sammy picked one and popped it whole into his mouth, Katie hesitated. 'We can't eat them here. We'll gather some into my skirt, and we'll look for a sheltered place.'

After they pulled as many as she deemed would be good for them, they walked on, and it wasn't long until she saw a big barn separated from its owner's house by a small cluster of trees. 'That should be safe enough,' she told Sammy. He was off like a shot, sliding the huge door open and smiling as he beckoned her in. They sat down on the earth floor, their hunger making them wolf into the strawberries, and Sammy giggled at the mass of stains on her skirt when they were finished.

'What a mess I'm in,' she sighed, 'and I feel filthy. I wish I could have a wash.'

On their way to the barn, Sammy's keen eyes had taken in the details of the surrounding area. 'There's a burn,' he beamed. 'I'll show you.'

He darted out, and because it was still daylight, Katie made sure that no one was about before she ran after him. He was hunkered down lapping water from his cupped hands when she reached him, and she let herself relax – the bank was so high it would screen them from unwanted eyes. She washed her face and hands and made Sammy do the same, though he mumbled that he wasn't dirty, then she took off her skirt, sluiced the juice from it and scrubbed until most of the stains were gone. Back in the barn, she hung it over a rickety wooden box to dry. 'I think we should stay here tonight. I can't walk about half undressed.'

Sitting down, Sammy said, a little wearily, 'I hope we don't have to go much farther, my feet's awful sore.'

Katie could sympathize with him over this, for her own feet had sprouted blisters the size of pennies. 'Take off your boots, then,' she advised him, 'and stuff them with some of that straw in the corner. That'll dry up the sweat, and you can put in some fresh in the morning.'

She filled her own shoes and then spread a heap of straw on the floor. Sammy lay down first and, feeling quite cold with only her thin petticoats round her legs, Katie curled in behind him. He turned to face her and put his arm round her like a child cuddling his mother, and she was so tired and worried that she hadn't the heart to reprimand him.

'What the hell are you two doing in there?'

A stout man was glowering at Katie when she woke with a start. 'We came in for a rest,' she mumbled, pushing Sammy's arms away. Then she caught a glimpse of her skirt where she had spread it out to dry, and, her face crimson, she tugged at her petticoats to pull them over her bared legs. 'I'd to wash my skirt . . .'

'You're trespassing,' the man growled. 'Do you know that, you little tart? You and your fancy man.'

Rallying her wits, Katie tried not to show how shaken she was. 'He's my brother.' She turned to the boy, cowering away from the angry intruder. 'Aren't you, Sammy?'

Sammy's solemn nod enraged the man even more. 'Brother? Good God! What's things coming to?'

'We just wanted a place to sleep. We're looking for work.' She knew they couldn't go on as they had been doing, and even if the hue and cry for them had started, the bobbies surely would never think of looking for them here.

'What kind of work can you do?'

'We're willing to try anything. You see . . . our father died not long ago, then our mother died, and we've been walking for days.'

Katie's anxious expression did the trick, and the man let his breath out slowly. 'Aye, well . . . there might be something here for you.'

'Will you take us to the farmer then, so I can ask him?'

He gave a loud chuckle. 'I'm the farmer, lassie. Can you milk a cow?'

'I can easy learn.'

'I bet you can, you look real quick on the uptake, and it's like this. My dairymaid walked out when she took the huff at something I said, and my wife's been complaining about having to do the milking herself this past four days, so she'll be pleased somebody's taking on the job. She'll show you what to do.'

Katie jumped to her feet eagerly. 'Is there something my brother can do, and all?'

The man turned to Sammy, standing uncertainly, and looked him up and down. 'Are you willing to work hard, lad?'

Katie answered for him. 'He's a good worker. He's a bit scared of strangers, and he doesn't speak much, but he used to do all the gardening at . . . home, and all the odd jobs.'

'There's aye a lot of odd jobs at Struieburn, and he looks sturdy enough. So he's Sammy? What's your name?'

'Katie Mair, what's yours?'

He grinned at her pertness. 'Davey . . . Mr Sutherland to you. Come on, then, you'll be needing some breakfast, no doubt.'

'Yes, please, Mr Sutherland.'

In the farmhouse kitchen, Madge Sutherland's face lit up when she learned that Katie was taking over the dairymaid's job, and she fussed over Sammy as if he were one of the motherless lambs or calves she hand-reared. 'You can chop some sticks for me when you're finished eating,' she smiled. 'Mr Sutherland'll tell you where we stack the logs.'

He returned her smile shyly until she said that he would be sleeping in the bothy with the other single men and Katie would share a room in the farmhouse with the housemaid, at which he stood up, scowling. 'Sammy sleeps with Katie.'

Mrs Sutherland glanced at her husband, who muttered, 'They were lying together when I came across them.'

'We've been sleeping together for days,' Katie explained.

72

'We couldn't pay for beds anywhere, and we went into any old sheds or barns we saw when we were tired.'

The frankness with which she spoke was enough to convince Madge Sutherland that they had done nothing wrong, and she looked at Sammy again. 'Katie'll be sleeping with Susie,' she said, gently, 'and you'll have a comfy bed in the bothy, so be a good laddie and stop arguing.'

His stricken eyes went to Katie, who said, 'You don't have to look out for me now, and we'll see each other every day.'

He looked a little happier when he went out to chop the sticks, and the farmer's wife took Katie to the dairy to teach her how to skim the cream off the milk already in the wooden 'coggies'. Showing her how to churn the cream, Mrs Sutherland said, 'When the butter comes, put the buttermilk – that's what's left – in a jug, for I make scones with it, and Davey drinks what I don't need.'

Her day fully occupied – making the butter, dividing it into workable lumps for use in the kitchen, sterilizing all the utensils, scrubbing the work surfaces in the dairy, then milking the cows at five o'clock and beginning all over again – Katie was glad to lie down in bed with Susie Clark, the little housemaid. They had liked each other on sight when they met at lunchtime, and had got to know each other a little better over supper, but Katie discouraged Susie from asking any questions by saying she was too tired to talk that night. She *was* tired, but her mind had filled with images of the two bodies she had left lying on the landing at Fenty, and even when she did drop off, it was into an uneasy sleep.

Chapter Six

✤✤

Mary Ann's hand flew to her breast when she saw a policeman standing on her doorstep, but she recovered quickly. 'What are you wanting here, Johnny Martin?' she demanded, scowling at him.

'Can I come in, Mary Ann?' PC Martin had grown up in the Seatown part of Cullen and knew that her bark was worse than her bite.

Mystified, she opened the door wider to let him in, and her husband stood up in alarm. 'Is it about Katie? Dinna say something's happened to my lassie, Johnny?'

Removing his hat, the constable shuffled his feet. 'I came to see if she's here. I can't say any more than that.'

'Is she nae at the Howe o' Fenty?'

'No, she ran off with the laddie Gunn, and that's all I'm saying. I shouldn't really be telling you that.'

Although shocked by this, the old man's thoughts were still on his grand-daughter's welfare. 'Is she all right?'

'I can't tell you that, either, for we don't know where she is. It's three days since they disappeared, and I was told to find out if she'd come home.'

'She hasna been here since October,' Mary Ann told him, 'and that's nine month ago. She said she'd be back in April, then she wrote saying Mrs Gunn was laid up in her bed and she couldna get off, so we didna expect her.'

William John bit his lip. 'Her letters were cheery enough, but it's a great pity she's been stuck there. I'm dying to see her again.'

After clearing his throat nervously, Martin returned to the

matter in hand. 'When she was here, did she tell you about Sammy Gunn?'

William John stroked his chin. 'She said he was a bittie simple, and he sometimes went walks wi' her at night . . .'

'Did she say anything about his father and mother? Like . . . was there any trouble?'

Mary Ann was annoyed at being kept in the dark, and spoke impatiently. 'She said she got on fine wi' Mrs Gunn, but she never said much about him. Can you nae tell us what . . . ?'

'No, it's confidential information. Have you heard from her lately?'

'We havena had a letter for near three weeks,' William observed, sadly.

'Oh, well, that's it, I suppose. I'm sorry if I've upset you, but my hands are tied.' PC Martin made for the door.

As soon as he left, Mary Ann turned to her husband. 'Like mother, like daughter!'

The jibe made William John forsake his usual no-arguments-at-any-price doctrine. 'No, no!' he cried, 'Katie's not a bad lass.'

His wife pounced in triumph. 'Ha! So now you admit Lizzie Baxter was bad?'

'I never said that. She wasna bad, any more than Katie is, though you blamed her for enticing your precious son away. Her nor naebody else could have made him go, if he didna want to.'

'She likely forced him into it.'

There was a long, uncomfortable pause, into which William John made one last effort. 'You should have told Katie the truth when she was old enough to understand.'

'What could I tell her? That her mother left her on our doorstep? It would have broken her heart.'

This was a revelation to him. He hadn't for one minute guessed that she'd been trying to shield the lass. 'Is that why you never said? I thought . . .'

75

'You thought I didna care? Neither I did, nae at first, then – oh, I'll never forget that poor mite's eyes looking up into my face . . .' She broke off, shaking her head. 'She was hurt enough as an infant, and when she was old enough I just couldna tell her. You ken, I often wondered what made Lizzie Baxter . . .' She broke off, then said, her tone much harder, 'Ach, we'll never ken why, and what does it matter now, any road? She's tainted wi' her mother's blood and I never want to see her again.'

William John wished that his wife would admit, just once, that she loved Katie, as he was sure she did, but it was just the way she was made, and nothing would change her. 'It wouldna be so bad if Johnny Martin had said why he . . . I can hardly think she's done something bad enough to have the bobbies after her.'

'Mr Gunn likely reported her for taking his son away.'

William John let her have the last word, though he was sure that there must be more to it than that. He pondered over the matter for some time, and came to the conclusion that, whatever Katie had done, it would likely remain as much of a mystery to him as the whereabouts of his son.

Awake long before Susie stirred, Katie lay wondering if she had made a big mistake in ending the flight so soon. She and Sammy might have been better to keep going . . . but how would they have lived? They would have had to beg food, and the more places they stopped, the more people would be able to pass on the information to the police when the newspapers came out with the story of the double murder. Nobody would know that it was Mr Gunn who had killed his wife, nor that his death was really an accident, and everybody would think she and Sammy had killed them both then run away.

Her heart suddenly ached for her grandparents. They would wonder what had happened when they got no more letters from her, especially Granda. But she couldn't chance writing, for Cullen would be the first place the bobbies would look for her, and though she would stake her life that he wouldn't tell them where she was, she wasn't so sure about Grandma. She would just have to make up her mind that she would never see either of them again, she thought, mournfully. They were safer at Struieburn than anywhere else. The farmer's wife had taken a shine to Sammy and believed that they were a brother and sister whose parents had just died, so she would never suspect anything.

Suspicions had already formed in the farmer's mind, however. 'There's something queer about Katie and Sammy,' he observed to his wife as they were dressing. 'She told him he didn't need to look out for her now, but I'd have thought it was her that looked after him – him being . . . well, a bit daft.'

Hooking her corsets round her ample figure, Madge said, 'He's not daft, just backward, and maybe she just lets him think he looks out for her, to keep him happy, like. She's a good lassie.'

Davey sighed. 'You're too easy taken in, though I must admit the laddie worked hard. He chopped that whole pile of logs and swept the yard like his life depended on it.'

'She worked like a trooper, as well.' Madge paused, then added, thoughtfully, 'Mind you, she'd a look on her face sometimes . . . like she was feared of something . . . or somebody, and she jumped a mile when I went to tell her to come in for her supper.'

'You'd make anybody jump, the way you bang about.'

Madge ignored this. 'She's bound to feel strange till she gets the hang of things, and she'll still be grieving for her mother and father. No, you've picked up the wrong end of the stick there, Davey. There's nothing queer about them.'

*   *   *

When the harvesting began, Sammy was in his element, working even harder, and faster, than any of the other men when it came to building the different stacks of wheat and oats. The construction of these was an art for those with experience, building from raised stone foundations so that air could circulate underneath, but he was allowed to help by sending up great forkfuls of the grain to them. So speedily did he work that those engaged in the intricate business of shaping the huge stacks had to tell him to take it easy, and he slowed down obediently, his face one big smile. When he first started working on the farm, he had been the butt of many, at times rather cruel, jokes, but he had taken all the snide remarks with a grin, and, after seeing how well he acquitted himself during the harvest, the majority of his fellow workers had come to respect him.

Seeing how angry it made him, they had stopped teasing Katie when they were in the kitchen at mealtimes, and, in any case, Susie Clark was a far better target – she more than fulfilled the promise in her shining blue eyes. She was a winsome young girl, her fair curly hair a direct contrast to Katie's long, wavy brown tresses, and although she was a few months younger than her room-mate, her figure was fully matured. She was out for as much fun in the evenings as the young lads were, romping in the hay with several at a time, giggling in delight when rough hands strayed where they shouldn't, and finally giving in to one – not always the same one – and going up to the hayloft with him. Those left below passed the time by sniggering and making rather crude comments – some even bragged about their own performance with her – and a great cheer went up when at last the two participants climbed down, dishevelled and flushed, but quite unabashed.

When Susie discovered that Katie was not conversant with all the facts of life, she had deemed it her duty to teach her, often using humorous, graphic anecdotes she had heard from other girls – which left nothing to the imagination – to explain what took place before, during and after the act of procreation. At first, Katie had been quite shocked, but she had learned to take the stories with a pinch of salt.

'I think the lads put bets on to see who's going to be lucky wi' me,' Susie confided when she came in one night.

Katie felt obliged to remind her of the risks she ran. 'If you're not careful, you'll land in trouble.'

'I make sure they stop in time,' Susie giggled. 'You dinna ken what you're missing, Katie, you should try it.'

'Not me.'

'Sammy just sits and laughs, but likely he wouldna ken where to put it, any road. Maybe I'd better show him?'

'You leave Sammy alone, Susie!' Katie snapped.

'Would you be jealous? I've seen the way he looks at you. Do you let him . . . ?'

'Don't be stupid! He's my brother! And I'm not jealous, it's just . . . you know he's not quite right, and if you start doing things like that with him, he'd want to do it every night, and he likely wouldn't stop when you told him.'

'I suppose no', and I wouldna want a daftie's bairn.'

After a short silence, Susie gave a wicked chuckle. 'But I've the feeling he could gi'e me a bigger thrill than ony o' them, for I'm sure he's hung like a bull.'

Katie was outraged at this. She liked Susie, liked the way she could make even Davey Sutherland laugh while he was berating her for something she had forgotten to do, but the housemaid would have her bedfellow to reckon with if she tried to corrupt Sammy. Still, it had likely just been talk. With so many other young men about, Susie couldn't really want to have anything to do with him.

After this, Katie, having convinced herself as time went past that this farm was the best refuge she could have, was more conscious of the farm hands, and when they were all gathered round the big table in the kitchen one night at supper-time, she couldn't help casting her eyes around them. They were all sturdy – men and boys – with red weatherbeaten faces and manners that would have her grandmother tutting in disgust, but their very roughness held an attraction for her. She didn't want to be like Susie, but it would be nice to have a lad to walk out with.

Becoming aware that one youth was regarding her with some amusement, she blushed and lowered her head. Lachie Mooney was real nice, with wavy hair the colour of ripe corn, his rugged face tanned a deep bronze, his mouth always turned up in a smile. Glancing up at him again, she found that his keen eyes were still on her and returned his grin shyly.

Susie nudged her. 'I think you've clicked wi' Lachie. He's looking at you like he'd never seen you afore.'

'Is he . . . has he . . . ?' Katie didn't want Susie to know she was interested in him, but she had to find out. 'Have you and him ever . . . you know?'

'Oho! So it's like that? Well, you'll maybe nae believe this, but Lachie's never fell for my charms – and it's nae for the want of trying.' Susie let out a doleful sigh. 'I think he's had a lang eye after you since he started here.'

'Don't be daft.'

'I'm telling you!'

Katie wondered what she would do if Lachie ever asked her out. Would she let him kiss her if he tried? She had never been kissed before, not a real kiss, not from somebody so young and handsome.

When Susie came in that night, Katie said, 'What's it like being kissed?'

The other girl shrieked with laughter. 'It depends who's doing the kissing, but it's best if it's somebody bigger than you, it spoils it if you've to stand on your tippytoes. And aye look first to see if they've ony bad teeth, for sure as death they'll ha'e bad breath. Mind you, kissing some o' the lads here's like being sucked inside a tunnel, though they think they're the bee's knees.'

Katie sighed. 'Have you never kissed somebody you really liked, though?'

Susie's face straightened. 'Aye, I was only thirteen and I

loved Matt . . . my he'rt used to thump like a steam mill when he kissed me . . . and even though I could hardly thole it the first night he rammed inside me, I let him carry on . . . till I found out he was a married man, wi' six bairns and a wife that thought the sun shone out o' his backside. Oh, Katie, it still hurts.' After a moment, she threw back her head with a raucous laugh. 'So you see why I take up wi' ony man that wants me now, married or single.'

'But all men aren't the same. You'll meet somebody decent some day, and you'll fall in love and wish you hadn't been so stupid.'

Susie took some time to answer, then she murmured, 'Aye, I suppose I'll never get onybody decent if I go on like that. I could fancy that new lad, Lachie, but he never looks the way o' me. D'you think he'd take notice o' me if I stopped my carry-ons?'

'He might. I wouldn't think any boy would want a lass that lets everybody have their way with her.'

'So you think it's worth a try? Right! That's me finished having quick thrills up in the loft.'

'I'm glad to hear it.'

On the following evening, Katie couldn't believe her ears when Susie said she was going over to the bothy. After what she'd said, surely she wasn't still up to her old tricks?

Only five minutes later, the girl skipped in again, blonde curls bouncing, blue eyes twinkling with mirth. 'I told them, Katie! I opened the door and bawled, "As from today, Susie Clark's bloomers will not be taken down by any hands but her own."'

'Good for you!'

'None of them said a word, but you should have seen their faces! I just about pee'd mysel' laughing. I suppose some o' them'll still try it on, but a knee in the knackers'll stop their capers.'

They both spluttered with laughter at that.

*　　*　　*

In November, the end of the term, Katie and Sammy, like all the other workers at Struieburn Farm, were given their wages – four months for them instead of six, since that was all they were due. Sammy laid his on the table and pushed the coins around with his finger until Katie said, 'I think I'd better keep them for you, or you'll be losing them.'

Watching Sammy handing them over, one of the young men gave a sarcastic laugh. 'Folk that didna ken better would think you two was man and wife,' he began, but stopped, colouring, when he caught Madge Sutherland's stern glare. 'If you stopped biking to Mintlaw every night and wasting your money on drink, Fobbie Littlejohn,' she rapped out, 'you'd have some left at the end of every term, instead of having to sub for weeks from them that's soft enough to let you. Let Sammy be, he's more sense in his pinkie than you've got in your thick skull.'

Sammy, who had been looking in a perplexed manner from one to the other with his mouth slightly open, now lifted his hand and flexed his little finger mischievously at the other boy. This raised a howl of laughter from the others, Fobbie himself joining in after a moment of looking shamefaced.

'That put his gas doon to a peep,' Susie whispered.

Katie hoped that he would not take it out on Sammy, and for the next few days, she watched her 'brother' closely in case Fobbie said something nasty to him in the bothy, but he looked as carefree as always, and she gradually relaxed.

Susie was the only close friend Katie had ever had, but she didn't dare tell her anything about her life before coming to Struieburn. At times, Katie almost forgot why she had left the Howe of Fenty, she was so happy at the farm, but occasionally the memory of that awful night surfaced in her dreams, making her wake up shivering yet sweating, her heart clattering painfully against her ribs. Not wanting to disturb Susie, she would lie as still as she could, thanking her lucky stars that Mr Sutherland had found them hiding in his barn.

She tried not to think of her grandparents now. She had

considered writing to let her grandfather know that she was well and working on a farm, but she remembered in time that, even if she put no address at the top, the postmark on the envelope would be a clue to her whereabouts.

As they did every Hogmanay, the Sutherlands invited all their workers to the farmhouse in the evening, laying on a huge meal and refilling glasses with brown ale even before they were empty. Afterwards, the table was shifted into the passage to make room for the dancing, music provided by the first horseman on an accordion and the ploughman's son on a penny whistle. Most of the wives were there to keep an eye on their husbands, but there was a surplus of men, and some of the young bachelors danced with each other, the 'lady' mincing about with an exaggeration that made the spectators go into wild paroxysms of laughter.

At first, Sammy sat forward in his chair with his eyes – brighter than ever with the beer he had consumed – popping out of his head, his feet tapping rhythmically, but the urge to join in grew too strong. Jumping to his feet, he cavorted round the floor with his arms in the air, grinning happily.

'You're supposed to have a partner, Sammy, man,' somebody shouted, and he stopped in confusion until Mrs Sutherland took his hands and skipped along with him.

'Are you enjoying yourself?' she asked, grimacing as his heavy boot crunched down on her toes.

'It's fun, this,' he beamed. 'Dancing's easy.'

'Not so easy on my feet,' she groaned.

When the music stopped, he stood waiting for it to begin again, but his partner had hobbled away and the musicians had set down their instruments. 'Katie?' he yelled, suddenly realizing that he was the only one left on the floor and unsure of what was happening.

She went across to him. 'They're all taking a rest now. Go and sit down.'

'Gi'e's a song, Mrs Sutherland!' a voice called from the back of the room, and needing no further persuasion, the farmer's wife stood up with her back to the range to face her audience. A deep contralto, she launched unaccompanied into an old favourite.

> Oh, sing to me the auld Scots sangs,
> In the guid auld Scottish tongue,
> The sangs my faither liked to hear,
> The sangs my mither sung
> As she rocked me in my cradle,
> Or held me on her knee,
> And I wouldna sleep, she sang so sweet,
> The auld Scots sangs to me,
> And I wouldna sleep, she sang so sweet,
> The auld Scots sangs to me.

Looking round, Katie saw that several of the men – reminded of their mothers – were wiping away sentimental tears, and she wished that she had memories of a mother singing to her. She felt even more sorry for herself when she remembered that she had nobody at all now, for she could never go home again. Thrusting aside the deeply distressing thought, she joined in the shouts of 'More! More!'

The requested encore was forgotten when the brass clock on the mantelshelf chimed midnight. This was the moment the men had been waiting for, and flat, half-pint bottles of whisky were dug out of pockets to toast the birth of the new year and begin on the business of serious drinking. Raucous voices now vied with each other to make their good wishes echo from every corner of the room.

'Here's to 1924!'

'To us, wha's like us? Damn few and they're a' dead.'

'Lang may your lum reek wi' other folk's coal!'

This old chestnut still raised a laugh, then a deep bass voice began to sing and everyone joined in.

A guid New Year to ane and a',
And mony may you see,
And during a' the years to come
Oh, happy may ye be.

Backs were thumped, hands were shaken, each man kissed all the ladies and the celebration carried on, although, as time passed, first one and then another reeled across the floor to go outside to be sick. Sammy, too, was feeling a little under the weather, but in his fear of missing something, he held himself rigidly on his chair, his fixed smile making him look more simple than ever. Katie, not drunk but quite merry, was whirling round with one man after another in the Strip the Willow, but when the dance ended, Lachie Mooney, who had been her most frequent partner, put his arm round her waist and, laughing with him, she let him lead her outside. Sammy made a move to stand up to follow them but, discovering that he had no control over his legs, he was forced to sit back with a thump.

At two o'clock, Madge Sutherland waved to the musicians to stop and addressed those of the company still there. 'You'll not be fit for your work unless you get away to your beds for a while,' she said, loudly, then added with a grin, 'And will them that can still walk, help them that can't.'

It was Fobbie Littlejohn who hoisted Sammy up and held him steady as they staggered out. 'Where'sh Katie?' Sammy asked, his unfocused eyes sweeping the farmyard.

'In her bed if she's ony sense.'

In the bothy, Sammy looked in vain for Lachie, the boy who had disappeared with Katie, and not noticing that there were others missing – those sleeping off the drink where they had fallen down – he jumped to the conclusion that Katie was in danger. Even in his present state, however, he knew that he would be stopped from going to look for her and waited until he thought everyone would be asleep. The twenty-minute rest helped him, and he found that his legs were steadier when

85

he attempted to walk, though he had to concentrate on avoiding the boots and trousers scattered all over the floor.

Her brain pleasantly hazy, Katie did not resist when Lachie took her into an outhouse, nor when he pulled her down on the floor, and she soon discovered that being kissed was even better than she had imagined. It was the most thrilling experience she'd had in all her sixteen-and-a-half years.

After about ten minutes, Lachie moaned, 'Oh, Katie.'

Something telling her that it hadn't been such a good idea to lie down with him, her body tensed.

'Let yourself go,' he coaxed, 'I'll nae hurt you.'

She relaxed as his hands stroked her neck, long caresses that sent exciting messages all over her body, and when they slipped down and cupped her breasts, she gave a long sigh of delight. Encouraged, he tightened his grasp until she gasped in pain. Then suddenly, instead of the handsome Lachie, it was Mr Gunn's mad face she saw hovering over her, and she struggled in fear, but the squeezing strengthened. 'No! No!' she shouted.

'You've never been wi' a man afore, have you?'

The voice was Lachie's, but it was thick with passion, and his leg was prising her thighs apart. 'No! No!' she yelled, again, 'and you're not getting to be the first.'

Recalling Susie's remark about 'a knee in the knackers', Katie moved her leg sharply up, at which Lachie jerked back with a cry and she was free. Scrambling to her feet, she raced back to the farmhouse, past the table still in the passage and up the stairs. Susie looked at her archly when she burst into their room. 'What's Lachie been doing?'

'Not what he wanted, any road. Oh, I forgot you fancied him . . .'

Susie grinned. 'I wasna caring. They were shit mirack, the lot o' them, and it's funny the way the drink takes them –

some o' them was as happy as pigs among treacle and some would've hit you as soon as look at you if you said a wrong word.'

'Was Sammy fit to walk to the bothy?' Katie had not given him a thought since she left the kitchen.

'He must've been. I didna see him lying in the yard.'

Undressing quickly, Katie jumped into bed, not bothering to snuff out the candle, and both girls were asleep when their door crashed open. Susie sat bolt upright. 'What the hell . . . ? Oh, it's you, Sammy! What are you doing here?'

Intent on making sure that his beloved Katie had come to no harm, Sammy had forgotten she shared a bed, and he moved in the direction of the voice. A little afraid of him at the best of times, Susie let out a piercing skirl when his arms went round her, but believing that she was Katie, he stroked her head and crooned, 'Don't be scared. Sammy's got you.'

Susie gave him a push that sent him staggering. 'Get aff me, you great lump!'

Katie had been struck speechless by the sight of Sammy clad only in his semmit and drawers, but now she got up and ran round the end of the bed. 'What's the matter, Sammy? Did somebody say something bad to you?'

He turned to her, his anxious eyes clearing. 'Katie, are you all right? Is Lachie in your bed?'

'He must have seen you and Lachie going out.' Susie tried to keep back a laugh at the incongruous figure he cut. 'It's me that's in the bed wi' her, Sammy. Lachie's likely spewing his guts up some place else if he's nae in the bothy.'

Giving a sob, Sammy threw himself at Katie, knocking her off her feet and falling on to the bed with her. Susie, not sure whether or not he was attacking Katie but too scared to intervene if he were, jumped to the floor and stepped well clear, and at that inopportune moment, the farmer ran in to find out why there was such a rumpus. He halted when he saw the bodies on the bed, legs entwined, his face registering his disgust. 'So you two are at it again, are you?' he roared. 'I should damn well never have believed you that first time I saw you.'

Horrified at being caught in such a compromising position, Katie rolled out from under Sammy, quite unaware that more of her was on display than was decent. 'Mr Sutherland,' she gasped, 'he just came to . . .'

'I can see what he came for, you little tart, and you'll get out of here this minute, the pair of you! I'll not put up with your carry-ons in my house.'

Standing behind him, his wife burst out, 'Oh, Davey, I'm sure they haven't . . .' She stopped, his heaving chest and crimson face telling her it was useless trying to make him see reason, and when he stamped out she laid her hand on Sammy's shoulder. 'Go and put on your clothes, lad, and take the rest of your things back to the kitchen. You've time for a cup of tea before the men come in for their breakfast.'

Susie, who had been cringing against the wall all the time Davey Sutherland was ranting, stepped forward when the woman went out. 'I'm sorry, Katie. I couldna say onything. He'd his mind made up, and it did look as though . . . your goon was up round your hips, and Sammy's backside was bare.'

Giving a sobbing sigh, Katie looked at Sammy. 'Tie up your things like you did last time, we'll have to leave.'

'Was it Sammy's fault?'

'No, it was my fault. If I hadn't . . .' She couldn't trust herself to say more.

Pulling up his drawers so that he wouldn't trip over them, Sammy left, and Katie dressed and wrapped her clothes in her shawl again. Susie, silenced by the awful turn events had taken, sat down on the bed and watched her, but when she saw Katie ready to go, she muttered, 'I couldna help screaming when he grabbed me. If it hadna been for me . . .'

'It's all right, Susie. I know you got a scare.'

'I'm awful sorry, though.'

Katie shook the outstretched hand to show she bore no ill will, and went down to the kitchen, where Mrs Sutherland had set out some thick slices of bread and a pot of jam. 'I know Davey was wrong in what he thought,' she said. 'Sammy's just got the mind of a bairn, and I admire you for trying to look after him. I was thinking, though. You'll not find another place so easily, but my brother's the manager of a hotel in Peterhead, and I've often heard him saying he can't get good workers. So I've written him a letter, a kind of reference, saying you and Sammy are honest and dependable. The address is on the envelope, so if you let him read it, he might give you both jobs. You'll get a bus on the turnpike . . .' She stopped and looked at the clock. 'Oh, it's hardly five yet, so you'll not get a bus for a while. You'd better just keep walking and keep a lookout for one coming.'

Katie was too choked up to speak, but her eyes showed her gratitude. Sammy came in then, and when he had eaten his fill – she was too upset to take even a cup of tea – they lifted their bundles and Mrs Sutherland saw them to the door. 'I've put your wages in the envelope, as well.'

'Thank you.' Katie had not forgotten this time to take the money she kept in a drawer with her underclothes, but more would always be welcome.

'Good luck.' The farmer's wife patted Sammy's still-smooth cheek and went inside.

Sammy said nothing for a long time, walking with his head down as if he were trying to figure out the reason for their abrupt departure from the farm, then he said, 'Have we far to go, Katie?'

'To the main road,' she told him, relieved that this was all he had on his mind, for she had been half afraid that he would ask her why Mr Sutherland had been so angry. 'I'm not sure how far.'

It did not take them very long to reach the main road, and they had walked along it for little more than thirty minutes when Katie heard the sound of an engine. When the vehicle came in sight, she was disappointed to see that it was an old lorry, not the bus she had hoped for, and pulled Sammy to the side to let it pass. The driver, however – a middle-aged man wearing a cloth cap and a jacket with holes in the elbows – stopped as he came abreast of them. 'D'you want a lift?' he asked, eyeing the bundles they were carrying.

'We're making for Peterhead,' she told him, 'so if you're going that way, we'd be . . .'

'I've a load o' tatties for the prison, but there's room for the two o' you.'

He jumped out and let down the backboard for them, Sammy scrambling up first and giving Katie a hand. She was glad that they would not be sitting in the cab with the driver; he might have asked too many questions. Their journey was not very comfortable, but they leaned against the bulging sacks and Sammy, for one, was satisfied with this mode of transport. With having little or no sleep the previous night, the rocking motion made them both doze off, until Katie sat up abruptly. 'We must be near the sea!' she said in delight, poking her companion.

'How do you know?' Sammy asked. 'I can't see it.'

'I can smell it.'

At the next crossroads, the driver drew the lorry to a halt. 'I'm turning right here,' he said, as he let them off, 'and you've to turn left if you want the town.'

'Thanks,' she smiled, knocking lumps of dry soil off her skirt. They watched him drive away, then turned in the other direction. She felt quite excited now. She had forgotten that Peterhead was a fishing port; it would be nearly as good as being at home.

Her elation vanished when she discovered that Peterhead was much larger than Cullen; a place this size was bound to have a big police station and more bobbies. Should she risk taking a job here? But it wouldn't matter where they went, for all the police forces in Scotland would be looking for them by this time. If they were recognized, she would tell the truth, and surely they wouldn't hang Sammy when they learned what had happened? The trouble was, they likely wouldn't believe her, whatever she said.

Her mind took another turn. Even if nobody connected them with the murders, could she trust Sammy to behave himself? But whatever it cost her in heartache, she would never ever desert him. He had nobody else to look after him, and she owed him her life, after all.

Squaring her shoulders, she stopped a passing workman and asked how to get to the Temperance Hotel.

PART TWO

Chapter Seven

❖❖

1924

Still not accustomed to his maroon livery although he'd worn it for three weeks, the night porter was admiring himself in one of the plate-glass doors of the hotel when Katie came out of the kitchen. 'You look smart, Sammy,' she smiled, 'but you'd better not stand there or Mr Leith'll be after you.'

Puffing out his chest, he boasted, 'I carried four lots of luggage in last night and I took one out this morning.'

'Good for you, but I haven't time to speak to you just now. It's time to start the breakfasts.'

His happy face fell. He hardly ever saw her now – he was ready to go to bed when she was just starting work – and if he did see her, she was always too busy to speak to him. She looked prettier than ever in her black dress and white cap and little apron, though, and he liked it here. A hotel was even better than a farm. He never got his hands so dirty, for one thing. The people – guests they were called – gave him money for carrying their cases and bags, and he'd a lot of shillings and sixpences in the tin Katie had given him to keep them in. When he was off duty, he built them up on top of the chest of drawers in his room, shuffling the piles about until they fell down, then he put them all back in the tin. If only he knew where her room was, he could go up and speak to her sometimes, but she wouldn't tell him, not even though he was her brother.

Something else had begun to annoy him. Katie never paid any attention to him, but she was always speaking to that waiter, Dennis, and touching his hand. She never touched his hand now, Sammy reflected, not like when they used to be walking together to . . . ? He couldn't remember where they'd been going, nor why, but he could remember the long walking, and eating berries and turnips, and hiding in sheds, and sleeping on floors. He'd liked cuddling up to her, and maybe some day she'd let him do it again.

Now and then he got a queer feeling that he hadn't always been her brother, and then the dream started; a lovely dream it was, and it could easily come true, for Katie could make anything come true. She would be his mother, and he would sit on her knee – like in a song he had heard somewhere – and she would stroke his hair and say nice things to him, like mothers are supposed to do.

Hearing Mr Leith's heavy footsteps, Sammy scuttled away like a startled rabbit. If he was caught wasting time, he'd be in trouble.

In her room on the top floor, Katie gave a happy sigh. She had been attracted to Dennis McKay as soon as he smiled to her on her first day, almost three months ago. His shining black hair was slicked close to his head with Brilliantine – one of the chambermaids had told her he tried to look like Rudolph Valentino, the film star, not that she'd ever seen him – and he had a long lean face. His eyes were deep brown, twinkling when he laughed, but they could be quite serious at times. To begin with, she had thought he was too smarmy, flashing his white teeth at the diners and almost fawning over them, but she had soon realized that it was part of his job to make them believe they were special, and they seemed to lap it up, the ladies most of all.

He'd been a bit distant to her for a start, but for weeks now he'd given her his attractive smile when they passed on their ways to and from the dining room. Then he'd started talking to her, standing in the passageway from the kitchen with her for a few moments, and asking her if she'd settled in, how she liked the job, what she thought of the other people who worked in the hotel. There had been nothing more than that until today. They'd been clearing the last of the lunch dishes when he came over and touched her shoulder.

'Katie, how would you like to come out for a walk with me tonight after we finish the dinners?'

Her knees had nearly buckled under her, for she had heard one of the chambermaids telling the other to stop fancying him, for he never went out with any of the female staff, and here he was, actually asking her. She had pretended to think about it, of course – she hadn't wanted to show how eager she was – and then she'd said, as casually as she could, 'I was going to wash my hair . . . but I suppose I could.'

'Wait for me at the end of the street, that'll save any of them seeing us. They'd just torment us.'

Katie could barely contain her excitement as she ferried the dinner dishes backwards and forwards, but at last she was free and ran up for her coat. Peterhead always seemed to be much colder than Cullen, or even Fenty or Struieburn, and the March wind held a touch of sleet as she walked up and down for the ten minutes before Dennis arrived, looking most apologetic.

'I'm sorry I've kept you waiting,' he said, 'but Leith collared me when I was coming out and I couldn't get away.'

The felt hat sitting at a rakish angle on his head made him look more handsome than ever, she thought, suave, a man of the world, yet he had asked her out, so he must like her. Her pleasure increased when he took her down to the harbour, for she had always loved the sea, even though the wind had cut through them as soon as they turned the corner into Jamaica Street. While they stood looking out at the array of moored fishing boats, he told her his plans for the hotel he meant to own one day, then he gave a self-conscious laugh. 'You'll be fed up listening to what I want to do. Have you any plans for the future, Katie?'

'I hadn't thought about the future,' she said, shyly. She had been too concerned with forgetting about her past.

'Maybe you're like all the other girls I've been out with, desperate to get married and have babies?'

'I suppose I'd like to get married some day.'

'And so you will, once you meet the right man.'

She was disappointed, though he wasn't to know that she'd half hoped he might be the right man. 'Do you not want to be married yourself?'

'If I find the right girl.' He took her hand and turned her round. 'We'd better go back before we're locked out.'

They walked in silence for a bit, then he said, 'How old are you, Katie.'

'I'll be seventeen in June. How old are you?'

'I was twenty-one in January. Have you been out with a lot of lads?'

Her pride stopped her from telling the truth. 'Some. Have you been out with a lot of girls?'

'Some.'

They both chuckled at that, and he added, 'I've been going steady for about six months, but I gave her the elbow last week. She was getting too serious for my liking, and I don't fancy being tied to a nagging wife and a bunch of squawking brats. Not for years yet, anyway.'

Katie couldn't help admiring him for his honesty. He was warning her not to expect marriage, but with any luck, she might be able to make him change his mind.

When they reached the hotel, Dennis said, 'I'll let you go in first.'

'All right. Goodnight, Dennis.'

'Goodnight, Katie.' He leaned against the wall and took a slim silver cigarette case out of his pocket.

Having thought he would kiss her, she felt despondent as she went upstairs, but she brightened when it struck her that he might be going canny in case she got serious about him, like the girl he had told her about. What had *she* looked like?

Did he miss her? It might be a while before he forgot her, but Katie was willing to wait.

Next morning, a pain shot through her when she saw Dennis bending over a fat, over-dressed, middle-aged woman who was smiling coyly up at him and fluttering her eyelashes like a young thing. When he straightened up and saw Katie watching him, his false smile became genuine, and her heart sang as she laid down the toast-rack she had been carrying. She was glad that not many women stayed in the hotel, most of the guests being fishbuyers or something to do with fish, and a few commercial travellers. Some of them did take their wives with them, or maybe the wives didn't trust them being away from home on their own, but thank goodness there were never any young, single females.

John Leith was waiting for Katie in the kitchen when she went back, and she hoped he wasn't going to complain about Sammy. His smile reassured her. 'Will you manage the lunches and the dinners on your own today, Katie? Dennis got word that his mother's ill, so he's going to Fyvie to see her and he'll not be back till late.'

'I'll manage, Mr Leith.' She would be rushed off her feet, but she would do anything for Dennis.

As soon as she saw him next morning, she asked, 'How's your mother?'

'My mother? Oh . . . she's not too bad, better than I thought from what my sister said in her letter.'

'That's good. I . . . I missed you.'

'I missed you. Will you come out with me again tonight?'

Her head was in the clouds all day, and she spent her time off duty in the afternoon in day-dreaming about a courtship that would develop into lasting love and wedding bells.

They strolled past the prison that evening, and as they passed the long, high walls, Katie gave a shudder. 'This place gives me the creeps.'

Putting his arm round her, Dennis said, 'Don't be scared. I'll save you if any wicked murderers jump out.'

All her joy at being with him vanished. This was where Sammy would be sent if he was caught and found guilty, and maybe they would put her there, too, if not for attempted murder, for helping him to escape justice. 'Don't make fun of me, Dennis,' she pleaded.

'I wasn't making fun of you.' He squeezed her waist. 'I'd never make fun of you.'

They walked on a little faster until they were well clear of the jail and the warders' houses, then Dennis halted at the side of the windswept road and pulled her against him. 'I couldn't stop thinking about you yesterday, Katie.'

Her spirits took an ecstatic leap. 'Couldn't you?'

'I couldn't get you out of my mind. Look, it's maybe a bit early for you to believe this, but I like you an awful lot, and . . . oh, Katie, I'd hate to think you went out with anybody else. Will you promise to go steady with me?'

'Oh, yes . . .'

His lips stopped her, and the kissing went on for quite a while until he drew away with a long satisfied sigh. 'I've wanted to do that for weeks, Katie. That's why I got rid of my last girl.'

This was very flattering, but she wished that he had said he loved her, though maybe he thought his kisses would tell her. She'd been thrilled with Lachie Mooney's, but they had been nothing compared with Dennis's.

When they were returning to the hotel after hurrying past the prison again, Dennis said, 'I don't think we should go out every night. We see each other every day, anyway, and you'd soon get tired of me.'

'I'll never get tired of you, Dennis,' Katie protested.

'You might, so what about making it three nights a week?'

It wasn't enough for her, but she nodded. 'Which three?'

'Um . . . Monday, Wednesday, Friday?'

'All right, Monday, Wednesday, Friday.'

On the top floor where the resident female staff had rooms – Mr Leith took no chances of any shenanigans by housing the males in the basement – Katie went over the past hour and a half in her mind, but, even with Dennis's kisses fresh on her lips, she couldn't forget her fears for Sammy outside those awful high walls. The Temperance was not as safe as Struieburn. Very few strangers had ever gone to the farm, but so many different people came and went here, and Sammy was moving around in the foyer and the front stairs from seven every night; it would only take one off-duty policeman to see that he fitted the description of a wanted criminal and he'd be a goner.

She undressed and lay down, but her mind was too active for sleep. She should really take Sammy somewhere he would not be seen so easily, but that would mean leaving Dennis. Sammy or Dennis? Oh, it was impossible. She was very fond of Sammy, but she loved Dennis. Would that be enough to salve her conscience if she stayed at the hotel to be near him and Sammy was caught?

She agonized for some time before it crossed her mind that the police would be looking for a girl and a backward young man together, and none of the guests or those who came in for a meal would connect the night porter with the waitress. Being so much in the public eye was probably the best thing for him. The police wouldn't think of looking at him twice.

The relief was almost a physical pain, a welcome pain, and she relaxed to recall again the thrill of her lad's kisses.

It was some weeks before Sammy overheard something that made him prick up his ears. He had often heard the chambermaids giggling together and usually paid no attention to what they were saying, but this time was different.

'Dennis isn't half laying it on thick with Katie.'

'He's going out with an older woman as well as her. I've seen him going into her house in Queen Street.'

'Oh, well, it's Katie's funeral.'

His blood curdling, Sammy went down to his room. He

could hardly believe that his Katie was going out with the waiter, but it must be true, and if she was going to need a funeral, Dennis must be trying to kill her when he was laying into her. Well, not if Sammy could help it!

His sleep was troubled that day, visions of Dennis taking an iron bar over Katie's head making him wake in a sweat so often that he rose long before he needed to. When he was washed and dressed, he looked at the little clock Katie had bought him off her first week's wages. He was not very good at reading the time, but he could recognize the o'clocks and it was just coming up to five. He didn't have to be on duty till seven, so he had plenty of time to think.

Should he tell Katie that Dennis was going to kill her? But the two maids were always giggling and making jokes he couldn't understand, so for all he knew it could be a joke about Dennis. If it wasn't true, Katie would be angry with him, and he didn't like when she was angry. She would likely be angry if he said anything to Dennis, and all, so he'd be better to keep quiet. He didn't even know if it was true about them going out together, but he could easily find that out. All he had to do was watch the service door. That was the one the staff had to use.

After the dinners were over, he went to stand where he could watch the rear entrance without being seen, and sure enough, Dennis went out just a minute after Katie. Sammy thought of following them to make sure no harm came to her, then he remembered that he wasn't allowed to leave the hotel while he was on duty. He would wait till they came back.

He had been allocated the responsibility of locking the rear door at ten o'clock, so when both hands of the clock in the foyer were nearly on ten, he knew they would have to be in soon. Slipping outside, he took up his stance behind a big bush by the gate, ready to pounce if he saw Dennis doing anything bad to Katie.

*   *   *

Although they had stopped in several doorways during their walk, Katie was looking forward to their last few minutes together. They had been keeping company for over a month, and it was when he took her back to the hotel that Dennis was at his most passionate, running his hands over her in such a way that her whole body tingled, kissing her with a fervour that made her long for something more. She had meant to keep herself pure for the man she married, but she loved him so much she didn't think she would be able to refuse if he wanted to go further than that. Why should she refuse, in any case? She was sure he'd be her husband one day.

Hand in hand, they went through the gate where a clump of rhododendron bushes screened them from the windows at the rear of the hotel, and as usual, he drew her into his arms. Their lips had hardly met when a great shout arose and Sammy hurled himself at the young man, his clenched fist cracking against a bony eyebrow.

As Dennis cried, 'God Almighty!', Katie yelled, 'Stop it, Sammy! Stop it!'

His arms falling, Sammy watched Dennis scampering inside with his hand clapped over his injured eye, then he turned to Katie. 'He was going to kill you.'

'He was just kissing me! Why did you have to hit him?'

'Has Sammy been a bad boy?'

She couldn't scold him, not when his eyes were fixed on her so sorrowfully, and after all, he had believed he was defending her. 'No, Sammy,' she sighed, taking his arm and pulling him inside, 'you weren't bad.'

He wasn't even a boy, she thought, as she went up the back stairs. He was nineteen now, a young man. Surely he didn't have a man's jealousy of Dennis? If that was it, she would have to make sure he didn't see them together again. That was, if Dennis ever asked her out after this, which seemed highly unlikely.

*　　*　　*

Holding a wet towel against his eye, Dennis wondered if he should give up on Katie. The rich widow he'd been seeing on Tuesdays, Thursdays and Saturdays – and Sundays, sometimes – wasn't all that bad, but her body was flabbier than Katie's. He didn't love Beth Morton, but telling her he did was the only way he knew of getting his hands on her lovely money. He had known she must be well off when she stayed so long at the hotel, but it hadn't been until she told him she meant to settle down in Peterhead and asked if he knew of a house she could buy, money no object, that his interest was aroused – just his interest.

Once established in her new home, she had invited him to visit her, which was when he realized that she was attracted to him. She hadn't said it in so many words, of course, but he could tell. A man can always tell when a woman fancies him. He had known Katie fancied him as soon as she looked at him that first morning in the dining room, but he had been involved in trying to get off with Beth at that time. Once he saw that he had her in the palm of his hand, he had felt free to get entangled with Katie.

It was really quite exciting, having two strings to his bow, especially after that second long afternoon and evening he had spent with Beth – both days Katie thought he had gone to Fyvie to see his 'ailing' mother. Beth was a good-looking woman – almost an older version of Katie – with thick brown hair she wore piled high, a creamy, unlined skin and dancing blue eyes, but his sights were set on her cash, whereas it was Katie's body he was after. He knew she wasn't the kind to give up her virginity easily and he'd been working up to it gradually, but he might be best to mark time for a while to let her idiot brother simmer down. He didn't want the damned fool jumping on him and knocking him for six again.

Chapter Eight

❖❖

The other hotel workers were pleased that Dennis McKay had been taken down a peg, whoever had given him the black eye. When Chris, the chef, first saw it, he had laughed, 'It beats me why somebody didn't dot you one long ago. I've heard you've pinched more girlfriends than I've cooked hot dinners.'

In spite of his mortification, Dennis tried to be cocky. 'You're jealous because you can't pull the birds like me.'

'Maybe it was a bird that clouted you?' The idea had just struck Chris. 'Were you a naughty boy?'

Dennis gave a lewd snigger. 'The birds don't think I'm naughty. They like it.'

'I saw you out with Katie Mair one night. Was it her?'

This coming dangerously near the truth, Dennis screwed up his mouth in feigned derision. 'I went out with her once or twice, but I like them with a bit more spunk, you know what I mean? The kind that pretend they'll be annoyed if you try anything, but they're really just waiting for it.'

Chris snorted. 'Huh! You'd better watch out, m'lad. I went with a girl like that a couple of years back.'

'I thought you were married.'

'That's what I mean. It was months before she let me touch her, then the next thing I knew, the banns were cried and I was standing in front of the bloody minister!'

'I'll not get caught like that. Once I've had my fling, I'm going to find myself a girl with money.'

'You could find yourself a father with a shotgun,' Chris said, darkly, from the depths of experience.

Knowing that he'd found the girl – or to be accurate, the

woman – with money, Dennis was grinning as he went into the dining room, and he kept well away from Katie. She had told him once that she was an orphan, so there would be no father to contend with, but her brother had a right hook like the kick of a horse, and he was taking no chances.

In her room that forenoon, Katie was downhearted because Dennis hadn't looked at her once during the breakfasts, yet she couldn't really blame him. If only Sammy hadn't been so ready with his fists. If only she could be free to live her life the way she wanted, but she was tied to him through gratitude. She would be stuck with him for as long as he lived, with no hope of ever marrying, for no man would take on a wife with a simple-minded brother – and not really a brother, at that.

When she went down for the lunches, Sammy was hovering on the first landing of the staff stairs. 'What do you want?' she sighed. 'You should be in your bed.'

'That Dennis didn't hurt you, did he?'

'I told you last night he wasn't trying to hurt me, and any road, I don't think I'll be going out with him again.' Leaving him standing, she ran downstairs.

Sammy was still making his way down when John Leith came out of the dining room. 'Why are you on the stairs to the girls' rooms?' he demanded. 'You've no business up there.'

It did not occur to Sammy that honesty would be the wisest answer, and his confusion made him shuffle his feet and hold his head down. His employer tutted. 'You won't be fit for your work tonight if you don't get some sleep.'

'That Sammy!' he exploded, when he went into the kitchen. 'I know he's soft, but I can only stand so much.'

'What's he done, Mr Leith?' Katie asked, anxiously.

'I don't know, that's the trouble. I found him coming down the back stairs, but he wouldn't tell me where he'd been.'

'He was speaking to me on the landing, that's all.'

'Why couldn't he have said that, then? He was smirking as

if he'd been up to something, and when he saw me, he turned bright red and looked guilty.'

'He'd been scared he'd get into trouble. He knows he's not supposed to be up there.'

Katie thought nothing of the incident, but she did warn Sammy, the next time she saw him, that Mr Leith was angry at him for being on the stairs to the female staff's quarters. 'You must never go up again. If you want to ask me anything, wait down here.'

When the discolouration round his eye faded to a yellowing purple, Dennis began to talk to Katie again, and although it was only about the running of the dining room, she was glad that he was not ignoring her any longer. Once his injured pride recovered, he might take up their relationship where he had left off. Without his goodnight kisses to relive when she went to bed, thoughts of her grandparents had returned. The police would have called on them months ago to see if she had taken Sammy there, so they would know what had happened and would be shocked at what she had done. She would have liked to let her grandfather know that she was well, but she couldn't write to him. He had likely been told to contact the police if he heard from her, and as long as he knew nothing, he could pass nothing on.

It dawned on her that it would soon be a year since that dreadful night, so maybe the police had given up the search for them ... if they ever gave up on such a wicked crime as murder? It was unlikely, she reflected, woefully, and Mr Leith, and all the hotel workers, knew that she and Sammy were connected, though they believed they were brother and sister. She would never be free of the fear of a heavy hand falling on her shoulder and a deep voice booming in her ear, 'Katie Mair, I arrest you for ...'

It was not the first time that someone had reported a theft, but before today there had always been room for doubt that something had actually been stolen, not merely mislaid. John Leith knew that this was different. A gold pocket watch and a gold tie pin? No man, however careless, could have mislaid two such valuable objects on the same day, and they had been taken from a room on the first floor, next to the door to the back stairs, which pointed to a member of his staff, banking on making a quick getaway without being seen. Fortunately the victim did not want the police to be called in – he had admitted that the woman he had signed in as his wife was not really his wife, and he preferred that no fuss be made – but the manager wanted to get to the bottom of it, and there was only one thing for him to do.

Having asked his entire staff to assemble in the kitchen, he cast an accusing, but regretful, eye around them and told them what had happened. All of them stared at him in wide-eyed amazement except the night porter, who turned a deep crimson and hung his head. Recalling that he had caught this same young man on the back stairs two days previously, John Leith was sure that he had found the culprit and went across and grabbed the lapel of his jacket. 'So it was you!'

The firm accusation galvanized Katie to action. Jumping to Sammy's side, she shouted, 'He's not a thief!'

'Look at him!' exclaimed the hotel manager. 'He has guilt written all over him.'

'It's you holding on to him,' she said, desperately. 'He doesn't know what you're going on about.'

'He knows, he stole those things.'

Despite Katie's protests, Sammy was searched, then his room was searched, but there was no trace of the missing articles. 'Now do you believe he's not the thief?' Katie cried. 'He wouldn't steal anything.'

Angry because it appeared he had been proved wrong, and wishing that he had not engaged the half-wit in the first place, Leith snapped, 'I'm still not sure he isn't guilty, and I'd rather he left. He embarrasses the guests.'

Katie's blood boiled over. 'He does not embarrass them!'

she shouted. 'They give him big tips so they must like him, but if that's how you feel about him, I don't want to work here any longer, either.'

'Now, now, Katie, don't be hasty. I've no fault to find with you or your work.'

Ignoring his attempt to pacify her, Katie turned to Sammy. 'Go and pack your things, and I'll meet you outside as soon as I've packed mine.' She pushed him out, watched him going down to the basement and then stamped up to her own room.

Her fury gradually cooled down, but she knew that she had done the only thing possible, though Sammy would never find another job and they would have nowhere to live. Still, they had managed without a roof over their heads before, and they would manage again, somehow. Having tied her clothes into the old shawl again, she marched downstairs determined that no one would see how distressed she was, and strode along the ground-floor corridor and out through the service door as if she owned the place.

'Katie.'

She was taken aback to see Dennis, and although she could see that Sammy was eyeing him in deep distrust, she gave a bright smile to prove that she hadn't a care in the world. 'Cheerio, Dennis. I don't suppose I'll see you again.'

'No, worse luck, but it's maybe better this way.' He cast a meaningful glance at Sammy. 'I'm really going to miss you, though, Katie. What are you going to do now?'

She struggled to keep hold of her fragile composure. 'I don't know yet, but we'll be all right.'

'Listen, Katie. A couple of nights ago, I heard they were a waitress short at the Salutation. Why don't you go and see if the job's still going? They maybe won't take Sammy on as well, but it's worth a try. Cheerio, and good luck.'

Her spirits soared as he clasped her hand. He had cared enough to come and say goodbye, and not only that, he was trying to help her to find a job. She would always have that to remember. 'Thanks, Dennis.' She moved before he could see the tears glistening in her eyes. 'Come on, Sammy, we're going to the Salutation.'

The proprietor of the other hotel – a short man with a pleasant, open face – told her that he was very sorry but the post of waitress had been filled, and Katie was turning sadly away when he added, 'Would you be willing to work as a chambermaid? I've a vacancy there.'

'Oh, yes, I'm willing to do anything. Um – what about my brother? Is there a job for him, and all?'

The man stared doubtfully at Sammy, whose bottom lip was sticking out sullenly. 'What can he do?'

Katie decided to be honest; the man could easily find out what had happened. 'He was night porter at the Temperance, but some things went missing, and Mr Leith blamed Sammy. I know he's not a thief, so that's why I left.'

'You're sure he can be trusted?'

'As sure as I'm standing here. He'd never touch a thing that didn't belong to him, and he's strong as a horse and willing to work.' Remembering another of Sammy talents, she added, 'And he's good at gardening.'

'Ah! I could be doing with a gardener. My present man is nearly seventy and crippled with arthritis, but he's been here so long I don't like to pay him off. The work's a bit too much for him now, so if your brother's willing to do most of it himself and to keep out of the hotel itself . . . ?'

'He won't mind that, will you, Sammy?'

At the mention of gardens, Sammy's face had undergone a swift improvement. 'I like gardens.'

'So, that's settled.' The man hesitated, then added, 'On a trial basis.' Then, noticing their bundles, he asked, 'Have you nowhere to live?'

'We lived in at the Temperance,' Katie said, hopefully.

'I'm sorry, I only employ locals, so I don't have any rooms for staff. Couldn't you find lodgings somewhere?'

'I'm sure we can. When do you want us to start?'

'Eight o'clock, Monday morning?'

'We'll be here, Mr . . . ?'

'My name is Noble, and I'll see you on Monday.'

'Thank you, Mr Noble.'

Out in the street again, Katie gave a deep sigh. 'Well, Sammy, we've got jobs, but where are we going to sleep?'

'In a bed.'

Knowing he wasn't trying to be funny, she made no attempt to explain. 'Did you remember to take your money with you?'

'Yes, I've got my tin in my pocket.'

She, too, had taken the money she had saved and the wages she had made Sammy hand over in case he lost them – she had let him keep his tips – so they could easily afford to pay for lodgings and anything else they needed. This thought cheered her a little, but they still had to find somewhere. She had no idea where to start looking, and kept on walking until she could think about it properly.

They were going down Broad Street when they passed a baker with a card in the window saying that it was also a café and the appetizing smell wafting out made Sammy say plaintively, 'I'm hungry.'

Katie was too worried to think about food, but, to humour him, she took him inside. There were two women behind the counter – the younger skinny and a little slow at serving, the other plump and brisk – and only one item on the chalked menu on the wall. Katie ordered two servings of the mince, peas and boiled potatoes and they sat down at one of the three tables. When the older woman brought their order, she asked, conversationally, 'Are you on holiday?'

Katie shook her head. 'My brother and me have got jobs at the Salutation Hotel, and we're looking for lodgings.'

The woman regarded her thoughtfully. 'I don't know anybody round here that takes in lodgers, but I could maybe help you. My man's got some property in Marischal Street, just along a bit, and one of his tenants died in the hospital last week. She was an old body, no relations and no money, and we paid for her to have a decent burial. I gave her clothes to the Salvation Army, and we were thinking about letting the place furnished. If you'd like to see it, I'll give you the keys.'

It had never entered Katie's head to rent a house, but it would be far better than lodgings, and probably cheaper in the long run. 'I'd like to take a look at it, thank you.'

She found that Marischal Street was a continuation of Broad Street, and to reach the house, they had to go through a pend with house doors and windows along one side and what looked like shed doors, painted dark green, along the other, She had been told it was the last house, and when the first two keys on the ring did not fit, she thought she must be at the wrong place, but the third key turned in the lock, and she and Sammy went inside. It was an old house, packed with old furniture, and had a musty smell, but she didn't care. It had probably been standing empty for a while, and once the windows were opened to let in fresh air, the smell would soon go. Discovering that there were two bedrooms as well as the kitchen, she breathed a sigh of relief. 'What d'you think, Sammy? We'll be fine here, won't we?'

'Is this where we'll be sleeping?' He bounced on the high bed like a little boy.

'If you want this room, I'll have the other one.'

'You'll be sleeping next door to me.'

A perplexed frown furrowed his brow, and Katie knew that he was trying to remember another life, another time when they had slept in adjoining rooms. She often felt irritated with him for having such a short memory, but she was glad that he had forgotten the Howe of Fenty. 'We'll go and tell the woman we'll take the house, then.'

Fifteen minutes later, the rent agreed on and some items of food bought, they were back in their new home, and the first thing Katie did was to open the casement windows as far as they would go. Then she said, 'We'd better make the beds ready first. I'll have a look and see if there's clean sheets and blankets anywhere.'

They were still making the second bed when the woman

from the café knocked and walked in. 'I forgot to say you've to share a wc with Ella Brodie next door, though you've got a coalshed to yourself. I'd better show you. Have you got the keys handy?'

'I wondered why there were three,' Katie smiled.

She was pleased that the lavatory was so clean and bright – tiled from cement floor to white-washed ceiling, and more delight was to come. The shed – last in the line of green doors – was stacked high with coal. 'There's enough to see us right through the winter!' she exclaimed, clapping her hands, then her expression changed. 'I'm sorry. You'll be wanting to take it.'

'No, no, you might as well use it.' Locking the door, the woman returned the keys to Katie. 'If there's anything you want, you know where to find me. Oh, and I'll need your name for the rent book.'

'I'm Katie Mair, and my brother's Sammy.' Katie had always said it that way, leaving the person who had asked believing that Sammy's surname was also Mair, and praying that nobody ever asked him first, though he had likely forgotten that his was Gunn.

'My name's Lottie McRuvie, and I'd better get back to the shop. Kirsty's dead slow and stop, and we're aye busy.'

Katie now began on the mammoth task of making the kitchen presentable. Sammy was detailed to lift the rugs and shake them outside while she scoured the grate and lit the fire. Then she asked him to shift the furniture to let her scrub every inch of the linoleum. He hadn't complained once, but when they were having a meal of corned beef and potatoes, he couldn't stop yawning. 'Oh, Sammy!' she exclaimed. 'I forgot you didn't have any sleep today. Off you go to bed.'

Once she had seen him settled, she washed all the dust-covered ornaments and polished the furniture. Her mouth was bone dry when she called it a day, and she sat down to drink a last cup of tea. She had been on the go since six in the morning, and the wag-at-the-wa' was showing a quarter to eleven – she had pulled up the weight to start the mechanism and set the hands at the correct time when she heard a clock outside striking four. It was no wonder she was so tired.

Getting to her feet wearily, she went through to her own room, but, as she undressed, it dawned on her that she and Sammy were in an even more dangerous position than when they were at the Temperance. They had always been in uniform there – the only time she had been out was with Dennis – but, as from Monday, they would have to walk together to the Salutation in their ordinary clothes. What if a policeman recognized them?

Chapter Nine

❖

Because it was licensed, the Salutation generally housed more commercial travellers than the Temperance, but Katie rarely came in contact with any of the clientele. She had to wait until the occupant had left the room before she could go in to make the bed and tidy up, although there was the odd occasion when someone returned for something he or she had forgotten, and it was then that Katie was made aware of the difference in her status. As a waitress, the guests had smiled to her and talked to her, but as a maid, it was as if she were invisible. She didn't mind, for it took her all her time to get round her quota of rooms without being hindered by chattery guests.

Apart from missing Dennis, she was quite content in her new job, and Sammy seemed to get on very well with Hairy Cameron, the old gardener, who was as bald as a coot and whose nickname had been bestowed on him with gentle irony by some long-forgotten employee. Every day when he came home, Sammy would begin, 'Hairy said . . .' and she was forced to listen to another of the far-fetched tales of his youth that the old man spun to his assistant. At least, she thought they were far-fetched, but maybe they weren't, and Sammy lapped up every word.

Finished at the hotel by half past two, she did her own housework in the afternoons, and Sammy helped when he came home by taking in coal, chopping sticks, and, once a week, polishing the cutlery from the table drawer. He had learned how to make his own bed now, mitring the corners as Katie taught him and not being satisfied until blankets and top cover were scrupulously smooth. He was a good pupil and beamed proudly when she praised him.

They had been in their new jobs barely two weeks – her fear of being caught not so acute since two policemen had walked past them in the street on different days without looking at them – when she was disquieted by what Sammy said one evening. 'Are you my wife now, Katie?'

Sick inside, she exclaimed, 'What made you ask that?'

'Well, Hairy says he takes in coal and chops sticks for his wife, and cleans the spoons and forks for her, like I do for you, so I thought you must be my wife.'

Her tension eased a little. 'You're my brother, and that means I'm your sister, not your wife.'

'My sister?' Never having made this connection, Sammy took a moment to chew it over, then dismissed it. 'Hairy and his wife sleep in the same bed, and she heats her bloody great feet on his legs. If we slept in the same bed, I'd let you heat your bloody . . .'

Even knowing that he was only repeating what the old man had said, Katie had to stop his train of thought. 'Brothers and sisters can't sleep in the same bed. It's not allowed.'

That satisfied him – he knew there were things he was not allowed to do – but her jangled nerves took a long time to settle.

With the shops being so handy, Katie often popped into the baker's shop and was now very friendly with Lottie McRuvie. She bought their supper on her way home each day, and at first, she had taken Sammy with her on Saturday afternoons to stock up on heavy items such as oatmeal, flour, bleach, etc. After a few weeks, she felt that he could manage by himself, which gave her time to attend to all the chores she usually had to leave until the weekend.

At first, Sammy had been a trifle hesitant to tackle the weekly shopping, but now he trotted off happily, the money wrapped in the list she wrote out and placed at the bottom of a string bag she had bought for the purpose. He was very proud of being her errand boy, and the shopkeepers gave him a few sweets or a biscuit, as they did to the children who shopped for their mothers; even the butcher gave him the odd bowl of potted head, which pleased him immensely, for he was quite partial to it.

He and Katie were sitting together one Saturday night, a few months after they had come to live in Marischal Street, when he heaved a long deep sigh. 'What's wrong?' she asked, anxiously, afraid that someone had said something to him about being backward.

'Nothing.' His smile was blissful. 'I like this house.'

She relaxed. 'So do I.'

'I like it being just me and you. Sammy's happy, Katie.'

'Me, and all.'

'The happiest I've ever been in my whole life.'

Aware that he had no recollection of his earlier life, or indeed of any time before they came to live there, she still leaned over and patted his hand. 'I'm glad.'

Sammy's happiness was shattered when he caught a cold which developed into a feverish influenza. He had never been ill before, and Katie had difficulty in persuading him to stay at home. At last, she said, 'You'll make it worse if you're outside all day, and you could end up having to lie in bed for weeks.'

'If I don't go to work today, will I be better tomorrow?'

'Maybe not tomorrow, maybe in two or three days.'

He gave in, but she was worried about leaving him on his own for so long and issued some instructions before she went out. 'I've left soup in a pan for your dinner, and you'll have to keep the fire going so you can heat it up. Will you manage that? Don't try lighting the gas stove, and don't bother answering the door if anybody knocks, it'll likely just be a gypsy selling pegs.'

Sammy was never far from Katie's thoughts that morning – she pictured him letting the soup pot drop and scalding himself, or turning dizzy when he was putting on coal and falling into the fire, or trying to light a gas ring and blowing himself up – and the bedrooms at the Salutation had never been cleaned so superficially as she rushed through them in order to get home to make sure he was all right.

Her work finished, she ran as fast as she could, and she was in the Longate when someone on the opposite side of the street shouted, 'Katie!'

Not wanting to stop, she gave a quick glance across, but came to an abrupt halt at the sight of the familiar figure. 'Dennis!' she cried, all concern for Sammy forgotten.

He came across to her. 'I heard you got a job.'

'Not a waitress's job, though, just a chambermaid, and Sammy helps the gardener. Mr Noble said he couldn't give us rooms and I thought we'd have to go into lodgings, but I found a house to rent.'

'A house? My, you're coming up in the world.'

'It's quite nice, three rooms in Marischal Street, all furnished.' It dawned on her that there was nothing to stop her inviting him there. 'I'd be happy if you wanted to visit me some night. I've . . . missed you.'

'I've missed you, and all, and I'd love to visit you . . . oh! Will your brother be there?'

Her heart sank. 'Yes, he will. He's got the 'flu just now, that's why I was hurrying home, so I'll have to go, Dennis.'

'I'll come with you, so I'll know where to come.'

Katie's renewed worry for Sammy vanished again when Dennis slid his arm around her. 'It's like old times, isn't it,' he murmured.

As they sauntered down Broad Street, he said, 'By the way, about a fortnight after you left the Temperance, Mag Stewart – remember, the wee chambermaid with the Eton crop? – well, she was caught red-handed taking money out of a wallet, and she owned up to stealing the other things. Leith sacked her on the spot.'

'I told him it wasn't Sammy,' Katie burst out, 'and I hope he's ashamed for what he did.'

The young man smiled. 'You know, I got a shock at you that day. I didn't think you had the guts to stand up to Leith, and I like girls with a bit of spirit. It made me like you a lot more, Katie.'

'Oh, Dennis, I'm glad, for I like you an awful lot.'

He regarded her seriously. 'If you can tame your brother, we might get together again.'

'I'll make sure Sammy knows I . . . I like you. It'll be all right, Dennis, I promise. Here's my house. Through the pen' and it's the last door. Do you want to come in now?'

'I suppose I could, it's my day off, but only if you're sure Sammy won't fly at me.'

'I'll make sure he understands you're my . . . friend.'

She told Dennis to sit down by the fire till she talked to Sammy, and when she came back, she said, 'He won't bother us. I told him I'd my . . . friend in, and I'd never speak to him again if he came through, so he won't bother us. You can stay for your supper, can't you? There's pork left over from yesterday.'

While she mixed a sponge pudding and put the bowl into a steamer, then prepared some vegetables to eke out the pork, Dennis told her what had been happening at the Temperance, and she found that she wasn't really interested in hearing about her ex-workmates – she had never known any of them very well – but she took good care not to let him see how she felt.

'We have our supper at half past five,' she said, when he ran out of stories. 'That's when Sammy usually comes in, so I hope that's all right with you?'

'Any time's all right with me,' he smiled.

'How do you get on with the waitress who came after me?' This was something she had often wondered.

'Peggy? She's gorgeous! Curves that make me want to grab hold of her every time she passes, lips made for kissing, and her legs! Her skirt's so short, I can see the backs of her knees every time she bends over a table.'

119

'Have you . . . taken her out?' Katie faltered, wishing that she had never asked, and dreading his answer.

His loud roar of laughter told her that he had only been joking. 'Oh, you!' she exploded. 'What's she really like, this Peggy?'

'She's fifty, if she's a day,' he grinned, 'with no curves at all and skirts down to her feet, but she's a good enough waitress. Oh, Katie, you should have seen your face!'

She was hurt by his teasing, even more so because he had enjoyed seeing her discomfiture. 'I'm glad you think it's funny,' she said, huffily.

'I'm sorry, Katie, I didn't mean it. Listen, I'll tell you something that'll maybe cheer you up. I've never looked at anybody else since that last night with you. I used to be a great one for the girls, but you changed that.'

She was flustered by the way he was looking at her. 'I'd better light the gas under the tatties,' she said, turning away. 'Supper won't be long now.'

He said nothing personal while she set the table and put plates in the oven to heat, nor during the meal, except to congratulate her on her cooking, but when she turned from laying past the dishes he dried for her, he stretched out his arms. 'Come to me, my lovely, lovely Katie.'

After only a fractional hesitation, she gave a happy sigh and almost swooned against him. 'I used to dream about us being together like this. It's better than when we were in the street having to be careful nobody saw us.'

'It might be even better if we sat down on the couch.'

It was better, far better, and she responded to his kisses and caresses like a drowning person responds to a lifebelt. Suddenly, he leaned away. 'I'll have to stop, Katie. I might do something . . .' He disengaged her arms from his neck, and when she pressed herself against him again, he gave her a gentle push. 'No, it's not right, and anyway, it's time I was going. It's twenty to ten already.'

'You'll come back to see me?' she begged.

'After I finish work on Friday?' He gave her a quick kiss, then lifted his hat from the dresser and left.

Katie did not go through to see if Sammy needed anything; she couldn't face him just yet. She was hot and bothered, her whole body tingling from the touch of Dennis's hands. The love she had felt for him before was as nothing in comparison with what she was feeling now. This wasn't a girlish infatuation, it was a woman's love, crying out for fulfilment. It didn't matter that he hadn't tried to get in touch with her. Nothing mattered except that they were together again.

Going up Broad Street, Dennis was wondering if he'd been too cautious in refusing what was blatantly on offer. Katie had been his for the taking, but not tonight, Josephine. Tonight he'd been preparing the ground for a bumper harvest – he didn't want to scare her off at this early stage. Besides, it gave him a feeling of power to make her wait, just like teasing a dog with a bone.

But he'd gone too far for his own good, and he didn't have time to satisfy himself with Beth. He was sick of having to keep to Leith's rules and be in by ten. Wait! Why hadn't he thought of it before? All he needed was a place to live, and now he had the choice of two houses. Asking Beth Morton was a bit dodgy, for she had an old-fashioned outlook on things, and she probably wouldn't agree unless he promised to marry her. That might be the only way he'd get his hands on any of her cash, but as his wife, she would keep a tight rein on him. In any case, was it wise to tie himself to a woman so much older?

No, Katie was the answer. She might balk if he asked right out if he could sleep with her, but surely he could string her along and make her think the idea was hers. Once he was in, say in a few months when he'd be bored with her, heigh-ho! She'd be so much in love with him, she'd believe any excuse he gave for being late home. He could go on seeing Beth or any other bit of skirt he took a fancy to. It would be dangerous, but by God he'd enjoy the challenge.

When Dennis arrived on Friday, Katie warned him at the door, 'Sammy's in the kitchen, so don't kiss me in front of him.'

'It's hardly worth my while coming, then, is it?'

'It'll just be till he gets used to seeing you here . . . then it'll be all right. Anyway, he always goes to bed at nine, so we'll have a wee while on our own.'

Sammy, however, did not go to bed at nine, and kept his eyes fixed on the other man. 'That's been a waste of time,' Dennis observed, sourly, when Katie saw him out.

'He'll come round,' she muttered, miserably.

'He'd better. It puts me off when he glares at me like I'm doing something wrong. I'd be as well not coming at all.'

'Oh, Dennis, please don't stop coming.'

'You'll have to do something about him, then.'

'I'll try, honest I will. I'll see you on Monday?'

He took her in his arms and kissed her, passionate kisses that left her gasping, then he said, 'Monday,' and walked through the pend.

She kept standing after he waved from the street and went out of sight; she couldn't get over Sammy recognizing him. She had thought he wouldn't remember, but when she took her 'friend' in, he had shrunk back into his seat, not in fear, but more as if he were trying to make himself invisible so that he could keep watch. Angry at him now, she went inside to have it out with him. 'That was a fine way to carry on!' she scolded. 'Did you have to glower at Dennis like that the whole time he was here? He didn't like it, you know, so why didn't you go to bed?'

Sammy's eyes filled with the pain of one whose motive had been misunderstood. 'I wanted to see he didn't hurt you.'

'He won't hurt me, and I'll be really angry with you if you

stay up so long again. Nine o'clock's been your bedtime ever since we started at the Salutation, and you need all your sleep so you'll be fit to help Hairy in the gardens.'

He trailed out to the lavatory sadly, and when he came back, he made for his bedroom. 'Will he be here again?' he asked, before he opened the door.

'He'll be here every Friday,' she said, firmly, 'and every Monday and Wednesday, and all, so just remember.' Wondering where Dennis went on the other nights of the week, she knew that she couldn't ask him. She didn't have the right . . . yet.

On Monday when Sammy came home, she reminded him that he had to go to bed at nine, and after sitting morosely silent for nearly three quarters of an hour after Dennis appeared, he stood up and went into his room without saying a word.

Grinning, Dennis put his arms round Katie. 'Thank God that's him out of the road.'

His kisses were not quite so passionate as they had been on the first night, and she supposed that he didn't want them to get so worked up . . . not until they were married.

When the familiar knock came on Wednesday – da-di-di-da – she ran to let Dennis in, sliding briefly into his arms before taking him into the kitchen, where Sammy – having been told to try to be more friendly – gave him a half-hearted smile. Dennis patted him on the shoulder and sat down. 'You been busy today, Sammy?'

Katie did not know that Dennis had only asked this to get in her good books, but she did know that making conversation wasn't easy for Sammy. 'You trimmed the hedges, didn't you?' she prompted.

A proud grin lit up his face. 'Yes, and Hairy said I did a grand job.'

'Good for you.' Dennis pulled Katie down on the couch and put his arm around her. 'And what have you been doing today, my sweet one?'

'Just the usual,' she said, uncomfortably conscious that Sammy was scowling darkly now. 'Bedrooms and bathrooms.'

'And I'm sure you did a grand job, and all,' he teased.

To fill in time until he had Katie on her own, Dennis gave her the latest gossip from the Temperance, and at last Sammy stood up. 'I'm going to bed now.'

Once they were alone, Dennis drew Katie towards him and kissed her hungrily. 'I hate having to waste nearly an hour waiting for him to go to bed,' he murmured in a few moments. 'If I didn't live in at the hotel I wouldn't have to be back by ten. If I could only find a room somewhere . . .'

'You could live here. It's not far from the Temperance.'

'Do you mean that?'

His astonishment at the suggestion pleased her; it had obviously not occurred to him. 'Yes, I mean it, as long as you don't mind sleeping on the couch.'

He gave her a troubled stare. 'I likely wouldn't be able to sleep knowing I was so near you. I'd feel like going in beside you. No, I'd better try and find somewhere else.'

So tempted by the thought of sharing a bed with him, Katie took no time to think. 'It's all right,' she murmured, 'I'll not make you sleep on the couch.'

'You're sure?'

It wasn't what she had meant originally, but did it make any difference? After all, she was ninety-nine per cent sure that she would be giving herself to her future husband. 'Yes, Dennis, quite, quite sure.'

With a low moan, he crushed her to him. 'Oh, God, Katie, I'll be the happiest man alive. I'll tell John Leith in the morning I've found lodgings. When can I move in?'

'As soon as you like.'

'Not tomorrow but the next day?'

'That's fine.'

For the next half hour, Dennis gave Katie a foretaste of the passion they would soon share nightly, taking off her blouse and bodice to fondle her, but going no further than that, and when he left, she was a trembling mass of longing.

Lying down on the couch again, she could still feel his hands on her, his fingers gently kneading her. She let her own fingers emulate his, stroking each breast, running her thumbs round her nipples as he had done, until the same thrills started, and shamed by what she was doing, she shut her eyes and let her thoughts dwell on a future with Dennis. She didn't hear Sammy coming in, and he stood looking down at her over the back of the couch. Her top half was totally exposed, and although he had a boy's mind, he had the body of a man now, with a man's responses to seeing a woman's naked bosom, especially for the first time. At last, he said, 'Can I feel them?'

Startled, Katie jerked her head up. 'Feel what?'

'Them.' His index finger pointed.

Remembering her condition too late, she covered herself with her arms and cast her eyes round desperately to find where Dennis had thrown her blouse and bodice. 'Give me over my clothes, please, Sammy.'

'But I don't want you to hide them.'

'You mustn't look at them.'

'Is it because I'm your brother?'

'Yes, and it's not allowed.'

The magic words were all he needed, and he handed her the garments. 'Go back to bed, Sammy,' she ordered, keeping her arms firmly across her chest.

'You're not angry? You still like me?'

'I'll always like you, but go back to bed now.'

When he moved clear of the couch, she was dismayed to see his hand at his crotch, and when he opened his mouth as if to say something, she snapped, 'Right now, Sammy!'

'I came through for a drink of water,' he wailed. 'That yellow fish we had made me awful thirsty, and I waited till I heard Dennis going away.'

'Go on, then, but straight to bed after that.'

She watched him fill the tumbler at the sink, but her horror grew when he turned and she saw his swollen organ poking out of his drawers. Noticing where she was looking, he said, 'D'you want to see my thing? It's got great big.'

She averted her eyes hastily. 'No! Go to bed!'

Sick at what had happened, she began to shake even before his door closed. Would she be able to cope with him now he had discovered his sexuality? He was too strong for her to fend off if he tried anything, and even when Dennis moved in, he wouldn't be home till after eight every night.

Another fear caught at her. How on earth would Sammy react when she told him that Dennis would be sleeping with her?

Chapter Ten

❦

After a restless night, Katie rose wondering which would be worse, facing Sammy after what had happened, or telling him about Dennis, and when she heard him going into the kitchen to wash, she primed herself to take the bull by both horns.

He looked round when she went in, but not by one flicker of an eyelid did he show that this morning was different from any other, so that was one weight off her mind – though she still had to deal with the other matter. 'Sammy,' she began, nerves making her voice a trifle high, 'I've asked Dennis . . . he was fed up having to be in at ten every night, so I said he could come and live here with us.'

Sammy digested this information for a moment, then said, his mouth sulky, 'He'll not be sleeping in my bed, will he?'

'No, he'll be . . . in my bed.'

If Katie had been thinking more clearly, she might have realized that her guarded statement would be misconstrued, but as it was, she could hardly believe that there was no explosion. After a moment's deliberation, Sammy merely said, 'How long's he going to be here?'

'I don't know. Maybe for ever?'

This meant nothing to Sammy. 'When's he coming?'

'Tomorrow night.' Katie was thankful that there had been no scene, no hint of jealousy. Of course, he must know by now that Dennis would never hurt her, and with three of them in the house, she would feel she had a family again.

When she went to the baker-cum-café on her way home that afternoon, she told Lottie McRuvie that she was taking in a lodger, ending, a little uncertainly, 'It's not against the rules, is it?'

Having grown fond of the girl, the baker's wife gave her a reassuring smile. 'I don't mind, but I'd have thought you'd enough on your plate with Sammy, without saddling yourself with a lodger, and all.'

Katie coloured a little. 'Sammy's no bother, and Dennis'll not make much more work.'

'Dennis? Isn't that the lad you told me you had when you were at the Temperance? Him that Sammy thought was killing you and punched his face? I thought you said you never saw him again after you left?'

Feeling guilty because she hadn't mentioned her renewed romance with Dennis, and even guiltier because of what she intended to do, Katie's cheeks flamed. 'I ran into him one day, and he's been coming to the house a lot.'

Lottie said nothing as she wrapped the requested loaf, but as she dropped the six softies into a bag, she looked at the girl doubtfully. 'I only hope you know what you're doing.'

Just then, another customer came in, and Katie paid for her purchases and went out, wishing that Lottie had not been so quick to put two and two together.

Carrying out her duties one morning, Katie was thinking as usual about Dennis. She had never slept with any other man – except Sammy and that was different – but she was certain that Dennis must be the best lover in the whole world. She had been apprehensive the very first time, and, recalling what Susie Clark had said about her first experience, more than a little scared. But he hadn't rushed her, and now, after six weeks, she waited impatiently for Sammy to go to bed so that she and Dennis could go to theirs. Just lately, though, he had started petting her in front of Sammy, and he wasn't pleased when she stopped him. She had to stop him, though, for she could see that a jealous anger was building up in Sammy, and she was afraid that it could erupt at the least provocation. If it wasn't for that – and the lingering shred of worry that the police might still find them – she would be truly happy.

The last bed made, the last bathroom cleaned, Katie made her way down to the staffroom, and was putting on her coat when Melvin Noble came in. 'I want to ask you two things, Katie. First, do you think your brother would take on the gardens himself?'

'Without Hairy, you mean?'

'Cameron's just told me he's giving up. He's hardly been doing anything for months, so it won't mean much extra work for Sammy, but is he fit to do it without being told what to do, without being supervised?'

'He used to do a garden before, Mr Noble. He knows what's to be done, and when.'

'So you think I'd be safe to leave him? Or should I give him a young lad to help him?'

'He'd manage himself, but he likes having company.'

'Right, I'll hire a fourteen-year-old. Now to the other thing. You said you'd been a waitress, and Francie's got a higher-paid job in the Saltoun Arms in Fraserburgh, so how do you feel about taking over her job? Any Tom, Dick or Harry – or maybe I should say Jeannie, Mary or Bella – could make beds, but a waitress needs to have the looks and the figure, and if you don't think I'm being personal, you'd be an asset to my dining room. What do you say, Katie?'

'I wouldn't mind being a waitress again.'

'That's settled, then.'

At that moment, Sammy came in, as he usually did, to say goodbye to his 'sister' before she went home, and Mr Noble said, 'I'll leave you to tell him, Katie. It'll mean more wages for you both, and you'll start this coming Monday.'

'What have you to tell me?' Sammy asked, as their employer went out.

'I'll tell you when you come home.' Katie wanted him to be where his inevitable jubilation wouldn't disturb anybody.

Her own jubilation was such that she popped her head into the McRuvie's shop as she passed to tell her friend the good news. 'Oh, I'm right pleased for the pair of you,' Lottie beamed. 'What's Sammy saying about it?'

'He doesn't know yet.'

'How's things between him and Dennis?'

'So-so.'

Lottie's face sobered. 'Your neighbours are speaking about you having your lad biding with you. Ella Brodie says it's a downright disgrace among decent folk.'

Katie tossed her head. 'I don't care what they say. It's nobody's business.'

'That's what I told her, but she's a narrow-minded besom. When you went in there first, she thought you were sleeping with Sammy, and I put her right about that, but Dennis is that good-looking . . . and with just two bedrooms . . .' Lottie shrugged expressively as the girl went out.

Although it hadn't bothered her, Katie had wondered why the woman who shared the lavatory with them had never been friendly, and now she knew, she felt angry. What right had Miss Brodie or anybody else to sit in judgment of her? But she couldn't help chuckling when she thought of how shocked all the women in the pend had been when Dennis moved in.

When she told Sammy about his promotion, she was glad she had made him wait, because he hadn't come down to earth by the time he went to bed. 'I've got Hairy's job,' he said, for the umpteenth time, as he stood up, 'and he says he's head gardener, so I'll be head gardener now.'

'That's right,' she laughed, 'and you'll have to tell the new laddie what to do.'

'What's his name, the new laddie?'

'I don't know, but you can ask him on Monday.'

Dennis had passed no comments on their promotion, but as soon as he and Katie were alone, he observed, 'I hope he doesn't get above himself. Noble's mad to give him so much responsibility.'

'Sammy doesn't know he's got responsibility. He'll go on

working the way he's always done, except he'll have a boy to help him.'

'I sometimes wish . . .' Dennis paused, looking at her rather warily. 'If you . . . put him in a Home and told them he likes gardening, they'd likely let him . . .'

'Dennis McKay!' Katie was absolutely appalled. 'How could you say such a thing! I couldn't put Sammy in a Home.'

'I'm sorry. It's just . . . there's something about him that gets up my nose, and I'd like to have you all to myself. I love you, Katie Mair, that's what.'

She let him kiss her and pull her up off the couch, but as they went into their room, she said, 'Don't you ever tell me to put Sammy in a Home again.'

'Get into bed, my dearest one,' Dennis soothed, 'and I'll show you how sorry I am for upsetting you.'

His love-making succeeded in cooling her anger, but when he fell asleep, she lay considering what she would do if she ever had to choose between the two men, and came to the conclusion that, much as she loved Dennis, she would rather give him up than put Sammy away . . . but would she, if it came to the point?

From the minute Katie first started to work alongside Keith Robb, she knew that the waiter resented her, and it took her only another minute to discover why.

'I thought Sally would get Francie's job,' he said, while they put starched napkins in rings and set them on the side plates. 'I don't know why Noble gave it to you.'

Guessing that Keith fancied Sally, the other chambermaid, Katie stood her ground. 'He knew I was a waitress before I came here.'

'So you put your oar in as soon as you knew Francie was leaving?' he sneered.

'I didn't know she was leaving till Mr Noble said I could have her job.'

This took Keith aback, and he blustered, 'You'd better do what you're told, then. I like everything running smoothly.'

'So do I.' Seething, Katie turned away, but she knew that he would be on the look-out for any excuse to complain about her, and was determined not to give him one.

During the breakfasts, she couldn't help comparing Keith with Dennis, and had to admit that he was just as efficient, though he didn't have Dennis's charm. In her off-duty time before the lunches, she sat in the staffroom and wished that she had thought of buying a magazine to read. At last, she stood up and looked out of the window, a smile crossing her face when she saw Sammy talking animatedly to the young boy beside him and gesturing with his hands as if demonstrating something. At least he was happy in his new job, and maybe she would be, too, once Keith accepted her. When he saw that she was competent in her work, he would be more friendly.

When she began serving lunches, she was surprised that first one person and then another complained that an item of cutlery was missing. She apologized and furnished them with replacements, but she couldn't understand it.

They were making the tables ready for dinner when Keith sidled up to her. 'Make sure you set all the places properly this time.'

'I set them properly before,' she retorted.

'You couldn't have.'

He walked past her with a sarcastic swagger, and the truth dawned on her. He had removed the cutlery himself so that it would appear as if she had been careless, and she would have to make sure that he didn't try the same trick again.

Just before the dining room doors were opened for dinner, she went across to him respectfully. 'Keith, will you please check my tables before anybody comes in?'

She had placed him in a difficult position, and smiled to herself as he made a quick inspection. 'Everything seems to be there,' he said, truculently.

'It was all there last time.'

Their eyes met and held briefly before he turned away, and she knew that she had made an enemy of him.

Dennis McKay was well pleased with himself. He had let Katie see he didn't like Sammy being in the house with them, and she would surely get rid of her daft brother before she'd give up the man she loved. He had never been in so much clover. Having told Beth Morton that he was being sent to Glasgow as a relief waiter for three months, he considered that he had allowed himself enough time. Katie was madly in love with him already, and while he was still finding her body exciting, he knew the novelty would wear off – it always did – and three months would be just about right.

Beth hadn't seemed too happy about not seeing him for so long, but he had promised to make it up to her when he came back, as he had expressed it, but in reality, when he got tired of Katie. Beth had never let him go all the way, but he was sure that once she did, she would soon start giving him money to keep him sweet – as a thirty-five-year-old widow, she would think he was her last chance of love. She was bound to be far more experienced than Katie, who had been a terrified virgin that first night, but she'd got over it, like all the rest.

When the three months were up. he would be his own man again, dallying with Beth for as long as he wanted – even all night – and Katie was so naive, he could palm her off with any old excuse for his absences. Life was good, and it would be even better when Beth presented him with the wherewithal to splurge out and have a harem of girls on the side. Speak about Casanova, Dennis McKay could have taught him a thing or three.

He arrived home before Katie, something he tried to avoid, because he didn't enjoy being alone with her brother. 'I'm first, am I?' he asked, brightly.

Giving him the usual scowl, Sammy said, 'Katie shouldn't be long now.'

Wishing that he could persuade Katie to put him out of the way, Dennis was struck by an idea. If he got Sammy angry enough to punch him again, maybe that would do the trick, for Katie wouldn't like to see her lover being injured. It was worth a try, and the sooner the better.

Katie came in only a couple of minutes later, and when she told them what Keith Robb had done, Dennis stood up and took her in his arms. 'Oh, my poor poor sweetheart,' he murmured, pressing the small of her back so hard that she was arched against him, and following this with a passionate kiss that made her struggle upright in embarrassment. 'Not in front of Sammy, Dennis,' she hissed.

'Why not? He knows I love you.' He cupped her breast with one hand, using his free arm to hold her still, but he kept an eye on her brother while he kissed her again.

Sammy's eyes were glittering alarmingly, and his hands were balled up into the fists which had lashed out at Dennis once before, but they unclenched slightly when Katie broke free. 'Did you remember to buy a hot pie for your supper?' she asked him, breathlessly.

'Lottie gave me the biggest one she had,' he muttered, his brows still down.

'I saw you with your assistant today,' she said, to take his mind off Dennis. 'Have you found out his name yet?'

'Jackie.'

Katie drew him out to tell her what he and Jackie had done that day, and Dennis thumped down sullenly, wondering if she was worth the effort. But if he went back to live in at the Temperance, he would cook his own goose. He didn't think he would get Beth to part with any cash unless he wangled his way into her bed, and he couldn't do that if he only had an hour and a half with her every night. No, dammit! He'd have to put up with the simpleton a while longer.

When Sammy went to bed, Katie said, a little sharply, 'I didn't like what you did tonight, Dennis.'

Bugger, he thought, and tried to sound hurt. 'You didn't like me kissing you?'

'You know that's not what I mean. You just did it to annoy Sammy, didn't you?'

'Oh, Katie, that was the last thing on my mind. I wanted to kiss you, so I kissed you. What's wrong with that?'

She stroked his cheek. 'Nothing, I suppose, but don't kiss me like that again when he's here.'

'Brothers don't usually get jealous when somebody kisses their sister.' He couldn't help saying it. Sammy's attitude had puzzled him for ages.

'Sammy's not . . .' She paused and started again. 'We've been on our own so long he thinks I shouldn't look at other men.'

Her slight hesitation held no significance for Dennis. 'He doesn't mind us sleeping together.'

'I can't understand that myself,' she said, thoughtfully.

Katie was aware that Keith Robb still resented her and would do everything he could to have her sacked. She often caught him looking at her speculatively and turning away when he noticed that she had seen him, and the past two weeks had been like standing on the edge of a volcano waiting for the eruption. He hadn't tried anything else to discredit her, but he was so unfriendly she was surprised that the diners couldn't sense how constrained the atmosphere was. He was always polite to them, of course, so they probably didn't notice that he ignored her. Apart from that, she liked her job. She had got to know some of the men who came regularly, also the women who sometimes accompanied them, be they wives or lovers, and Mr Noble was satisfied with her, which was all that really mattered.

Sammy seemed to be happy working with young Jackie, for he spent every evening talking about the things the boy had said. Jackie's stories – swaggering accounts of girls he went out with – were nothing like Hairy Cameron's, though Katie suspected that they were every bit as fanciful. She did worry in case they might make Sammy take an interest in girls, but she didn't think it likely. He was in a class by himself, with no thought for the opposite sex. There had been the time he had . . . but that had been her own fault for letting him see her half-undressed.

Having convinced herself of this, she was all the more alarmed when Sammy observed, one night as they all sat by the fire, 'Sally's got fine big tits.'

Dennis convulsed with laughter, but Katie turned on her 'brother' furiously. 'Who did you hear saying that?'

'Jackie's always looking at girls' tits,' he explained, 'and Sally's is bigger than Molly's.'

'Who's Molly?' Dennis spluttered.

'She's the girl that got my old job,' Katie told him. 'I don't want to hear you saying things like that again,' she warned Sammy. 'It's not nice, and you shouldn't be looking at girls' bodies, any road.'

'I only look at their tits, like I . . .'

Terrified that he was about to say he had seen hers, Katie shouted, 'Don't, then.'

'Och, let him have some fun,' Dennis giggled. 'He's a big boy now. What's the harm in it?'

'You know perfectly well what harm there could be,' she said, coldly. 'Just do what I tell you, Sammy.'

He looked puzzled, but nodded sadly. 'I'll tell Jackie we shouldn't look again.'

'You do that.'

When they went to bed, Dennis said, 'He's fairly coming out of his shell, isn't he?'

'I don't want him coming out of his shell,' Katie burst out. 'He wouldn't know how to control himself if he . . .'

Dennis looked at her suspiciously. 'You sound jealous, and all. What goes on between you two?'

'There's nothing going on between us. I've looked after him for years, and I don't want to see him hurt, that's all. He could lose his head and . . . rape somebody.'

'You *are* bloody jealous!'

'I am not!'

'Then why are you so annoyed? I get a kick myself out of looking at girls' tits, all men do. It's just a bit of fun.'

'It's maybe fun for other men, but Sammy's different.'

'Is it *your* tits you want him to look at? Are you scared he'll get to like somebody better than you?'

It was their first quarrel, and Katie was so upset – both about Sammy and about the things Dennis was saying – that she started to cry.

Dennis did not move for a moment, then he turned abruptly away, shifting as far from her as he could. Heart aching, she wondered if this was the end. There *was* nothing between her and Sammy – not in the way Dennis meant – but he didn't believe her. Would he pack his things in the morning and leave? This thought made her weep all the more. Her whole body was shuddering with the sobs that were ripped from her, when he whipped round with a groan of repentance and took her in his arms, smothering her wet face with kisses. 'Oh, God, I'm sorry, Katie. I know you're just worried for him.'

He rocked her until her body stilled, and when his hands started to fondle her, her raw emotions made her turn to him with a hiccupping moan.

He gave a long satisfied sigh when it was over. 'That was good! We should quarrel more if that's what it does to you.'

'No, Dennis,' she whispered, snuggling into the crook of his arm. 'I don't want to quarrel with you ever again. It's a horrible feeling.'

He was asleep in no time, but she couldn't settle. Sammy and Dennis would never get on, that was obvious, but she couldn't put Sammy in a Home, not even for Dennis, and they would have to learn to live peaceably with each other. She gave a slight shiver as she recalled Sammy's contorted face when Dennis had been baiting him. It reminded her of his father's on that terrible, terrible night.

Mr Gunn had killed his wife and would have strangled her, as well, if Sammy hadn't saved her. Was it possible that he was capable of murder, too? In his jealousy, would he end up by killing Dennis? Or would he turn on her?

Chapter Eleven

❧❧

Unable to sleep, Sammy was thinking. He didn't like Dennis, he didn't like him living here, he didn't like being alone with him, even if it was only a few minutes till Katie came home. He knew she had to work till eight every night, and Dennis worked in a different place, so they couldn't be together, but he wished he could have a little while with her without Dennis being there.

He was a long time on his own every day, that was another thing he didn't like. He finished work at five, so he was by himself in the house for three hours. He did things for her, and sometimes she patted his shoulders for having the fire lit. He swept the floor every night, and dusted, and chopped sticks, but it still left him a lot of time to think. That was why his old dream had come into his mind again. It was a good dream, the very best dream, and he was still sure Katie would make it come true one day.

He had remembered it one night he was trying to remember other things, for he didn't have a good memory and Jackie had said something about a secret place he went to when he wanted to think. It had nagged at him for a while, till a picture came to his mind, a picture of walking in a wood with Katie and showing her his secret place. He hadn't been able to remember anything else, except he hadn't been her brother at that time. But she had made him her brother, so that's why he was sure she would be his mother some day. He really wanted a mother, only it had to be Katie, and she would just be his mother, not Dennis's.

His mind went back an hour and a half to when Dennis had come home from work. He had stood on the hearth rug heating himself, then he'd said, 'You've got a grand fire going.'

Sammy was never sure about the praise he got from Dennis. There was something about his face when he said anything nice, as if he didn't mean it. 'I lit it at six, so it would be burning bright for Katie.'

'Everything you do's for Katie, isn't it?'

Again, there had been this funny smile that puzzled Sammy. 'Katie's my sister, and . . .' He had felt muddled then. He had nearly said she'd be his mother some day, but he didn't want Dennis to know that.

'Aye, she's your sister, worse luck.'

Recalling the incident, and taking the remark to mean that he would have liked Katie to be his sister, too, Sammy felt a surge of pride that he was better than Dennis. But he wished he could sleep. It was awful to lie in bed and not to be able to sleep. It made the night twice as long. Maybe if he rose and took a drink of water – but Dennis had Katie's bed and she would be sleeping on the couch, so he'd have to be careful not to make a noise and waken her.

Creeping through to the kitchen, Sammy opened the cupboard to get a tumbler, then turned on the tap in the sink enough to let a quiet trickle of water come out. Knowing it would take a long time to fill the glass, he swivelled round to make sure that Katie hadn't heard him, and nearly dropped the tumbler in his dismay. She wasn't there! Stricken with fear for her, he set the tumbler down and burst into the other room to ask Dennis if he knew where she was, but the words dried in his mouth when he saw them in bed together.

Katie had been on the verge of sleep when Dennis started to stroke her again. 'Don't you ever get tired of it?' she asked, drowsily.

'No, do you? Is that why you put your nightie back on.'

'I was cold.' But she let him slip it off over her head.

'That's better.' He flung back the covers.

'We'll freeze,' she whispered, but desire flooded through her as he kissed her breasts and let his hands slide down her stomach, and they were both panting in mounting passion when the door was flung open.

She turned her head, dishevelled and angry. 'What do you want, Sammy?'

'I was looking for you, Katie,' he mumbled. 'I got up for a drink and you weren't on the couch.'

Stopping his thrusts, Dennis gave a high-pitched giggle. 'Did you think she slept through there? That's a good one, eh, Katie?'

Katie frowned at his laughter. 'Be a good boy, Sammy, and go back to bed.'

'Aye, Sammy,' Dennis mocked, 'get back to your bed, for me and Katie are busy.' He bent his head to kiss her nipple.

She couldn't help a momentary smile of delight, but when she heard Sammy go out, she said, 'I feel terrible about him seeing us.'

'He couldn't have seen much from where he was standing, and anyway, even if he had, he wouldn't have known what we were doing. Maybe we should have made him watch.'

'Oh, the things you say,' she managed to whisper before he took her mind off Sammy again.

The next day being Sunday, Sammy's day off every week and Katie's once a month, Dennis was the only one who had to go to work. He hadn't been out much more than five minutes when Katie noticed Sammy eyeing her speculatively, and her heart sank. 'Will you take in some coal, please?' she said, in an effort to distract him. When he didn't move, she knew he was going to ask questions, and braced herself to answer.

'Why did you and Dennis not have any clothes on?'

So it hadn't been too dark for him to see, she thought. 'We felt hot.' It was all she could think of.

'But it wasn't hot, it was cold, and why were you smiling when he kissed you? Do you like him doing that?'

'Yes, Sammy, but just him, nobody else.'

'Why just him?'

'Because I love him.'

'But you love me, and all, don't you?'

'Yes, but . . .'

'You never let me kiss you. Will you let me, Katie? I bet I love you more than him.'

'Sammy, it's different with Dennis.'

'You don't love me.'

'I do, but . . .' He was on the verge of tears, and pity for him got the better of her. 'All right, then, you can give me one kiss, but that's all.'

She shuddered when his slack lips came towards her, but in the next moment, his arms were round her and his kiss was not the kiss of a backward boy, it was the kiss of a man on fire. 'That's enough, Sammy,' she cried, trying to push him away, but his hands delved inside her wrapper, rough and rasping against her skin, for she hadn't been able to find her nightgown among the tangled bedcovers.

When he tore off the flimsy garment, she screamed, 'No, Sammy!' and kicked out with her foot, wishing that she had taken time to put on shoes, or even slippers, for she was only hurting her own toes and making no impression on him.

'They're nice,' he mumbled, his fingers squeezing, his voice thick and his breath coming in loud gasps. 'Sammy needs to kiss them, and all, like Dennis.'

She was struck with a comforting thought then. He only wanted to be as good as Dennis, and even if he'd seen more than the kissing, he wouldn't have understood. It might be best to let him fondle her for a minute so he wouldn't be jealous any more. When he stopped, she would tell him it wasn't allowed between brother and sister, and that would prevent him ever doing it again.

But Sammy gave her no chance to tell him anything. After running his tongue over her nipple, he lifted his head and enveloped her mouth with his, his breathing, always some-what noisy, becoming more and more laboured. His arms held her imprisoned, like iron bands round a barrel, as he hoisted her off her feet and carried her through to his room, and her desperate struggles could not break his hold. He laid her on his bed, and kept her down with his knees until he opened his trousers, and only then did she remember that he had seen what his father had done to his women, or maybe it was something that came naturally to a man consumed in the fire of lust. At first, she fought like a tiger, but his need had given him extra strength and she couldn't stop him.

He wasn't tender. He didn't whisper words of endearment. He had no thought for anything except his own gratification, his excited grunts growing louder and louder as he pounded into her. Mercifully quickly, she recognized the signs of approaching climax and at last it was over.

As he lay sweating and panting at her side, it dawned on him that she was weeping as if her heart was breaking, and he said, looking perplexed, 'Have I been a bad boy, Katie?'

'Oh, yes, Sammy,' she sobbed. 'You've been a very bad boy, and you must never do that again. Never!'

'But Dennis was . . .'

'It's different with Dennis. He's not . . . oh, Sammy, you're . . . my brother, and he's not.' It was the only way she could make him understand.

'Is a brother not allowed . . . ?'

'No, and you must never let Dennis know what you've done. He'd be awful angry. Now, get my wrapper, and go out for a walk or something to let me get washed and dressed.'

She lay, weeping uncontrollably again, for a long time after he left the house, but eventually the sobs quietened and she stood up shakily to pull on her wrapper. It wasn't his fault, she thought, wretchedly. She couldn't blame him for what he had done, but she had learned one thing from it. Sammy's brain had never developed beyond that of a child, but the same wasn't true of his private parts.

Susie Clark had been right in what she said about him when they were at Struieburn – he *was* hung like a bull.

Chapter Twelve

❧❧

Beth Morton was feeling very low. It had been one of those days when she felt her age, felt older than her age, and she wondered if she should pack up and leave Peterhead. A change of scene might be all she needed, and she hadn't meant to stay so long, in the first place. Picking up the Ethel M. Dell she had been trying to read, she started the same page for the fourth time and had actually reached the next page when the da-di-di-da knock made her look up in disbelief. Dennis? After all this time? She would soon tell him where to get off. In the next instant, however, it was as though she had been given an injection with some kind of elixir that made her cast off her anger, her despondency, and her heart quickened at an alarming rate. But, as she went to answer the knock, she made up her mind not to let him win her round too easily, and forced a frown on her face when she opened the door. 'Well, well! Dennis McKay! I didn't think you'd have the brass neck to turn up here again.'

'Don't be like that, Beth.' He gave her his well-practised smile of apology-cum-heart-rending-entreaty. 'If you let me in, I'll explain everything.'

Savouring the unease he was doing his best to hide, she opened the door wider. 'It'll take a lot of explaining.'

He sat down and laid his felt hat on the arm of a chair. 'I'm sorry. I know I should have written, but I never had a minute to call my own. They made me stay on in Glasgow for longer than I was told, so I only got back this morning, and I came as soon as I finished work.'

'You only got back this morning?' Beth's voice was icy. 'I'm disappointed in you, Dennis. Can't you come up with anything better than that?'

'It's true, I swear it!'

'Well, that's funny. I didn't believe that the best hotel in Glasgow would take a waiter from Peterhead as a relief, so I went to the Temperance to check up, and I must have been dreaming when I saw you there a month after you were supposed to be away.'

'Oh,' he floundered, 'oh, that! Well, I'd to come back for one day, but I'd to leave again that night . . .'

'Why can't you just be honest and say you told me a pack of lies? I'm not a fool, you know.'

He had the grace to look ashamed. 'That's that, isn't it? I should have known you were too smart to believe it.' He picked up his hat. 'I'd better leave, I suppose.'

'Before you go, I'd like the whole truth. Who was she?'

'Who was who?' he blustered, but her expression warned him that she would not be palmed off. 'She was only . . . Beth, I'm truly sorry, but I couldn't help myself. Katie was mad about me, and she pleaded with me to move in with her.'

'So you've been sleeping with this girl . . . this Katie? Are you still living with her?'

'Yes, I'm still there, but we're not sleeping together any more. I share a bed with her brother.'

'What happened? Did you tire of her? Do you expect me to be grateful that you've come back to me?'

In spite of her sarcasm, he could tell that she was coming round. 'I never wanted her, not really, and I know where I am with you, don't I?'

'You think I should be glad to have you because nobody else would look at me at my age?'

'That's not what I meant. You're a beautiful woman, Beth, but I've a weakness for young girls. It's like . . . how can I explain? I love you, but I get a kick out of them for a wee while. Have pity on me, please, Beth? I need you.'

'Till another young thing catches your eye?' Baiting him

suddenly lost its appeal, and she sighed, 'Dennis McKay, I know I'm a silly old bitch, but . . . welcome back!'

He jumped up to fling his arms round her. 'I don't deserve it, Beth, but thank God you didn't throw me out.'

'I can't think why you bother with me when I'm old enough to be your mother.'

Dennis gave a throaty chuckle. 'Hardly. I'm twenty-one . . .'

'And I'll be thirty-five in October, maybe not old enough to be your mother, but still too old.'

'I don't think of you as old, Beth. As soon as I saw you, I knew you were special, there was something about you . . .'

'My money?'

'Oh, Beth, that's not fair.' Dennis looked hurt. 'Have I ever asked you for anything?'

'No, I'm sorry, I'm just a bit touchy about it. You see, I've come up against some nasty money-grabbers in my time.'

'I'm not like them, Beth, and I think I'm falling in love with you. Let me show you.'

She let him pull her down on the sofa, her heart speeding up as he took her in his arms. He was really just a boy, but it was nice to be loved, to feel that she meant something more than a meal ticket. His gentle lips finding hers, she gave herself up to pretending she was as young as he was. If she could be sure he was serious about her, she could even be persuaded to marry him . . . if that was what he wanted.

'Oh, my lovely, lovely Beth,' he whispered. 'I'll never love anybody but you.'

It was the first time she had let any man hold her since her husband died three years before, and his firm boyish body was so different from Tom's that she felt no shame when his hand found her breast. The almost-forgotten pleasure of being gently caressed was so great that she didn't want him to stop, although a cushion, rumpled into a hard lump, was digging into the small of her back. The fondling became less gentle and her breathing had quickened with delight when his hands delved downwards. 'No, Dennis,' she said, sharply.

'Oh, come on, Beth,' he coaxed. 'It's not as though you're an innocent young girl.'

Pushing him away, she sat up, still trembling. 'I'm not innocent and I'm not young, but I'm not an easy mark.'

'Oh, God, I'm sorry, Beth. I couldn't help myself, but I promise I won't do anything like that again.'

Feeling as she did about him, she did not stop him when he kissed her and slid his arms round her once more. She was almost certain that he was only amusing himself with her and would probably stop seeing her if she refused him too often, but she wasn't going to give in to him just yet.

Hopefully, Dennis said, 'I'm not tied to hotel rules now I'm living out, so I can stay with you as long as I want, all night sometimes, if you let me.'

Beth felt a momentary pang of pity for the young girl who had given Dennis a home – and probably her virginity – only a momentary pang, because it was so good to have him back.

It had all turned out perfectly, Dennis gloated, as he made his way back to Marischal Street. Hoodwinking Katie had been the first thing, and it had been easier than he expected. He had held back until he was certain she was well and truly hooked and would believe any lie he gave if he stayed out late, and then, in bed last night, he had said, casually, 'I ran into some of my old pals on the way home. I used to go for a drink with them at one time, and we'd have a game of dominoes or darts to pass the odd hour or two, but I dropped them for you.'

'You shouldn't have dropped your friends,' she said.

He hadn't understood why her voice was so flat – he still couldn't – but he had gone on with his plan. 'You wouldn't mind if I started seeing them again?'

'Please yourself, Dennis.'

Her lack of interest rankled even yet. She shouldn't take it out on him if Sammy had done something to annoy her. As long as they didn't involve him in their quarrels, he didn't care what they got up to when he wasn't there.

His ego had been even more bruised when she turned away from him when he tried to kiss her. She'd been lukewarm with him ever since the night Sammy had burst in and caught them . . . no, he was wrong. She'd been all over him the next night, clinging to him as though she couldn't get enough, pleading with him not to stop; not that he'd needed much coaxing, for he'd been as randy as she was. He'd had high expectations when they went to bed the following night, and that was when she refused him first. She had actually shuddered when he put his hand on her, as if she couldn't bear him to touch her, so the sooner he got away from her the better.

He'd been doubtful about how Beth would receive him after his long absence, but he needn't have worried. She had been stroppy at first, which was only natural, but it only took a ladleful of flattery and a few ardent kisses and caresses to bring her almost to boiling point. Another hour or two like that and she'd be putty in his hands. She'd likely end up begging him to go and live with her, and then it would just be a matter of time before she started giving him the odd backhander to keep him there.

Visions of his rosy future were pushed aside when he came to the pend. He would have to stop on with Katie till Beth came up trumps, much as he hated the idea of sleeping with a girl whose hot blood had turned to ice for no reason. Still, it wouldn't be for long, and the end result would be worth any sacrifice.

Katie hadn't been sure at first, but after missing a second time, she couldn't go on fooling herself. She was definitely in the family way, and she meant to tell Dennis tonight when he came home from the pub, though he'd been staying out late an awful lot lately. She wasn't sure how he would take it, for he often said he didn't believe in marriage, but surely, with a baby coming, he would change his mind. He couldn't be so heartless as to leave her to bring it up on her own?

Sick at the thought, Katie wondered miserably if his love for her had cooled off. She had blamed the drink for his lack of interest, but maybe it wasn't the drink. Maybe he was tired of her, and who could blame him when she stopped any advances he did make? Maybe he wanted to finish with her and telling him about the baby would make him leave her all the sooner? She still loved him, though, and didn't want to lose him, so it might be best to wait until she was showing before she said anything. That would give her a few more months with him, and even if he did walk out on her when she told him, she would have his child to ease her heartache.

His child. She had often heard the Cullen wives saying they could pinpoint the exact time their men had put a bun in the oven. She hadn't understood at the time, but now she did. It had happened about six weeks ago, and the glory of her mating with Dennis had exceeded all other times; he had said it was the best night they'd ever had. She could recall how she had clung to him, her emotions so raw that all she could think of was getting rid of the feel of Sammy inside her body.

She jerked up, aghast. Sammy had raped her earlier that same day! His seed had been inside her before Dennis's! Oh, dear God, it wasn't Dennis's child she was carrying, it was Sammy's!

Chapter Thirteen

❖

On her next day off, demented by the thought of having an imbecile child, Katie decided to ask advice from the only person she would dare to tell. Lottie wouldn't breathe a word of it to anybody else.

The shop was busy with women snapping up the loaves and rolls Bob McRuvie put through still hot from the bakehouse, and Katie beckoned Lottie to the end of the counter. 'Could I have a private word with you?'

The baker's wife smiled. 'There's no chance of privacy here, but I suppose I could leave Kirsty on her own for a wee while after the rush is past. Say . . . the back of two?'

It was ten past two when she arrived. 'Now, what's up with you?' she asked, as soon as she sat down. 'I could see there was something. Has that Dennis been ill-using you?'

'It's nothing to do with Dennis.'

'Has Sammy been getting into trouble at the Salutation?'

'It's worse than that, Lottie. I'm . . . I'm expecting.'

'I some thought that would happen. Well, you'll just have to tell Dennis he'll have to marry you. Hang on, though! You said it had nothing to do with him.' Lottie's round, cheery face darkened, her eyes filled with horrified suspicion. 'It's not Sammy's, is it? My God, Katie, surely you didn't let him . . . ?'

'I didn't let him, I couldn't stop him.' Tears were edging down Katie's cheeks now.

'Don't upset yourself, lass. How are you so sure it's his? You've been sleeping with Dennis for a good while now.'

Unlike Katie's neighbours, mostly devout members of one

religious denomination or another, who had treated her like dirt because she was living in sin with Dennis, Lottie had never condemned her, so she told her everything.

After hearing the sequence of events on that fateful night and morning, the baker's wife screwed up her nose. 'Aye, I see your trouble. You're not sure whose bairn it is?'

'I'm nearly sure it's Sammy's,' Katie sobbed. 'Oh, Lottie, what am I going to do?'

'You could tell Dennis it was his. He'd never know.'

'He would if the baby wasn't right in the head.'

'Aye, maybe it's not worth chancing it. Well, there's only one thing for it . . . you'll have to get rid of it.'

'Could I do that?' Katie's face held a hint of hope.

'Lord bless you, lassie, of course you could, but mind, it depends . . . how far on are you?'

'Six weeks, not any more.'

'Aye, well, that'll not be so hard to shift. A double dose of castor oil or liquid paraffin should do the trick.'

'You think so?'

'Well, it might, and then again, maybe no, but we'll keep trying, lass.' Standing up, Lottie gave a low chuckle. 'I'd better get back, but I was thinking, it's a good thing I'm not one of them Brethrens or Catholics, for this would be against their beliefs, but me? I look at it this road. The Lord made a mistake when he gave Sammy a boy's brain and a man's needs, so it's up to us to sort out the consequences.' Laughing loudly, she went out.

Katie did not feel like laughing, but she did feel a lot better, and lifting her purse, she ran along to the chemist for a big bottle of castor oil. Back inside, she forced down two large tablespoonsful, gagging over the thick, cloying liquid, but determined to make it stay down.

That evening, unfortunately for the poor girl, was one on which Dennis did not 'go out with his mates', and she was ashamed at having to grab the torch and go to the lavatory so often. The purgative was giving her pains so severe that it was all she could do to stop herself from doubling up in agony, yet there was no sign that the remedy had worked.

Dennis frowned when she trailed back in after her fourth visit in twenty-five minutes. 'What's up with you?'

'I've got diarrhoea.'

'Keep away from me, then, in case it's catching.'

At bedtime, she lay down on the couch, not undressing because she knew she would be kept on the move, but around three in the morning, when the effects of the castor oil wore off, she finally managed to get some sleep.

She was still awake first, and had the kettle boiling when Sammy came through to shave the whiskers which had started to sprout on his upper lip. He had been very proud when he first noticed them, and even prouder when she bought him a razor. After lathering his face with soap, he turned to her. 'Shaving means I'm a man, doesn't it, Katie?'

She nodded sadly. She had no doubts about him being a man – she had living proof of it inside her.

When Dennis came through, he asked, 'How's the belly?'

She wondered what he would say if she told him what was really wrong with her belly. 'It's a lot better now.'

'I'll not be home till late tonight. We're playing another pub at dominoes.'

'That's good.' It *was* good, Katie thought, because it meant she could take some more medicine in the afternoon, and he wouldn't be here to see her tearing outside every few minutes in the evening.

On her way home, after eight, she went to the McRuvies' house door – the shop was closed – to tell Lottie that the castor oil had failed in its intended purpose. 'I took some more at half past four,' she added, 'so I'll keep my fingers crossed that it works.'

Looking at the girl's wan face and drawn cheeks, Lottie said, 'You know, I was right angry at Sammy at first, but now I've had time to think . . . it's Dennis I blame. He should have stopped when Sammy came into your bedroom.'

Katie heaved a despondent sigh. 'It's too late to worry about whose fault it was. I'd better go though, or Sammy'll be wondering why I'm late.'

Beth having sent him away because she was not feeling well, Dennis was in a vile humour when he arrived home, scowling when Katie said, 'Why are you in so early?'

'The dominoes were off. One of our team was ill.'

Fired by the whisky he had drunk on his way home, he pulled Katie down on the couch, and despite her struggles of embarrassment because of Sammy's presence, his kisses grew more and more passionate until he opened her blouse buttons and slid his hand inside.

'I've seen them.'

At Sammy's announcement, Dennis whipped round in surprise. 'What d'you mean? What have you seen?'

Sammy's smirk held deep self-satisfaction. 'Katie's tits.'

Furious now, Dennis turned back to her. 'You surely to God didn't let him . . . ?'

Fastening her blouse with fumbling fingers, she said, 'I didn't . . . oh, Sammy, please don't say any more.'

'There's more, is there? Go on, Sammy, tell me.'

Delighted at annoying Dennis, Sammy went on jubilantly, 'I kissed the pink bits that stick out.'

'Stop it, Sammy,' Katie pleaded, but Dennis put his hand over her mouth. 'Go on, Sammy,' he repeated, harshly.

The heady exhilaration of boasting was too much for Sammy. 'My thing got great big and I knew where it had to go, so I put her on my bed, and oh, it was good! I felt like I was going to burst, and I did burst! Is that what happens when you do it, Dennis?'

It was a moment before the full impact of what Sammy was saying struck Dennis, then he roared, 'Great God Almighty, Katie! You let this damned idiot . . . ? I don't know how could you let him near you!'

She tried to keep her panic under control. 'It was the morning after he saw us . . . he wanted to kiss me, and I thought it would stop him being so jealous of you . . . and I couldn't find my nightie so I'd nothing on under my wrapper and he took it off . . . and I let him . . .' Her voice broke now, and the rest came tumbling out between hysterical sobs. 'I thought he'd be happy just doing that, but he got all worked up and I couldn't stop him.'

His face livid, Dennis yelled, 'You let him kiss your tits and you were surprised you couldn't stop him? Christ, Katie, you were asking for it! Were you comparing him with me? Is that what you've been up to? I knew something was going on, but I never thought you'd sunk as low as that – with your brother!'

'No, Dennis,' Katie wailed, 'it was only once.'

'He'd never have stopped at once.'

She clutched his sleeve. 'It's the truth, Dennis!'

Jerking his arm away, he snarled, 'You're a bloody liar! You've been at it for weeks. I should have known that was why you wouldn't let me . . . does he satisfy you better?'

His open hand hit her across the mouth, and at that Sammy gave a menacing growl and lumbered to his feet, his fists flailing, but being more agile, Dennis dodged to avoid being hit and made for the door.

Trying to restrain Sammy, Katie cried, 'Dennis! Where are you going?'

'To a woman that wouldn't let the likes of him come within a mile of her.' He fled as Sammy broke free.

As the door slammed, Sammy looked at Katie uncertainly and tried to put his arms round her, but she screamed, 'Don't you dare touch me! It's all your fault!' Sinking down on the couch, she burst into another flood of tears, and he stood for a moment, his face showing the pain her accusation was causing him. Then he turned slowly and went into his room, and Katie could hear his sobs over the sound of her own.

In only a few minutes, she had to grab the torch and fly out to the lavatory, noticing, even in her haste, that there was no sign of Dennis in the pend. He really had gone, and he likely wouldn't come back.

The castor oil continued its work several times over the next half hour, and her insides were so sore from the many purgings that she wished she could die. Suddenly, she began to recognize a different pain, a pain which started lower down and increased in strength until, at last, something slipped out between her legs. Standing up, she shone the torch down the pot, and saw – nestling among the watery mucus which was all that was coming from her bowels now – what looked like a lump of liver, but she knew that at its core was the tiny foetus that would have developed into a baby – Sammy's baby.

She felt a lightness inside her, as if all her internal organs had been removed, not just the unwelcome inhabitant of her womb, then she was gripped by guilt and hesitated before flushing it away, but the deed was done and she could do nothing to undo it even if she wanted to.

There was no sound from Sammy's room when she went in, and she went to bed wondering if the abortion had actually been the result of the castor oil or of her shock at what had happened. Then, recalling what Lottie had said, she was sure that God had used Sammy himself as the instrument to undo the consequence of His mistake in the young man's physical make-up – but why hadn't He taken into account the effect Sammy's revelation would have on Dennis?

Chapter Fourteen

❧

'I keep thinking about Katie,' William John said, somewhat cautiously, for his wife had a habit of changing the subject when he mentioned their grand-daughter. 'It's two and a half years come Monday since she was here.'

Mary Ann compressed her toothless mouth and gave just the suggestion of a nod. 'Aye, October 1922.'

Her precision should have surprised him. but it failed to register. 'I'm awful worried about her.'

'What is there to worry about? She ran off wi' the laddie Gunn.'

'So Johnny Martin said, but maybe it was the laddie that forced her. She said he was simple, mind? For all we ken, he could've killed her and hidden her body somewhere.'

The blood drained from his wife's face. 'You surely dinna think that's why we havena heard from her?'

'I'm nae saying it is, I'm only saying it could be. Katie wouldna have bidden away as long as this without letting us ken where she was – nae if she was still alive.'

Each seeking reassurance from the other, the elderly man and woman stared at each other for a few moments, then he said, decisively, 'No, no! We're imagining things, and we'd better nae let other folk hear us saying things like that, or they'd have us locked up in an asylum.'

The clock ticked away the long minutes of silence, then he burst out, 'I still canna understand it. Lizzie Baxter wasna the kind o' lassie to leave her bairnie like that.'

'What I canna understand is our William John letting her. It was his bairn, and all.'

157

Her husband felt driven to make one thing clear. 'William John wasna as good a laddie as you thought. Maybe he didna like being tied down wi' an infant? He could've made Lizzie leave her here – maybe it was him that left her.'

Mary Ann's brows knitted. 'He did once tell me he wanted to go to America, that was afore him and Lizzie Baxter . . .'

'And you never said a word to me?' William John felt angry and hurt that his wife had known this all along. 'That's it! Do you nae see? If his mind was set on America, that's where they'll be, for he got everything he wanted – you made sure o' that. He'd have thought the infant would hold them back, and Lizzie would have done anything for him, even gi'e up her bairn.'

Mary Ann gulped. 'And now we've lost Katie, and all.'

Her husband regarded her thoughtfully. 'I aye wondered why you tell't folk they were both dead.'

'They were dead to me,' she defended herself, 'and it was best that naebody could tell Katie different. It was a good thing our William John didna set up house wi' Lizzie Baxter in Cullen, so folk here didna ken he wasna lost at sea and she didna die after the bairn was born. It was the only thing I could think on to explain why we had Katie, and they took it for gospel.'

'I wouldna be ower sure about that, you ken what the folk round here are like, and I still think you should have told Katie the truth.'

'I could never've done that to her. Nae that it makes much difference now, for we'll likely never see her again.'

'Maybe she'll come back some day.' He regretted letting her see how pessimistic he had felt earlier. His Katie couldn't be dead! She just couldn't!

When the urgent knocking started, Beth Morton sat up in bed, startled and puzzled. She had sent Dennis away well over an hour ago because she didn't feel well, so it couldn't be him.

Getting up, she opened the bedroom window and called down, 'Who is it?'

'It's Dennis! Let me in!'

Wondering why he'd come back, she slipped on her dressing gown and went down to open the door. When she switched on the light in the sitting room and saw him properly, she gasped, 'What's wrong? You look awful.'

'I feel awful,' he muttered.

'Did that Katie girl throw you out?'

On his way to Queen Street, Dennis had invented what he deemed to be a credible explanation. 'Remember I told you I slept with her brother? He's not right in the top storey, and he turned on me tonight for nothing. If I hadn't managed to run out, he'd have killed me.'

Knowing his capacity for lying, Beth did not believe this. No man, however soft in the head, would turn on anybody else without provocation, and Dennis must have done something to trigger the poor soul off. He'd been angry when she sent him away, so he'd likely gone home and taken it out on the girl, which could have annoyed the brother. Not feeling up to arguing, however, she said, 'So you'll have to go back and live in at the hotel again?'

'Could I not stay here?'

She had given quite a lot of thought to this since their association started, and had decided against it. 'I'll let you stay tonight, that's all. I like being my own mistress and pleasing myself what I do and when I do it, and I'm not giving up my freedom.'

He sighed hopelessly. 'That's telling me.'

She gave a light laugh. 'Oh, Dennis, you're priceless. You thought I'd take you in? I know you, don't forget. I know you can't keep away from the ladies, but this lady's got a splitting headache and wants to get back to bed. You can sleep in the spare room or on the sofa, whichever you like, but only for tonight.'

'The sofa, I suppose,' he mumbled, ungraciously.

'Right, I'll throw you down some blankets. Goodnight.'

She had let him see where he stood, she told herself as she went upstairs, and it was up to him now. If he promised to reform and asked her to marry him she probably would, and if he didn't? She'd likely just let things go on as they were, though it was coming up to Christmas, and the festive spirit might encourage her to take them a few steps further.

It was impossible for Katie to remain angry with Sammy. He had looked so chastened when he came through in the morning, she had almost put her arms round him to assure him that she didn't blame him for what he had done, but it would only have been asking for more trouble. The one thing she would have to do before she would feel easier with him was to make him understand how wrong it was for him to even think about her in any way other than as a sister, which would be far from easy. Not only that, would he remember?

Neither of them spoke over breakfast, and they walked to the Salutation together in silence. She could tell that he was waiting for her to say something, and it would do him good to be kept waiting for a while yet. When they came to the bakery, she said, 'I'm going in to speak to Lottie for a minute. I'll catch you up.'

Opening the door, she walked past the customers and leaned across to whisper to her friend. 'It worked, Lottie.'

Mrs McRuvie gave a wide smile as she wrapped a high plain loaf in tissue paper. 'Thank heaven for that.'

'But something else happened and I can't tell you here, and not in your house in front of Bob.'

'I'll come and see you when you get home. Dennis won't be in tonight, will he?'

Katie shook her head sadly. 'Dennis won't be there.'

Sitting in the staffroom to ease her feet that forenoon, she told herself that she should be thankful for having a decent job and a house to live in, after what she had done. She had made Sammy run away, which made her worse than he was, because she had known what she was doing and the poor soft thing had just done what she told him. Not only that, she had struck at Mr Gunn with her scissors when he maybe hadn't been going to kill her at all. He could have been after something else and she'd been too innocent at the time to realize it ... though he must have killed his wife.

Confused, she wished she had someone to lean on. If she could speak to her grandfather, he would take all her fears and worries away ... but she only had Sammy, who was the root of them. Even Dennis hadn't lived up to her expectations. She had loved him so much, and he'd sworn that he loved her, yet he hadn't believed her last night. She had thought he would ask her to marry him once they had been together for a while, and it was obvious now that he'd had no intention of that ... but she would still take him back if he asked.

She gave her head an abrupt shake. She would manage to survive without Dennis; she had done it before. It was more than two years since she left Fenty with Sammy, and the police would never find them now. They would gradually get back to the old footing of brother and sister, and be as happy as they had been before Dennis came into their life ... but the trouble was that Sammy couldn't control his emotions. Anger, jealousy, lust, he gave in to them all.

When she went home that night, Sammy was sitting with his head down, and she knew that she only needed to say a kind word to him and his shame would be forgotten, but she was determined to keep him in suspense for a little longer. It was the only way to teach him a lesson.

When his head rose, slowly and uncertainly, the entreaty in his eyes was too much for her. 'Oh, Sammy,' she sighed, 'what am I going to do with you?' The softness of her voice made his face brighten and she went on, musing to herself, really, 'I wish there was still somebody at Fenty for me to take you to.'

'Fenty?'

He obviously didn't remember his real home, and probably it was just as well, she thought. 'I should really put you away,' she gulped, 'but not to Fenty.'

'Don't put Sammy away.'

He was speaking in his old babyish way, which proved how distressed he was, and her heart cramped at the thought of him in a Home. She would never rest easy if she had him committed, and, in any case, the minute any institution got a hold on him, the powers-that-be would make enquiries about where he came from. It would be as good as putting a noose round his neck. 'You'll have to behave yourself if I let you stay with me,' she told him, very firmly.

'Sammy can behave.'

'You don't always.'

His eyes filled with tears. 'When Dennis went away, you said it was my fault. Was Sammy bad, Katie?'

'Very bad, but I suppose you couldn't help it, and I'm sorry I was nasty to you. I was upset about Dennis.'

'Will he be coming back?'

'I don't think so.'

'Will it be just me and you again?'

'Yes, just us, and you're my brother, remember that, and brothers don't touch their sisters. No kissing, no anything at all. Do you understand what I'm saying?'

He nodded vigorously. 'No touching, no kissing.'

'And no anything else . . . especially no anything else. That was the worst, Sammy, and if you try it again, I *will* have to put you away.'

'No touching, no kissing, no anything else.'

'Don't forget, then, for I mean what I say.'

He lowered his head for a moment, then looked up with an impish grin. 'No touching, no kissing, no anything else, no Dennis! Eh, Katie?'

'That's right,' she agreed, sorrowfully, 'no Dennis.' Christmas was only two weeks away, and she'd been looking forward to spending it with Dennis, but there would be no celebrations now.

Lottie McRuvie came in just after nine, having waited until she knew Sammy would be in bed. 'What's troubling you, lass? I'd have thought you'd be pleased you managed it.'

Tearfully, Katie gave her a detailed account of what had taken place the previous evening. 'So I don't know if it was the castor oil that did it, or the row,' she finished.

'It doesn't matter, does it, as long as you got rid of it? And you're better off without Dennis. I wouldn't trust him as far as I could spit, and that's not far.'

'I still love him, Lottie, and it must have been a shock to him when Sammy told him . . .'

'I'm sorry, lass, but it doesn't change the way I feel. I think he was getting cold feet and he goaded Sammy into a fight to get an excuse to leave you.'

Katie gave a deep sigh. 'You could be right, Lottie.'

'Ach, cheer up, lass. You'll meet somebody else.'

'I don't want to meet anybody else.'

'Eh . . . I don't like to say this, but are you sure you're safe with Sammy? Now he knows how to get his thrills, he could jump on you any time. Maybe you should have reported him to the bobbies for raping you. It would be a worse crime seeing he's your brother.'

'No, no, I couldn't tell the bobbies! He understands now that brothers and sisters can't do that, and I'm sure he'll not touch me again.'

'I hope no.' Lottie shook her head. 'Poor devil, I can't help feeling sorry for him.'

That was her problem, too, Katie reflected, as her friend went out. She would never feel properly safe with Sammy now, but she was so sorry for him she couldn't send him away. At least he'd be happy with the tie she'd bought weeks ago for his Christmas.

*   *   *

In his old room at the Temperance, Dennis was wallowing in self-pity. It had all been going perfectly for him; he had been on top of the world until that bloody awful night, and now he wouldn't touch Katie Mair with a barge pole. It was disgusting to think she'd been having it off with her idiot brother when he wasn't there. She'd pretended to be little Miss Prim, and all the time she ... ach, he should put her out of his mind. If only he could get round Beth Morton. He was practically sure she was waiting for him to say one word – marriage – before she let him take up his abode at Queen Street, and maybe that was his best bet.

He wouldn't even have to go through with it. Once he had his feet under her table, as the saying went, she'd find it damned difficult to get rid of him, not that she would want rid of him. If she suspected he was seeing other women, she would likely bribe him not to leave her.

He sometimes wondered where Beth's money came from. She didn't work, yet she never seemed to go short, and she had the best of clothes and jewellery. Her late husband must have been rolling in it to leave her so well heeled, and maybe he *should* take the plunge and marry her.

At nine that night, he gave the old da-di-di-da knock, smiling sardonically when Beth flung her arms round him as soon as she opened the door; he had purposely stayed away for over a week knowing that she would miss him.

'Where have you been?' she asked, when she sat down beside him on the sofa.

'John Leith's had me working like a slave over Christmas and the New Year. My waitress is off ill, so I've had to do all the meals on my own, and I totter downstairs to my room every night not fit for anything.'

'Oh, poor Dennis. Let Beth massage your tiredness away.'

Her supple fingers, rubbing his shoulders and down his back as far as his buttocks, were almost his undoing, and he had to fight back the urge to grab her and show her that he wasn't in the least bit tired.

'Is that better?' she asked, as the grandmother clock in the corner gave a silvery chime for the half hour.

'Oh, yes,' he breathed, wondering, wryly, just who he was punishing most by his little charade, Beth or himself? 'But I'll have to go in about ten minutes, worse luck.'

'Oh, Dennis, not already?'

Her farewell kiss was loving, not passionate, but he went back to the Temperance Hotel feeling triumphant. It would only take a few more nights like that, and he'd have Beth Morton exactly where he wanted her.

Since Sammy's young assistant had exhausted his very limited knowledge of girls, they now discussed the comics they read, played marbles in their short breaks, or wrote down unusual registration numbers on the guests' cars. Katie was glad that Jackie was introducing Sammy to the boy-world he had missed out on; it was a welcome change from old Hairy's reminiscences, sprinkled too liberally with oaths. He, like Jackie originally, had been a bad influence on Sammy. Her own situation was far from happy, however. Keith Robb had been unfriendly to the point of rudeness for weeks, and just lately he had begun to find fault where none existed. Not only that, he often jogged her elbow when she was passing, thus making her spill whatever she was carrying.

Aware that he still resented her having the job instead of his girlfriend, Sally, and that he would have her sacked if he got half a chance, Katie held back her protests, though she could tell that most of the people in the dining room could see what was going on and were on her side.

As she said to Lottie one night, 'Most folk keep out of arguments with the management, and I don't suppose they'd stick up for me if it came to a showdown.'

Lottie gave the fire a poke with the toe of her shoe to break up the coals. 'You should look for another job.'

'If I leave, Mr Noble would likely make Sammy leave, and

all, and he loves his job. It would be a shame to spoil it for him, and he wouldn't get another job as easy as me.'

'Aye, I grant you that. Can you not tell Mr Noble what's going on? If you got your word in first, he'd believe you.'

'I don't think he would. Keith's been there a lot longer than me. No, I'll have to put up with it, for Sammy's sake.'

'Well, I admire you for that, after what he did to you.'

A frown of annoyance creased Katie's brow. 'I'm trying to forget about that.'

'Aye, I'm sorry. He's lucky he's had you to look after him since your mother died. Not many lassies would take it on.'

Going towards her own house, Katie wished she could tell her friend why she was tied to Sammy, but it was far too dangerous. Lottie wouldn't mean to, but she could easily let the story slip out to somebody in the shop. It only needed to reach the ears of the police, and she and Sammy would be arrested.

He looked up with a smile when she went in. 'You've been a long time. Did you go in to speak to Lottie?'

'Aye, and I couldn't get away. You know what she's like.'

It being Saturday, when Sammy only worked until one, he had the kitchen as neat and shining as a new pin, and a fire crackling merrily in the grate. Katie looked round the room in approval. 'I don't know what I'd do without you.'

His childish pleasure at this made tears come to her eyes. In spite of what he had done, in spite of her fear of him, she still held a deep affection for him, and she was duty-bound to keep protecting him from . . . She was almost sure that the danger was past, but now and then, in the stillness of a night when she couldn't sleep, she wondered what she would do if she opened the door to a knock and found a bobby on the step. She could almost feel the dryness of her mouth, the panic in her breast, and saw herself standing in front of Sammy with her arms flung wide to shield him. They would have to shift her before they could get at him . . .

She shook her head at her own foolishness. She could do nothing to save him if the police came, but they would never come now . . . would they?

Chapter Fifteen

☙☙

1926

On his way to his room after the lunches, Dennis spotted Freddie, the porter, showing two policemen into the new manager's office and bending down to listen at the keyhole after the door closed. Waiting until he moved away, Dennis asked him what was going on.

The porter shrugged. 'All I heard was something about a girl and a boy missing from somewhere near Huntly.'

This did not interest Dennis. 'Is that all? I thought it would be some sort of crime.'

'They said she'd been a servant, and the son had abducted her. That's kidnapping, isn't it? That's a crime.'

Dennis gave a scoffing laugh. 'What do they think he's done to her? Taken her into white slavery?'

Not having much of a sense of humour, Freddie said, quite seriously, 'I'm not sure they think it was white slavery. He was just two years older than her.'

'Love's young dream, then?'

'It wasn't that, either. One of the bobbies said he was just sixpence to the shilling, so he must be a bit soft.'

'A bit soft?' This did engage the waiter's interest. 'What else did you hear?'

'Nothing else.'

'Did they mention any names?'

'Not that I heard.'

When he reached his room, Dennis sat down on the bed to think. It couldn't be Katie and Sammy – they were brother and sister. Lifting a slim electro-plated case from the high chest of drawers, he took out a cigarette and tapped it on the case before putting it in his mouth. Flicking the lighter Beth had given him at Christmas, he inhaled deeply.

It was queer the bobbies coming here, though likely they had to check all hotels and boarding houses. He had never heard Katie speaking about Huntly, but he didn't know much about her, only that she was an orphan and had been brought up by her grandparents in Cullen. Could she be the girl they were looking for? If Sammy wasn't her brother, it would explain a lot. Spitting out a fragment of tobacco which had worked loose, it dawned on him that, if Katie was the girl they were after, the cops would likely question him, because some of the staff had known they kept company for a while.

Having an inborn distrust of policemen, Dennis did not want to be drawn into giving evidence in court – he couldn't risk Beth finding out he'd two-timed her – so he decided to deny any relationship with Katie. He wouldn't have minded landing Sammy in the soup, but he suddenly remembered that one of his late father's mottoes was never to spill the beans about anyone else to save your own skin, not even your worst enemy. It had a habit of backfiring on you. A third generation, highly proficient poacher, Jock McKay had always managed to talk himself out of trouble. As he often told his son, 'It's best to stick as near the truth as you can without giving anything away, for the bobbies can check up.'

With this in mind, Dennis thought he would be best to admit to being friendly with Katie and wait to see where to take it after that. What he did not know about the success of his father's creed, however, was that although Jock made no secret of having walked along the river on a certain night, his denials of catching and selling salmon were backed up by the local hotelier and publican, whose wives had already cut the fish into steaks and distributed some to the doctor and the minister, who both knew where they came from but kept quiet. The policeman also knew Jock was guilty, but because he was not above accepting a cut of salmon himself, he made a show of trying to trace the thief and told the gamekeeper it must have been a gang from Glasgow or Edinburgh. What was a salmon or two to a man as rich as the laird?

A rap at his door made Dennis jump. 'Yes?'

'You're wanted in the office.'

So it was Katie, he thought. Stubbing out his cigarette, he ran upstairs, ignoring the porter's blatant curiosity. Freddie, like the manager, had only recently come to the Temperance and hadn't known the backward Sammy.

'Ah, Mr McKay,' the police sergeant began, 'we are looking for a Katie Mair, grand-daughter of William John and Mary Ann Mair of Seatown, Cullen. I've been told you were quite friendly with her when she worked here?'

Dennis answered cautiously. 'We went out a few times.'

'Do you know where she went when she left here?'

'I'd stopped going with her before that.'

'You don't know where she works now?'

'No, I'm sorry.'

'Nor where she is living?'

'No, I haven't seen her since.'

'One of the chambermaids said you'd been living out for a few months, it wasn't with Katie Mair, then?'

'No, I was lodging with a widow . . . to tell the truth, we had a thing going, you know, but she got a bit too serious, so I got out quick.'

The sergeant's eyes twinkled understandingly. 'I see. Now, do you think Katie Mair could be working in another hotel?'

It occurred to Dennis that it might be a good idea to put them on a false trail, at least until he could warn Katie. 'No, I don't. Before we split up, she told me she was fed up being a waitress, and, if I remember right, she said she was looking for a shop job with decent hours, but I don't know if that's what she did.'

'What about the boy she had with her?'

'Sammy? What about him.'

'Did you know he wasn't her brother?'

'No, is that a fact?' Having figured that out for himself, Dennis hoped his show of surprise was convincing. 'Good God! I never dreamt . . . I didn't have much to do with him.'

'Katie didn't say anything to you about him forcing her to run away with her?'

'Never, and if that's what all this is about, I'm sure you're wrong. She was real fond of him.' Too bloody fond of him, he thought, savagely.

The sergeant shot a troubled glance at his constable, who was standing by the door. 'There's something damned fishy about this, if you ask me. The message from Huntly said the boy had abducted the girl, but it looks like she went with him of her own free will. There's more to it than we've been told, and we'll have to start on shops now, not hotels. It's a bigger job than we thought.' He turned to Dennis again. 'Thank you, Mr McKay, you've been very helpful.'

His legs shaking with relief, Dennis returned to his room and lit the half cigarette from the ashtray. He had got away with it, and he had explained away all the things they could have tripped him up on, but he'd better warn Katie tonight. Whatever the big lump had done that had the police after him – and it couldn't have been abduction, they were wrong there – she'd be bloody grateful to him for telling her. Not that he wanted to go back to her – his innards still turned at the thought of her letting Sammy's slobbery lips touch her. That alone would have put him off her for ever, never mind what else she had let Sammy do.

It had been a hard day, and Katie sat down thankfully on the couch to read the paper. The front page held nothing of any interest to her – it was mostly about the miners complaining about their wages again – so she turned to the Women's Page and was reading, with some envy, about the Marcel Wave which was popular with those women who could afford it, when she grew conscious of Sammy fidgeting in his chair and hoped he would go to the lavatory before it was too late.

She was on to the next page when she thought she'd better make sure that there was nothing wrong with him and held the newspaper down. 'Sammy!' she shouted. 'What on earth . . . ?'

He was sitting with his trousers wide open. 'See how big my thing is?' he smirked.

Gripped by the fear of being raped again, she did her best to hide how she felt. 'I don't want to see it, put it away.'

He fumbled for a moment, then said, 'It won't go. Jackie told me how to make it grow, and mine gets bigger than his.'

She silently cursed the absent Jackie. He knew too much for his own good. 'Go through to your room.'

'Jackie says if I do this,' he demonstrated with his hand, 'it'll burst and get little again.'

'Stop that!' she cried. 'It's rude!'

His hand halted. 'Rude? Like farting?'

'Worse than that. Stop it!'

'It's too nice to stop.'

'Do it in your bedroom, then. You shouldn't let anybody see you.' She held the paper in front of her eyes as he went past her, but after his door closed an appalling thought struck her. Had he told Jackie what he had done to her? Was that what had led to the comparing of sizes? Oh, God! What if the boy had told some of the other hotel workers? She would never be able to look any of them in the face again. And it would be just what Keith Robb was waiting for – an excuse to have her dismissed.

A tight knot had gathered in her throat and she was still considering the awful prospect when Sammy came back, looking in dismay at the wet patch on the front of his trousers. 'It burst all over my breeks.'

She could hardly keep her voice steady. 'Take them off and I'll wash them. Now listen, Sammy! You must never do that again. Do you hear me? Never!'

'Jackie says he does it a lot.'

172

'I'm sure he doesn't do it in front of his mother. Take off your breeks and get to your bed. This minute!'

While she plunged his trousers up and down in hot soapy water, Katie's stomach was churning. She couldn't possibly cope with him if he was going to do things like this. He had satisfied himself tonight, but how long would it be before he turned to her again? She had better buy a lock for her bedroom door, or she would never sleep for worrying that he would come in and jump on her.

It might have comforted Katie to know that Sammy was lying in bed sure that his dream had come true. When Jackie had said, a few days ago, 'I'm lucky having a mother to wash my clothes and cook all my food,' Sammy had boasted, 'Katie does that for me.'

'She's acting your mother, then,' Jackie had told him.

He hadn't been too sure what acting meant, but Katie had said tonight she was his mother. She hadn't exactly said it, but she'd said Jackie didn't do it in front of his mother, so that meant she was Sammy's mother. The pain he always felt when she scolded him was replaced by the deep emotion of mother love, though he did not recognize it as such. He did know, however, that he couldn't touch her again – a man never touched his mother – and he didn't need to, for he could get the lovely thrills without touching anybody. But he'd better not let Katie see him at it again.

Dennis had waited until Sammy would be in bed, and without thinking, he gave his usual knock on Katie's door. Her look of joy when she opened it made him say, hastily, 'I've only come to tell you something I thought you should know.'

His serious expression alarmed her. 'What is it, Dennis?'

'The police were looking for you at the Temperance today.'

'Oh no! Not after all this time?' She slumped down on the couch, her face chalk white.

'You knew they'd come after you?'

'I've been expecting them ever since...' She broke off, then clasping her hands together in an attempt to stop their shaking, she murmured, 'I'd better tell you, Dennis.'

As she described Angus Gunn's cruelty, Dennis jumped to the conclusion that she and Sammy had run away because they were afraid of the man, but he felt most uneasy when she told him about the night of the thunderstorm. Had that been the start of them being lovers? But... no! She'd definitely been a virgin the first night he'd gone to bed with her.

Katie hadn't finished, and from the way she hesitated in mounting agitation, he gathered that there was worse to come. Her voice sank to a whisper when she spoke of Mr Gunn coming to her room, and sure of what she was going to say, Dennis was completely flabbergasted by what she actually told him. The Peterhead police had made a helluva bloomer! Sammy wasn't wanted for abduction, he was wanted for murder!

'So you see,' Katie went on, babbling now because it was such a relief to speak about it, 'I'd to make Sammy run away ... if they'd caught him he'd have been hung ... and they'd have seen I'd stabbed Mr Gunn, and I was scared they'd arrest me for attempted murder.'

Aware that it was hysteria and not amusement, Dennis fought back an urge to laugh and tried to reassure her. 'You couldn't have done much damage if he was able to get up and fight with Sammy.'

Her voice was steadier when she took up her story again, and it came as no surprise to Dennis to learn why they'd had to leave Struieburn. Anybody would have thought the same as the farmer.

'So how did you end up at the Temperance?' he asked.

'Mrs Sutherland was John Leith's sister, and she gave us a letter for him, a kind of reference, she said.'

'Nobody else knew that's where you were going?' When Katie confirmed this with a shake of her head, Dennis went on, 'So it must have been her that told the cops where you'd gone.'

'I don't think she'd have told them,' Katie wailed. 'She was so nice . . .'

'You can't trust anybody,' Dennis interrupted, wishing he had never involved himself in her troubles, but how could he extricate himself without making it obvious? Then an idea occurred to him. 'I think your best plan would be to go to Cullen.'

'I can't go back to my Granda and Grandma . . .'

'Yes, you can. Just tell them the same as you told me, and they'll likely go with you to the police station, and once the cops know Sammy didn't mean to kill his father, they'll not charge him with anything, or you either.'

'Do you really think so?'

He thought it highly improbable, but said, 'Well, I'm not sure, but there's always the chance.'

'Oh, Dennis, thank you for coming to tell me. I thought you'd never want to see me again after what happened. If the police do let us go free, we'll come back to Peterhead, and . . . would you come and live with us again?'

Positive that the police would not overlook their crimes, he felt safe to say, 'Like a shot, and we could get spliced in a month or two, if you like?'

He returned to the Temperance in high spirits. He would never see Katie again, but at least Sammy would be where he belonged . . . swinging at the end of a rope.

Nemesis having overtaken Katie, she had no sleep that night, and she lay in bed wishing that she had Dennis's confidence in the outcome of her trip to Cullen. The search for Sammy and her had gone on for three whole years, which meant the police were convinced of their guilt, and not even Granda's silver tongue would save them. Should she risk making the journey? Or would it be best to run away again? She had some money laid by, so they could take a train or a bus and be hundreds of miles away before the bobbies found out where they'd been living.

But she was tired of this thing hanging over their heads. She couldn't go through life being afraid of discovery every minute of every day ... and what about Sammy? Uprooting him again could unsettle him, maybe unhinge him altogether, and she could be putting herself in terrible danger. God knows what he might do to her. It might be best to face up to what they had done, and pray that her story would be believed.

Early the following morning, she told Sammy that they were going somewhere on a train, and after combing his fly-away hair he stood meekly until she inspected his hands and the back of his neck, which he often didn't bother to wash. At last she decided that he was quite presentable, for she was so used to his vacant expression and loose mouth that she no longer noticed them. 'That's us ready, then.'

He walked at her side proudly, as a son should walk with his mother, and sat down next to her in the carriage when the train came in. 'Where are we going?' he asked.

'Somewhere you've never been before,' she told him, hoping that her grandmother would be more understanding than she used to be. She still wasn't sure that she was doing the right thing, but she had no option, and Granda would do all he could for her.

Her heart outpaced the clickety-clack of the train as they neared Cullen, and by the time they alighted, she was so tense that she forgot to show their tickets and was called back. She prayed that no one she knew would see them, but luck was not on her side, for they had just left the station when the local constable cycled past. His bike wobbled when he turned to look at her, and she held her breath when he came to a halt. Surely he wouldn't arrest them here?

'Katie? Katie Mair?'

'Yes,' she whispered, for what was the use of denying it? Johnny Martin had known her since she was a little girl.

The PC turned his bicycle round. 'I'm afraid I must ask you to accompany me to the police station. Him, and all,' he added, when Katie gave Sammy a little push as if urging him to run for it.

Her feet dragged as they went along the street, and her heart was in her mouth when they were shown into a small room, bare except for a table and two chairs. When she was asked by Sergeant Thom if Sammy had threatened her if she did not run away with him, she answered truthfully that he had not, that it was she who had made him leave Fenty. Then he asked where they had been hiding, and she explained in some detail.

At last, pushing aside his notebook, Thom laid down his pen. 'There's some sort of misunderstanding here, Katie. We were told the boy had abducted you, but you say you went of your own accord, and what you've told me has corroborated what we'd already learned.'

Believing that he was about to come to the real reason for the search for them, she burst out, 'We ran away because I didn't want Sammy to be hung for the murder.'

Johnny Martin's mouth fell open. 'Murder? What murder?'

'His father. Isn't that why you've arrested us?'

Glowering at his constable for forgetting his place, the sergeant said, 'It was Mr Gunn that laid the charge against his son.'

This unexpected information took a little time to sink in, then Katie's blood started to pound inside her head and she could feel her body shrivelling with shock. But it couldn't be true! She must have misunderstood. Gripping the edge of the table, she forced her swimming brain into some semblance of rationality and managed to gasp, 'Are you saying . . . he's not dead?'

Thom smiled reassuringly. 'Anything but. He made a

damned nuisance of himself to my colleagues at Huntly for a long time for not being able to find you.'

Katie was in such a state now that she lost track of what he was saying. To think she had worried all this time about Sammy being charged with murder, when all the time Mr Gunn was alive and pestering the police to find them. What would he do to them now they *had* been found? This was too awful to contemplate and she concentrated on the sergeant again.

'. . . and when they told him they'd discovered you'd worked at Struieburn for a while, he went there himself and got it out of the farmer's wife that she'd sent you to the hotel in Peterhead.'

Doing her best not to give way to the hysteria threatening to overtake her, Katie could visualize Mr Gunn forcing the woman to tell him, and couldn't blame Mrs Sutherland. Then another scene floated into her reeling mind. There had been two bodies on the floor when she and Sammy left Fenty. One had apparently not been a corpse, but what about the other? Why hadn't the sergeant said anything about that? 'Um . . . Mrs Gunn?' she mumbled.

'Aye, I forgot you wouldn't know about her.' Thom gave his head a sorrowful shake. 'According to the Huntly sergeant, the poor woman died in her bed. Her doctor said he'd been expecting it, and there was nothing suspicious about it.'

'But . . .' Katie began, then thought better of it. She knew that Mrs Gunn hadn't died in her bed. She had definitely been lying dead on the floor of her bedroom, there was no question about that, but who would believe her if she accused the husband of killing her? And how had the old devil pulled the wool over the doctor's eyes? Too confused to think about it any more, Katie gave a long, shivery sigh.

Thom, however, wasn't finished with her yet. 'It beats me why you thought Mr Gunn was dead, Katie. What happened that night, exactly?'

She didn't want to talk about it, but he was looking at her

in such a perplexed way that she told him why Sammy had been fighting with his father, and how Mr Gunn had fallen down the stairs. 'There was so much blood, I thought . . .'

Her head had been down all the time she was speaking, but now she looked up and was surprised to find Thom smiling at her. 'So that was it? You made a mountain out of a molehill, Katie, and you're free to go. I suppose I should give you a lecture about running away from what you thought was the scene of a murder, but I can't help seeing the funny side of it.' Sergeant Thom let out a few loud guffaws, then said, 'Of course, the laddie'll have to go back to his father.'

'Oh, no!' Katie cried. 'You can't send him back there! Mr Gunn used to hit him for nothing, and send him to his bed without any supper.'

Thom looked at Sammy. 'You want to go home, don't you?'

Sammy nodded eagerly. 'Yes, home with Katie.'

'No, I mean home to your father.'

'My father?' Sammy's nose crinkled.

Still shaken by what she had been told, yet weak with relief that they were no longer wanted by the police, Katie quavered, 'He doesn't remember anything about Fenty.'

'Aye, I can see that, but I'm afraid . . . you see, he's not responsible for his actions, so he'll have to go back there, back to his father.'

Although Katie knew that her life would be easier without Sammy – especially since Dennis was waiting in Peterhead for her – she hated the thought of him being ill-treated again, but there seemed nothing she could do. 'You'll have to go with the sergeant,' she told him, tremulously.

He grabbed her arm. 'Are you coming?'

'No, I'm going to see my Granda, and you're going back to where you used to live.'

'No!' he screamed. 'I'm going with you!'

It took the combined efforts of the sergeant and the constable to restrain him as Katie walked out, tears flowing copiously when she heard the rumpus he was kicking up, but she dried her eyes resolutely when she arrived at her grandparents' door, and remembered in time to knock before she went in.

Mary Ann looked up from darning the knee of her husband's knitted drawers. 'Oh, my God! It canna be! Katie!'

Struggling stiffly to his feet, William John took the girl in his arms with a strangled cry. 'Oh, Katie lass, we didna think we'd ever see you again.'

They stood for some time, their joyful tears mingling, and Mary Ann lifted the corner of her apron to catch hers. Then, William John held the girl away from him. 'Let me look at you. Ah, thank goodness you're still the same Katie.'

'Did you think I'd change so quick?'

Mary Ann's dry voice broke the magic. 'So you've decided to come back? Not a word in all this time and you walk in like you just went away yesterday – wi' no explanations.'

'I'm sorry, Grandma.' Katie went over with the intention of kissing the old woman's cheek, but Mary Ann averted her head, so she said, 'Will I make a pot of tea? Then I'll sit down and tell you everything.'

Not surprisingly, she didn't tell them everything. With her grandmother's beady eyes fixed on her, how could she say that Sammy had been in her bed, that Mr Gunn had tried to kill her, or even rape her? So she told them only of Mr Gunn's cruelty to his son, hinting vaguely, to make them think that was why she had run away, that she, too, had been at the receiving end of the man's anger at times.

Naturally, William John was up in arms at the thought of anyone hitting his Katie, but Mary Ann, with her usual perception, put her finger on what the girl had overlooked. 'But why did you not come home here? And why did you never write? You must have ken't we'd be worried out o' our minds about you. I think you owe us the truth.'

Turning from the accusing eyes, Katie looked at William John. 'Aye, lass,' he said, 'I think there's still something you're not telling us.'

And so, with many hesitations and tears, she told them how Mr Gunn had come to be lying on the landing. 'I couldn't come here and I couldn't write, in case the bobbies found us, and we were . . .' She meant to say that the police *had* found them the minute they set foot in Cullen, but Mary Ann didn't give her the chance.

'Where have you been all this time?'

Katie had just said that she had been in Peterhead when an imperative rap on the door made her stop, fearfully.

William John took her hand in his. 'If that's the bobbies, I'll not let them take you away, Katie lass.'

'Aye?' said Mary Ann to the policeman on her doorstep.

Walking past her, Sergeant Thom looked at Katie. 'There's a bit of a problem. We couldn't get the laddie into the police van, so we phoned through to his father's shop in Huntly to ask if he would come and collect him, and Mr Gunn says he wouldn't want to upset his second wife by making her look after a mental defective. He wanted us to put him in a Home, but there's no charge against the laddie now and we have no reason to have him shut up anywhere.'

'Thank goodness for that,' Katie said. 'I wouldn't let him go into a Home, anyway.'

Thom seemed somewhat at a loss. 'The only thing we can do is leave him with you.' Opening the outside door, he gave a signal with his hand, and Sammy walked reluctantly inside, his sullen face lighting up when he saw Katie.

'You'll be responsible for him,' the sergeant told her, 'but we need to know where we can contact you.'

After writing down the address she gave him, he said, 'I think that's it all cleared up, but if you have any trouble with him, let us know – here or at Peterhead.'

When the sergeant went out, Sammy flung himself at the girl. 'Oh, Katie! I thought you didn't want me!' Noisy sobs burst from him as her arms went round him.

'Whisht, whisht,' she soothed, stroking his back. 'It's all right. We're together again, and we'll be going home to our own house.' Over his shoulder, she saw the dark scowl on her grandmother's face. 'I have to take him,' she said. 'He can't manage on his own.'

'The two o' you could bide here,' William John suggested, but Mary Ann cried, 'No! I wouldna feel safe wi' him. I'm surprised at you, Katie. By law, his father's bound to have him back . . .' She stopped, puzzled. 'You said he'd killed his father, but Thom said he spoke to Mr Gunn on the telephone.'

Katie shrugged. 'I thought he was dead, but it seems he wasn't. I'm still glad we ran away, and I'm glad Sammy's not going back there. Oh, Grandma, can you not understand?'

'I understand a lot more than you think,' Mary Ann said, grimly, 'and if you go back to Peterhead and bide in the same house as him, you needna bother coming here again.'

'Oh, now!' William John exclaimed, in dismay. 'She's just doing what she thinks right, you canna blame her for that.'

'She'll not get inside this door again if she goes off wi' him. Can you not see what'll happen? If it hasna happened already,' she ended, eyeing Sammy with distaste.

It *had* happened already, Katie thought wryly, knowing what was in her grandmother's mind, yet she couldn't desert Sammy now. 'Come on,' she told him. 'We'd better go.'

William John stood up. 'I'm sorry, Katie lass.'

'It's not your fault, Granda, and we'll be fine. I wasn't going to stay here, anyway, even if I didn't have Sammy.' At the door, she suddenly ran back and kissed him, then walked out with her head high, tears glistening but not shed.

William John turned on his wife. 'You were awful hard on her,' he muttered.

Mary Ann sighed. 'It wasna easy, but did you not see the way that daftie looked at her? She's storing up trouble for herself, and I dinna want to be landed wi' looking after her when she has his bairn, for that's what it'll come to.'

'Katie wouldna let him . . .'

'Laddies like that have great strength when they're roused – their bodies or their anger – and if he wants her, she'll not be able to stop him. But she's made her bed and she'll have to lie on it, though she'd better not let him in beside her again.'

'You should have let her bide here, then, where we could keep an eye on her.'

'She didna want to bide here, and like I said, I wouldna feel safe wi' him about the place.'

Her husband closed his mouth quickly. Mary Ann would be safe from even the vilest fiend, but it was more than his life was worth to say it. This was his house, though, and he should have put his foot down and said Katie and the laddie were welcome in it, but he hadn't been feeling well this past day or two, and he wasn't up to fighting with her.

Katie tried to keep calm while she and Sammy walked to the station. Mr Gunn wasn't dead! The words screamed inside her head, and even when they were on the train, the clickety-clack of the wheels on the sleepers changed to 'Gunn isn't dead, Gunn isn't dead', until she almost asked Sammy if he could hear it. She tried to think of something else, but all that came to her mind was what the sergeant had said about Mrs Gunn. Yet her death hadn't been natural. If her husband had strangled her, of course, there would have been marks, but he might just have held a pillow over her mouth, he was crafty enough. And the rhythm of the wheels took up the new refrain, 'Crafty enough, crafty enough'.

Oh, God! she thought in despair. He was bound to want revenge on her and Sammy for what they had done, that was why he had pestered the police to find them. He hadn't known where they were before, but Sergeant Thom had likely given him their address when they spoke on the telephone. Her fear of Mr Gunn was growing much greater than when she had worked at the Howe of Fenty.

Then she remembered something that nearly made her swoon with relief. How could she have forgotten that Dennis was coming back to live at Marischal Street? He would help

Sammy to throw Mr Gunn out if he turned up, and once he saw he was wasting his time, he would give up all thoughts of revenge. In any case, she wasn't quite so sure now that he would come after her. Maybe she had been over-reacting. The sergeant had said he had married again, and he was probably happier than he had been with his first wife. She had been worrying herself for nothing – seeing danger where none existed.

She turned to Sammy as the train pulled into Peterhead. 'It's good to be home again, isn't it?'

Chapter Sixteen

❖❖

Livid with anger, Angus Gunn slammed the earpiece back into the upright receiver of the telephone, and sat for a moment glaring at it. Then, with a loud exclamation of disgust, he jumped up and stamped through his shop. Not caring that it was early afternoon and he still had four hours of business to conduct, he locked the door, hauled down the blinds and returned to the small back room.

It was abominable! He had banished Katie Mair and his son from his thoughts on the day he married Betty Runcie, and it been the unwelcome visit from the police last week that had stirred everything up again. Leaning forward with his elbows on the table and his hands at his temples, he let his mind travel back to that morning three years ago.

Wondering what had happened, Angus pulled his head free of the sticky substance that was holding it to the floor. His whole body was aching with excruciating pain, especially the side of his head. He touched the area gingerly and when he took his fingers away, they were covered in blood. For a moment, he thought that he was on the battlefield again, or in the military hospital, then, noticing a familiar zig-zag crack on the ceiling, he realized that he was lying on the landing of his own house and remembered that he fallen down the stairs during a fight with his son. He must have hit something which had opened up his old wound.

He tried to stand up, but it took him some minutes to get to his feet, and he had to lean against the wall until his head stopped spinning and his stomach settled down. He was getting over the dizziness when he noticed that his wife was lying in the doorway of her room. She must have heard the commotion and tried to come out to find out what was going on, but he did not have time to bother about a woman in a faint. He had more important things to do.

Picking up the spar of the bannister which his fall must have dislodged, he went upstairs to give his son a good beating, and, discovering that both garret rooms were empty, he gave a sardonic laugh. They imagined they would escape his wrath by running away, did they? Back in his own room, he flung on his clothes and picked up the keys of his car. Wherever they were, they could not have gone far, and he would soon catch them.

Recalling only the most important events, Angus skimmed over his six hours' search of every road within a ten-mile radius of Fenty, and his cool reception by the Huntly police when he laid charges of assault and abduction against his son, although he did eventually convince the sergeant that Sammy had assaulted him and had then abducted Katie, which should have been enough to have him locked up in an institution. He had said nothing about Katie's attack, as he had wanted to deal with her himself, and had intended to continue his search for them once he cleaned himself up and had something to eat. Things had not gone according to plan, however.

Angus gave a gasp of horror when he saw his reflection in the hallstand mirror. No wonder the police sergeant had given him such a strange look. If his eyelids swelled any more they would prevent him from seeing, his right cheek was a solid mass of bruises and the left side of his face was so encrusted with blood that he could not tell how badly it was damaged. Before bathing his injuries, he went upstairs for some of the cotton wool his wife used to remove the cold cream she rubbed into her face at night. He was a little surprised that she was still lying unconscious, but he had no compunction about having left her, and no inclination to do anything for her. Stepping over her, he made for the table by her bed, and with the long roll in his hand, he walked across the room again. Only then did he notice that Marguerite's skin, always pale and unhealthy, had a definite blue tinge now. He bent to touch her with trembling fingers, and jumped away clutching his chest when he found her brow ice cold.

Reeling back, he thumped down on her bed, wishing that his brain would function, but the side of his head was throbbing worse than ever, and his heart was hammering so erratically that he expected it to run out of power and grind to a halt at any second. His shocked body slowly recovering, he did not feel sorry that Marguerite was dead – she had never been a proper wife to him – but she might have chosen a better time for her demise. How would he explain why he had left her lying there for so long?

If he could lift her into bed, he could go and tell the doctor that she was worse, and pretend to be shocked when they returned to the house and found her dead. He was amazed at how heavy she was, but after trailing her across the floor, he eventually succeeded in his purpose, although his final, desperate heave started his heart palpitating again.

Downstairs, he dabbed his face clean and when he saw the gaping three-inch wound on his left cheek, the wound Katie had made with some sharp weapon, anger boiled up in him once more. Camouflaging it with a strip of sticking plaster, he went out to his car.

It had all been so easy, Angus recalled. His show of shock and grief when they found Marguerite dead had made Doctor Graham quite concerned for him. 'I will ask the undertaker to call,' the man had said, 'but do you want me to contact someone to help you make the arrangements for the funeral?'

'I would rather do everything myself,' he had replied, as brokenly as he could. 'I owe it to Marguerite.'

He had owed her nothing, he thought now, and because of her, he had been forced to remain in the house for the next four days – until after the funeral. It would have looked bad to be scouring the countryside when he should be acting the grieving husband. That was why the scent had gone cold, and the police had been no help.

Oh, God! Thinking about that girl had started his blinding headaches again. Raising his eyes to the small mirror on the wall, he shuddered at the sight of the ugly scar. Until last week, he had completely forgotten how he had come by it – he had presumed it was another wound from the war – although he was very conscious of it. Too conscious, Betty often told him. Betty? Yes, he should stop remembering that awful time and think about Betty.

The café where he usually went for lunch had been very busy, and he asked a woman sitting alone if she minded him sharing her table. She said, 'Please do,' and while they waited to be served, they introduced themselves, smiling rather sadly when it turned out that she was a widow and he a widower. Over the meal, they talked of local happenings, discussed current affairs, and when the conversation flagged, he said, 'It is good to have someone to talk to, someone sensible. My housekeeper is not blessed with brains, and I would send her away tomorrow if I thought I could find someone better.'

He had only been making conversation, and was surprised when Mrs Runcie laid her hand on his sleeve. 'If you don't think I'm too pushy, Mr Gunn, I wouldn't mind the job. Jim did leave me some money, but after a year and a half, it's nearly all gone, and I'll have to take a job of some kind.'

'You mean . . . you would be willing to come and keep house for me?' He could hardly believe it, because she was such an attractive woman, with rich brown hair and lovely blue eyes. He had felt drawn to her as soon as he sat down beside her.

'If you think I'm suitable.'

And so it had been arranged, Angus reflected. At first, he had supposed that she, like the girl he dismissed, would not be averse to sharing his bed, but she had rather Victorian morals, and so he had proposed marriage a few months later. At the time, he had wondered if he was being too rash. Women were notorious for changing their ways once the wedding ring was on their finger. Docile creatures became shrews, or else they withheld their sexual favours, like Marguerite. The making of their son had been no pleasure for him, with her weeping all the way through it, and it had been the same on every one of the rare occasions she had let him near her, until he sickened of her and looked elsewhere.

Betty had not turned out like Marguerite. She had made him happy; she had made him forget . . . until the police had come and rekindled his old need to take revenge on Katie.

When Sergeant Begg walked in, Angus thought he had called as a customer, or to acquaint him with another of the new rules for shopkeepers which always seemed to be coming into force, and when the policeman said, 'We traced them, Mr Gunn,' he could not think who the man was talking about. Then he felt like telling him to go away, that he wanted nothing more to do with them. But . . . he had pestered the police for months after their disappearance, and it was bad policy to get on the wrong side of the law. 'Y-yes?' he faltered.

'Let me tell you how it came about. I went to see an aunt of mine last night on my bike, and she's a real gasbag, you know the kind, going a mile round to tell you something? I was that fed up when I came away, I went into the first hotel I came to, just for a pint, you understand, for it wouldn't do for me to be seen drunk in charge of a bicycle.' He stopped to laugh at his own witticism. 'Any road, I got speaking to a farmer . . .'

Thinking that the sergeant was every bit as bad as his aunt for prolonging a story, Angus interrupted, 'Does this have any bearing at all on . . . ?'

'I'm telling you how I came by my information.'

His interest rising in spite of himself, Angus said, 'Then you do have some information? About my son?'

Sergeant Begg scratched the back of his neck. 'It could be. Well, as I was saying, this farmer and me were speaking about the state of the world today, and how the young ones take the law into their own hands, and I happened to mention we'd been looking for an eighteen-year-old laddie that had abducted a sixteen-year-old lassie . . .'

His pause for effect had the wrong effect on Angus. 'For God's sake, man,' he burst out, 'get on with it!'

With an apologetic smile, the sergeant got on with it. 'So he tells me he farms at Struieburn, on this side of Mintlaw, and he hired a brother and sister about the time . . .'

Angus felt his back sagging with disillusionment. 'I fail to see what all this has to do with . . .'

'I'm coming to it.' Begg, a rather stolid countryman, was enjoying making this man sweat, for he had been a thorn in their flesh at one time, hinting at police incompetence. 'So Sutherland, that's the farmer, he says he hired this . . .'

Angus listened with increasing nauseous excitement to the sergeant's repetition of what Davey Sutherland had told him, using the same graphic words to describe how the 'brother and sister' had been found in the barn, and, later, in bed together. Looking at him in triumph, Begg ended, 'And he threw them out!'

By this time, Angus was almost frothing at the mouth with rage. He had been right about Katie all along! She *had* been interfering with Sammy, because the stupid fool would not have been the instigator of their fornication. But even in his anger at Katie, Angus knew he had to go carefully. 'You believe that this alleged brother and sister were really my son and the girl?'

'It looks that way to me, Mr Gunn. The descriptions fit.'

'Then no time must be lost – do you not understand, man? I am afraid for the girl's safety. My son does not know right from wrong, and he could easily ... if he loses his head, if his lust grows too strong, he might kill her. Did you find out where they went after they left the farm?'

'Sutherland says he doesn't know, and it happened on the night of Hogmanay, or really the morning of New Year's Day, 1924, and that's a fair time ago. We didn't think to check farms when we were looking, and I don't suppose they'd be anywhere round there now. I've got the Mintlaw constable checking all the farms in his area, but it looks like a dead end to me.'

Angus could still feel the anger he had felt at the finality in Begg's tone, which had decided him to go and question the farm workers himself. He had been sure that he could make a better job of it than any plodding flatfoot.

After some difficulty in finding the farm, Angus found the farmer easier to locate, but it was obvious he could tell him nothing he did not already know, so he said, 'Would you let me ask your men if any of them heard them saying where they were bound for?'

'None of my men saw them that morning, but you're welcome to ask them.'

Angus spent the whole forenoon trailing from one field to another to talk to the workers, his shoes filling with mud, even with horse and cow dung, his smart suit soaking up the rain which had apparently waited for him to arrive before it began. Unfortunately, most of the men and boys who had been at Struieburn at the relevant time had left to work at other farms. Only two had known Katie and Sammy, and neither of them knew where they might be.

Angus squelched back across the field. The only one to whom he had not spoken was the farmer's wife, and she would likely be no more help than the others. Reaching his car, he unlocked the door and sat inside, but before he started the engine, a woman came dashing out of the farmhouse.

'Davey said to ask if you'd like a bite of dinner? You'd have time before the men come in for theirs.'

'Oh, thank you, that would be very acceptable.' He was too despondent to feel hungry, but he did not like to refuse.

When he sat down at the table, set with well over a dozen places, Angus said, half-heartedly, 'I do not suppose you know where Katie and Sammy went?'

'They went away in a terrible hurry.'

Because she had not given him a definite negative, he looked at her speculatively, and was pleased to see a deep flush creeping up her neck. She was keeping something back. 'I have been told why they left,' he said, encouragingly, 'and what I asked was if you knew where they went.'

Extremely agitated now, Madge Sutherland said, 'I told the bobbies I didn't know.'

'But you do know, don't you?'

Stubbornly, she shook her head, but he could see that she was weakening. 'Katie must have told you.'

'Katie didn't tell me anything.'

Noticing that she was plucking at the fluff-balls on her old woollen cardigan as if she couldn't keep her fingers still, Angus pressed home his advantage. 'I will ask you one more time. Do you know where they went?'

Her eyes held his for a moment, then dropped. 'Yes.' she murmured, faintly.

It was all Angus could do to contain his excited triumph, but she said no more. 'You may as well tell me,' he snapped, 'otherwise I will make sure that the police come and get it out of you. Withholding evidence is a crime.'

Madge Sutherland was not so easily browbeaten. 'The bobby said Sammy had abducted Katie, but I can tell you, he didn't abduct her. Maybe they weren't brother and sister, but they loved each other like they were, and Katie was the driving force. She spoke for Sammy, she sorted things out for him. He would never do anything to hurt her.'

Angus was nonplussed for a moment or two, but soon found his tongue again. 'He is mentally backward, as you must be aware, and your husband told me he threw them out because he found them in bed . . .'

'But that was all a . . .'

'Please let me finish, Mrs Sutherland. Some time ago, I, too, found them fornicating in bed, which is why they ran off, and I am sure you can imagine what could happen if she ever refused him.'

Her eyes held uncertainty now. 'Are you sure that was what they were doing when you saw them?'

Angus gave a grim half-smile. 'Quite sure. Perhaps if you and your husband had been a few minutes later in going into the room that night, you would have been left in no doubt, either. I am afraid for Katie, Mrs Sutherland, and I want to find them before he does something dreadful to her. Even now it may be too late.'

'Oh, my God!' Her hand on her bosom, Madge said, 'I'd a soft spot for Sammy, and I was sure Davey had made a big mistake, that's why I didn't say anything to the bobby when he came. I told Katie my brother would likely give them jobs . . . he runs the Temperance Hotel in Peterhead. Mind you, I never heard if he did, for we never write to each other, but I'm near sure that's where they'll be.'

His blood pounding fierily through his veins, Angus drew a loud, shivery breath. He had done it! He had actually done it – at long last! Once he passed this information on to the police, it would be next to no time before Sammy was under arrest, and Katie Mair would be brought back to Fenty to face retribution for what she had done.

That had been another pipe-dream, Angus mused. The Peterhead police had called at the hotel but the birds had flown, as Begg had expressed it when he came to tell him. He had been furious and had made up his mind to carry out his own investigation without saying anything to Begg. Someone at the Temperance Hotel must have known where Katie and his son had gone after they left there. But before he had the chance to do anything, he received the final slap in the face.

The sergeant at Cullen had just telephoned to say that they had arrested Katie and Sammy coming out of the railway station. She had sworn she had not been abducted, and, with the length of time since the assault charge was made – there would be nothing left to prove that it had ever taken place – it too had been dropped, and Sammy was free to go home to his father. It was the girl Angus wanted back, not his son, so he had refused to have him, but it was galling to think that Sammy was still with Katie, both of them at liberty to do what they liked. It still riled him to think that she had preferred an under-developed cretin to a man in his prime ... but perhaps Sammy had not been so under-developed in that direction.

When he felt a little calmer, Angus glanced at the clock on the wall. Good heavens! It was after six! How quickly the time had passed. Betty would wonder why he was late.

Passing the mirror he provided for his customers, Angus stopped to admire himself, as he often did. He still cut a fine figure. His body had not gained the avoirdupois of some middle-aged men, nor had he lost any of his hair. Admittedly there were several silver threads through the black, but he looked all the more distinguished for that. His smirk faded as his eyes fell on his left cheek. How could he overlook what Katie had done when the evidence was there to remind him?

He couldn't let her off. He must think of a way to take her back to Fenty so that he could put his mark on her, as she had put hers on him.

Chapter Seventeen

❖

When Katie went into the Salutation Hotel on the morning following her trip to Cullen, Mr Noble was waiting for her. 'Where were you yesterday?'

Her heart sank. 'I got word my . . . our grandmother was ill, so I took Sammy to see her.'

'I wasn't bothered about Sammy not being here, Jackie kept himself busy, but you should have let me know you wouldn't be here and not left me in the lurch. Keith said he couldn't manage on his own, so I'd to put Sally into the dining room, and he . . .'

Katie sighed. 'I suppose he said she was better than me.'

'That is what he implied, and they certainly did seem to get on better. There was none of the usual mishaps.'

Katie could have told him that the mishaps were engineered by the waiter, but she was sure he wouldn't believe her. 'So you want me to leave?'

'You could have the chambermaid's job back.'

'And have them all laughing at me? No thank you, Mr Noble, I'll leave right now, though I'm sorry I wasn't suitable as a waitress.'

'I've the feeling it wasn't all your fault, but you see the position I'm in? Keith's the best waiter I've ever had, and I don't want to lose him. I'm sorry, Katie, but if your mind's made up, you'd better come to the office and I'll pay you for the three days you worked this week.'

'Thank you.' She felt a pin-prick of satisfaction at his patent discomfort, but she was not going to knuckle down to being shunted around because of Keith Robb. She should have known she had played right into his hands, though it would have likely been only a matter of time till she lost her job, in any case. If Sammy had told Jackie what he had done to her, the young boy wouldn't keep it to himself, and once Keith heard about it, he would have gone right to Mr Noble ... she was probably better out of there.

Five minutes later, she walked into the gardens. 'I've got the sack, Sammy.'

'Me and all?' he asked, his eyes widening in apprehension.

'Just me, and I'm leaving now, so I'll see you when you come home at suppertime.'

'Aye.' He bent his head to carry on weeding.

On her way home, Katie went into the bakery. There was a queue of women at the counter, and when it was her turn, she asked Lottie for four morning rolls and then whispered, 'I'd like to see you when you've time.'

'Are you not working today? The back of two, then?'

'That's fine.'

After tidying her house, Katie remembered that she should have let Dennis know she was back. He would be wondering what had happened in Cullen, and he'd be delighted that the police had made a mistake, and that she and Sammy weren't wanted any longer. Looking at the wag-at-the-wa', she saw she would just have time to go to the Temperance and be back before Lottie came.

She felt like an interloper when she went into the place where she had once worked, not that there was any reason to be scared, because she had left of her own accord, but it would be awkward seeing anybody she knew. Dennis was attending to three men in the far corner of the dining room, and didn't seem pleased to see her standing in the doorway. He came across to her with what she knew was a forced smile and shepherded her into the lobby. 'Well?'

She assumed that he was annoyed at being interrupted at work and said, hastily, 'Everything's all right, and I'll tell you about it tonight.'

'I'm busy tonight.'

'Oh, have you arranged to meet some of your friends? Well, tomorrow, then?'

'I'm busy tomorrow, as well.'

This did disconcert her, but she asked, hopefully, 'The day after tomorrow?'

Getting no reply, it suddenly dawned on her that he hadn't expected to see her again. His promises to come back to her and to marry her had been made because he'd been sure he would never have to keep them. But she had to hear him saying it. Sick at heart, she whispered, 'You thought Sammy and me would be locked up, didn't you?'

He couldn't meet her eyes now. 'Why weren't you?' he said, harshly.

This question confirmed what she thought, and the pain it caused her was evident in her voice. 'You should have been honest with me, Dennis.'

Looking her right in the face, he snarled, 'You want me to be honest? Right! You disgust me! You were carrying on with that idiot and he wasn't your brother at all, though you let me believe he was. Speak about being honest? It's the pot calling the kettle black! I don't want to have anything more to do with you! I've got somebody else!' He whirled round and walked away.

Realizing that she couldn't keep standing there, Katie went outside on legs that would scarcely bear her weight, wishing that she was dead. This last shock, coming so soon after she had been sacked from her job, and just the day after being told that Mr Gunn wasn't dead, had been too much for her, although she wasn't capable yet of reasoning this out. Her thoughts were totally engaged in recalling the horrible things Dennis had said. She had been longing for his comfort, his love, and without them, there was nothing left for her.

Then she remembered, with a tightening of her chest, that she would only have Sammy to protect her when his father came after her. She was positive that Mr Gunn wouldn't have forgotten what she had done, even though three long years had gone by, and she'd be wise to keep the outside door locked all the time.

Back in her own house, her bruised heart gradually started to recover, and she told herself that Dennis wasn't worth being upset about. He had only wanted her for one thing, and he was getting it from another girl now. As Lottie had said, she was better off without him . . . though it would take her a long time to get over being used. And what would she tell Lottie about yesterday? Maybe it would be best to tell her what she had told Mr Noble, to save her asking questions.

When Lottie arrived and learned why the girl had lost her job, she was quite indignant. 'I never heard the like! He gave you the sack just because you took a day off?'

Katie shrugged. 'I should have asked him first.'

'Aye, I suppose you should. What are you going to do now?'

'I'll have to look for something else. Maybe I should try at Crosse and Blackwell's.'

'Would you consider working for me? I could be doing with somebody that's used to serving at tables.'

'Oh, you can't give Kirsty the sack just to let me . . .'

'I was going to get rid of her, any road. You'll need to serve behind the counter as well, of course.'

'When would you want me to start?'

'I'll have to give her notice, so not this first Monday but next? You'd need to be there by seven, that's when Bob has the first batch of rolls ready, and there's aye a rush on them. He'll be glad to see the back of Kirsty, for he's aye said she's *a useless lump.*'

'I'll be there at seven sharp, a week on Monday. Thanks, Lottie, you've taken a weight off my mind.'

It had started off as a cold, but Mary Ann was growing more and more concerned for her husband. None of the mixtures the doctor prescribed had helped, and William John had started to complain about a terrible pain in his chest. At first, she had thought it was a result of the coughing, but she soon realized that it was worse than that. He was steadily weakening, and she felt absolutely helpless.

Sitting at his bedside while he slept, as she did every afternoon, she rose to make herself a cup of tea, trying not to disturb him, but his eyes opened. 'Write and tell Katie the truth,' he said, hoarsely.

'What good would that do?'

'Maybe none, but she should ken.' Another cough made him hold his chest as if the pain was too much to bear.

His wife waited until he seemed easier. 'Tell her she was dumped on our doorstep? How d'you think she'd feel about that? All her life she's thought her mother and father were dead, and it'll not hurt her to keep thinking that. Now, I was going to make some tea, would you like a cup?'

When she returned with the tray, she held his cup to his lips because his hands were too shaky to hold it himself. 'Telling her the truth now would be like opening Pandora's Box,' she murmured, carrying on the conversation as though there had been no break. 'Can you not see how hurt she'd be? Things is best left the way they are.'

Too weak to argue any more, William John sighed, 'Aye, I suppose you're right.'

But he had made his wife think. Had she been wrong all along? Should she have told Katie from the beginning that her mother had abandoned her? But how could she, without explaining the rest? Even William John didn't know why she had taken such an ill-will at Lizzie Baxter. If she had been more friendly to the lassie, they wouldn't have gone away. It was her fault, Mary Ann thought remorsefully, she had always known that, and she had done what she could to salve her conscience – something her man knew nothing about and never would now – but was it enough? And would poor Katie understand when the time came?

*　　*　　*

On the Sunday three weeks after she started work at the baker's, Katie was sitting by the fire knitting a pair of socks for Sammy – who was leafing over a comic Jackie had given him – when someone knocked. Thinking that it would be Lottie, her only visitor these days, Katie rose to unlock the door. Her welcoming smile froze when she saw, not the familiar cheery face, but the saturnine features of Angus Gunn, Her legs turned to jelly and the knitting fell from her nerveless fingers.

'Well, well!' he sneered, shoving past her and standing just inside the door. 'You and Sammy have a cosy little love-nest here.'

The sound of his voice stirred a far-away memory in Sammy, a memory that made him cringe and put his hands over his eyes, and Angus gave a wicked laugh. 'So you remember your father, do you, boy?'

'Wh-what are y-you d-doing here?' Katie stammered, her heart pounding.

Advancing into the room, he waved a finger at her. 'That's not a very nice welcome.'

His sarcastic smile made her flesh creep, but she found the courage to say, 'You're not welcome.'

Another spine-chilling laugh. 'I think it's time you and I had a little talk, Katie.'

His teeth baring now like a wolf ready to pounce, her bravery deserted her, and afraid to move in case her legs gave way, she muttered, fearfully, 'We've nothing to talk about.'

He still had the horrible grin on his face. 'Sit down, my dear, and tell me why you ran away with my son and left me lying unconscious. That was not very charitable, was it?'

Rooted to the spot, she had difficulty forcing the words out. 'I thought . . . you were dead.'

This had obviously not occurred to him, and his expression became less evil. 'Ah! I begin to see things more clearly. You thought that my son had killed me, and you made him run away to escape justice?'

'Yes.' Her lips were stiff, every inch of her body felt as though it had been anaesthetized, and she desperately longed for outright oblivion.

He smiled encouragingly. 'You can relax. I have not come to do you any harm.'

'What did you come for?' Noticing the long jagged scar on his cheek, she shuddered at the memory of how she had raked his face with her scissors.

'Please sit down. You make me feel that you are afraid of me, and I can assure you that you have nothing to fear.'

She flopped into her chair again. 'What did you come for?' she repeated.

'I am going to take you back to Fenty.'

She cast a beseeching glance at Sammy, but Mr Gunn's soft voice having reassured him, he had picked up his comic and was paying no attention to them. 'You can't force me to go back,' she said, hoping that she sounded confident enough.

'Hear me out, my dear. As you probably know, I married again after poor Marguerite died, and it is for Betty's sake that I came here. I want her to have some help in the house, and I am offering you the position of maid again, Katie.'

'Me?' Terrified as she was of him, Katie couldn't help laughing at his audacity. 'You'd have to be kicking up the daisies before I'd set foot in your house again.'

An ingratiating smile followed his brief frown. 'It would be on a different footing this time, Katie.' Stretching out his hand, he stroked her knee.

She sprang to her feet. 'Keep your filthy hands off me!' she shouted. 'I don't want to be on any kind of footing with you!'

When he jumped up and made a spring at her, she wished she still had the steel knitting needles in her hands, not just to jab at his face, but to plunge them into his heart. But she was powerless against him, and he had her pinned against the wall with her arms behind her, his face close to hers as he hissed, 'This is where I should say, in the words of the old melodramas, "Come to me, my fine beauty".'

Giving a sneering giggle, he forced her legs open with his knee and put his arms round her neck, but at that, Sammy, who had been keeping an eye on him since Katie raised her voice, leapt out of his chair roaring, 'Leave her! You leave Katie alone!'

Angus did not move, but his body was tensed in readiness for the onslaught. 'Go on then, boy! Hit me! The police will not overlook a second charge of assault against you.'

Realizing that this was what he wanted, Katie screamed, 'Don't hit him, Sammy! Put him out and lock the door so he can't get in again!'

Grinning happily, Sammy grabbed his father under the arms from the back and hoisted him off the floor in one seemingly effortless heave. 'Let me go, you idiot,' Angus squealed, threshing his legs about, but he was carried to the open door and flung out with such force that he landed on his knees on the flagstones. The door slammed and the key clicked in the lock, but he knew that he was beaten and picked himself up to scurry through the pend to his car.

Trembling uncontrollably, Katie held on to the nearest chair for support, her knuckles turning white from gripping so fiercely. 'Thank goodness you were here, Sammy,' she breathed.

His chest puffed out with pride. 'He was trying to kill you, wasn't he, Katie?'

'I think he was.' She knew he hadn't been, but it was best Sammy did not know what his father *had* tried to do. She was scared enough as it was that he might try the same at any time.

'And I saved you?'

'Yes, you saved me, but I want you to sit down again and read your comic.'

Crossing obediently to his chair, he said, 'Will that man be coming back?'

'Oh, God, I hope not!' Seeing his agitation at that, she said,

'No, no, he'll not be back. It's all right, Sammy, just read your paper.'

When she was sure that he was engrossed once more in the *Wizard*, she sat down in her own seat to think. That old devil had likely waited three weeks after he discovered her address so she would be off her guard. And what about Mrs Gunn – the first Mrs Gunn? He couldn't have strangled her, because the doctor – or the police or the undertaker – would have seen the marks. He could have smothered her, but how had he got her back into bed? However he had managed, she had no proof of anything, and what did it matter now?

He would be mad enough at her as it was, without raking that up, and she would have to find out who was at her door in future before she opened it to anyone.

Chapter Eighteen

❖

'You've been here every night for weeks,' Beth observed, with a smile. 'Have you no other girls on the go just now?'

'Not one,' Dennis laughed, then added, seriously, 'I don't want anybody but you.'

'What about the girl you lived with before . . . Katie?'

'That was all finished ages ago. I told you, I'm living in at the Temperance again.'

'I never know when to believe you.'

'Now, Beth, that's hitting below the belt. I told you one little fib . . . Listen. I love you with all my heart, truly. I know I've said it before, but I mean it this time. I've come to my senses and I'll never look at another girl.'

'If I could only believe that, I'd . . .'

'I'll prove it. I didn't mean to say it yet, but . . . will you marry me, Beth?' He was fed up with his present life and she was the only way out he could see.

'Well!' she gasped. 'I wasn't expecting that. I was going to say I'd let you move in with me.'

He wished he hadn't been so impetuous, but she would throw him out if he retracted the proposal and he'd have to stand by it. 'You haven't given me an answer.'

'I'll have to think about it. Oh, Dennis, it's not that I don't love you, I do, but you're so much younger.'

'I don't give a damn about age, I want you to be my wife, so think about it if you have to, just don't take too long.'

Walking back to the Temperance, Dennis felt glad that he had burned his boats. His whole lifestyle would change once he was Beth's husband. No more suits off the peg, no more cheap shoes and shirts. Best of all, once they had been married for a month or two, he would hint that he'd like a hotel of his own and she would likely fork out the needful. Once he got it established, he could start spending the odd night with any girl he fancied . . . at Beth's expense.

The encounter with Mr Gunn four weeks earlier had made Katie long for the comfort of her lover's arms, and the more she thought about Dennis, the more miserable she became. She had tried to convince herself that he was a waster and that she was better off without him, but she still loved him. Night after night, she cried herself to sleep, and she knew she would be ill if she didn't stop. Of course, worrying about Sammy didn't help. She had often noticed him with his hand in his pocket, his face red, his breathing fast, and then he would jump up and go into his bedroom. She was well aware of what he was doing, and was thankful that she'd paid a joiner to fit a lock to her bedroom door. She would never let him see her in her wrapper again, so surely he wouldn't try anything during the day.

In the room next door, Sammy was lying wide awake. He hadn't had peace to get a good night's sleep for ages. Why was Katie always so unhappy? She hardly ate a thing nowadays and that wasn't good for anybody. She was awful short-tempered with him, and all, even when he did everything she told him. She'd once said she would have to send him away – that had stuck in his mind – and every time she'd been angry with him after that he'd been scared she would do it. He didn't like it when she lost her temper, but he'd rather put up with it than have to live in some other place without her.

Sammy propped himself on one elbow to plump up his pillow, hoping that Katie wouldn't go on like this for much longer; it was an awful long time already. Was it Dennis she was crying for? But she hadn't been so bad till they came back from . . . that place where the bobbies had tried to get him into their van. Was she upset because he hadn't gone? Did she want rid of him?

At this thought, a dull ache started inside him, so bad that he had to get out of bed. He would never know if she wanted him out of her house unless he asked her. Barging out of his room, he tried Katie's door, but it wouldn't open. His need to speak to her made him rattle the handle. 'I want to come in, Katie,' he shouted, 'but the door's stuck.'

'Go away, Sammy!'

His mouth fell open in surprise. He had to get in; he had to ask her. Banging on the wooden panel with his knuckles now, he roared, 'I need you, Katie!'

'You can't have me! Go away!'

When he put his shoulder to the door it didn't budge, but Katie screamed, 'I put a lock on to keep you out! Go away, you can't get in!'

More hurt than he had ever been in his life, he returned slowly to his own room and sat down on the edge of his bed. His head was going round and round, and he felt like a horse had kicked him in the guts. Bending over, he dropped his head into his hands and rocked backwards and forwards until his dim brain started to work again. He didn't need to ask her now. She'd told him she wanted him to go away! She'd even locked him out! But where would he go? Katie was the only person he had; she was his mother. How could a mother send her son away?

Ten more minutes passed before he remembered the man that had come to see them, the man Katie had made him throw out. He had said he was Sammy's father. He wasn't a nice man, but he had wanted to take them to a place called Fenty. Fenty? Sammy had a vague recollection of hearing that name before. He could go there and let Katie be on her own, and maybe she would get tired of being here by herself and she might come to Fenty some time, and all. A mother and father should be together.

Getting off the bed, Sammy put on the clothes he had been wearing the day before and made a bundle of the rest.

When Katie was calm enough to think over what had happened, it occurred to her that maybe Sammy had not been trying to get in to rape her. What was it he had said? 'I need you, Katie,' that was all. Maybe something had scared him? Maybe he just wanted to tell her something. If he got an idea into his head, he usually couldn't wait to tell her. She had been all upset anyway, crying about Dennis, and she had jumped to a wrong conclusion with Sammy. Poor soul, he must have been hurt by the things she'd said.

Wondering if she should go and say she was sorry, she decided to wait until rising time. Her nerves were all to pieces just now, and she had better try to get some sleep.

When she woke up some hours later, she was surprised that she had slept so well. She had been needing it, of course, and she felt a lot better for it. Making up her mind to forget about Dennis in future, she got up and went through to the kitchen, knocking on the other bedroom door as she went past. Then she knelt on the hearthrug to clear out the grate, but even by the time she had lit the fire Sammy had not come through. Wondering why, she rose to empty the ashes into the pail in the coalshed, and when she came in, she rapped on his door again. 'Come on, Sammy, or you'll be late for your work.'

When she got no reply, she turned the handle and looked in, then stood stock still in dismay. He wasn't there! He must have got up earlier, she thought, and ran to see if he was in the wc, but the key was still hanging on its hook by the outside door. Could he have gone for a walk? Yes, that's where he must be. She had better make the breakfast, for he'd be hungry when he came in.

When the porridge was ready, she filled two plates and sat down to sup hers, but by the time she was finished, there was still no sign of Sammy. Panicking now, she tried to think where else he might have gone. Could he have gone to work? Had he been so hurt by what she had said last night he had left without speaking to her? She would have to go and find out. On her way to the Salutation, she went in to tell Lottie that she would be late for work, and when her friend heard what had happened, she said, 'Off you go and see if he's there. I'll easy manage here myself till you're back.'

The heavens opened as Katie went out, and she was soaked to the skin by the time she returned from her fruitless errand, frantic with worry. She went straight home to change her clothes, then had an urge to check Sammy's room. It was the same as always: the old patchwork quilt pulled up over the neatly made bed, the cross-stitch runner smooth on top of the chest of drawers, the little alarm clock he had been so proud of when she bought it though he couldn't read the time, the teddy bear she had bought for him the Christmas before last because he had been taken with it in a shop window.

When she opened the drawers, her heart sank. Most of his underclothes and shirts were gone. Remembering that he kept his money tin under the bottom shelf in the cupboard, she put her hand in to search for it, but it, too, had gone. There must have been quite a bit in it, for when the lid wouldn't shut on the coins, she had always changed them for notes which didn't take up so much room. He had definitely meant to go away for good, but maybe he would come back if he didn't like being on his own. He must come back, for anything could happen to him and she didn't know where to start looking for him.

Blaming herself for being nasty to him, she felt too upset to go to work, but she didn't like to let Lottie down. Her distress, however, was so great when she went to the bakery that Lottie told her to go home again. 'You're in such a state you'll not be able to put your mind to things anyway. And it's best you're there in case Sammy comes back. Stay off as long as you like, lass, and stop worrying. I'm sure he'll turn up.'

Katie was a little soothed by Lottie's optimism, but she was so afraid that Sammy would go away again if he came home and she wasn't there that she didn't leave the house at all for the next few days, except to go to the lavatory or take in coal and sticks.

On the afternoon of the fourth day, her eyes were sunken from lack of sleep, her face was drawn when she went to answer a knock at the door and her hand flew to her mouth when she saw the constable.

'Can I come in?'

Numb with fear, she followed him inside. 'Is this where a Samuel Gunn lives?' he asked.

'Sammy?' she whispered. 'Yes, but he's not here.'

'I know that. The Banff police picked him up last night.'

'Picked him up? What for?'

'I'm sorry, but I'm not at liberty to tell you. My orders were to inform you of his whereabouts.'

'How did you know where he lived? He can never remember.'

'They found a ticket in his pocket with his name and address on it.'

'I wrote that in case he got lost. Can I go to see him?'

'Nobody said anything about that, but I could take you.'

When she ran into the police station at Banff around half an hour later, the sergeant glared at the PC from Peterhead. 'You weren't told to take her here.'

'I wasn't told not to,' the younger man defended himself.

'He's not in a fit state to see anybody.'

'He'll want to see me,' Katie said, firmly.

'Are you his sister?' Sergeant Tait demanded.

'He thinks I am.' It was out before she realized how odd it must sound and felt obliged to explain why she and Sammy were together, adding that they could check with Sergeant Begg at Cullen if they didn't believe her. 'Now will you let me see him? He'll be confused, and I'll be able to calm him down.'

'I'd advise you not to go near him, lass. He's mad, ranting and raving and shouting for his mother.'

'His mother?' Katie was astounded, and hurt. 'His mother's dead, and anyway, she never had much to do with him. It's me that's looked after him for years, and I'd like to see him.'

'Do you know why he's been locked up?'

'I suppose he was wandering round lost?'

'He'd been showing himself to a thirteen-year-old lassie, and another two had reported him earlier for the same thing.'

'Oh no! But I still want to see him.'

After more explanations about why she and Sammy had been together, she was told to wait until Sergeant Tait found out if the prisoner wanted to see her, and when he came back he was shaking his head. 'I told him you were here but it's his mother he wants, and he's just like an animal. He's punched my constable, and he's kicked me a few times, and all. He's not fit to be among ordinary folk. He belongs in an asylum.'

'Please let me go to him,' she begged. 'He'll be all right once he sees me.'

Shrugging, Sergeant Tait took her through to the cells, but even Katie could not get through to Sammy, and she could see for herself that his mind was completely gone. Sadly, she turned away. 'What happens to him now?' she asked, as she was led back to the desk.

'Who's responsible for him?'

'Me, so the police at Cullen said. His father lives at the Howe of Fenty, near Huntly, but he doesn't want him.'

'There's not much point in us charging him with indecency. We'll have him certified by a doctor, but we'll need your signature as well before he can be put away.'

'Where would they put him?'

'Ladysbridge, likely. It's nearest.'

Having reluctantly appended her signature to a form, Katie was driven home by the Peterhead constable, who let her weep without saying anything, but when he stopped to let her out, he said, kindly, 'It wasna your fault, lass. He's far better locked away.'

She could not answer, and walked through the pend with tears streaming down her cheeks. When she went into the house, she made straight for her bedroom and flung herself down on the bed. How could she live with the guilt of having Sammy locked up? It was her fault. If she hadn't been taken in by Dennis, Sammy would still be as innocent as when she first met him.

After another sleepless night, Katie dragged herself to the bakery and poured out her tale to Lottie, who let her customers wait until she had heard everything before she opened her shop. 'I'd like to get a hold of Dennis McKay,' she said, grimly. 'I'd tell him what I thought of him, but he'll get his just deserts some day.'

It was a full week before Katie felt any better. 'I'd like to go to Ladysbridge,' she told Lottie. 'If Sammy's settled in, I'll let him stay there, but if he's not happy, I'll take him home with me.'

'Well, I'd tell you to leave well alone, but you'll not take my advice, so I'd better say nothing.'

Up at the crack of dawn the following day, Katie set off on the bus for Ladysbridge, just beyond Banff. She had some fruit and some sweets to give to Sammy, and was sure that he would be calmer and would be glad to see her. How could he forget her after what they had been through together? When she saw him last, he'd been muddled by being held in a cell, and likely the policemen had been rough with him when they picked him up on the street. She didn't know if the asylum had strict visiting times, but was confident that whoever was in charge would allow her in once she explained the situation.

The superintendent was not available when she got there, but one of the attendants, soft-spoken and understanding, said that he thought it would be all right as long as she didn't stay longer than fifteen minutes.

'They get a bittie agitated after that,' he explained.

When she entered the long room and saw the inmates, most of them old men with slavering mouths and vacant eyes, grinning slyly at her as she passed, their hands coming out to pull at her skirts, she was certain that Sammy did not belong there. He wasn't nearly as bad as that – there had always been something in his eyes that had told of thoughts behind them. Shivering, she kept looking for him, but it wasn't until she came to the far end that she found him. Holding out her hand, she said, 'Hello, Sammy.'

When he lifted his head, she was alarmed to see that his eyes were as vacant as all the rest. 'It's Katie,' she told him. 'You remember me, don't you?'

Slowly he shook his head, and she sat down beside him. 'I brought some sweeties for you, and some apples and bananas.'

There was still no sign of recognition, nor anything else, but she persevered. 'I got jelly babies, for I know you like them.' She took one from the bag and held it out, but his hands stayed in his lap. 'Do you want to come home with me to your own room, and . . .' Trying to think of something to jog his memory, she went on, 'And your clock, and your teddy bear? Remember? They're both waiting for you.'

It was like talking to a brick wall, but she did not give up. 'And the gardens'll be full of weeds. Jackie needs you to tell him what to do.'

His head had gone down again, and she burst out, 'Sammy, you must remember. We ran away together. We ate berries. We slept in barns.'

He gave no sign that he had heard. 'Do you not remember the farm?' she persisted. 'Mrs Sutherland?'

There was not even a faint movement at the mention of the woman who had been so kind to him. 'She danced with you one Hogmanay, remember? When we were all in the kitchen having a good time?'

Recalling what had happened after that, Katie thought it wisest not to pursue it any further. 'Oh, Sammy, you must remember me. It's Katie. Katie.'

With no warning, he stood up and roared, 'Mother! Mother!'

The attendant came running up and grabbed his arms. 'It's all right, lad, it's all right. Just sit down and be good.'

Turning to Katie, he said, 'He was shouting for his mother when he was brought in.'

'His mother's dead,' she murmured, 'and, any road, they were never very close.'

'I think you should go now, lass. Once they get upset, it takes them a while to settle down again. He was a handful when he came in first . . . in a straitjacket for a couple of days, but he's been quiet since . . . till just now.'

The implication that she was the cause of Sammy's distress made Katie leave abruptly. When she reached the main road, she decided to walk to Banff to find out when she would get a bus to Peterhead, and if she had time, she would go into a café for a cup of tea. She needed something.

She didn't feel the cold as she strode along head down. She could think of nothing but Sammy. If only she could take him home to his own room, to things he would recognize, he might get better . . . but she couldn't cope with him the way he was. She couldn't even cope with her own emotions at the present moment, never mind his, and her tortured mind turned to her grandfather. He would have advised her what to do.

She was on the outskirts of Banff when the sound of an engine made her look up to see a bus chugging towards her with BUCKIE on its destination board. Without stopping to think, she ran across the road and held up her hand for it to stop. As she jumped aboard, she was sure that it was no coincidence that a bus which went through Cullen should appear at that minute. It was Fate!

Her insides were churning wildly as she got off and stood watching the bus move away, then, her heartbeats drumming in her ears, she ran down the hill to Seatown and burst into the little house. 'Where's Granda?' she demanded, not taking in the fact that it was unusual for her grandmother to be sitting by the fire in the middle of a forenoon. 'I want to speak to him.'

Mary Ann's startled eyes hardened. 'You'll have some job, then, for he's been in the kirkyard this past three days.'

At first, Katie didn't understand, and when comprehension did dawn, she shouted, 'Granda can't be dead! I need him!'

'You should have let him ken, then,' came the dry retort, 'and he'd have held on till you came afore he passed ower.'

Almost hysterical, Katie collapsed into her grandfather's chair, and the old woman waited for her harsh tearless sobs to stop. It was fully five minutes until they began to tail off and Mary Ann could say, gently, 'I dinna suppose you'll want to tell me . . . ?'

At a normal time, Katie would never have dreamt of telling her grandmother the things she heard herself saying, but they poured out of her like water from a burst dam – about everything except Dennis; she couldn't bear to mention him – and the old woman listened until she came to a sobbing halt.

'I suppose you think I'm shocked,' Mary Ann remarked then, with the hint of a smile, 'but at my age there's little left to shock me. I ken't that laddie would bring you nothing but trouble, and to tell you the truth, I some thought you'd end up bringing an imbecile bairn here. I'm glad you'd the sense to get rid o' it. Dinna blame yourself for him being put in Ladysbridge. He'd likely have landed in some asylum or other come time, any road, for his kind aye grow worse the older they get.'

'Is that true, Grandma, or are you just trying to stop me feeling guilty?'

'I thought you ken't me better than need to ask that.'

She should have known, Katie thought. Her grandmother had never been one for considering other people's feelings. 'I'm awful sorry about Granda,' she murmured, rather belatedly.

'Aye, well, it's a queer thing. Here's me lost the man I wed near half a century ago, and you left without the man that's

215

been your companion for years. Was there a purpose to it? You wouldna think on . . . ?'

'Are you asking me to come home again, Grandma?' Katie could hardly believe it. 'For good?'

'I ken we never saw eye to eye about things, but we'd be company for each other.'

Katie couldn't help a watery smile. 'You mean you'd rather be fighting with me than sitting on your own?'

'Something like that.' Mary Ann had a twinkle in her eye.

'I'd have to go back to Peterhead and work my notice to Lottie, and give up my house.'

'I can wait another week or two.' The twinkle was even more pronounced.

'Well,' Katie said, pensively, 'there's nothing for me there now, so I suppose . . . all right, then.'

It was no surprise to Katie that her grandmother let her go with no sign of affection. There had never been any, and she guessed that there never would be.

On Tuesday morning, after describing her experiences at Ladysbridge, Katie told Lottie that she was going back to live with her grandmother. 'I'll wait till you get another assistant, though.'

Her friend and employer looked at her sadly. 'I'm going to miss you, Katie. Are you sure you're doing the right thing?'

'I'm not sure, and before I'm back a week, I'll likely be wishing I hadn't gone, but I think it's what my Granda would have liked.'

'Poor Sammy,' Lottie said, suddenly. 'I can't get over him ending up like that.'

The house in Marischal Street having been furnished when Katie went in, all she had to do was ensure that the next tenant would have no complaints as to its cleanliness. She spent all her evenings scrubbing, polishing, laundering the bedding and curtains, and slept the last night on the couch with her coat over her.

In the morning, she handed the keys to Lottie, who was

too busy to be sentimental over the parting. 'You'll write and tell me how you're getting on?'

Katie hesitated. 'I'd better not. I want to forget . . . but I'll never forget you and your kindness.'

Smiling, Lottie held out her hand. 'Good luck, lass.'

Katie kept a fixed smile on her face as she walked to the railway station carrying the cardboard box Bob McRuvie had given her to hold her belongings, but alone in the carriage, thoughts of her bleak future made her put her handkerchief to her eyes.

She was going home disillusioned with life – and there was no Granda now to shield her from her grandmother's cutting tongue.

PART THREE

Chapter Nineteen

❧

On Katie's first night back in Cullen, she felt a compulsion to let the Three Kings know of the tribulations that had beset her since she last spoke to them; only then would she feel free to take up the reins of her new life. Afraid that their magic might have worn off for her, she did not make her usual bee-line for them, but walked instead along the water's edge – the blown spume wetting her hair and face – and waited until she was in line with them before turning to make her way up the shingle. As she came to each huge mass, each 'friend', she put her hand out to make contact with it, to remind it who she was. Her damp, unpinned hair was flying all over the place now, her skirts billowing up like a hot-air balloon ready to take off, and a lump rose in her throat at the old familiarity of it all.

When she ended the saga of her misfortunes, she said, 'I don't know if I should have come back. Grandma'll soon start finding fault with me again, even though I'm older now. The trouble is, she's older, and all, and I feel sorry for her now Granda's gone. We'll rub each other up the wrong way like we always did, but it's just how we're made. I think I must have a lot of her in me.'

Pausing briefly to consider this new thought, Katie gave an amused gurgle. 'She wouldn't be pleased to think we've got the same nature, and we haven't really, for I can love other people, and I'm sure she's never truly loved anybody in her life, not even Granda. Oh, I wish he was still here. He'd have known the right things to say so I wouldn't feel so ashamed of putting Sammy away or letting Dennis make such a fool of me. I didn't know there were men like him, and he must have laughed at me for being so easy taken in. But I've learned from it, and I'll not be taken in again by any man.'

She shivered as the iciness of the winter evening finally pierced through all her layers of clothes. 'I'd better go now, but I'll be back, I promise.'

When she returned to the house, Mary Ann said, 'I suppose you'll be needing a cup of tea?'

'Yes, please, but I'll make it.'

'I can manage, I can still boil the kettle and fill the teapot.' Dropping her sarcasm, she barked, 'You'll have been along the shore?'

Having forgotten how quickly her grandmother's mind could switch from one subject to another, Katie was taken aback by the abrupt question. 'It's my favourite walk,' she said, a little defensively, then wished she had been more positive. They were in different positions now – she was doing Grandma the favour by living here, not the other way round.

'You'll need to stop your childish nonsense. Folk'll think you're off your head if they see you speaking to rocks.'

Katie sighed gustily. Nothing was changed. Nothing would ever change, no matter how old she was.

She was home before she realized that she hadn't mentioned Mr Gunn to the Three Kings this time, not that it mattered. They couldn't protect her from him if he turned up in Cullen. But would he come? He wouldn't know Sammy was in Ladysbridge. He'd think they were still living together in Marischal Street, and he wouldn't risk going back there. He would likely never find out she had left . . . and even if he did, he wouldn't know where she was.

As soon as she heard Angus drive off, Betty Gunn went up to the top floor. He had told her once that the garrets were just stores for old rubbish and she needn't bother about them, and she had taken him at his word, but she was positive he had hidden the letter up there somewhere. He had taken it in his hand when he went upstairs and he'd gone right up the two flights of stairs, and she wanted to know what was in it that had upset him so much. He shouldn't keep secrets from her. Jim had never kept anything from her in all the fifteen years they had been married.

She had something of a shock when she went into the first small room. Instead of the jumble of junk she had expected to find, there was a rumpled bed, the blankets flung back as if the occupant had left in a hurry. There was little else except a chair thick with dust and a trunk where the film of grey powder had recently been disturbed. Her heart racing, she went down on her knees to lift the lid, feeling like a thief as she rummaged through torn handkerchiefs and socks with big holes in the heels and toes. Then she came on some well-worn shirts, their necks far too small for her husband. At the bottom of the trunk were some boys' comics, which, going by their dates, couldn't have been his, either. Her perplexity deepened when she found some items that made her recall the things her brother had hoarded when he was a boy. Angus must surely have a young brother, but why had he never mentioned him?

Annoyed that her search had been in vain, Betty was trying to replace the contents exactly as she had found them when she noticed a bound slit in the striped twill lining – a secret pocket? Her stomach lurched as her fingers took out a sheet of paper as well as the envelope she was looking for, and trembling with guilty excitement, she sat back on her heels to read them.

The loose sheet looked as if it had been lying for some time, so she unfolded it first, and was amazed to see the name Katie written several times in her husband's flamboyant hand, and at the foot, circled by an elaborate pattern of whorls and curlicues, he had written 'Mrs Katie Gunn'. This shocked her. His first wife's name had been Marguerite! Had he married again after she died? Had he committed bigamy when he married her, Betty?

Three addresses were scribbled on the other side: Seatown, Cullen; Struieburn Farm, near Mintlaw; Marischal Street, Peterhead. Were they places where Katie Gunn had lived? Was it to one of them Angus had gone that Sunday he had said he had some business to attend to? He was in such a state when he came home that she had been afraid he was having a heart attack, and when he calmed down, he said that the deal he'd been trying to negotiate had fallen through. Was it possible that he had been trying to get his legitimate second wife to come back to him and she had wanted nothing to do with him? That would explain his agitation.

It crossed Betty's mind that she could be thrown out if he ever succeeded in bringing Katie to Fenty, and in the worry of this, it was some time before she remembered the letter and was so on edge that she nearly put it back unread. Then, thinking that it might contain information about Katie – which would be why Angus had acted so strangely – she took the single page out of the envelope. It shed no light on Katie but was another great shock to Betty.

She read it a second time before she returned paper and envelope to the secret pocket and shut the lid of the trunk. Then, on an impulse, she went into the other attic, where a bed had also been left rumpled, with a chair at one side and a small table at the other. Instead of a trunk there was an old chest of drawers which drew her like a magnet. The top two drawers held only linings of yellowing newspapers, but in the lowest lay a pair of ripped stockings and a faded, torn petticoat. Were these Katie's? But surely she would not have slept up here if she was married to Angus?

About to slide the drawer in, Betty saw that the lining paper was not lying flat at one corner and curiosity made her lift it to see what was underneath. To her astonishment, there was a small collection of coins and three ten shilling notes. In all, it could not amount to much more than two pounds, and the owner must have forgotten about them.

When Betty went down to the kitchen, she tried to put the

pieces together in her mind. The letter, from Banff police station, had said that Samuel Gunn had been apprehended in the street for indecent behaviour, and also that he had been certified as insane and was now in Ladysbridge, the papers committing him having been signed by his recognized guardian and the police doctor. The writer had felt, however, that the young man's father should be told, although he had been informed by his colleagues at Cullen that Mr Gunn had, some time earlier, refused to take his son back.

Betty felt a surge of anger. Angus had never told her that his son was still alive – she had assumed that the imbecile he had spoken of once had died at birth – but it explained the contents of the trunk. Then it occurred to her that Katie could be Samuel's wife. She might have been a maid who had fallen in love and eloped with him, and left him when she found out that he was mad. Angus could be anxious about her, that was all, and was trying to find her to make sure that no ill had befallen her.

Yes, Betty decided, it all fitted in. Katie had slept in one of the attic rooms and Samuel in the other. The letter had shocked Angus at first – he would hate the idea of his son being in an asylum – then he'd been pleased that no harm had come to Katie, for, being Samuel's wife, she must have been the other person who had signed the form to commit him.

Betty rose to make herself another cup of tea, but, while she waited for the kettle to boil, the doubts came flooding back, and she knew that she could never rest until she knew the truth. She would have to ask Angus . . . but not yet.

Mary Ann seemed to have recovered so quickly from the death of her husband that Katie wondered if she had ever mourned at all. After being married to him for so many years, she should have been lost, bewildered, but her tongue and her eyes were as sharp as ever. The only hint of advancing age was her occasional comment that her knees were as stiff as boards in the mornings with rheumatics.

Katie knew better than offer to share the housework, and so, to pass her time, she took bus trips to Buckie, not far along the coast, and once as far as Elgin; it was like being on a never-ending holiday. After three weeks, however, this began to pall, and she reflected, sourly, that holidays should come to an end some time, otherwise there was no pleasure in them.

It was worse having to sit through the long evenings with her grandmother, neither of them having anything to say to the other. Mary Ann, who had always kept her hands busy by knitting socks, drawers and ganzies for William John, did not have this to occupy her any longer and sat with her hands in her lap, staring into the fire. At last, Katie could bear it no longer. 'Couldn't you knit a cardigan for yourself, Grandma?'

'I've plenty cardigans.'

'Aye, but it's just the darns that holds them together,' Katie retorted.

Even having suggested it, she was still surprised the next morning when Mary Ann said, 'If you're going to Buckie, I'll gi'e you money to buy some black wool and a pattern for me. You'll get a better selection there.'

Katie bought wool for herself, too, and from then on, the evening silence was broken by the click of knitting needles. She sometimes went out for a short walk before she went to bed, along the harbour wall or across the golf course, but not to the Three Kings. There was nothing to tell them any more. She still felt guilty about putting Sammy away and often wondered how he was. She even dreamt of him one night, reliving her brief visit to Ladysbridge, feeling again the deep pain she had felt when he had looked blankly at her and shouted for his mother. She couldn't understand that, for he had never mentioned his mother after they left Fenty. Maybe she should go back to see him? He could be better now. The

226

shock of being accosted by the police and locked in a cell was enough to make even the most balanced of men lose their reason.

When Katie told her what she meant to do, Mary Ann was very much against it, but the young woman stuck to her guns. 'Sammy could be wondering why I've never been back to see him, so I'm going, whatever you say, Grandma.'

'And if he's got back what little sense he had? You surely wouldna think on taking him out o' there?'

'If he recognizes me, I'll ask how I should go about . . .'

'You're nae taking him here! Have you lost your wits, and all? He might have clear spells, but they wouldna last and then he could be worse than ever. He's best where he is, for they ken how to deal wi' the likes o' him, and seeing you could easy upset him.'

'I have to go, Grandma!'

Mary Ann sagged back in her seat. 'So be it, then.' In her displeasure, her compressed lips vanished inside her gummy mouth, leaving the impression that there was only a puckered hole in the middle of her face.

As it turned out, the two women need not have bothered to argue, because there was no change in Sammy's condition, and when, after ten minutes of trying to jog his memory, Katie turned to go, he shouted for his mother. The attendant came running up to quieten him. 'He hasn't done that since the last time you were here,' he said, accusingly.

Bitterly disappointed, she walked away, presuming that she must remind Sammy of Fenty and Mrs Gunn.

When she went home, Mary Ann did not need to ask what had happened, and uncharacteristically, she made no reference to the girl's long face and melancholy eyes.

The days passed so slowly for Katie that she eventually had to say, 'I can't go on like this, Grandma. I've got nothing to do all day and I've used nearly all the money I'd saved. I know you give me all my food, but I've been paying a lot of bus fares, and I've had to buy stockings and other things I needed. I'll have to get a job.'

Mary Ann bridled. 'You should have said and I'd have paid for the things. Besides, there's precious little jobs to be had round here, and I'm not having you going away again. I kept you till you were fourteen, and I can still manage.'

'But Granda was working when I was younger, and you've only your old age pension coming in now. Ten shillings a week's not enough to keep us both.'

'Your grandfather didna leave me penniless. I got what his father left him, and I . . .' Mary Ann broke off, then ended, a crafty smile flitting across her face, 'Nothing'll come ower you when I go. You'll be well provided for.'

'But I could provide for myself if I had a job,' Katie objected. Her grandmother had no idea how quickly money went down when there was less coming in than going out.

'You'll get the house, and all, when I pass on.'

'You won't be passing on for a long time yet.'

'I hope no', but you never ken.'

Mary Ann's pessimism worried Katie, and she wasn't sure if she would want to stop on in Cullen if her grandmother died. There was nothing for her here. She would be better to go to a city, Aberdeen, or Edinburgh, or even London. She might get the chance of working for a lady with a title there.

She was unwilling to waste money on bus trips now, and when she returned from one of the long walks she had started to take – strolling through the grounds of Cullen House or visiting her grandfather's grave in Seafield Cemetery, or, as today, going up the Bin – Mary Ann observed, 'When I was up at the baker's in the Square this forenoon, young Alice Burnett was telling me she's getting wed next Saturday.'

Katie knew that there was something behind this apparently

innocuous remark, but it took her a minute or two to realize that her grandmother was telling her to apply for Alice's job. There was no point in trying to thank her, for her head was bent over a pot at the fire.

'I thought I'd never be happy again after Tom died, but I'm happier than I've ever been.' Beth McKay gave her husband a loving smile.

'I'm pretty happy myself,' Dennis smirked, 'though I was a bit embarrassed about you paying for everything – the ring, my clothes, the honeymoon.'

'I wanted it to be perfect, and it was. I was proud of you in Strathpeffer, you looked so distinguished. Some of the old dears in the Hydro looked at you like you were royalty.'

'King Dennis, that's me,' he grinned. 'I never thought I'd be in a place as swanky as that, but being a waiter, I knew the right knives and forks to use.' His face straightened. 'I'll be back to serving other people tomorrow, though.'

'I've been thinking about that, Dennis. What would you say to running your own restaurant?'

After the initial soaring of his spirits, he decided to go carefully. 'How do you mean?'

'I could buy a place for you, and you could hire your own staff, and do anything else you wanted.'

'Just a minute, Beth.' He had meant to wait a while before hinting that he'd like to have his own hotel, but she had only said a restaurant, and he didn't know what she had in mind. 'What kind of place were you thinking of? A poky wee cafe, a tearoom?'

She gave a tinkling laugh. 'Much better than that, Dennis. A proper restaurant, with good food reasonably priced, but not cheap. The kind of place a businessman could take his wife, or a solicitor might take his clients. You know what hotels serve . . . that's what you could aim at to start with, then once you saw how it was going, you could engage a chef to specialize in a certain kind of cuisine.'

He smiled derisively. 'In Peterhead?'

'Why not? There's a lot of moneyed people here, skippers and fish-curers as well as the businessmen and solicitors, and so forth. I'm sure you could make a go of it.'

Dennis felt his interest stirring. A restaurant would be easier to run than a hotel. As long as he found a decent chef, he could do the rest standing on his head. 'So how do we go about it? I mean, getting premises and that?'

'Leave that side of it to me. After I've found the right spot, it'll be up to you and I promise I won't interfere.'

He heaved a sigh of satisfaction. 'I can't believe you'd do this for me, Beth.'

'Can't you? You should know how much I love you.'

'Not half as much as I love you.' As he said it, he felt a slight prickle of conscience, because he didn't love her at all. He liked her, but he had married her purely for her money, though he had never thought she would cough up so quickly. He would make a go of this restaurant, which would lull any doubts she might harbour about him, make her think he was a reformed man, but once he had it running smoothly, he meant to have a good time amongst the girls again.

Betty Gunn had been waiting to catch Angus in a good humour. She had not been able to get Katie, whoever's wife she was, out of her mind, and when Angus came home one night looking pleased with himself, she made up her mind to tackle him.

'I sold three skirts to one woman today,' he crowed.

Betty smiled admiringly. 'You're a good salesman.'

'Yes, I think I have a good way with the women.' Full of bonhomie, he asked, 'What have you been doing today?'

It was the perfect opening and she took it. What did it matter that what she was about to tell him had taken place nearly a month ago? 'Well, I'd finished all the housework early, and I was stuck for something to do in the afternoon, so I tidied up one of the attics.'

A frown appeared on his forehead. 'I told you not to go up there. Which one did you do?'

'The nearest one.' She waited for the eruption and when it didn't come, she added, 'There's a lot of stuff in the trunk that could be thrown out.'

He took a moment to answer. 'Yes, I have not been in there since my son left.'

'Oh,' she said, feigning great surprise, 'I thought your son died when he was born.'

'It would have been better if he had.'

'It was his bedroom, then?'

'For a time.'

'Who slept in the other one?'

His face registered deep annoyance now. 'So you went in there, too, did you?'

His anger made her regret broaching the subject, but she had started and was determined to get to the bottom of it. 'I just had a look. There's some ripped stockings and an old petticoat in one of the drawers.'

'Er – yes. They were left by a young maid we had.'

'Katie?'

His eyes flashing, he shouted, 'Damn you to Hell! You had no business up there! You were interfering with things which do not concern you.'

Her legs trembling, Betty still persisted. 'Anything about you concerns me. I told you I was tidying up, and I saw the pocket in the trunk, so I put my hand in to see if there was anything inside. Why did you write that name so many times? What's Katie to you?'

Not answering her question, Angus said, in a voice as cold as steel, 'I suppose you found the letter from the police, too? You knew my son was in a mental institution.'

'I can't understand why you didn't tell me yourself, it's

nothing to be ashamed of. And you still haven't told me what Katie is to you.'

'She is nothing to me! It was she who . . . turned my son's brain altogether. She interfered with him, and when I caught them one night and ordered her to leave next morning, she ran off and took Sammy with her.'

He was shaking so violently that Betty was sure there was much more to it than he was saying. 'Did you fancy her, and all? Was that why you . . . ?'

He grabbed her arms roughly above the elbows. 'Oh, Great God, woman! Yes, I fancied her, as you so crudely put it, and she spurned me! Are you happy now that you have wormed it out of me?' He paused, his fingers digging into her flesh, then sneered, 'Since you seem to be so interested, I may as well tell you that Marguerite's death was a direct result of Katie taking Sammy away. If I ever get my hands on her, I'll . . .'

Betty was relieved when he stopped and let his arms fall. 'I warn you,' he muttered, 'do not goad me again.' Then he turned and went out.

She sat down, rubbing her arms. What kind of man had she married? She had never seen him so angry; he had been on the verge of striking her. After giving it a little more thought, however, she realized that she had asked for it, reminding him of things he would rather forget. She just wished she had found out why he had written Mrs Katie Gunn, but she would be wise never to mention that name again. Enough was enough.

When Angus came back from wherever he had gone to cool off, it was he who brought up the subject again. 'Katie was a trustworthy maid, and I would like to bring her back here. I have learned that she now lives in Peterhead, and I have been meaning to go to see her, to show her that I bear her no malice. Perhaps, if you came with me, she would be more willing to return.'

Betty contemplated refusing, then she remembered that he

had said he would like to get his hands on Katie for what she had done to his son. If he was out for vengeance, she could warn the girl if she went to Peterhead. Besides, she wanted to find out what she looked like. 'All right,' she smiled, 'I'll go with you.'

'Shall we make it this coming Sunday?'

Never having been told of the wartime injury to his head, nor of the fall which had further damaged his brain, Betty was blissfully unaware that her husband was teetering on the borderline between sanity and insanity.

Too wound up to sleep on Saturday night, Angus was recalling his first visit to Peterhead. The indignity of being thrown out had mortified him, and the excruciating headache and the intense pains in his chest had made him sure that he was in the throes of a fatal heart attack. It had been more than an hour before he felt fit to drive home, and he had decided to put Katie and what she had done out of his mind for good.

The arrival of the letter from Banff, however, had put a different perspective on things. With Sammy out of the way, his long-nourished dream of putting his mark on Katie could soon be fulfilled, but first he meant to force himself on her, give her a taste of what a red-blooded man could do. Betty would suspect nothing as long as he could contain his feelings in front of her, but he would have to guard his tongue tomorrow. If he let slip that he had bought a whip . . .

His imagination ran wild now, and screams rang in his ears as he pictured the thongs cutting into the helpless naked body. He was revelling so much in the enjoyment of this that he was infuriated when an unwelcome voice in his head kept insisting that his wife would not allow it. What right had she to interfere? If she tried to obstruct him, she would find herself at the receiving end of the crop too. It was about time Marguerite was punished for refusing him night after night

233

for so many years. She deserved more than just a whipping. But ... was it Marguerite he would be whipping? If not, who was it?

His evil thoughts now too confused to make sense even to himself, Angus drifted into the arms of Morpheus.

Chapter Twenty

❖❖

1927

The mornings were always fairly hectic in the baker's shop, especially Saturdays, when the housewives stocked up for the weekend on bread, rolls, cakes, meat pies and fruit tarts, but Katie liked being busy, the time passed more quickly. She was totting up some purchases on one of the paper bags when another customer said, sharply, 'Hey, wait your turn! I'm next!'

Not wanting to lose count, Katie did not raise her head, but she couldn't help smiling. There was always somebody trying to push her way to the front, but whoever it was never got away with it. 'Two and tenpence ha'penny, Bella,' she said, after checking the total twice.

While the woman fumbled in her purse, Katie looked to see who had been reprimanded, and guessed that it had been the young man now gazing out of the window. She wondered who he was, for very few men ever came in, and she gave a start of recognition when he turned his head and their eyes met. When his turn came, she said, 'Was it you got told off, George?'

He smiled sheepishly. 'I'm sorry for trying to barge in, Katie. Ma's up to her elbows spring cleaning, and she needs a half-loaf.' Watching her break a double loaf down the middle and wrapping it in tissue paper, he said, 'The last time I saw you was the day we left school.'

'I've been away, but I came back after my Granda died.'

'Aye, I was real sorry about William John. I was at sea at the time, so I didn't hear about it till I came home.'

'I hope you two's not going to stand there blethering the whole day,' came an annoyed voice from behind him.

'I'm just going.' He held out a half-crown and waited for his change, saying as he went out, 'No doubt I'll be seeing you again, Katie.'

'George was in the same class as me at school, Mrs Reid,' she explained, as she served the impatient housewife.

'Aye, well, some o' us have bairns coming in for their dinner. I'll take that other half-loaf, Katie, and a couple o' fly cemeteries.'

Opening another bag, Katie popped in two of the currant-filled pastry slices. 'The bairns dinna like them,' Mrs Reid confided, 'but me and my man does.'

When she went home at half past twelve and sat down at the table with her grandmother, Katie said, 'You'll never guess who came into the shop this forenoon? George Buchan, and I haven't seen him for years.'

'Ina Green's laddie?' Mary Ann, like all the other older women, still used the maiden name, however long the woman in question had been married.

Katie had been well schooled in this. 'That's right, and he goes to sea now.'

'George was aye a nice laddie. He used to carry my basket for me, though it must have been heavy for him sometimes, and him just a wee toot o' a thing.'

Having only half an hour off, Katie was soon running back up the hill, and it was well on in the afternoon before she had time to think about George Buchan again. He was a few months older than she was though they had been in the same class, and when the older boys said nasty things about her having no mother – with so many fishermen lost at sea, being fatherless was quite common – it had been George who had bloodied their noses and given her one of his sweets to stop her crying. He had been a nice boy, and he seemed to have grown into quite a nice young man – not that she had any interest in men, young or otherwise . . .

Mary Ann gave Katie an arch look when they were having supper that night. 'So am I to be hearing more about him?'

'Who, George? I hardly know him now.'

'That doesna mean – would you like to ken him better?'

'I hadn't thought about it. He only came in for a half-loaf, and he'll likely never be back.'

'Mmmphmm.' Mary Ann looked sceptical, then said, 'And was there any other news at the shop?'

Since she had started working, Katie had fallen into the habit of keeping her grandmother up to date with the gossip that went on between the customers – which girl was seeing which boy, which young wife was in the family way, which girl was in the family way though she wasn't a wife, which wife had been seen with somebody else's man, which man had been seen with somebody else's wife – so the clicking of their knitting needles was now accompanied by speculations about who was taking up with who.

When they ran out of gossip, Mary Ann returned to a more interesting topic as far as she was concerned. 'Would you go out wi' George Buchan if he asked you?'

'He'll not ask me, Grandma.'

'You could do a lot worse.'

'I don't want anything to do with men.'

Her grandmother hesitated. 'Was there a lad in Peterhead that let you down?'

Katie burst out laughing. 'You're as bad as the rest of the women, wanting to know everything about everybody.'

'Well,' Mary Ann said, defensively, 'them that don't ask, don't get told.'

'And them that do ask, sometimes still don't get told.'

The old woman's mouth rose at the corners. 'So you're not telling me?'

'There's nothing to tell.' Even when she'd been spilling her heart out to her grandmother, Katie recalled, she had said nothing about Dennis. Mary Ann would be shocked if she knew that her grand-daughter had slept with a man she wasn't married to. The old woman had been understanding about what Sammy had done to her – she had been powerless to stop that – but Dennis was a different matter.

When George Buchan went home, he said, 'You didn't tell me Katie Mair was working in the baker's.'

Mrs Buchan, née Ina Green, pulled a face. 'I clean forgot. She's been there about three or four month now.'

'She's grown into a right bonnie lass.'

His slight flush made his mother's brows fly down, and she said, sharply, 'I hope you're not getting any ideas there, George, for there's a mystery about her.'

'What do you mean?'

'Well, Mary Ann aye made out she was young William John's bairn, and she said he was lost at sea a week afore his wife died in childbirth, so her and her man had to take Katie.'

'I knew she was an orphan . . .'

'Aye, well, that's the story Mary Ann put out, but me and a lot o' other folk have our doubts about it.'

George's nose screwed up. 'Why would she say that if it wasn't true? Katie *is* their grand-daughter, isn't she?'

'Maybe she is, and maybe she's nae. A lot o' stories went about at the time.'

'Such as?'

'Such as Katie's mother was some lassie young William John had bairned and the Mairs took in the infant and gi'ed the mother money to go away and say nothing.'

'Katie would still be their grandchild, though.'

'Aye, if that was the way o' it, but another story was she wasna young William John's at all, she was his father's.'

George struck his fist on the table. 'Ach, that's havers! Mary Ann would never have taken in her man's by-blow, even if he had one, and I don't believe that. Why do folk always think the worst? It's likely true that Katie's mother died when she was born.'

'Maybe it is, but I'm near sure young William John wasna lost at sea. He'd had a row wi' Mary Ann and he was biding wi' a lassie in Portknockie and . . .'

'They weren't married?'

'Well, Mary Ann never said onything about a wedding. Ony road, as I was saying, naebody here heard o' a Portknockie boat going doon about the time Mary Ann said, or a man going overboard, so he couldna have been drowned at sea. Some folk say he went to America wi' the lassie that had his bairn . . . but I canna understand ony mother leaving her poor infant.'

'Well, I don't care. Katie's a nice lass, whatever's the truth about her.'

Ina played her trump card now. 'She was in trouble wi' the bobbies a while back.'

'Ach, another story!'

'It's true, for she was seen being lifted. Janet Findlay was waiting for a parcel she was expecting, and she seen Katie coming aff the train wi' a man that looked like he wasna right in the heid, and Johnny Martin the bobby stopped them in the road and took them to the police station.'

'What for?'

'Janet wasna near enough to hear.'

'What a shame.' George couldn't help being sarcastic. Like his mother, Janet Findlay was notorious for poking her nose into other people's business.

Ina carried on unabashed, her long, thin face showing her pleasure at passing on the scandal. 'I did hear they let her out and kept the man, but we never found out what they'd been up to.'

'It doesn't matter to me. All this because I said she was a bonnie lass? That doesn't mean I've got my eye on her.'

'Just as well.'

* * *

Sunday morning, although fair, was bitterly cold, making the loathsome blue-white scar on Angus Gunn's cheek show vividly in his shaving mirror, and he was pleased that he would soon have Katie where he could pay her back for stabbing him. He waited until he and his wife were on their way to Peterhead, then said, 'I suppose you must have wondered how I came by the mark on my face?'

'I did wonder,' Betty murmured, 'though it's not nearly as noticeable as you think.'

'Of course it is noticeable, and it was Katie's doing.'

Many things became clear to Betty as she listened to his version of what had happened, and when he finished speaking, she said, quietly, 'I can't understand why you want her back at Fenty. You're surely not thinking of trying to punish her for what she did to you?'

Realizing that he had said more than he should, Angus gave a light laugh. 'What put that into your head? She was a good maid, that is all I was thinking of.'

'I don't want a maid, especially not a girl you admitted you once fancied. Maybe you still fancy her? Is that it?'

His smile vanished. 'I have no need for any other woman now I have you.'

His secretive expression alarmed her. 'I think you should forget about her, Angus.'

'Forget?' he cried, caution thrown aside. 'After what she did to me, and to my wife and son?'

'But it was so long ago. Aren't you happy with me?'

'It has nothing to do with happiness, it is a matter of principle. I cannot let her get away with it.'

Betty knew now that her qualms as to his intentions had been justified, and tried again to dissuade him. 'After what she did, she'll be too scared to come back to Fenty.'

'Oh, she will come back. I can be very tenacious when I have to be.'

Having often wondered why he used words a small shopkeeper wouldn't normally use, and wanting to take his

240

thoughts off Katie, Betty said, 'What did your father work at?'

'My father?' Angus looked somewhat put out. 'What has my father to do with this?'

'Nothing really, I just wondered.'

'My father was a man of some means, with an estate in the Highlands and a large house near Inverness.'

'Do you have any brothers or sisters?'

'I had one brother, who inherited almost everything when our father died.'

'Had a brother? Is he dead now?'

'He was killed in the last stages of the war.'

'Did you not fall heir to the estate when he died?'

'He left a wife and son, who now live in luxury while I slave in a run-down little shop.'

'Is your mother still alive?'

'She died a few years after Father. What you see before you, Betty, is a man who was deprived of his birthright.'

'Second sons don't usually get . . .'

'I was not the second son, I was the elder, but I blotted my copybook. My father kept me extremely short of money when I was a young man, you see, and I had rather a predilection for the opposite sex, so I stole from some house guests in order to buy expensive gifts to impress the ladies.'

'And you were found out?'

'Not for some time. My father's friends were reluctant to accuse his elder son of robbing them, but it eventually came out. Father settled up so that I should not be imprisoned, or perhaps to save his name being dragged through the court. He cut me out of his will and banished me with just enough to start a small business. I lost everything because of one youthful prank, and as if that were not enough, I married a girl who thought it was vulgar to make love. Imagine what that did to a man of my virility. To let me have the son I longed for, she suffered my attentions until she was with child, then I was deprived of that, too, and I was forced to go

241

elsewhere for pleasure. To crown it all, when our son was born, he was not a son of whom I could be proud, and she gave me no chance to make another.'

Betty touched his hand sympathetically. 'You've had a hard life, Angus, it's no wonder you're . . .' She broke off, having almost said 'twisted', and changed it to 'bitter'.

'I had come to terms with my lot when Katie came on the scene, tempting me with her charms, flaunting herself in front of me until I could control myself no longer, but she preferred my idiot son. You know the rest.'

He said no more until he drew the car to a halt in Marischal Street. 'I shall go in by myself first, to see how the land lies, and if I need you . . .'

'No, Angus,' Betty interrupted, quietly. 'You asked me to come with you and I'm not going to stay in the car.' She had to keep her eye on him in case he did something crazy.

He darted ahead of her through the pend and knocked on the last door, his whole body quivering. When there was no reply to his second knock, he peered through the window. 'Everything is still the same, except that the fire is not lit. She must be at work.'

He stood for a few moments, unsure of what to do, then gave a shiver. 'There always seems to be a wind whistling through this damned alleyway.'

'Yes, it's too cold to stand about,' Betty agreed. 'I think we should give up and go home.'

'If I could remember the name of the hotel . . .' Breaking off with a self-satisfied smirk, he moved swiftly along to the door nearer the street, composing his features as a thin-faced woman in a black coat and hat answered his knock. 'Ah, excuse me, madam, but I am looking for . . . my . . . um, niece, Katie Mair. I expected her to be at home on a Sunday, but I had forgotten that she works in a hotel. If you would be so kind as to tell me which one, I will keep you no longer.'

His oily manner cut no ice with Ella Brodie, a staunch member of the Close Brethren, and she snapped, with a touch of malice in her gimlet eyes, 'She gave up the house a good while since, and I've nae idea where she's went, or where she's working.'

'But ... but ...' Angus was completely disconcerted. 'Surely she left a forwarding address for her mail?'

'She never got nae letters as far as I ken. None o' us here had ony trock wi' her, for it was a right disgrace the way she carried on. As if one man wasna enough for her, she took in another ane ...'

He would have liked to hear more about the second man she had mentioned – the first had been Sammy – but Betty stepped forward. While Angus had been speaking, she had looked at the nameplate on the door and had also seen that the woman wore no wedding ring, so she was able to be more personal. 'I can see you were going out, Miss Brodie,' she said gently, 'and I'm sorry we've troubled you.' She pulled at her husband's sleeve. 'Come on, Angus.'

His body stiffened briefly as if he were preparing himself for battle, then relaxing, he lifted his hat. 'Thank you for giving up your time, madam.'

He was glad of Betty's hand under his elbow as they walked out of the pend, and his hand fumbled with the car key before he could open the doors.

Betty sighed with relief as she sat into the passenger seat. 'So that's it, then?'

He ignored her and started the engine. Red lights were flashing behind his eyes, and he was quite frightened by the increasing discomfort in his chest. 'I will have to stop some-where for a short time,' he managed to get out, when they were clear of the town. 'I do not feel at all well.'

'What's wrong, Angus?' she asked, though she guessed that he was only suffering from pique that his plan had failed.

'Do not fuss,' he gasped, as he drew in to the side of the road. 'It will pass. Just leave me.'

His hands clenched round the driving wheel, he slumped over, unable to think for the pain in his chest and the awful sensation that his head was about to explode, while his wife waited unconcernedly until he got over it, praying that this would make him forget about Katie.

Chapter Twenty-one

❖❖

1928

For months, Katie's life had been quite placid, too placid sometimes, with not even an argument with her grandmother to break the monotony. George Buchan had not come into the shop again, and she had overheard his mother saying that he had gone with the herring fleet in March, which had not bothered her one way or the other. During the summer, she had taken advantage of the long sunlit evenings by going for long walks; filling her lungs with the tang of the sea or the freshness of the country air was luxury after long hours of breathing in the oppressive heat from the baker's ovens. But she had been forced to give up that pleasure once winter made its grip felt. With the onset of the damp, cold weather, Mary Ann's rheumatism had worsened, and Katie didn't like to leave her all day and all evening, too.

The pain made her grandmother's temper as brittle as an eggshell, and in order to keep the peace, Katie often had to suppress the retorts she felt like making. She was not going to let her life be made a misery, however, and when it came to the point where she could bear it no longer, she would stand up for herself.

When Mary Ann complained one morning about how hard it was for her to go down on her knees and worse still to get up again, her grand-daughter said, 'I'll rise earlier in the mornings to light the fire, and I'll do the housework when I come home at nights.'

'I've kept this place clean from the day I was wed,' Mary Ann barked, 'and I'm not letting it go to rack and ruin.'

'It wouldn't go to rack and ruin,' Katie flung back. 'I can keep it as clean as you ever did.'

'You're not getting the chance. Once I'm away, you can please yourself what you do, but as long as I'm able, I'll do things my way. I'm still mistress of this house.'

Katie stopped arguing. Her grandmother would have to give in sooner or later.

Mary Ann, however, kept on doggedly, and it was almost the end of November, when Katie was about to go back to work one afternoon, before she muttered, 'I'll need some vegies for the broth the morrow.'

Knowing what it was costing the old lady to admit to being unable to walk to the shops, Katie just said, 'If you write out a list, I'll hand the basket in to Jimsie on my road to the baker, and I'll collect it when I'm coming home.'

Later that day, she was struggling with the load of leeks, carrots, turnip and potatoes the greengrocer had packed into her basket when someone took it from her and a deep voice said, 'You're nearly down on your knees with that, Katie. Let me carry it for you.'

She looked round gratefully. 'You're home again, George? Thanks. If I'd known how heavy this would be, I'd have asked Jimsie just to put in half a stone of tatties.'

'What's wrong with Mary Ann that she's not doing her own shopping? Is she laid up?'

'Not exactly, but her knees have bothered her for a long time, and she's hardly able to walk at all now.'

'I'm sorry to hear that. I used to carry her basket and all, when I was a young laddie.'

Katie smiled. 'Aye, she told me.'

'She used to make out she was a real tartar, but she aye gave me a ha'penny for helping her.'

'I hope you're not expecting a ha'penny from me.'

They both chuckled at that, then George said, 'Would you mind if I came in with you to have a word with her?'

'No, I'm sure she'll be glad to see you again.'

246

Mary Ann was glad. 'Come away in, George,' she beamed, 'and Katie'll make you a cup o' tea.'

'Don't bother, Katie. Ma'll have my supper ready.'

'I'd better do what I'm told,' she smiled. 'Grandma still thinks I'm a wee lassie to boss around.'

The old woman shook her head. 'You're getting ower big for your boots. It's a man you need, to keep you in about.'

'Oh, Grandma,' the girl protested, 'what'll George think?'

'I think she's right,' he grinned.

Katie blushed, and Mary Ann sat back. 'And how long are you home for?' she asked the young man.

'I've got another week before we start the painting and doing all the things that need to be done. The *Jean Nutten*'s not a bad old tub, but every time we come back off a trip, there's more and more to be done on her.'

'The *Jean Nutten*?'

'The skipper named her for his wife. I'm thinking about signing on a Cullen boat, though, for I'm tired of being away so long at a time, when I could be home every weekend.'

Mary Ann's pointed glance in her direction made Katie's colour deepen even further. 'Do you take sugar in your tea, George?' she asked, not daring to look at him.

'Two spoons, please, no milk.'

'How's your mother keeping?' Mary Ann took his attention back to her.

'She's fine, thanks. How are you, yourself?'

'I'd be fine if it wasna for my knees, though I suppose I shouldna complain at my age.'

'You haven't changed much since I was a laddie.'

She took the compliment with a nod. 'I canna say the same for you. You used to be a wee nickum wi' a dirty face and holes in the knees o' your breeks, and look at you now – a fine upstanding young man. You've still got the same taking way about you, though. Hasn't he, Katie?'

Looking at him – tall and broad, with an attractive smile

that made her heart beat a little faster – Katie could only agree. 'Aye, I suppose he has,' she mumbled.

He gave a self-conscious laugh. 'And Katie's as bonnie as ever . . . maybe bonnier.'

While they drank the tea, George told them about his trips to Shetland and down the east coast as far as Yarmouth, and Mary Ann let Katie ask the questions, smiling to herself at how things were going.

At last, George said, 'I'm keeping you from your supper, though, and Ma'll think I'm lost.'

Mary Ann held out her hand. 'You'll come back to see me?'

'Aye,' he smiled, 'I'll do that.'

'See him out the door, Katie.'

The kitchen door opening straight on to the road, Katie knew what her grandmother was up to, but did as she was told. 'I'm sorry if she embarrassed you,' she said when they were standing outside.

'I wasn't embarrassed. She made my mind up for me.'

'What about?'

'I was wondering if I should ask you to come for a walk with me later on.'

'And what did you decide?'

'I decided not to ask you.' He gave a mischievous grin and added, 'I'm telling you – I'll come for you about eight.'

Annoyed at him for teasing, she said, cuttingly, 'What if I tell you not to bother?'

His face fell. 'Oh, you're not turning me down, are you, Katie? Surely you'll come out for a wee walk?'

'I'll think about it.'

His grin returned. 'All right, I'll give you five seconds. One, two, three . . .'

She gave him a push. 'Oh, go on with you, George Buchan.'

She was shaking her head in amusement when she went inside again, and Mary Ann said, 'You're going out wi' him, then?'

'You were listening?'

'I couldna help hearing. I'm nae deaf yet.'

'You won't mind being on your own?'

'It looks like I'm going to be, whether I mind or not.'

'I'll not go if you . . .'

'Ach, just go, and stop your havering.'

Not aware that George's mother had been angry when he told her where he was going, Katie wondered why he was so subdued when she went out in answer to his knock, and was glad when his spirits lifted in a few seconds. 'Where do you want to go?' he asked. 'To the Bin . . . but maybe that's too far. What about along the shore? Or is there anywhere else you fancy?'

'I love going along the shore.'

As they walked, they reminisced about their schooldays and speculated as to the whereabouts of their classmates who had left Cullen. When they came to the Three Kings, Katie said, shyly, 'Have you ever . . . ?' She halted, then whispered, 'Ach, you'll think I'm daft.'

'No, go on.'

'Have you ever thought they're something more than just rocks?'

'Have you?'

'I used to think they were the Three Kings in the Bible.'

'The Wise Men?'

'Aye, and I spoke to them and told them things.'

'What kind of things?'

He sat down at the base of the one nearest them, and she sat down beside him. 'Childish things, mostly about being annoyed at Grandma. Not Granda, though, for he was always good to me.'

'Was your Grandma not good to you?'

'She wasn't wicked, if that's what you mean, but she never loved me, not like Granda. I knew he loved me.'

George opened his mouth as if to say something, but shut it again, so Katie went on, 'I was working for the doctor's wife at first, then Grandma put me into service miles away without even asking me if I wanted to go.'

'Did you not like being in service there?'

'I didn't mind Mrs Gunn, and Sammy was my friend, but Mr Gunn . . .'

'Sammy? Was he their little boy?'

'He was their son, just two years older than me.'

'Oh!'

The word conveyed dismay, and, realizing what he thought, she hurried on, 'I was sorry for him . . . he was a bit simple and he's in Ladysbridge now.' Her guilt about Sammy reared its head again, and she burst out, 'I don't want to speak about him. What were you going to say a minute ago?'

'I was going to ask if you wanted to come back to Cullen, or if you just came to keep Mary Ann company when William John died?'

Katie pulled a face. 'I didn't really want to come back. Grandma and me never got on, but . . . well, things happened to me that made me want to get away from where I was.'

'From service?'

'No, I left there years before, and I'd a few different jobs in different places.'

Although they fell silent now, each was electrically aware of the other, as if some invisible cable joined them, and Katie could not – did not want to – draw away when George's hand slid over and covered hers. They kept sitting thus for some time, then he lifted her hand to his face. 'You'll come out with me again, Katie?'

The humble pleading made her feel as if she were floating on air, giving her a sense of power. Her hand still tingling from contact with his rough cheek, she suddenly remembered her experience with Dennis. It was as almost as if she were being given a warning, and she knew she had to be careful. About to say, once again, that she would think about it, she realized that it wouldn't be fair to tease George this time. 'All right,' she smiled. 'I do like being with you . . .' She paused, then added, firmly, 'just as a friend.'

He let out his breath. 'That's all I wanted to know. Now, we'd best get back, it's too cold to be sitting about.'

He helped her to her feet, and they stood facing each other, so close that his breath stirred her hair, his brown eyes, more serious than she had ever seen them, locked with hers, then he turned away abruptly. She was sure that he had been going to kiss her and was quite glad that he hadn't. He was an old school friend she liked talking to, and anything more than that would spoil it.

At her door, he squeezed her hand. 'Tomorrow same time?'

'If you want.'

Inside, Mary Ann eyed her with interest. 'Well, did you enjoy yourselves?'

'Aye, we'd a walk along the shore.'

Her lack of excitement told her grandmother that nothing had happened between them. 'I'm away to my bed then, so mind and turn out the lamp when you go to yours.'

'I'll not forget.' Katie poured herself a cup of tea and sat down by the dying fire. She suspected her grandmother was hoping she would fall in love with George, but a girl couldn't turn love on and off like a tap, though she *was* attracted to him, she couldn't deny that. When they left school, he had just been an inch or so taller than she was, and he seemed to have shot up since then, for her head only reached his shoulder. His face had lost its chubbiness, the puppy fat had gone from his body – he looked better without it – and he wasn't a boy any more. His hands were calloused, and his light brown hair looked as if he had hacked at it himself – or maybe one of the men he sailed with had cut it for him when they were away. He didn't seem to care about his appearance, which was a good thing, for it showed he wasn't vain like Dennis had been.

Thinking about Dennis started the old ache in her heart –

not an ache for a lost love, but anger at having been duped by the man she had believed loved her – and she stood up and turned out the lamp.

George was pensive as he walked home. Why hadn't he kissed Katie? He had wanted to, but something had held him back. Was it what his mother had said about her? At the time, he had thought it didn't matter that she might have been born out of wedlock, now he wasn't so sure. He had been brought up in a religious household, and had been taught to believe that no decent woman would allow a man to touch her before they were married. If Katie's mother hadn't been married to young William John, if she'd been a girl he'd just played around with, would it mean Katie had inherited loose morals from both parents? He might be wise not to get too deeply involved with her, for he would expect the girl he chose as a wife to be a virgin, and he didn't know what she'd got up to when she was working away from Cullen.

His mother pounced on him as soon as he went inside. 'I hope you didna try onything wi' that lassie?'

'Her name's Katie,' he said, sharply, 'and she's too nice for me to try anything, even if I'd felt like it, which I didn't. We were just walking, and speaking.'

'You'd best be careful. Did she tell you about that man she had wi' her at the station?'

'Him that looked soft? She told me who he was.' George told her no more because there was little more to tell.

Not having expected Katie to mention the man at all, Ina was taken aback, but she said, tartly, 'Dinna forget she could be a bastard.'

Despite what he had been thinking on his way home, George burst out, 'It wouldn't be her fault if she was, and I've aye been real fond of her.'

'As long as that's all. If you ever think on taking her as your wife, I'd . . .'

'If I want her for my wife,' he said, firmly, 'I'll take her, though I doubt if it'll ever come to that. We're just friends, and I'll keep on seeing her, whatever you say.'

Ina flounced out of the room, and George sat down, wishing that he knew what Katie and the man – Sammy, she'd called him – had done that made Johnny Martin arrest them. She had apparently been released quickly, so it couldn't have been anything bad, but maybe it was why Sammy had been sent to Ladysbridge. George wasn't surprised that his mother was doing her best to put him off Katie. Since his father died, he'd been the be-all and end-all of her existence, and she would likely think no girl was good enough for him. Mary Ann, on the other hand, had seemed to be encouraging him, though he hadn't made up his own mind what to do.

Ella Brodie opened her door just wide enough to see who had knocked. Having overslept for the first time in years, she was ashamed to be seen in her nightgown at nine o'clock in the morning and was glad to find it was only the widow from next door. 'Aye, what is it?' she asked, testily.

Mrs Frain held out a letter. 'It's addressed to Katie Mair, and I minded you saying she bade in the house afore me. The postie put it through my door, and I thought you'd ken where she was.'

Ella was about to refuse to take it when she noticed that it looked official, and thinking that it must be important, she decided to let bygones be bygones. Whatever Katie Mair had been, it wasn't Christian to keep her letters from her. 'I've nae idea where she is, but her and Lottie McRuvie was awful friendly, so she'll maybe ken. I was going up to the baker's any road, so I'll take it.'

Before she went out, Ella had another change of heart. It maybe wasn't such a good idea to be handing Katie's private correspondence over in a crowded shop, with so many gossips ready to broadcast it to the four winds. It would be best to

253

go to the Temperance Hotel and give it to that waiter Katie had lived in sin with. He'd likely know where she was.

As soon as he was free, Dennis opened the letter Ella Brodie had given him. He had no reservations about reading it; he wanted to know what it said before he sent it on to Cullen – he was sure Katie had gone home to her grandparents.

His eyebrows shot up in astonishment when he discovered that it was a notification of Samuel Gunn's death in the Mental Institution at Ladysbridge. So the daftie had landed in the asylum? After Katie always swearing she would never have him put away, she had actually gone and done it. Dennis felt quite resentful. She wouldn't do it for him, but she must have done it for some other man. That hurt his pride. It bloody well did, and he would let her find out for herself that the daft blighter had kicked the bucket. She didn't mean anything to him now, so why should he go out of his way to post on this letter? With an evil grin, Dennis held his lighter to the corner of the paper, watched while it flared up, and then dropped it into the ashtray before it burned his fingers.

Chapter Twenty-two

✦

The *Jean Nutten* being berthed at Peterhead, where her crew carried out the necessary maintenance, George Buchan saw quite a lot of Katie over the winter. There were times when he wondered if he was being fair to her – he wasn't ready to tie himself down – yet he couldn't bring himself to break off with her, for there was something about her that drew him like metal to a magnet. He told himself that he hadn't fallen in love with her, but he always felt put out when she turned her head away if he tried to kiss her goodnight and his lips met her velvety cheek.

The only good thing about it was that he could answer his mother honestly when she asked him if anything was going on between him and Katie Mair. 'Nothing's going on,' he told her one night. 'We're just good friends, and it looks like that's all she'll ever want from me.'

'Aye, well,' Ina muttered, 'she's more sense than I gi'ed her credit for.'

After one miserably wet evening spent with Mary Ann's eyes darting back and forth from him to her grand-daughter as if searching for signs of blossoming love, George looked at the girl quizzically when they were saying goodnight outside the door. 'I think your Grandma's hoping . . .'

'She'll be disappointed, then,' Katie declared. 'I don't want anything to do with men.'

He should have been relieved at this, but a pain started somewhere inside him, cramping round his heart and telling him he'd been fooling himself to think he didn't love her. 'You've been coming out with me for ages, and I'm a man.'

'You're just an old school chum,' she laughed, 'and that's different.'

It was as if she had knifed him. 'Can't you see how . . . I'd like to be more than . . .'

She covered his mouth with her hand. 'No, George! You're my friend, and that means a lot to me. Don't spoil it.'

She went inside before he could say anything more, and he walked up the hill slowly in spite of the rain to give himself time to face the truth. He had thought himself in love before, but his heart had never been affected like it was now. What he felt for Katie had nothing to do with sex – the usual starting point for his feelings – it was above any lusts of the flesh, absolutely pure. It was an inner need, a need of the spirit, a need to protect and care for, and to be cared for in return. He had to make her love him.

On Hogmanay, George persuaded Katie to join him and his pals at a dance in the Town Hall, and, reluctant as she was to go, she found that she did enjoy herself. After the bells chimed midnight, his friends suggested that they go round each other's houses 'first-footing', but she said, 'If you don't mind, I'll just go home. I don't like leaving my Grandma so long, and you'll likely all get drunk, any road.'

George gripped her arm to stop her walking off. 'Mary Ann knows you're with me, she'll not be expecting you back yet, and I promise I'll just have a couple of drinks.'

None of the people they visited, however, would take no for an answer, and after his fifth dram – and the hosts were never stingy as to the amount they poured out – he could see Katie eyeing him reprovingly. 'I'm all right,' he whispered. 'I've drunk a lot more than this and still been on my feet.'

'It's up to you,' she said, stiffly, 'but I'm going home this time, and don't bother coming with me.'

The cold air hit him as soon as they went into the street

and he could hear his words slurring slightly when he spoke. 'I took you out, and I'll see you home.'

She shrugged off the arm he tried to slip round her waist, and said nothing on the way to her house, then she turned to him with her hand on the knob. 'Goodnight, George.'

Her eyes were shining in the clear moonlight, her mouth soft and inviting, and he couldn't let her go like that. 'Give's a kiss, Katie?' he begged. 'One for the New Year? So I'll know nineteen twenty-nine'll be a good year for me.'

She laughed and gave him a quick peck, but pushed his arms away when they went round her. 'Goodnight, George.'

Opening the door, she slipped inside and he was left with the tantalizing memory of his hands almost spanning her tiny waist, of the fragrance of her breath. 'Damn you, Katie,' he muttered as he made his way unsteadily up Castle Street.

His anger and frustration had gone by the time he woke up, sober, later that day, but he knew that he could not go on for much longer with this yearning in his heart. He had been thinking of signing on one of the cod boats so he wouldn't have to leave Katie for the whole summer, but it might be better to go with the herring fleet again when it set off for Lerwick in March, for one last time. Maybe if she missed him enough, she would see she loved him.

Dennis had been somewhat disgruntled that Beth wouldn't let him have a say in fitting out the premises she had finally chosen, but now that the restaurant was nearing completion, he could see that it was in far better taste than anything he could have thought up. The plain white walls – which he had said would be too stark – were broken up by pot plants in brass brackets; the four tables were covered with pale lemon cloths and the dishes were white with a delicate green and lemon pattern. The carpet was a deeper shade of green – not too dark – with swirls of what was not exactly lemon but not quite strong enough to be called yellow, which blended in and seemed to tie everything together.

It wasn't as big as he'd have liked, but it had a touch of class about it, and the chef he had hired had been impressed by the arrangements in the kitchen at the back. In any case, it was only temporary, because the lease of the shop next door would run out in less than a year, and Beth had made the owner promise that she could take it over, too, when the time came. So, Dennis thought, happily, it was up to him to make this small place pay, to prove he was fit to cope when it was extended. Meantime, in addition to the chef, he had engaged a young waitress – though he would likely have to help out himself during busy spells – and a woman to wash the dishes.

When he went home after the last satisfied inspection, he grabbed Beth round the waist and twirled her round. 'It's perfect, my dearest, and I've been wondering what to call it. It needs something quirky and striking, so how about joining our names – Dennibeth?'

Beth shook her head. 'That's a bit contrived. Something foreign would be better, French maybe, to appeal more to the clientele we're after.'

His knowledge of French confined strictly to saying 'wee, wee', which he wouldn't have recognized if he saw it written down, Dennis shrugged. 'I'll leave it to you.'

Some days later, when he saw the sign his wife had ordered to be fixed, he went home furious. 'Denis? They've spelt my name wrong in the first place, and folk'll likely think it's a bloody fish and chip shop.'

Beth smiled fondly. 'It's pronounced Dennee, the accent on the last syllable.'

'How many folk would know that?' he asked, churlishly.

'All those that matter. Trust me, Dennis, it'll attract the people who feel they're a cut above the common herd, but if you like, I can have it changed to Le Denis. Would that make you any happier?'

'It's a bit better.' He brightened suddenly. 'I can hardly wait till I open on Monday.'

'Neither can I, and I'll likely pop in sometime. I want to see how it's going.'

Dennis had a moment's misgiving. Beth having said that he could choose his own staff and that she would not interfere, he had picked his waitress for her looks – a pert blonde with a ravishing figure – and he was almost sure that his wife would disapprove. 'You said you'd leave me to run the place by myself.'

'I will, but you can't grudge me one look, surely?'

'Just one, then. It'll make me nervous if I think you're checking up on me.'

'So you've got a nice young thing as a waitress?'

'It needs somebody attractive to pull the customers,' he blustered, annoyed that she had hit the nail on the head. 'Somebody that can laugh with them, and flirt with them a bit . . . you know.'

'Yes, you're right, but keep your hands off her, Dennis. I don't trust you around young girls.'

'I don't need any young girls when I've got you, and my wandering days are over.' For a while, anyway, he thought, until she gave him a restaurant to put all others in the shade, not an apology of an eating place.

Halfway through his lunchtime opening on Monday, Dennis knew that his judgment of his waitress had not been wrong. Trudie's brightness with the customers had them all smiling, and the eyes of the men followed her wiggling rear end as she made her way amongst the tables. He could hardly keep his own eyes off it, come to that, and he'd have to take care, for he didn't know when Beth would come in.

When she appeared, she asked, 'Have you been busy?'

'Not bad . . . a steady stream.'

'Your waitress seems efficient. I see what you mean about having somebody young and attractive. She'll draw the men.'

'That's what I thought, and don't get jealous. I wouldn't dream of messing around with her.'

'I don't think she'd mind if you did,' Beth smiled, then added, with a touch of warning, 'but I would.'

During the first two months of 1929, George had endured the frustration of not being allowed to kiss Katie properly by telling himself that it proved his mother wrong in what she thought about her. Katie was as pure and innocent as any man could wish his future wife to be, and he was determined to marry her when the herring season was over.

On the night before he left, he told Katie that this was the last time he would be away for such a long spell. 'I'm going to sign on with Alickie May when I come back. He goes to the fishing grounds off Iceland, so I'd be home every ten days or so.'

Hoping that he wasn't doing this for her sake, Katie still couldn't help feeling pleased about it. 'How long will you be away this time?'

'Till November, and I'm really going to miss you, Katie.'

'I'll miss you, and all.' She hadn't meant to say it, in case he got the wrong idea, it had just come out.

They were walking along the harbour wall, so close that his hip sometimes brushed against hers, and the contact made her heart beat too quickly for comfort. She didn't want to fall in love again, she didn't want the pain that love could bring. She had liked George from their first day at school, when they stood wide-eyed together waiting to be told where to sit, and she preferred her feelings to remain at liking.

The early March winds were unusually cold, but he stopped suddenly and turned her to face him, walking his fingers up her arm as he said, 'Katie, would you mind if I kissed you?'

She couldn't hurt him by refusing, not when he was going away for eight months. 'I wouldn't mind,' she whispered. It wasn't a lover's kiss, more a kiss between good friends, and she was torn between relief and disappointment.

'I'm going to ask you something when I come back,' George said, softly, 'so I want you to think about it.' He took her face between his hands and looked at her earnestly. 'I don't want to rush you into anything, Katie lass.'

Tears sprang to her eyes at his last two words, and he snatched his hands way as if she had bitten them. 'Oh, I'm sorry, I didn't mean to upset you.'

'It was just . . . Granda always called me Katie lass.'

'I'll not say it again then, I promise.'

'I like you saying it, George.'

His second kiss, although longer, was just as undemanding as the first, then he ran his index finger down her cheek. 'I'll be thinking about you all the time I'm away, Katie.'

She should have stopped him before it went so far. 'You'll be too busy to think about me, and I'll be the same.'

'You think I'm going too fast? Maybe I am, and I'd better take you home.'

She let him take her hand. They had walked hand in hand when they were five-year-olds, and it meant no more to her now than it did then. No, if she were strictly honest, it was entirely different.

When they reached her house, George drew her towards him. 'I'll wait, Katie lass. I can wait as long as you want.'

Mary Ann's eyes, a little rheumy now but still missing nothing, lifted from her knitting when her grand-daughter went in. 'You'll nae be seeing him for a while? I hope you didna do anything you shouldna?'

'No, Grandma, he just kissed me.'

'Men dinna usually stop at kissing.'

Katie was annoyed at her persistence. 'There's nothing between me and George. We like each other, that's all.'

'Maybe it's just as well.'

'I thought you were trying to push us together.'

'So I was, at first, but I minded something when you were

out. There's not a man on God's earth that can be trusted, and that goes for George Buchan, and all.'

This slur on him made Katie say, angrily, 'You've never a good word to say for anybody, and you're wrong about him.'

'Time'll tell,' Mary Ann said, darkly, bundling up wool and needles and getting stiffly to her feet. 'You've never listened to me, and you'll live to regret it some day.'

Katie went into her room thoughtfully. She had made up her mind not to get serious about George, but her grandmother's unexpected condemnation of him had changed it. She would prove the accusation wrong. George would keep any promises he made. He would never make a fool of her. He would never break her heart.

A shiver went through her. Why had her grandmother turned against him? What had she remembered? Was it something she had heard about him in the past? Or was it something in her own past that made her distrust all men?

Chapter Twenty-three

❖

Sleety November winds were blowing in Yarmouth when George Buchan saw her – a slim girl with her fingers bound with cloths to prevent them being slashed by the razor sharp knife she was using. Her movements were so quick and fluid that it was impossible to follow what she did, for each fish was lifted from the farlan – a huge trough – and thrown into the proper bin minus its innards in only a second. He had stood on the Denes in other years, marvelling at the speedy skill of the lassies as they gutted and graded the herring so that the packers could place them in the correct barrels – he had even amused himself with some of them for an hour or two in the evenings – but there was something special about this one. She was an exact replica of all the others – hair completely covered by a scarf tied gypsy-style, face pinched with the cold, legs and feet encased in long rubber boots, curves concealed by an oilskin apron – yet she stood out like a beacon amongst them.

A vision of Katie came to his mind. Katie in her neat dark skirts and pale blouses, her shining brown hair pinned up, her plump cheeks with tiny dimples at the corners of her mouth. But Katie was hundreds of miles away, and there were only a few yards separating him from this girl. Sensing someone watching, she glanced up, and in the brief moment before her head went down again, he couldn't judge whether or not she had seen his smile. He'd have to wait until she finished work before he spoke to her. Like all the fisher lassies she was paid by the amount of bins she filled and interruptions wouldn't be welcome. Besides, he didn't have to sail until the morning tide tomorrow. There was all the settling up to do first, and since he had bought a share in the nets this year he'd have extra money coming to him.

Turning away, George hurried to catch up with the rest of the crew of the drifter *Jean Nutten*. 'Aye, George, man, have you got your eye on one o' the lassies?' asked one.

'Maybe,' he laughed, 'but I'll need to bide my time.'

'I think we were last in, so once they've finished wi' our catch, they'll be through till the morn.'

This was good news to George. Their catch had been quite a few crans less than usual, which meant that the girl would finish work all the sooner. For the next two hours, he walked around, never straying far from the quay and checking each time he was near enough as to the amount of fish still to be done.

When he saw the gutters start to move, he knew they were about to go back to their lodgings. Tired though they were, and blue with the cold, they came past him in a laughing gang, and his eyes skimmed over them until he found the one he sought.

'There's a lad after you, Lizann,' one of her companions told her, and she looked round shyly.

He fell into step beside her. 'Lizann? That's a bonnie name. Mine's plain George.'

'It suits you.'

Although he was well-practised in picking up fisher girls, he had to pluck up his courage before he said, diffidently, 'Would you come out with me later on?'

After a slight hesitation, she smiled. 'Gi'e me an hour to wash and change and have my supper.'

That hour, unfortunately for George, gave ample time for his conscience to start bothering him. This trip was not the same as other trips. He was in love with Katie now, so why on earth had he arranged to meet Lizann?

When she appeared, her oval face shining, her black curly hair tied up with a red ribbon, she bore no resemblance to Katie, but his heart stirred in the same way when she smiled up at him. It couldn't be wrong to spend a little time with her when he felt like this. She likely had a lad at home, in any case, and was just wanting somebody to speak to, the same as he was.

Walking at her side, he had a compulsion to be frank, to let her know his position. 'Lizann, I'd better tell you . . . I've got a lass at home in Cullen.'

He had been afraid that she would be angry at him and was relieved when she said, 'I've a lad in Buckie.'

'Are you promised to him?'

'Not exactly, not yet. Are you promised to her?'

'Not yet.'

Too aware of each other, they strolled on in uncomfortable silence for a short time until George felt he had to say something and asked her about the girls she worked with. This broke the spell and they went on to talk about the crew of the *Jean Nutten*, their homes, their relatives, the things they liked, the things which annoyed them.

After another awkward break, Lizann murmured, 'I've never been out with anybody but Peter. He works in the shipyard and he doesn't like me being away so long, and I think he's going to ask me to marry him when I go home this time.'

'I'm going to ask Katie to marry me.'

'Will you tell her you've been out with me?'

'Aye, why not?'

'Will she not be jealous?'

'Will your Peter be jealous of me?'

'He would be, if I told him.'

'But we'll not see each other again after tonight.'

Their eyes met, and what he saw in hers made him swallow painfully. Katie had never looked at him like that, and he had to fight against the need that surged up in his loins. 'I'd better get you back,' he muttered.

When they arrived at her lodgings, his arms slid round her before he could stop himself, and he drew her gently towards him. 'A first and last kiss, Lizann?' he smiled.

He got the feeling that she didn't want to stop at one, but he knew it was safer for both of them that way. 'That's it, then,' he sighed, when, reluctantly, he released her. 'I hope you and Peter make a go of it. Goodbye, Lizann.'

'Goodbye, George, and I wish you and Katie a happy life.'

As he walked away, he was pleased that he had only kissed her. Normally, the kissing would have been followed by the love-making, but Lizann wasn't like that. It was just a case of two people, missing their loved ones, keeping each other company for one evening. Katie wouldn't object to that when he told her. When he tried to picture her face, however, it was Lizann's that came into his mind, and he thought it was just as well he would be sailing in the morning, away from temptation and home to the girl he loved.

But things were taken out of his hands. While he had been wandering around, the *Jean Nutten*'s engineer had carried out his routine checks and found that one of the cylinders was cracked. When the skipper told him at breakfast time the next day, it struck George – superstitious like all seamen – that this was an omen. The ship, and her crew, would have to remain in Yarmouth until the repair was carried out, which meant that he could see Lizann a few more times.

She looked pleased when he showed up at the Denes in the late forenoon, and agreed to meet him at night, but when he set out for the trysting place, he was beset by doubts. Was it possible for him to spend a whole evening with her and not do something he'd regret later? Past experience had told him that only one kiss could spark off an undeniable need, but he couldn't leave her standing. He would have to fix his mind on Katie and keep his hands off Lizann.

All went well for the first hour they were together, just light conversation and a little teasing, but eventually the urge to taste Lizann's sweet lips again grew too great to ignore, and with a groan, he took her in his arms. After a little while, he muttered, 'I shouldn't be doing this.'

'I like it, George.'

'But what about Peter, and Katie?'

'They'll never know . . .' She looked at him and added, with an embarrassed half-smile, '. . . whatever we do.'

He hesitated. 'Do you mean what I think you mean?'

Her arms came round his neck, snapping his control. 'Oh, God, Lizann.' He kissed her hungrily, then pulled her down on the ground, his resolutions forgotten.

In his bunk that night, he felt sick at what he had done. Lizann wasn't a good-time girl like the others he'd had. She had been a virgin, had cried when it was over, and he'd been so ashamed he couldn't find words to tell her how sorry he was. Suddenly, the thought of Katie made him feel worse than ever. How could he have done this thing when he loved her so much? He should have turned away from Lizann the minute he set eyes on her, for he'd been drawn to her even then. No, he corrected himself, what he had felt was deeper than just attraction.

By morning, he had decided not to see her again, yet he found his feet taking him to the Denes once more, and she nodded when he raised his eyebrows in question.

Having resolved not to repeat what had happened before, he didn't even kiss her that evening, nor the next, although it took every ounce of his will-power not to put his arms round her, for he could tell that she was hoping he would. On his last night, she was very quiet as they walked side by side, listening without seeming to take it in when he told her how some of the seven-men crew had argued with the skipper about the amount of subs they'd had during the trip and insisted that they were due more at the settling up than he had given them. Eventually, her abstraction made him say, 'Lizann, are you angry about what I did the other night?'

'No, I'm not angry, and I'm not sorry we did it.'

He didn't notice that she was shouldering half the blame. 'What's wrong, then?'

'What are we going to do, George? After this, I mean.'

'When I go back to Cullen and you go back to Buckie?'

'I still love Peter, and I can't tell him.'

'No.' George thought for some time then said, slowly, 'I'm still going to marry Katie, and you'll marry Peter. What we did hasn't changed that, but I'd better get you back . . .'

'Not yet, George. I'll never see you again, and I want to have this last night to remember.'

Her eyes told what she wanted. 'Are you sure?' he asked, slowly, wonderingly.

'D'you think I'm awful . . . ?'

'No, I want it as much as you.'

Their bodies welded together, their kisses setting light to their smouldering passion, they sank down on the sodden, grassy bank and not even the wetness seeping through their clothes had any effect on the ecstasy they shared.

Outside her lodgings, George knew that he didn't want to say goodbye to her. 'Oh God, Lizann,' he groaned, 'I think I love you.'

'And I think I love you, and all, George.'

They looked at each other in awe for a moment, then she gave her head a vehement shake. 'No, I can't let Peter down now.' With a strangled sob, she ran inside.

George was filled with remorse as he walked back to his ship. Falling in love with Lizann was something he hadn't foreseen, and he was thankful that she'd been strong enough to nip it in the bud, painful as it had been to him. He had betrayed Katie, but please God she would never find out he had been unfaithful, or she wouldn't look at him again, like he would be finished with her if he thought she had ever let another man touch her. A girl should come to the marriage bed with her maidenhead intact.

Even in his rationalizing, it did not occur to George that he had spoiled the virgin Lizann for the unknown Peter.

Having plodded over hard-packed, rutted snow to get to and from her work, it was a very tired Katie who was lying in bed thinking of George. It must be awful out there on the North Sea, pulling in nets with hands frozen to the marrow and your body so cold it was difficult to move. They should have landed their catch at Yarmouth by now, though, and it wouldn't be long till he was home. He was going to ask her to marry him, and she'd have to make up her mind soon. She liked him an awful lot, but was that enough?

'George Buchan'll be back ony day,' Mary Ann observed the following morning, 'and he'll have had a high old time among the fisher lassies, if I ken the driftermen.'

'He's not like that,' Katie protested, her heart giving such a jolt at the thought of him with anyone else that she knew it was more than liking she felt for him. 'He said he'd something to ask me when he came home, and I'm sure I love him now. If he wants, I'll get engaged to him, but I'm not rushing into marriage.'

'If you're determined to have him,' her grandmother said, dryly, 'you'd better trap him afore he goes away again.'

Katie took umbrage at this. 'It's not a case of trapping him. He loves me as much as I love him.'

'Well, dinna count your chickens.' Mary Ann turned away.

Walking to the baker's shop, Katie felt angry. There was nothing for her to worry about. George did love her and he wouldn't have gone out with any of the fisher girls.

His last visit to Peterhead had given Angus Gunn cause to worry about his health, his heart especially. He had not told his wife of the fearsome pains which had gripped him as she sat beside him in the car, nor of the pressures which had triggered the red lights that flashed behind his eyes. He had thought – when he got over them – that it was a good thing she did not know how close she had been to being a widow, but perhaps that had been an exaggeration. There had been no recurrence of the chest pains, although he was still bothered by headaches, even after so many months.

He had decided that day, as he had done more than once before, to forget his need to avenge the attack Katie Mair had made on him, but his scar was showing up more with the cold weather, and he could not ignore what she had done. He was not confident of success now, and he did not wish Betty to witness another failure, but she would be suspicious if he went away on another Sunday, and his absence on a weekday would be difficult to explain.

'I'm having a problem with a wholesale firm in Aberdeen,' he told her one morning, this hopefully plausible excuse having occurred to him during the night. 'They say I am owe them for my last consignment of goods, but I paid it some time ago. I seem to be getting nowhere by writing, so I shall have to go to see the manager in person and show him the receipt. Do you think you could take over the shop for me? The sooner I get it sorted out the better.'

Betty gave a fond smile. 'How would tomorrow do?'

'That would be ideal. Thank you, my dear.'

Angus set off at his usual time the next morning, humming tunelessly after he dropped Betty off at the shop because he had the feeling that today was the day. He had remembered that the farmer's wife at Struieburn had said she sent Katie to the Temperance Hotel, so all he had to do was go there and ask to talk to her.

His spirits were dampened when he found the hotel and put his request to the manager – he had not known Katie. Angus had no option but to leave, his disappointment so great that a fierce throbbing started up inside his head. He could not think what to do next, and was cruising round the streets when he saw a small bakery which also laid claim to being a café, and hoping that a little refreshment might stop the alarming pounding in his head, he stopped the car and went in. The tea did help him, black and strong as he liked it. His brain clearer, it came to him that he had seen the café before and that it was quite near where Katie used to live. Perhaps the woman who served him had known her.

Lottie McRuvie did not like the look of this customer – a dark man with staring eyes, his conservative suit and hard-brimmed homburg suggesting he was a prosperous businessman. He looked out of place here, where the usual rig-out was a navy ganzy and rough serge trousers, topped by a cloth cap. Curious to know why he was there, she went eagerly to his table when he beckoned her over.

'I wonder if you can help me?' he began. 'I am looking for a Katie Mair who lived in Marischal Street at one time, and I thought, since her house was not far from here, that you may be able to tell me where she is now.'

His manner was pleasant enough, but Lottie knew that this didn't mean a thing, and she wasn't going to give anything away until she found out why he was asking. 'Katie Mair?' she said, pretending to think.

'She was living with a young man the last time I saw her – Sammy, I think his name was – but I mislaid her new address and I have something of great importance to tell her.'

Coming to the conclusion that he must be a solicitor with news of a legacy, Lottie still didn't altogether trust him. 'Oh, aye, I know who you mean now,' she said, snapping her fingers as if it had just dawned on her. 'It's a good while since she left, and she didn't say where she was going. But Dennis McKay might know, she was real friendly with him for a while, and I can tell you where to get hold of him.'

The man sat up, beaming. 'I would be most obliged.'

Watching the stranger coming in, Dennis could not understand the ripple of apprehension that ran through him – maybe it was the expression on the man's face, sort of secretive yet tinged with excitement. 'Lunch for one, is it, sir?' he said, stepping forward with the smile he always presented to new patrons of his restaurant. 'May I recommend the . . .'

'Ah, no, I did not come in for a meal. I merely wanted to ask you . . . you are Mr McKay, I take it?'

The smile fading, Dennis snapped, 'Yes?'

'My name is Angus Gunn, and I believe you knew my niece, Katie Mair.'

Dennis did not reply at once. The name had rung a bell, and he was searching his brain to place the man. Wasn't it Katie herself that had mentioned it? Sammy's father, that's who he was – the man she had believed was dead. 'Katie isn't your niece,' he snapped.

'So you do know her?' Angus sounded triumphant. 'Yes, I am afraid I was not entirely truthful, but I would like to know her present address.'

'What do you want with her?'

'You may not know that my son is in Ladysbridge . . .'

Astonished that Sammy's father had not been told of his death, Dennis played for time. 'Yes, I knew that, but I'd like you to tell me what you want with Katie.'

Angus had thought this out on his way to Le Denis. 'I want to hear about my son. Knowing what he thought of me, I did not go to visit him, it might have upset him, but I am quite sure that Katie goes to see him regularly.'

'Are you now? I wouldn't be so sure if I was you.'

'I do not care for your tone of voice, Mr McKay.'

Dennis gave a sardonic snigger. 'Is that a fact?'

'I came in here to ask you a civil question and I expect you to give me a civil answer.'

'Right you are, you asked for it. Sammy died months ago, so Katie wouldn't be visiting him. Is that civil enough?'

Taken unawares by this information, Angus staggered to a chair and thumped down, his sallow skin a yellowish white, and Dennis regretted springing it on him so suddenly. 'Are you all right? Will I get you some water? Or a whisky?'

'Water, if you would be so kind.'

By the time Dennis filled a glass from the carafe on the table, Angus was rather more composed. 'You will think it strange that I did not know, but I suppose I gave up my right to be informed of his well-being when I did not answer the letter telling me he had been admitted to Ladysbridge. I should have acknowledged it, but I had married again and did not want to run the risk of having him sent back to me. How could I burden my wife with the responsibility of looking after him? You must understand my position.'

'There's nothing about you I understand,' Dennis sneered, 'and if you're feeling better, I'd be glad if you left me to run my restaurant. I don't know where Katie is, though I heard she left Peterhead, and I'm sure she wouldn't want to see you, anyway.'

Angus tottered to his feet. 'In that case there is nothing more to be said.'

Watching him stumbling out, Dennis thought that, whatever Mr Gunn wanted with Katie, it wasn't to hear about Sammy, and he was glad he hadn't said she might be at Cullen.

'I should have wrung that impertinent young devil's neck!' Angus muttered, as he opened the door of his car, oblivious to the suspicious look a passing woman was giving him. 'He was making a fool of me, and he does know where Katie is.'

Starting the engine, he recognized the same pains in his chest that he had felt before. 'I can't let him see me like this,' he gasped, driving off slowly and praying that he could hold on until he was out of the town. He had only just reached the open road when he was forced to stop, doubled over the steering wheel in agony.

It was hours before the pains let up and he lay back in his seat sweating, but thankful that he was still alive. How ironic it would have been, he thought, if he had died as a result of trying to find Katie Mair. This had not occurred to him on the other two occasions, but he had learned his lesson now. Nothing – even the hatred he had harboured for years – was more important to him than his own well-being.

'Oh, George, I'm glad you're back,' Katie cried, when she opened the door to him.

Over her head, the young man caught Mary Ann's eye and was disconcerted by her unblinking stare. Wondering why she was glaring at him, he decided it could wait, for he had a very important question to ask Katie first. Turning to her again, he said, 'Put on your coat. We're going for a walk.'

They had not gone far along the shingle when he stopped. 'Have you thought about what I asked you before I left?'

'I've thought about little else,' she smiled.

'If I say I love you, what would you say?'

'I'd say I love you, and all.'

'Honestly, Katie?'

'Honestly, George. I love you with all my heart.'

He crushed her to him. 'Will you promise to marry me, then? It'll not be for a while yet, not till I save enough to set us up in a house, but we could get engaged.'

'We won't need to get a house, I couldn't leave Grandma. We'll have to live with her . . . I hope that's all right?'

'I'd rather we were on our own, but I won't mind as long as you're my wife.'

His kisses left her gasping for breath, and her whole body was aching with love as he pulled her down on the ground. Then, to her dismay, his mouth stopped being gentle, and she wrenched her head away when his tongue tried to prise her teeth apart.

'What's wrong?' he asked, his breathing unsteady.

'I don't like you kissing me like that.'

He pulled her face round. 'I was kissing you like a man, not a boy. God, Katie, I want you.'

'No, George, not till we're married.'

'What difference would it make?'

'You might . . . land me in trouble,' she faltered.

'What if I do? We'll get wed all the sooner.'

'But folk'll know . . .'

'I don't care a damn about other folk!'

'George,' she said, very quietly, 'if you love me enough, you'll wait.'

He struggled to regain control of his desire. If this had been Lizann she'd have . . . but he would never see her again. 'Righto, Katie,' he sighed, 'I don't want to force you.'

He kissed her again, very gently, teasing her so much that she felt like giving in after all, but when he said, 'It's getting too damned cold here,' she was glad that she hadn't.

'What was wrong with your Grandma tonight?' he asked when they were walking back to the house.

'What do you mean?'

'She was glowering at me like I'd done something wrong.'

'Never heed her,' Katie smiled. 'I think she's jealous of me being young and in love. She tried to put me off you, you know. She said you'd likely been taking up with one of the fisher lassies when you were away.'

'As if I would.' He couldn't give her a proper denial, and hoped she hadn't noticed.

Katie grasped his hand. 'I knew you wouldn't, any more than I'd take up with anybody else when you're not here.'

'Have you ever taken up with anybody else? What about that Sammy you told me about?'

'Sammy? I told you he was simple.'

'Well, he could have forced you. Can you swear to me you never went to bed with him?' Her gasp made him free his hand and glare at her. 'So you did! And you say he was simple? He couldn't have been all that simple if he knew how to . . .'

'I never *went* to bed with him,' Katie interrupted, wishing that she hadn't given herself away. 'He was scared of the thunder one night, and he . . . I told him not to, but he . . . came into my bed beside me.'

275

He pulled her to a halt. 'Oh, aye?' His voice dripped with sarcasm. 'Do you expect me to believe he was lying beside you and didn't touch you?'

'He didn't do anything to me. Oh, George, please believe me. He was like a little boy, and he didn't have the sense to know he shouldn't be there.'

'And you didn't stop him?'

'I tried to, but he was terrified and I just couldn't make him go back to his own room.'

'Likely you didn't want to. Maybe you'd been waiting for him. Maybe you'd been ready for him.'

'George Buchan! That's a horrible thing to say!'

'It's horrible to think the girl I loved let a daftie take her. What would you think if I told you I'd been with a girl down in Yarmouth?'

'Oh . . . you weren't, were you?'

Again, he couldn't bring himself to deny it. 'I just said what would you say if I had.'

They kept standing, both rigid with anger, then he said, 'That's it, Katie. We're finished.'

'George! I've told you the truth!'

'It's too much for me to swallow, and I'm not marrying a girl that's not pure.'

After waiting a moment for her to assure him that she was pure, he turned from her in disgust. 'I knew it. You did let him take you, and I couldn't bear to touch you now.'

As she watched him walking away, she reflected sadly that she had told him the truth as far as it went, but Sammy had eventually taken her, though it had been Dennis McKay who defiled her first.

She walked straight past her grandmother without speaking when she went in, and the tears did not come until she was in bed.

In the morning, Katie did not satisfy her grandmother's obvious curiosity, and when the old woman asked, 'Did you and him fall out last night?' she didn't answer.

'All right, then,' Mary Ann said, unfeelingly, 'keep it bottled up.'

Katie was glad that no one referred to her blotched face in the shop, for she couldn't have laughed it off, and the day dragged on for so long that by mid-afternoon she felt like running out and leaving all the customers standing. It was with great relief that she locked up at six o'clock.

After half an hour of toying with a plate of stewed liver and vegetables – unable to confide in her grandmother, she avoided her inquisitive eyes – she had a longing to be by herself. As she walked along the shore, she wondered if the Three Kings were offended that she had not talked to them for such a long time, and decided to chance telling them what had happened, though they likely knew, for the quarrel had taken place not far from them.

'George doesn't want to marry me now,' she gulped, as she stood looking at the rocks, 'and he'd be worse shocked if he knew the whole truth. Maybe I shouldn't have told him about the thunderstorm, but he'd have found out I wasn't a virgin once we were husband and wife. I wish I could have my time over again, knowing the things I know now. I'd have more sense than give in to Dennis, and if Sammy hadn't seen us making love, he'd never . . .'

Katie broke off. She had ignored Sammy for far too long, and for all she knew his mind could be back to what it used to be. He would think she had forsaken him.

She addressed her special friends again. 'I'll make a bargain with you. If you make George change his mind about me, I'll go to see Sammy, and if he's better, I'll take him home with me. Once George sees him, surely to goodness he'll believe I was telling the truth about that night.'

Going home, she doubted if George *would* understand, and remembering Sammy's jealousy of Dennis, she wondered if she would be storing up trouble in bringing them together? But she was duty-bound to do what she could for the poor soft thing, whatever the cost. Although her heart felt as if it was being riven asunder, Katie kept her tears at bay until she was in bed and spent another night weeping.

George was cursing himself. He shouldn't have finished with Katie last night, for he still loved her, and he'd surely get over his sickness at what she had told him. If only she'd been honest with him and admitted letting that Sammy make love to her, it wouldn't be so bad, for if he did marry her he'd know beforehand he wasn't the first with her. She wasn't the first for him, either, not by a long chalk, though Lizann was the only one who ever meant anything to him. In any case, it was different for a man.

When he went into the baker's shop the following morning, he was dismayed to see that Katie's eyes were puffed and red-rimmed. It gave him no pleasure to have wounded her so badly, and he wanted to make it up to her. She kept her eyes steadfastly on the customers she was serving, but she had to look at him when his turn came. 'Half a dozen bread rolls, please,' he said loudly, then leaned across the counter and whispered, 'I'm sorry, Katie lass, I lost my head. Say you forgive me?'

'Nothing's changed,' she muttered.

'I know, and I don't care. Do you want to see me again?'

Taking his money, she gave a nod and he grabbed her hand for a moment. 'I'll come for you at the usual time, and I swear everything'll be all right.'

He went cautiously when they were walking over the golf course later. He had to gain her trust again. 'I was plain jealous,' he said, when they sat down behind a bunker. 'I hated thinking another man . . .'

'You know something, George?' she asked softly. 'I went to the Three Kings last night and I promised them I'd go to see Sammy if they made you come back to me, and you have, so I'm going to Ladysbridge on Sunday.'

His stomach lurched. 'Oh, Katie, I wish you wouldn't.'

'I made a bargain.'

'With three damned rocks?'

'They're not just rocks to me, and I'm going to take him home with me if he's fit to come.'

'What are you trying to do to me, Katie? You know what I feel about you and him, so why . . . ?'

'Listen George. I love you, but if you can't take Sammy along with me, I won't marry you.'

'Katie, you can't expect me to . . .' He couldn't believe she could be so insensitive.

'It'll maybe not come to that,' she said, sadly.

'You're damned right it'll not come to that!'

She remained sitting long after he had stamped off, her eyes dry because she knew she had only herself to blame this time. What she had suggested would have been too much for any man to take, she should have known that.

When she went home, Mary Ann said, 'Have you been fighting wi' him again?'

The tears came now. 'I told him about Sammy.'

'The laddie Gunn? You didna tell George about that?'

'I didn't tell him everything, just about Sammy coming in my bed at Fenty and George thought we'd . . .'

'Aye, men are aye ready to believe the worst, for it's what they'd do themselves. I'd a lad once, Katie, afore I met your grandfather . . .' She broke off looking flustered, then shook her head. 'I'm saying no more, but believe me, Katie, it's stupid to tell the man you love about somebody that doesna mean a thing to you. If George ever comes back to you, dinna tell him what else the laddie Gunn did to you, for that would finish the two o' you good and proper.'

'We're finished good and proper now,' Katie's sigh ended in another sob.

On learning why, Mary Ann burst out, 'You're nae going to Ladysbridge on Sunday. Tell George the morrow you're sorry. Tell him you love him, and say you'll never think about the laddie Gunn again. See if that patches things.'

'I thought you wouldn't want me to patch things? You said I shouldn't trust him.'

'Maybe I was wrong about him, and I'd rather see you back together than put up wi' you moping for him.'

Katie suddenly tossed her head and said defiantly, 'I'm still going to see Sammy on Sunday. George did come back though he went away again, so I have to. I promised the Three Kings.'

Mary Ann gave a derisive snort. 'You promised three lumps o' stone sticking up in the air? And what could they do to you if you broke your promise, do you think?'

'I'm not going to break it, Grandma. Not for you or for George or even for God Himself, if He told me to.'

Giving a shocked gasp, Mary Ann levered herself off her chair, muttering, as she hobbled into her bedroom, 'May the Lord forgive you for taking His name in vain.'

Katie remained in her seat, thinking. Maybe she shouldn't have told George she was going to Ladysbridge. Maybe she shouldn't have told him about Sammy at all? But she couldn't leave him to rot in that place for the rest of his life. She still owed him a debt of gratitude for saving her twice from his father. Thank goodness she didn't have to worry about Mr Gunn now, for she'd more than enough worries as it was.

Rising to turn out the lamp, she wondered about the lad her grandmother had started speaking about. Something must have gone wrong between them, so was it because of him she had said men weren't to be trusted?

Chapter Twenty-four

❖❖

1930

On the bus to Ladysbridge, Katie wished that her grandmother had said more about her first lad. If he had jilted her and gone off with somebody else, it would explain why she was such a bitter woman. Her own position wasn't as bad ... there was no other girl in George's life. He had climbed down after their first quarrel, and she shouldn't have annoyed him again. If she had waited, she might not have needed to tell him about this visit at all. If Sammy was still the same, she would go to George straight off the bus when she went back and tell her she was sorry for going against his wishes – but maybe it was too late for apologies.

When she arrived at the institution, Sammy was not in his usual chair, and she went in search of an attendant to ask where he was. The white-coated man gave her a peculiar look. 'I'd better take you to Mr Welsh.'

Mr Welsh, who turned out to be the superintendent and was a middle-aged man with thick glasses and a genial, round face, told her to sit down. 'You are Miss Mair?'

Katie was puzzled. 'Yes?'

'Did you not receive the letter I sent some time ago?'

Alarm gripped her. 'No, I didn't get any letter.'

'It was sent to your address in Peterhead ... oh, it must be about a year ago. I can look up the date if you like.'

'It doesn't matter. It's a lot longer than a year since I left Peterhead ... not long after Sammy was put in here. What was wrong ... was he ill?'

Mr Welsh cleared his throat. 'I wrote immediately after Mr Gunn died, but ...'

'Sammy's dead?' Disregarding the spinning of her head, she asked, 'Did he . . . was he . . . ?'

'There had been no change since he came in, and he passed away peacefully in his sleep.' He pushed back his chair and stood up abruptly. 'Miss Mair, are you all right?'

'It's been a shock, I'm sorry.' Her teeth were chattering and the man's face was blurring.

She knew no more until she came round to find him holding her head down on her knees. 'I'll get someone to bring you some tea.' Mr Welsh pressed a bell on his desk.

Her face was so colourless, her eyes so anguished, that he said he would have someone drive her home when she came to herself, but, unwilling to face her grandmother so soon, she said she would prefer to go to Banff – adding untruthfully that she had relatives there.

She could see that the young driver was apprehensive when she told him to drop her off anywhere on the seafront. 'I'm not going to jump in,' she assured him as she got out of the van. 'I just want to clear my head before I see my auntie.'

After walking along to the harbour, she stood looking at the 'BF' registered trawlers – and two marked 'BCK' – and let her thoughts turn at last to what she had steadfastly tried to forget for the past twenty minutes. It was awful to think that poor Sammy had died in that horrible place with no friend beside him, even if the superintendent had said he had passed away in his sleep. She should have gone to see him more often. What would it have mattered if he didn't know her? He might have recognized her eventually . . . if she had gone regularly.

As she stood, ignoring the piercing wind, heedless of the chill seeping right into her bones, she recalled the years they had shared: the fear-filled days after leaving Fenty; the carefree months at Struieburn; the three see-saw years in Peterhead when contentment alternated with sadness, and happiness with despair.

'Oh, Sammy,' she sighed, mournfully, 'if I hadn't made you run away with me, you'd still be alive.'

She jumped when someone tapped her shoulder, and looked round into the anxious eyes of an elderly fisherman. 'Are you all right, lass?' he asked. 'You've been standing there for near half an hour.'

'I'm all right,' she assured him. 'Somebody I . . . cared for died over a year ago, and I didn't know till I went to . . . the hospital this morning.'

The man did not appear to find it strange that she had taken so long to visit someone she professed to care for and nodded sympathetically. 'That would upset you, right enough. You look frozen, lass, will you let me buy you a cup o' tea? I was on my road to get one for myself, and I'd be pleased to have somebody to speak to.'

Katie accepted gratefully, and as they walked along, he told her that his name was Donald Shewan and he was on the drifter *Deveron Lad*. 'We were to sail at twelve,' he went on, 'my last trip, but it was eleven afore the cook sent word he'd broke his arm, and the skipper hasna got another cook yet.'

Unable yet to contribute anything to the conversation, she was glad to listen to his thumbnail sketches of the other five members of the crew of the *Deveron Lad*, and they were finishing a third cup of tea when he said, 'Will somebody nae be expecting you hame, lass?'

Glancing at the clock on the wall for the first time, she gasped. It was almost five o'clock. 'Do you know when I'll get a bus to Cullen, Mr Shewan?'

'Ach,' he laughed, 'that's my Sunday name. Naebody would ken who you wanted if you asked for Mr Shewan, for I'm ken't far and wide as Dosh. I've nae idea when you'll get a bus, lass, but I'll ask Babbie.'

He went to the counter, and was back in a few seconds. 'Ten past, she says, so we'd best get going.'

After paying for the teas, he walked with her to the main

road, and when her bus appeared, she held out her hand. 'Thank you for the tea . . . Dosh, and for helping me. I feel a bit better now.'

His huge, rough hand engulfed hers. 'My pleasure . . . eh, you havena tell't me your name.'

'Katie,' she said, shyly. 'Katie Mair.'

'Will you take some advice from an old seadog, Katie? It seems to me you're blaming yourself for nae going to see your friend afore he died, and that's no good for you. Mind on him the way you ken't him, and carry on wi' your life. Will you do that for me, lass?'

Katie nodded tearfully, and he tipped the peak of his cap before walking away. Taking a seat, she felt deeply grateful to him; talking to him had been nearly as good as being with her grandfather again. Was it possible that he had been an angel in disguise? Had Granda sent him down from heaven to minister to her in her hour of sorrow? But whatever he was, angel or ordinary mortal, Dosh had done much to heal the cracks in her heart, the cracks opened by George and widened by the news of Sammy's death.

Not fully recovered from either, she forgot, when she came off the bus, that she had intended to try to patch up her romance, and ran straight down the hill. Bursting into the house, she threw herself at her grandmother.

Mary Ann, unaccustomed to the role of comforter, held the sobbing girl until her shoulders stopped heaving then pushed her gently away. 'Sit down and tell me.'

Katie thumped into a chair. 'He's been dead a year . . . and I never knew.'

Hiding the relief she felt, the old woman soothed, 'Maybe it's all for the best. George'll have nothing to be jealous about now.'

'I don't want to see George again, not after this.'

'Look, lass, you're all upset the now, but you'll get ower it. Gi'e it a week or two, then go to him and . . .'

'You don't understand. I'll never forget Sammy as long as I live, and if George ever said anything bad about him, I'd want to kill him . . . and what makes it worse, I wasn't there when he died . . . and I wasn't here when Granda died, and . . . oh, Grandma, I wish I was dead, too.' Covering her face with her hands, she dissolved into another paroxysm of tears.

Rather at a loss, Mary Ann said, sharply, 'Stop it, Katie! A young lassie like you, wi' all your life in front o' you? If you dinna want George, somebody else'll come along, and you'll get married and raise a . . .'

'I don't want George, and I don't want anybody else!'

'You dinna ken what you do want, that's your trouble. I think you'd best go through to your bed, and try to get some sleep or you'll not be fit for your work the morn.'

Wounded by her grandmother's lack of compassion, Katie dragged herself into her bedroom, but as she undressed, her shaking fingers fumbled so much that she yanked her bodice open in a temper, and scowled as one button flew off and hit the china chamberpot under her bed with a resounding ping. She didn't bother to hunt for it, and dropped each item of clothing on the floor with a fierce satisfaction.

Angus looked so tired when he came home that his wife told him to go to bed and she would take his dinner up to him. 'Why don't you let me help you in the shop?' she asked when she carried up his tray. 'For a while, anyway, till you feel up to it again.'

'Perhaps you should,' Angus agreed. 'It has been getting a little too much for me lately.'

Betty had collected his dirty dishes and had started to wash up when she heard him making a funny groaning noise, and, not even bothering to dry her hands, she raced up the stairs. 'What's wrong?' she gasped, when she saw that he was clutching his chest.

'It's my heart! I felt it coming on earlier ... I have had pains off and on ... for some time ... but they have never been as ... bad as this before.'

'Oh, Angus, I'd better go for the doctor, and it'll take me ages to walk to Huntly. We're so far from anything here, I wish we'd a telephone.'

'My old bicycle ... in the shed.'

She ran downstairs and grabbed her coat. It was many years since she had done any cycling, but it was something you never forgot. The bicycle was red with rust, the tyres were bald and flat, but she had no time to pump them. She had a little difficulty in swinging her leg over the bar, but after steadying herself against the door of the shed, she managed to get on and pedalled as fast as she could up the long track, her whole body jarring each time the front wheel hit a stone. By the time she reached the road, her lungs were prickly-tight, but she couldn't afford to ease off.

She was still pedalling furiously when she heard a car coming behind her, and, hoping that the driver would give her a lift, she stopped and jumped off. Letting her ancient steed fall to the ground, she stood waving both arms, and the car drew to a halt. 'I'm Mrs Gunn and my husband's ill,' she managed to gasp. 'He told me to get the doctor.'

The driver opened the passenger door for her. 'Would that be Angus Gunn?' he asked, smiling. 'I was his first wife's doctor, but I've never attended him. He must feel bad before he's asking for me.'

After making an intricate turn around, he observed, 'You were lucky catching me here, I was on my way home.'

Seeing that she was unable to answer, he said nothing else until she got her breath back. 'What seems to be the trouble with Angus?'

'He says it's his heart, and I've biked ... oh, I've left it lying in the middle of the road.'

'If nobody's come a cropper on it and mangled it, I'll pick it up later.'

They had barely two miles to go to reach the house, and he ran upstairs in front of her. Angus was still in great pain, and Betty watched while Doctor Graham sounded his chest and asked him if he'd had anything like this before. At last, he turned to her. 'If you come out to my car with me, Mrs Gunn, I'll give you something for him.'

'Give him one just now,' he told her, when he gave her a handful of small pills, 'and one before you go to bed, then one morning and night for the next week. He has had a fairly severe heart attack, and he is lucky to be alive. He will have to stay in bed for some time yet, and even after he thinks he is fit again, he should take it easy for a few months.'

'I'll make sure of that,' she vowed.

'I'll come back tomorrow, though there's really nothing more I can do, except give you some more pills. He will always need to keep some handy.'

When she returned to the bedroom with a glass of water, she waited until Angus swallowed the pill then said, 'It's bed rest for you for the next few weeks, and pottering round the house for a long time after that.'

'What about the shop?'

'Don't worry about the shop,' she said, brightly. 'I'll look after it. I can teach myself to drive . . . I'll take the car up and down the track tonight till I get the hang of it, I've a vague idea of how the gears work.'

It was significant that her husband did not even try to dissuade her, and it made her understand more clearly how much his brush with death had affected him.

George had walked past the baker's shop several times, but had been careful not to let Katie see him. He had heard no gossip about her being seen with a man, so he was almost sure that she hadn't taken Sammy back to Cullen, but he couldn't face her. He wasn't even sure that he wanted to speak to her again, for he had been thinking quite a lot about Lizann.

Should he go to see her? It wasn't far on the bus, and she might have changed her mind about Peter.

'You'll be pleased to know I've finished with Katie,' he told his mother.

Her thin mouth turned up in the semblance of a smile. 'I am that. I aye said she wasna the lass for you. You want somebody that had a proper mother and father . . .'

He rose automatically to Katie's defence. 'You don't know she hadn't. You're like all the old wives here, putting two and two together and making five.'

'I'm not an old wife!' she cried, indignantly. 'It's Mary Ann that's an old wife! A crabbit old wife that turned her back on her only son because she didna like the lassie he was going wi', and she needna think folk believed her lies. There's folk here ken . . .'

'Ach, Ma! There's folk here would say anything to make a scandal, and you've no need to worry. You'll not have Katie Mair as a daughter-in-law. I'm going to Buckie to see a lass I met in Yarmouth.' He knew his mother would make sure Katie heard about it, but he was past caring.

When George arrived in Buckie, he thought of buying a box of chocolates before he went to the Yardie – where Lizann had said she lived – but thought it might look as if he were bribing her to give up her lad. The cluster of old houses he came to was brightened by spotless white lace curtains at each window and brass knockers on most of the doors. Never having asked her, he didn't know what surname to look for, and had made up his mind to try every door until he struck lucky, but he was saved the trouble when Lizann came out of a house farther along.

A wide smile transformed her face when she spotted him. 'George! What are you doing here?'

'I've come to see you.'

'What about Katie? Does she know?'

'I broke off with her. What about Peter?'

'I've promised to marry him.'

Wishing that he hadn't given in to his whim – it had been foolish when he knew she loved another man – George said, as heartily as he could, 'Congratulations! And I hope you'll be very happy together.'

He made to walk away, but she held his arm. 'You can't go just like that.'

'I think I'd better, before I forget myself and kiss you.'

'George, I'm sorry,' she whispered.

'Don't be. I'm pleased for you.'

'But I still love you, and all.'

His gut twisting, he groaned, 'Don't say it, Lizann.'

'It's true, and I wish you could kiss me.'

Looking at her again, he could see the pain in her eyes, the same pain that was tearing him apart, but as they gazed longingly, hopelessly, at each other, a voice called, 'Who's that you're speaking to, Lizann?'

'It's my mother,' she whispered, then raised her voice to answer. 'It's a man asking how to get to Portessie. I've been trying to tell him, but it would be easier if I took him up and showed him.'

'Aye, that would be best, and you're going up to the High Street, ony road.'

So, over-aware of each other and unable to let even their hands touch, they walked back towards the main part of the town. 'She's waiting for me to take back some flour,' Lizann said, tearfully. 'She forgot to get any herself when she was up the town yesterday and she hasna enough for the pastry she's making. I'll have to hurry, I'm sorry, George.'

'I should never have come. We said all that had to be said in Yarmouth.'

'I'm awful glad to see you.'

'Forget about me, Lizann. Marry your lad and be happy.'

'Will you marry Katie now?'

'I don't think so. I said things to her that ... maybe I expected too much.'

When they reached the point where one road led up to High

Street and another went down along the sea-front, Lizann suddenly said, in alarm, 'Oh, here's my auntie. You'd better go down that way.' She pointed to the lower road, her voice changing as she said, 'Straight along there. You'll see all the big houses up on the brae, that's Portessie.'

'Thank you,' George said, politely, though he felt as if he were being slowly and effectively strangled.

He walked away quickly, not daring to look behind him and carrying on past the harbour until he saw the impressive layers of houses on the hill overlooking the bay. Giving a sigh that conveyed the misery he felt, he turned into the first opening. He may as well have a look round Portessie since he was here. It would pass some time and let him gather his shaken emotions.

When Ina went into the baker's, she waited until there was only one person in front of her, and then leaned over the woman's shoulder. 'My George is away to see a Buckie lassie he met in Yarmouth,' she announced in her ear, loudly enough for everyone in the shop to hear. 'He saw a lot o' her when they were doon there, and I think it's serious.'

Katie felt her legs shaking and tried not to show how the information had affected her. When it was Mrs Buchan's turn to be served, she moved to the counter and looked at Katie in obviously insincere apology. 'I forgot George had been going wi' you, but it's ower, isn't it?'

'Yes, it's over.' Katie's smile was crooked.

'Aye, well, you ken what the men are. They see a bonnie lassie and they're like a dog after a bitch on heat.'

'Was there anything else, Mrs Buchan?'

'No, that's the lot.'

When Ina went out, the next customer said, 'She's a bitch herself, that one. I wouldna believe a word she says. She was just trying to annoy you.'

Katie managed a laugh. 'It'll take more than her to annoy

me.' But her heart was aching at the thought of George with somebody else.

When she went home, she said, 'George has another girl.'

Mary Ann's eyebrows lifted. 'Already?'

'He'd been going out with her in Yarmouth, that's why he'd wanted to break off with me.'

'Did I not tell you? Well, there's better fish in the sea than ever came out.'

Despite her heartache, Katie had to laugh. 'I'm off fish for good, Grandma.'

'You'll meet somebody else.'

'I don't want to meet anybody else. It's better not to get married and settle down.'

Mary Ann pursed her shrivelled mouth. 'If I hadna married your grandfather after . . . you'd not be here the day.'

'It seems to me there's a lot of ifs about why I'm here,' Katie sighed, 'and I wish I knew what they were. I don't know anything about my mother and father.'

Her grandmother smiled mysteriously. 'You'll find out some day. Now, you'll have to dish up the supper, for I havena felt right the whole day.'

Katie rose and crossed to the range. 'Your legs again?'

'Them and all, but something else, a dizzy feeling, like I was going to faint, sometimes.'

'You'd better go to your bed, and I'll get the doctor.'

'You'll do nae such thing. I'll be better the morrow.'

That night, Katie lay thinking about George. No wonder he had been so ready to believe the worst of her, but he should have told her he loved another girl. She would have thought more of him if he'd been honest, but he had let her down and made a fool of her. She had nobody now but her grandmother, who was far from being in the best of health. If only she had a mother to tell her troubles and fears to . . .

When Katie went through to the kitchen in the morning,

Mary Ann was sitting by the unlit fire, still in her thick winceyette nightgown. 'I'm nae fit for a thing the day,' she complained.

'That's all right, Grandma. I'll soon have the fire going and the porridge made.'

'Aye.' The old woman leaned back and closed her eyes, but after a few moments they jerked open again. 'Dinna you go telling the doctor, mind. I'm nae as bad as that.'

'It wouldn't hurt you just to let him check you over.'

'He's not coming in here poking about at me. Once you let doctors start that, you're on the road out. I'm sure they've got an agreement wi' the undertakers – so many dead bodies a month.'

'Oh, Grandma, that's daft. Maybe you just need a tonic, or tablets, or something.'

'A blue pill, that's what I'm needing.'

Katie was horrified at this. 'Nothing of the kind! You'll last for years yet.'

'I dinna want to last if I canna do things. I dinna want to end my days a slavering, useless wreck.'

Certain that her grandmother felt much worse than she made out, Katie made up her mind to tell the doctor, whatever the consequences. Maybe it was nothing serious, but it should be seen to.

Passing the doctor's house on her way to work, she left a message for him to call, then went to ask the baker if she could have time off. 'My Grandma's not feeling well,' she told him, 'and I can't leave her on her own all day.'

John Walker shook his head. 'I'm sorry, Katie. The wife's away to Macduff to see her mother, she's sick, and all. She said she'd be back about twelve, and you can go the minute she comes in. Will that do you?'

'It'll have to.'

Katie was on edge all forenoon, and at one minute past twelve, when Belle Walker came in and relieved her, she flew down the hill and found Doctor Fleming in the kitchen with

Mary Ann, a very different Mary Ann, with frightened eyes staring out of a grey twisted face.

'It's a good thing you called me in,' he told Katie. 'Your grandmother's had a seizure, and I can't get her into bed by myself.'

It took them some time to lift the solid old woman through to her room, and when they got her settled, Katie eyed the doctor fearfully. 'How bad is she? Will she get better?'

'Well, I've been here over an hour, and I don't know how long it was before that when it struck her, so it's a good sign that she's still alive. However, she'll need constant care over the next few days until I can assess the damage done. Is there anyone to look after her?'

'Just me, and I'd have to ask the Walkers if I can have some time off.'

'Would you like to run up and ask them now? I'll wait with her until you get back.'

Mary Ann's crooked, shrunken mouth opened, but no words came out, and it dawned on Katie that the old woman couldn't speak. There was no time to ask Doctor Fleming anything, for he'd be anxious to get on with his round, so she raced back to the bakery where Belle Walker was most sympathetic and understanding. 'It's only right you should look after your Grandma, Katie, I'll manage myself for a few days.'

When she returned to the house, Katie went outside with the doctor, moving away from the window so that Mary Ann wouldn't hear. 'Will she ever be able to speak again?'

'Most stroke victims regain some power of speech,' he told her, 'it depends on the severity of the attack. She has the tenacity to fight, so she has a good chance, but she may never be able to walk or talk properly again.'

'She hasn't been able to walk properly for a while. Her knees are full of rheumatics.'

The doctor set his hat on his head. 'I'll get the district nurse to hand in a bedpan.'

'Thanks, Doctor.' Not having had time to think about the problem there would be because of the outside dry lavatory, Katie was thankful that he had solved it before it arose.

He gripped Katie's shoulder for a moment, then smiled broadly. 'I can't see Mary Ann being speechless for very long. I know how you must feel, Katie, but try not to worry. She could live for years.'

When he went out, the girl went back to her grandmother's room. 'I'm going to look after you, Grandma, and you're going to be fine.'

Noticing the agitation in Mary Ann's eyes, she explained, 'Mrs Walker's given me some days off, till you're on your feet again.'

That seemed to put the old woman's mind at ease, so Katie straightened the bedcovers and went through to make a pot of tea. She was pouring milk into the cups when the district nurse knocked and walked in carrying an aluminium bedpan. 'The doctor told me to hand this in,' she smiled, 'and I've taken a feeding cup, as well. You'll likely need it.'

'Oh, thank you.' This was something else Katie had not reckoned on.

Nurse Macphail offered to show Katie how to hold the patient's head up and tilt the spout of the feeding cup to her lips. That first drink proved to be a bit messy, most of the tea dribbling out of the stricken woman's twisted mouth on to the towel which had been spread over the bedcovers to protect them. 'Very good, Mary Ann,' the nurse assured her. 'You'll soon get up to it.'

Katie had just begun to learn how much her grandmother would have to rely on her, but by bedtime she understood that Mary Ann was totally dependent on her for everything, and that letting her use the bedpan was a mammoth task.

In the morning, Katie was pleased to see that the old woman's face and mouth were not so squint, and when she took a cup of soup through to her in the middle of the day, she was delighted to receive a grateful grunt.

Doctor Fleming called in every afternoon, Katie gladly reporting the daily improvement in speech. 'Sometimes she can't say the words clearly,' she told him on the fourth day, 'but I can understand what she's meaning. And she can move her left arm a little bit now.'

He nodded. 'Her speech is coming on nicely, but . . .' He broke off, shaking his head. 'There is no sign of progress in her legs. They seem to be completely paralysed, and I don't think she'll ever walk again.'

Katie gasped. 'Is there no hope at all?'

'There's always hope,' he sighed, 'but I'm afraid it would need a miracle.' His voice became brisker. 'I believe you could help her to regain the use of her left arm by making her exercise regularly. She'll likely fight against you, but just persevere. If you have a sponge ball, give her that to squeeze, which should get her fingers moving again. It will be hard work, Katie, but it's the only way.'

'Will she be bed-ridden for the rest of her life?'

'It appears that way to me. Do you feel that it will be too much for you? Can you afford to pay for her to go into a private nursing home?'

'I want to look after her myself.'

'It'll be a full-time job, Katie.'

'Yes, I understand that. I'll go to the bakery when she's having her nap and tell them I can't go back to work.'

'Good girl. Now, I won't be calling every day, but I'll come occasionally to see how she is.'

On her way home from giving up her work, Katie wondered how she would cope with attending to her grandmother every minute of every day for years. As the doctor had warned her, it would be hard work, but at least it gave her a purpose in life and there would be no time to think about herself . . . or about George . . . or about poor, dead, Sammy.

Chapter Twenty-five

❖❖

Before locking the day's takings in the safe for deposit in the bank in the morning, Dennis extracted twenty pounds and put them in his pocket. What Beth didn't know wouldn't hurt her. He had started off by taking a fiver once a week, then, getting bolder, he had tried ten, and when Beth still hadn't twigged, he made it twenty. He had been at it since a month after the restaurant was extended, and his wife still didn't suspect a thing.

Looking in the mirror, he adjusted his silk tie, then ran his comb through his hair, no longer worn oiled and slicked back. It looked natural now – a darkish brown with a thread or two of silver – much more distinguished and suitable for a man who could call members of the upper classes his friends, some of the females even more than friends. The trouble was that the more money these uppity bitches had, the less ready they were to part with it. They expected him to buy gifts and pay for the afternoon or evening sessions in hotels out of town.

Unfortunately, before he had thought of helping himself to cash, he had tried to get more by gambling with the paltry pocket-money Beth allowed him, and now he was well and truly hooked. He owed the bookies a packet, and there didn't seem to be any way of paying them. He had considered black-mailing some of his ex-paramours, but if they told their husbands, word would get round that he wasn't to be trusted and no one would patronize Le Denis.

He did manage to winkle a few extra pounds out of Beth now and then when he had exceeded what he could safely pocket from the takings, but she wasn't too happy about it, and it was dodgy. If she got the slightest inkling of his extra-marital activities, he'd be up to his neck in shit – if he wasn't out on his ear. Still, he'd managed to get by up to now, and if she ever called the restaurant and found that he wasn't available, his staff would cover for him.

Tonight, however, Beth was in Glasgow seeing her solicitor – she was always damned cagey about where her income came in from – and she wouldn't be back until tomorrow lunchtime, so he had the whole night free. He would be with a sixteen-year-old whose parents were off on a cruise somewhere, and money would be the last thing on his mind.

Being in the house alone every day for so many months had told on Angus Gunn. He now lived in a twilight world of his own, and had difficulty in distinguishing what was reality and what was the product of his weird thoughts. On more than one occasion, he had climbed the two flights of stairs only to stop on the top landing wondering why he had come up. One afternoon in March, things went a little further. He found himself in one of the garrets with a cup of water in one hand and a plate holding a dry slice of bread in the other.

His brow wrinkled in perplexity. Who had he thought he was feeding? There was no one here. After a moment, he shook his head and went back to the kitchen, fearful that his mind was slipping. Would there come a day when it would go altogether and he would not know what he was doing? What if his wife caught him up there, talking to an empty room? He knew that he talked to himself, but, so far, he had not done so while she was in the house – or had he, without being aware of it?

When Betty came home that night, he had the dinner set in the kitchen – she had refused some time ago to eat in the dining room, saying that it was a lot of work for nothing.

'Something smells good, Angus,' she smiled.

'Only because you are hungry,' he protested, simpering

nevertheless at the implied compliment as he took the roasting tin out of the oven.

'What have you been doing with yourself today, apart from making the dinner?'

He carved four thin slices of meat before answering, 'I tidied up, and did some weeding in the garden. Um, I was wondering ... have you ever heard me talking to myself? I have caught myself at it once or twice, and I felt so silly.'

'It's nothing. I used to do it all the time. Everybody does. Now, dish up the vegetables and sit down and eat your dinner before it's cold.'

When they were both seated, she said, 'I was really busy in the shop today, Angus, and two women actually got tired of waiting and left without buying anything.'

Having divorced himself from his business, he did not care if all the customers went out ... or never went in, but how would they live, in that case? He forced himself to consider what his wife had said. 'You have done very well since you took over the reins, so well that it may be feasible for you to engage someone to help you.'

'I do need somebody ... why don't you come back? You could deal with the men and I'd deal with the women, and if you felt too tired any time, I'd do both. You wouldn't even need to drive the car, for I've managed myself for months.'

He deliberated for only a short time. 'I do not feel like returning to the grind, and the stress of the shop may prove too much for me. I am sure you can find a capable woman, or perhaps you should employ a man to look after the menswear.'

'That's a good idea ... as long as you wouldn't be jealous of me working so close to another man all day?'

'In such a public place? There would be no cause for me to be jealous.' Fatigue sweeping over him suddenly, Angus said, wearily, 'Do as you think best.'

*   *   *

'Katie! I want a drink!'

Mary Ann's speech had returned as sharp as ever, if not sharper, for there was a whine to it now that aggravated her grand-daughter.

'You can't have used that whole jug yet.'

'I knocked it ower.'

'Damn!' Katie rubbed her floury hands on her apron and took a cloth with her to dry up the spillage. 'I wouldn't put it past you to do it on purpose,' she scolded, 'just to have me running after you.'

Mary Ann's eyes were as innocent as a child's. 'I couldna help it. I was trying to reach it wi' my good arm to pour some in my tumbler, and my sleeve took it.' Watching the young woman mopping up, she added, 'I was thinking about George Buchan the now. Do you ever see him when you're up at the shops?'

'I'd have told you if I had,' Katie snapped, holding the empty jug under the dripping cloth as she took it back to the kitchen.

Mary Ann looked at her slyly when she went through with fresh water. 'I'd rest easier if you'd a man to look after you when I die.'

'You'll never die,' Katie said, scornfully.

'I will, some day.'

'Some day.' Exhausted, and rattled by her grandmother's unceasing demands, Katie had a momentary thought that the day wouldn't come soon enough, then she was horrified at even thinking such a thing.

'Would you go out wi' him again if he asked you?'

'How could he ask me when he's keeping clear of me?'

'Would you, though?'

'I'd need to think about it.'

'You never heard if anything came o' him and that lassie in Buckie?'

Katie shook her head. Mrs Buchan's words still rankled in her mind. It had hurt her deeply to think that she'd trusted

George, when, all the time, he'd been seeing another girl in Yarmouth. 'Time for your exercises, Grandma,' she said, to change the subject.

'A waste of time,' Mary Ann grumbled.

'You can use your left hand now, so stop arguing.'

Taking the sponge ball off the chest of drawers, she put it into her grandmother's right hand. 'Grip and relax. Grip and relax. That's right. Now keep on going till I get the scones in the oven.'

When she was ready, she went back to the bedroom. 'Do you feel any difference in your hand?'

'Nae a bit!' Mary Ann relinquished the ball and lay back on her pillows. 'I'd like a fancy cake wi' my flycup in the afternoon instead o' a scone. Would you go to the baker and get something fine? Maybe a cream bun, or a doughnut.'

Alarmed at how quickly the money in her grandmother's old biscuit tin was dwindling away, Katie had pointed out to her several times that it wouldn't last long at the rate they were using it, but Mary Ann had always smiled and told her not to worry, there was plenty. She had supposed that the old woman had some more hidden away somewhere, but she had never come across it and was now very careful in what she spent. She had stopped buying any cakes and biscuits weeks ago . . . but Grandma deserved a little treat occasionally.

Katie was waiting to be served – there was the usual crowd of people in – when a hand touched her back. 'Hello, Katie.'

Her stomach gave a jolt, but she looked round. 'George! I didn't expect to see you.'

'I didn't expect to see you, either. Katie, I was sorry to hear about Mary Ann, but I didn't like to come and see her in case you . . .'

'You're welcome to come any time. It'll not bother me.'

'It'll bother me,' he whispered.

The look in his eyes made her heartbeats quicken, and she turned away in confusion. When she had paid for the cream bun and doughnut – she had decided to be generous for once

– George said, 'Wait for me, Katie, I won't be a minute. I've just to get a pan loaf for Ma.'

She wasn't sure if she wanted to talk to him, but she went out and stood in the street until he joined her. 'I know you must be in a hurry to get back to your Grandma, Katie, but I won't keep you long. I've been hoping I'd run into you some time, for I wanted to let you know how sorry I am for what I did. I was stupid and unreasonable. Is there any chance of us trying again?'

'What about the girl in Buckie?' She thought it was best to clear the air.

'She's marrying somebody else. They'll likely have tied the knot by this time.'

Katie felt angry now. 'So you come crawling back to me?'

He grabbed her elbow. 'It's not like that! It was just a chance I saw you today. Ach, we can't speak here, Katie. Will you come for a walk tonight?'

Her heart crying out for him, she didn't need to think about it as she had told Mary Ann. 'I can't go out, but come to the house and we can speak in the kitchen. Grandma can't get out of her bed.'

'I'll see you about half seven, then.'

He walked away, but his eyes had told her that he still loved her, and her own heart was telling her that she still loved him. They would have things to sort out, but surely it wouldn't be impossible.

'You've been a long time,' Mary Ann complained, when she went home.

'The baker was busy, and I was speaking to George Buchan for a minute. He's coming down after supper.'

'Will the two o' you be . . . ?'

'Don't ask, Grandma, for I don't know myself.'

'Hoity toity! I'll just have to wait and see, will I?'

'You and me both,' Katie smiled.

For the first fifteen minutes he was in the house, George stood in the bedroom talking to Mary Ann, then he went into the kitchen and sat down. 'I want you to know the truth, Katie,' he began. 'I couldn't help falling for Lizann, the girl from Buckie, and we only had a few nights together – no, evenings, not nights. I told her I loved you, and she told me she loved Peter, and that would have been the end of it . . . if you hadn't . . .'

'If I hadn't told you I was going to see Sammy,' she said, sadly.

'Aye, and I was so jealous of him . . .'

'You'd no need to be jealous of him, George. I never loved him . . . well, just like a brother, and I should have gone to see him long before I did, for he'd died over a year before with nobody near him to care.'

'Oh! I'm sorry about that, Katie, but can you understand why I said the things I did?'

'I thought you wanted to break off with me – and you did go to see that girl again, didn't you?'

'I shouldn't have. I was upset about you, for I did love you . . . I still love you . . . and it upset Lizann, and all. What happened in Yarmouth was . . . oh, a few hours' madness, that's all. We knew it couldn't come to anything, for I told her I loved you and she said she loved her lad, and it should have been left like that. It was only after I fought with you . . .' He paused briefly. 'I just spoke to her for a few minutes, Katie, and if I promise I'll never see her again, will that do for you?'

'Will that do for me? What for?'

'I'm asking you to be my wife, Katie. You likely feel you can't trust me, but I swear to you there'll never be another girl in my life now except you. I love you . . .' His voice breaking, he stood up and held out his arms. 'Can you try to love me again?'

'I never stopped.'

About half an hour later, a call came from the bedroom. 'It's awful quiet ben there, what are you two doing?'

With his arms still round Katie, George opened the

bedroom door and drew her inside, grinning as he said, 'We've been kissing, if you've no objections, Mary Ann?'

Her frown was not deep enough to be real. 'As long as you stop at kissing,' she cautioned.

'And what could you do about it if we didn't?' His eyes danced with mischief.

She burst out laughing. 'George Buchan! You're still as cheeky as you were when you were a wee laddie.'

'Aye, cheeky enough to ask Katie to marry me.'

'About time, though I need her and you can't take her away from me. Katie, if you're not ower taken up wi' him, can I get a cup o' tea?'

'You haven't asked if I've said yes.'

'I didna need to ask. It's written ower your two faces as plain as day.'

After settling her grandmother for the night, Katie was free to continue with the kissing, and it was coming on for ten when George said, 'I'd better go, Katie. I'm not sure I could trust myself if I stay any longer. I'll go tomorrow to see the minister about the wedding, so I'll not be leaving you like this for much longer.'

'I love you, George,' she murmured, when she went to the door with him. 'We've had our ups and downs, and maybe it's a good thing, for I love you more than ever now.'

'Me, and all. I didn't think I could love you any more, but . . .' he eyed her anxiously, 'I love you more now than I ever loved Lizann. I suppose it's a back-handed compliment, but I mean it, and I'll never mention her name again.' He turned to leave, then looked back. 'Will Mary Ann let you come with me to get the engagement ring?'

'It's hardly worth bothering with that when we're getting married so soon. A wedding ring's all I want.'

Before Katie went to bed, she peeped into Mary Ann's room. 'Are you not sleeping yet, Grandma?'

'How can a body sleep wi' folk kissing and speaking about love and weddings outside her window?'

Katie smiled blissfully. 'Are you not pleased for me?'

'I'll not be pleased till the knot's really tied.'

'It'll be tied, Grandma, don't have any doubts about it. George won't let me down now, and we'll have a long, happy married life with at least six bairns.'

'That'll make me a great-grandmother.' Mary Ann did not appear to be displeased about this as she stifled a yawn.

The marriage ceremony took place quietly in the house, Katie in a dusty pink dress George had got his mother to buy for her, and he in a new navy suit. Mary Ann and Ina Green – bullied into it and warned by her son not to make trouble – were witnesses, and Doctor Fleming gave Katie away. After their first kiss as husband and wife, the radiant couple handed round glasses of the whisky George had bought, and slices of the beautifully iced cake which was a gift from John Walker, the baker.

The Reverend and Mrs Taylor left first, followed by the doctor and his wife, Mrs Fleming saying, as she went out, 'You were the best maid I ever had, Katie, and I'm so glad you've found happiness at last.'

George sat with Mary Ann while his mother and Katie washed up in the kitchen. 'I wasna ower pleased about my George wedding you,' Ina told her new daughter-in-law. 'I'm a bit old-fashioned about folk being illegitimate, you see.'

Katie was puzzled. 'I'm not illegitimate. My father and mother were married, and so were my Grandma and Granda.'

Ina sighed. 'Well, I'll hold my tongue, for it's ower late to do anything about it. You're my son's wife now, and I'll have to accept it.'

Katie swallowed the retort that she felt like making. She didn't like George's mother any more than the woman liked her, but for his sake she would do her best to get on with her. 'Thank you, Mrs Buchan,' she murmured.

'I've nothing against you as a lassie,' Ina continued, a trifle self-consciously, 'and you've a hard life wi' Mary Ann by all accounts, and likely she'll make you jump to her bidding for years, so if you want to call me Mother . . . ?'

Katie smiled. Mother was not what she wanted to call this scraggy, unpleasant woman, but loyalty to George made her say, 'I'll try, but give me time to get used to it.'

Mrs Buchan became her usual brisk self again. 'Aye, we'll all need time to get used to this. Now, you'd best get back to your man, for he'll wonder what we're speaking about.'

Katie wondered if he knew what his mother thought of her, but she did not bring up the subject when at last they were left alone. It was enough that they were married, and she was determined to be a good wife to him. She looked up at him as they cuddled in the old armchair which had once been her grandfather's. 'What are you thinking about, George?'

'Nothing much, just how happy I am.'

'It's the happiest day of my whole life.'

'I wish we could have had a honeymoon, though.'

'I don't need a honeymoon.'

'I'll give you the next best thing. I've signed on with Alickie May, starting his next trip. They fish for cod off Iceland, and they're just away ten days at a time, so I'll be home a lot more. Does that please you?'

'Oh, yes, I was dreading you being away for months.'

'I wasn't looking forward to it myself.'

Their lips had just met when the summons came. 'Have you two forgot about me?'

'Don't heed her,' Katie muttered.

George pulled her to her feet. 'We've got all our lives to kiss, Katie lass.'

'When am I getting my supper?' Mary Ann demanded, when they went through.

'When I'm good and ready,' Katie retorted.

Turning to George, the old woman said, plaintively, 'You see what I've to put up wi'? Like I said once afore, she needs a man to keep her in about, so the quicker you start, the better.'

Giving a laugh, George took Katie round the waist and bent her back to give her a long kiss, then he looked impishly at Mary Ann. 'My wife has other things than cooking on her mind right now, so how about me getting some fish and chips?'

'That would do fine.'

When he went out, the old woman said, 'He'll be a good man to you, Katie.'

'I know, Grandma, so don't spoil it for me.'

'Me?' Mary Ann looked hurt. 'How could I spoil it?'

'Give us some time to enjoy being married, that's all I ask. If you keep interrupting us when we're . . .'

'I'll not interrupt anything again. I'll lie here starving to death and not say a word.'

Mrs Buchan's odd remark coming back to her, Katie said, 'George's mother seemed to think I was illegitimate.'

'She's wrong, then, for your mother and father was married near a year afore you were born.'

'Why did you never tell me anything about them, Grandma?'

Mary Ann sighed deeply. 'Your grandfather was aye at me to tell you the truth, but I couldna hurt you. Now you've got a man to care for you, though, maybe I will, some day. Now, go through and get plates ready for the fish and chips.'

While she set the table and a tray, Katie puzzled over why her grandmother had said the truth about her parents would hurt her. Why was there such a mystery about them?

When she and George sat down to eat, he said, with a wry grin, 'I'd have liked to give you a better wedding feast.'

'It doesn't matter. I love fish and chips.'

Mary Ann passed no sarcastic remarks when they told her they were going to bed, and Katie's heart soared when they were in their own room and George said, 'Maybe our wedding day wasn't all we'd have liked, but we'll not say that about our wedding night, eh, Katie lass?'

He had been almost sure that she wasn't a virgin, but he couldn't help feeling let down when it was proved to him.

Chapter Twenty-six

❧❧

When Mary Ann suffered another seizure, Katie was thankful that George was at home. He could soothe the old woman much better than she could, agreeing with her even when she came out with outrageous accusations, for her brain had been left affected this time. Her eyes, if they weren't vacant, had a baleful look when they fell on her grand-daughter, as though she resented her being there, and Katie was often reminded of how unloved she had felt as a child. She had hated her grandmother then, and hate – a far worse, adult hate – was building up inside her again. It was as if the old woman had made herself helpless deliberately, for spite.

'She does it on purpose,' she told George one night, after she had risen out of bed for the fifth time to give Mary Ann the bedpan.

'She can't help it, Katie.'

'Yes, she can. She can't need it as often as that. She knows we're in bed, and she's just trying to spoil it.'

He gave a rueful smile. 'She is spoiling things, but she doesn't know what she's doing.'

'She's bound to know. She never cared how I felt.'

'You're over-tired, lass.' George put his arms around her, and held her tightly. 'Let me go to her next time.'

'A man can't do that kind of thing.'

'I wouldn't mind.'

'She'd mind! Oh, George, we've been man and wife for two months and we've hardly had one night's peace.'

His kiss was enough to set both their bodies on fire, but once again, the whining cry came before they could do more than caress each other. 'Ka–ayt–ie!'

'Bugger!'

Katie caught her breath at her husband's exclamation. 'You see, it's getting to you, and all, George.'

She stamped through to the other room. 'Grandma! You've just newly been, you can't be needing again!'

'I am needing again, but you've nae time for me now you've got a man.'

Hoisting her up, Katie rammed the bedpan under her. 'If you don't do anything, you can shout till you're blue in the face next time, and I'll not bother.'

'Did she do it?' George asked, when his wife rejoined him.

'Aye, she did. I don't know where it all comes from . . . I'll have to stop giving her so many cups of tea.'

They had gone much further than petting when the next cry came, and he exclaimed, 'Oh, God, I can't stop now.'

The call was repeated three times before being answered, and Mary Ann looked up at Katie angrily. 'I've wet the bed and it's your fault! I ken why you didna come, for I heard what you and him were doing.'

Thoroughly embarrassed, Katie had to ask George to help her change the sheets, then she said, 'I'd better stay with her. This is getting beyond a joke.'

Unwittingly, Katie had made a stick to break her own back, as George told her before he went to join the trawler again. 'I'm sick fed up having a wife that never sleeps with me,' were his last words as he slammed out.

Katie was not left long to cry in the kitchen, and when she answered the summons which came, she said, 'I just hope you're satisfied now! You've made George fight with me!'

All that day, Mary Ann was even more demanding than she had been before, hardly letting Katie out of her sight, and when the young woman sat down in the chair at the side of the bed in the early evening, she was so exhausted that she dozed off almost immediately. When the hand touched her arm about five minutes later, she had to drag herself out of a deep sleep. 'What is it?' she asked, petulantly.

'I just minded I promised to tell you about . . .'

Dropping with fatigue and lack of sleep, Katie snapped, 'I'm too tired to listen. Tell me in the morning.'

'I'd like some cocoa,' Mary Ann wailed.

Furious, Katie stamped into the kitchen and put a pan of milk on to heat, then after she had taken a cup through to her grandmother, she sat down by the fire to drink her own. Once she got the old besom settled, she thought, she would sit here for a while. Surely she'd get peace for half an hour or so?

Feeling quite relaxed, Katie stretched out her legs, and realized that she was cold. She opened her eyes and was astonished to see that the fire was out. Surely she couldn't have slept . . . ? But it was daylight . . . She glanced up at the clock and was dismayed to see that it was almost eight. More than twelve hours without a single call? Bounding out of the chair, she ran through to her grandmother's room.

When she saw Mary Ann lying with her eyes shut, her first reaction was one of relief that the old woman had managed to get one whole night's sleep at last, then something made her bend down to touch the brow, and when her fingers came in contact with the icy skin, she jerked them back in alarm. This was not slumber. This was death!

A terrible horror gripped Katie then. She had left Grandma – like she had left Sammy – to die with no one near to care, and she would be haunted by that for the rest of her life. Still looking down at the bed, she saw now that the face was waxen, but it was more peaceful than it had been for a long time. This kind of death couldn't be so very terrible, she thought. Neither of them would have felt anything, or known anything. They had fallen asleep and some time later, they had slipped away. She shouldn't reproach herself. Even if she had been sitting by the bed, there was nothing she could have done. She wouldn't even have been aware of the exact time of death.

Going into the kitchen, Katie raked out the fire and set it

with paper, sticks and cinders, then put a match to it, and when it was burning properly, she put on the kettle. She didn't feel guilty any longer, but she needed a cup of tea before she went to tell the doctor.

On first watch, George was thinking about his wife. He shouldn't have taken his frustration out on her, she wasn't responsible for Mary Ann's condition. No one was. If he could afford it, he would willingly pay for a woman to sit with the old woman all night, but it was impossible on what he would make from small fishing trips like this. If he was a skipper, things would be different, but he'd never be able to buy his own boat, so there would be no chance of sleeping with his wife until her grandmother died, and for all her tantrums, he didn't wish the old woman dead.

It was just as well he wasn't with the herring fleet now. Feeling the way he did, he'd be looking for a tart in the first port they stopped at. No, he corrected himself. He'd never do that again, not now he was married to Katie. It had been bad enough with Lizann, and he couldn't explain that, not even to himself. Was it possible to love two women at once? It must be, for his gut still twisted when he thought of Lizann with another man. He hadn't seen her wedding in the papers, though, so maybe she hadn't married her Peter. Maybe, if he went to Buckie when he got back next week . . . ? God, what was he thinking?

'Hey, George, you're away in a dream, man.'

He looked up at the skipper with a smile. 'I was thinking about my wife.' And so he had been originally, he assured himself somewhat guiltily.

'Oh, aye, I forgot. It'll still be new to you, but wait till you've been wed for twenty year like me, and you'll be glad to get away from her for a wee while.'

'We'd a bit of a row before I left.'

'You're surely not fighting with her already?'

311

'It's her grandmother. It's too complicated to explain.'

'Ach, it'll all come out right in the end, I'm sure.'

Watching the other man walking away, George felt better. Mary Ann couldn't carry on like that for long, and likely, by the time he went home, her mind would be back to normal.

'You couldn't let me have fifty pounds, could you?'

Beth frowned. 'I gave you thirty last week. If you've been gambling again, Dennis, I've a good mind to let you stew in your own juice.'

'Once I've squared up the bookies, I'll not go near them again, and that's a promise.'

'You've said that dozens of times before.'

'I mean it this time, Beth, honest! I kept thinking I'd hit a lucky streak, but . . .' Shrugging, he added, 'You know what they say – unlucky at cards, lucky in love, and the same goes for the gee-gees.' He slid his hand up her arm, smiling appealingly.

Heaving a resigned sigh, she picked up her handbag, took a wad of notes out of the inside zipped pocket and counted some into his hand. 'Ten, twenty, thirty, forty, fifty.' Noticing that his eyes had lit up greedily, she warned, 'And that's the last. You needn't bother asking for any more.'

'Thanks, Beth, you're an angel.'

'I'm a sucker.' She knew he was watching her put the other notes back in her bag, and guessed what he was thinking, but he wouldn't get away with it if he tried to get his sticky fingers on them, for she knew exactly how many were left.

'I feel like going to bed for an hour or so, how about you?' Dennis winked at her suggestively.

'On a Sunday afternoon?' She tried to sound shocked.

'The better the day, the better the deed. Come on, my dearest one, let Dennis give you a proper thank you.'

'I was going to look over your accounts.'

'Oh, come on, Beth,' he coaxed. 'I'll be cut to the quick if you prefer doing that to coming to bed with me.'

She gave in. She didn't have to check the books to know he'd been fiddling. The profits had decreased steadily for months though the restaurant was busier than ever, but she wasn't going to confront him just yet. What was more, she was almost sure he was taking up with other women, and she'd have to get proof before she accused him of that. Besides – she still loved the thieving blighter, God help her.

The stir of the preparations and the funeral itself were over now, and Katie was sitting forlornly in the kitchen. It didn't feel right to have time to sit down when she kept imagining a voice calling for her. The house was like a morgue – no, she thought, sadly, not that, but it was cold despite the fire crackling up the chimney. If George had been at home, he would have got her out of this depression which had nothing to do with her bereavement – it was better that her grandmother was at peace – it was more a sense of foreboding. But he should be home for Christmas within a couple of days and everything would be all right.

Maybe she should clear out Mary Ann's things? That would be something to occupy her hands, and she might find the money she suspected the old woman had stashed away. When she had opened the tin to get money to provide the funeral tea, there had only been three pounds left, though Mary Ann had always said there was plenty more.

Although Katie emptied every drawer and shelf in Mary Ann's room, and laid everything on the bed ready to put in boxes to be thrown out, she found no secret cache, only another old tin with some papers in it. She took it through to the kitchen and sat down, tired and dejected. Why had she let the undertaker talk her into ordering an oak casket with brass handles and a brass plaque? Of course, she hadn't been thinking clearly at the time, and he had said it was what her grandfather had, but it was far too expensive. George had paid for everything since they were married, food, coal, paraffin, and had left her a few pounds to keep her going until he came back from sea. She couldn't expect him to pay for her grandmother's funeral as well, even if he did have enough money, which was unlikely.

She would have to sell the house, it was the only thing to do. George's mother would probably take them in until they could afford a place of their own, though she would tell everybody her daughter-in-law was feckless and couldn't face up to her responsibilities.

Remembering the old tin in her hand, she took off the lid to go through the papers. There was likely nothing important but she may as well look. On top, she found two blue birth certificates almost worn through at the folds, one for Mary Ann Bruce and the other for William John Mair. Under them was their marriage lines, and another birth certificate in the name of William John Mair, white this time and dated 1888, which must be her father's. Slipped inside this was a scribbled note in her grandmother's writing. 'William John wed Elizabeth Baxter in Portknockie on 20th December 1905', it read. So that had been her mother's name, Katie thought, pleased that she now knew at least that much about her.

But there was something else at the bottom of the tin – a piece of paper with a rusting safety pin stuck through it. She thought at first that it was blank, but when she looked closely, she could just make out the faded writing. 'This is your granddaughter. Her name is June.' Uncomprehending – the name meant nothing to her – she returned everything to the tin and went to bed.

The cost of the funeral niggled at her again as soon as her head touched the pillow, but a far greater worry hit her some minutes later. The note in the tin had obviously been pinned to some infant's clothing . . . but whose infant . . . and why? When the answer struck her, Katie was left gasping like a fish out of water, and a great sickness surged up inside her. Almost

314

paralysed with shock, she was certain that the baby had been the grandchild Mary Ann had taken in after its mother died ... June, not Katie!

Her thoughts jumped around wildly, trying to make some sense of it, until, at last, shivering with cold, she rose and went through to the kitchen. It was only half past two, and the embers in the fire were still glowing, so she piled on some sticks to make it burn up. Waiting for the kettle to boil, she took out the little note again. June? It was this girl who was the rightful owner of the house ... unless ... had she died as a baby? Had Mary Ann been so upset about it she got another infant from some poor unmarried girl to replace her? Was that why there had been so much secrecy about her birth? Was Katie Mair not Katie Mair at all? Was she Katie something else? George's mother had been right. She was illegitimate!

With a shuddering sigh, she stood up to put a spoonful of tea in the pot, then poured in enough water to fill one cup. By the time she sat down to drink it, she was beginning to feel angry. She shouldn't have been left to discover a thing like this at such a time. She should have been told when she was old enough to understand, and not been allowed to think that the house would belong to her. Just the same, who would know she wasn't the rightful heir? She had been raised as a Mair, everybody thought she was a Mair – damn it all! She *was a Mair*, no matter what!

Going back to bed, she slept like a log, and it was almost eight o'clock before she got up, refreshed and determined to clear out the whole house so that it could be sold. She went up to the grocer first to get some tea-chests then set about her task. She weeded out all the items she thought should be thrown out and put them in a big pile in the backyard. Then she packed the rest in the boxes. If George's mother didn't have room to store the things until they got a house, the Salvation Army would be glad of them, or she could give them to the Seamen's Mission.

315

She was so engrossed that it was half past three in the afternoon before she felt hungry and made herself a slice of toast and a pot of tea, then, anxious to be finished before she lost her nerve, she set to again. Only once did she falter, when she came across William John's sail-making tools tucked away in a corner of the press. Her grandfather – she would always think of him as that whether or not he'd been any relation to her – would be horrified if he knew she was planning to usurp someone else's birthright. The moment passed, however, and, squaring her shoulders, she carried on. If Granda hadn't been able to make his wife tell her the truth, he should have told her himself . . . but maybe they had become accustomed to thinking of her as their grandchild.

It was almost nine o'clock when she finally stopped. There were still some odds and ends to be packed, things she was using, but that wouldn't take long. Her back felt as if it would never be straight again, and her eyes were stinging with the dust she had disturbed in her all-out onslaught, but she had accomplished what she set out to do.

She was enjoying a cup of tea, letting it swill round her dry mouth and slake her parched throat, when the door was pushed open. 'George!' she cried, and promptly burst into floods of tears.

He rushed over to her. 'What's wrong, Katie lass?'

'Oh, God!' he groaned, when he learned that Mary Ann was dead. 'I'm sorry I wasn't here for you.' He knelt down at the side of her chair and put his arms round her, holding her trembling body against his chest. 'Oh, lass, I'm sorry. It must have been terrible for you.'

It was not until her sobbing stopped that he noticed that the room was bare. 'What happened?' he asked. 'Where's all the ornaments . . . and the cushions . . . Katie . . . ?'

'I'll have to sell the house.' she whispered. 'for there's no money left to pay for the funeral.'

Letting his arms fall, he stood up. 'What I made this trip wouldn't be enough, I don't suppose, and we'd have to wait till after my next trip before we got any more. But stop fretting, lass. If we've to give up this place, we can move in with my mother till I can afford to get another house.'

She hadn't meant to tell him the rest, but it spilled out of her – the money Mary Ann had made out there was but which hadn't turned up, Mary Ann's note, the slip of paper with the safety pin. 'I'm not who I thought I was,' she sobbed, 'and I don't know who I really am, and I'll be stealing if I keep the money I get if I sell the house.'

Even though his mind was in a turmoil with the things she had told him, he could understand how anxious she must be about her identity. 'You've no idea who this June is?'

'No, I've never heard of her before. I think she must have died, and they got me instead, but Grandma did say the house would come to me.'

'It's a real puzzler, but if she said you were to get the house, it's yours, Katie, and the money you get for it would belong to you.'

'You're not just saying that to stop me worrying?'

'No, I'm sure I'm right. Now, we'd something to eat the time we were settling up, and I'm not hungry, so what about going to bed? You'll feel better in the morning.'

It was the first night they had ever been alone in the house, but Katie thought she could feel her grandmother's ghost hovering over her, telling her she had no right to sell it, and she would be stealing if she kept the proceeds. She was thankful that George just held her in his arms and expected nothing of her.

Chapter Twenty-seven

❧❧

First thing next morning, George went out to buy some rolls, and while they were having breakfast, he said, 'If you'd waited till I got home, I'd have given you a hand to clear things out.'

More relaxed than she had been the previous night, Katie smiled. 'It's all done, except the loft, and Granda used to say there was just a lot of rubbish up there.'

'I'll make a bonfire and we can burn what you don't want to keep. We'll get started after we do the dishes.'

When they went up the rickety ladder William John had kept outside, Katie was astonished at the amount of things lying about. 'It's like Aladdin's cave,' she gasped.

'Nothing valuable, though,' George said, ruefully, lifting some old books. 'Love stories,' he added in disgust, laying them down near the open trapdoor.

'They can't have been Grandma's, any road, for she didn't know anything about love.' Katie looked thoughtful as she remembered something. 'She did say once she'd another lad before Granda, but maybe she made it up.' Recalling that it had been at the time when she was upset that George had quarrelled with her about Sammy, she didn't elaborate.

By lunchtime, George had built a big heap of junk in the yard ready to burn. 'We'd best stop for a wee while,' he puffed. 'I'm peching like an old horse with going up and down that ladder, and I could do with something to eat.'

'You should have let me carry something down.' Katie banged her hands against her skirt to get rid of the dust. 'I could take this box of rusty keys, goodness knows what they're for and they'll have to be thrown out. What do you want to eat? Will I run up to the baker for hot pies?'

'That'll do fine, and I'll go through this old kist till you come back.'

When she called him some ten minutes later, he came down with an old brass sextant in his hand. 'This should be worth a good bit,' he told her.

'Granda never went to sea, it must have been his father's, or his grandfather's.'

'We could sell it to an antique shop. We'd have to clean it up first, of course, though I'd like fine to have kept it. If ever I get my own boat – but there's not much hope of that. There's a sewing box, and all, a real bonnie bit of work, rosewood inlaid with mother-of-pearl, I think.'

'That's likely Grandma's, so put it on the bonfire.'

'Oh, Katie, it's too good to burn. Do you not want to keep it to remind you of her?'

'I want nothing of hers – she never wanted me here.'

'Don't be bitter, Katie. She must have wanted you when she took you in.'

'I can't help it, and I still feel guilty about selling the house. It's not mine to . . .'

'Mary Ann said it was yours.'

Noticing an edge to his voice, Katie thought, morosely, that the old woman was going to come between them yet.

They said no more, and went silently up the ladder again to clear away the remaining bits and pieces. At last, only the old sea chest was left, and they took a handle each and manoeuvred it down the ladder. Lifting the sewing box he had set on the table, George offered it to Katie, who snapped, 'I told you I didn't want it! Put it on the bonfire.'

She moved away to turn the piece of meat she had bought at the butcher's when she was out and had put in the oven to cook, and George sat down with the sewing box still in his hand. After a moment, he removed the sectioned tray holding the needles and threads, scissors and tape measure, and looked into the compartment underneath. 'Katie! Come here!'

'What is it? I was going to pare some tatties.'

'You'd better come and look at this. It's a bankbook.'

'So that's where she had her money.' Katie went to look, her eyes almost popping out of their sockets when she saw her name on the inside of the cover as the holder of the account. What they discovered in the next instant staggered them both, although there was only one entry. It showed that, on 1st July 1907, a deposit of £1500 had been made.

'It looks like Granda must have done it not long after they got me,' Katie gasped. 'Why, George? I'm no relation.'

'You must be. Oh, Katie, you'll not have to sell the house after all.'

'But I can't understand it.'

'There's no doubt about it. It's in your name, so it's all yours.'

While Katie puzzled over it, George slipped his hand into the sewing box again and drew out a fat envelope. 'It's for you,' he murmured.

She took out the pages to lay them on the table so that they could read them together. 'It's Grandma's writing,' she said, tremulously.

Dear Katie,

You will be well on your way to the Howe of Fenty now and with your grandfather out of the way, I am writing what I should have told you years ago, and I have to go back a long way so you can understand why I couldn't. Andrew Baxter and me fell in love when I was sixteen, he was from Portknockie but we went steady till he had to go back to sea. He said he would wed me when he came home from the herring, so I got the banns cried and everything ready. On Hogmanay, one of the lassies made me go with her to a dance and I let her brother see me home, for it was a wild and stormy night. That was all, but when I told Andrew he would not believe me, and he wed another lassie instead.

He broke my heart and I never got over him, and I wed your grandfather out of spite, really, though I did come to care for him. Any road, you can imagine how I felt when our son took a girl home, for her name was Lizzie Baxter and she was Andrew's daughter. I hated her for that, and I would not go to their wedding, and I never went to see her all the time she was carrying, not even when your father came and told me she had a bad time at the birth.

A month after that, your grandfather found an infant in a basket at our door one morning. There was a note pinned to the shawl. This is your grand-daughter, it said, her name is June. I made him go to their house, but they had gone away. We never found out where they went and we never heard from them.

I thought June was too fancy, so I called you Katie, after my grandmother, she was a strong-minded woman and I have the feeling you have grown up the same. I loved you from the minute I held you in my arms, but I could not show it, for I was ashamed at how I treated your mother. The only thing I could think on was put money in the bank for you, so you would be independent after I died. It was what my grandfather left me, he was captain of a whaler. The sextant was his, and the sewing box was my grandmother's.

It has helped me to write everything down, for it has been on my conscience, and I hope it will help you as well, but I will hide it away so you will not get it till I am gone. I was a foolish bitter woman, Katie, and I hope what is in the bank will help you to forgive me for the things I did.

I am, as I always have been,
Your loving grandmother,
Mary Ann Mair

Looking at her husband in amazement when they came to the end, Katie gulped, 'After all the bad things I thought about her . . . oh, George! Why didn't she tell me before?'

He took her hand. 'Aye, she should have. But it means you really were her grand-daughter, and you'll not have to sell the house when you've got all this money.'

Katie was not to be consoled. 'But I was nasty to her at the end, when she couldn't help being the way she was.'

'Aye, that'll be hard for you to bear, but she brought it on herself, when all's said and done. If you'd known she loved you, you'd have felt different. Look, lass, you've had as much as you can take, so I'll pare the tatties for you.'

When they had eaten – Katie only picking at the beef – she said, in a small voice, 'I want to be by myself for a wee while, George. You wouldn't mind if I went out, would you?'

'No, but are you sure you're fit to be out on your own?'

'I just want a minute or two.'

She walked along the shore for the first time in months. It felt strange to be sitting in the same old place looking out to sea, not like it used to do. She didn't know what to say, for she couldn't voice the thoughts that were coiling round inside her brain, each one twisting through another until it seemed they were in a knot she could never unravel. The letter had made her understand why her Grandma had been unable to speak of her love, for there came a point when it was impossible to communicate – she had reached it herself – and she wondered if she could transmit what was in her mind to the Three Kings.

Katie was oblivious to the passing of time, but gradually she could feel her thoughts untangling – or had her attempt at telepathy succeeded? 'I know who I am,' she reflected, aloud, 'and why Granda and Grandma brought me up. The only thing I don't know is where my mother and father are, but if they didn't want me before, they won't want me now, and I don't care. I don't need them.'

'I guessed this is where you'd be,' came a quiet voice from behind her.

She did not look round. 'George, I don't feel right about having all that money. I don't deserve it after what I used to think about Grandma. Should I give it away?'

Sitting down, he picked up a handful of sand and let it trickle through his fingers. 'Mary Ann meant it for you, but if you want to give it away, I'll not stop you. Pay for her funeral and do what you like with the rest of it.'

Still concentrating her eyes on the three blurring shapes, she was acutely conscious of her husband waiting silently beside her. She had a sudden urge to do something for him, to prove how much she loved him, to prove to her grandmother that she was strong-minded and could stick to any decision she made. Drawing her feet towards her, she clasped her hands round her knees. 'I know what I'll do.'

'Whatever you say, it'll be all right with me.'

'I'll give you the money, so you can buy your own boat.'

'Oh, no! I couldn't let you do that, Katie.'

'You said I could do what I wanted with it.'

'But not that!'

'Not even if it makes me happy? Please, George?' Jumping to her feet, she put out a hand to help him up. 'My mind's made up, and it's time we went home.'

He put his arm round her waist as they strolled back to the house. 'I was thinking when you went out, there would be . . . um . . . over twenty-three years' interest to go on to what's in the bank. I wouldn't be surprised if it was nearer two thousand by this time, maybe more.'

'You'll be able to get a bigger boat, then.'

'Are you sure that's what you want to do with it?'

'I've never been surer about anything.'

'I've always dreamt of having my own boat . . .'

'Well, then, that's it settled!'

'I'd have to see about how to get my skipper's ticket. I know I'll have to pass tests and prove I can . . .'

'You can ask Alickie May about it tomorrow, and you can go to the shipyards in Buckie to see about buying a boat, and all, and I'll start unpacking again.'

No ghosts bothered her that night, and it was a very happy, and very satisfied, Katie who murmured, just before she went to sleep, 'I don't care how much you've to pay to get a decent boat, as long as you call it the *Mary Ann*.'

Betty knew that Angus was going to the woods every day. All his shoes, except his best pair, had mud on the soles, or moss, depending on the weather, and she had picked up some twigs around the house. She'd been glad that he was taking walks to pass his time, but tonight, when she came up to their bedroom to change out of her shop clothes, she had noticed a few bits of bark on the next flight of stairs, which made her feel most uneasy.

'What were you doing up in the attics?' she asked when she returned to the kitchen.

His smile was quite open. 'I sometimes go up there and sit for a while. It's a change from sitting down here.'

She let it go at that. It had been a long winter, so it must have been boring for him being on his own all day, and he was probably telling the truth. Now spring had come, he would get out more.

Angus went to bed first and was asleep when she went up, so she undressed as quietly as she could and slid in beside him. He had been restless these past few nights and she did not want to disturb him. She lay quite still, thinking about the salesman she had employed a few months earlier. He had been by far the best applicant for the job, but she should not have taken him on, for she had felt attracted to him even then, and he felt the same about her, if she was any judge . . . not that he'd said anything. He was an honourable man and, although he was a widower, he would not let himself get involved with another man's wife.

Her mind on Henry Ferguson, Betty inadvertently dug Angus in the back with her elbow when she turned round, and was astonished when his hands lashed out at her. 'God damn you, Katie!' he roared. 'Keep still!'

She remained absolutely motionless, scarcely daring to breathe until she was certain that he had not wakened. She had thought he had forgotten Katie completely, but he must have been dreaming about her. A new suspicion forming in her mind, she knew she couldn't settle until she found out what he had been doing in the attics, so, edging herself out of bed, she crept across the room on tiptoe and closed the door behind her as quietly as she could.

They had had electricity installed some time previously, and although there was no switch in what had been Katie's room, the light from the stairs showed enough to make her sick with horror. Lined against one wall were sticks of varying sizes, on the chair next to the bed was a leather whip, and on the bed itself there were two coils of rope. Bile swirled into her mouth as comprehension came to her. Angus was still planning to take vengeance on Katie, and he must be acting out his fantasies even though she wasn't there.

Creeping downstairs, Betty stood outside the bedroom door wondering if she should chance going back to bed, or if she should get away from Angus Gunn altogether. He had told her when he was convalescing from the heart attack that he had been invalided out of the army during the war with a head wound, so maybe it had affected his brain. Or had he been born unstable, like his son? This line of thought presented her with another solution to her problem. She could have him certified and put away – the instruments of torture would be evidence enough.

But Angus was too clever to be trapped. He could probably fool even the most experienced psychiatrist into believing that he was involved in conducting some experiment . . . say, testing the durability of a mattress, or something like that. He would be proved sane, and maybe he was sane, except where

Katie was concerned. He was doing no harm to anyone, Betty concluded, and lots of men had secret fantasies, so it might be best to let him get his out of his system. It wouldn't affect her as long as he did it while she was at work.

Thank goodness for the shop, she thought, as she went back to bed shivering with cold. It took her out of the house for hours on end, although she did feel guilty at how her pulses speeded up every time Henry Ferguson squeezed past her to show something to a customer. Worse still, when she and her husband were sitting by the fire in the evenings, she sometimes let herself imagine Henry taking her in his arms. She was every bit as bad as Angus, really, though his mind was filled with a need for revenge and hers merely with imagining a romance that could never be, like a young girl.

It seemed they both had dreams, and she shouldn't judge him too harshly.

Chapter Twenty-eight

❧❧

1931

Before they set off for home, the skippers of many of the trawlers landing at Peterhead gravitated to a restaurant after settling with their crews, not only to have something decent to eat, but also to compare catches and have a good chinwag with others they knew. They generally ordered wine with their meal, had a glass of brandy or whisky afterwards and left generous tips for the waitresses, so Dennis McKay made a point of being friendly to those who came to Le Denis.

The latest arrivals seemed to be in high spirits, so he went over to talk to them – good humour meant good catches, good catches meant they had money to burn. 'Good afternoon, gentlemen. I hope everything is satisfactory?'

The oldest, jolliest one looked up and laughed. 'Aye, as always. I wish the wife could cook like this.'

Dennis let his eyes travel round the table, stopping when he saw an unfamiliar face. 'I haven't seen you in before, Mr . . . er . . . ?'

'George Buchan. No, I couldn't afford your prices before I got the *Mary Ann*.'

Dennis had a fund of questions to gain information which may, or may not, prove useful, and the boat in question was new and quite impressive. 'The *Mary Ann*? Would that be your wife's name, or your girlfriend's?'

'We called her after my wife's grandmother. She left a lot of money to Katie.'

Not by one flicker of a facial muscle did Dennis show that the names meant anything to him, but his fertile brain was working at full speed. Katie? With a grandmother called *Mary Ann*? It couldn't be coincidence, but he had to make sure. 'Are you a . . . Lossiemouth man, Mr Buchan?' He felt that it wouldn't do to be accurate in his supposed guess.

'No, I'm from Cullen.'

Hard pressed to contain his excitement, Dennis said, 'I hope to see you again next time you're in Peterhead.'

'I'm sure you will,' George smiled.

Dennis went into his small office mentally rubbing his hands with glee. Speak about landing on his feet! Katie Mair – no, Katie Buchan now – had money, a lot of money! And her husband had his own boat. A constant supply of money! The last time Beth had paid what he owed to the bookies, she had said it was definitely the last, though she'd been saying that from the first time he asked her. But he wouldn't need to ask again, for he had just learned of a new, bottomless, source of supply, and what was more, it had been handed to him on a plate – one of his own plates.

The *Mary Ann* had been so successful that George and Katie now had a joint bank account – he had been adamant about that since buying the trawler had practically emptied the one her grandmother had taken out for her. They had only a few hundred pounds so far, but that would soon grow. George, of course, had suggested having running water put in, and a bathroom, but she had said, 'Don't waste money on this old place. Once we start a family, we'll have to move.'

'There's brains inside that pretty head,' he had laughed.

She was truly happy, Katie thought one morning, as she rubbed wax polish into the already gleaming old furniture. Letting George buy his own boat was the best thing she could have done. He'd had to study for his skipper's ticket and learn all about navigation, but he had passed the tests the Board set in time to take over the *Mary Ann* when it was built. From the first, he had landed at Peterhead, where prices for fish were better, and he handed over everything he made to her, apart from what he spent when he went to some fancy restaurant for a meal with the other skippers. She didn't mind him treating himself; he worked hard enough for it, and his crew respected him for mucking in at all the jobs, and for always being fair with them when it came to the settling up.

She went to answer the knock at her door with a smile on her face. 'Mrs Buchan?' Her hand flew to her mouth, which had dried up the second she saw who it was. 'What do you want here?' she mumbled.

Dennis grinned. 'You're not going to leave an old friend standing on the doorstep, are you?'

He pushed past her, and she had no option but to close the door behind her. 'How did you know where I was?'

Sitting down, he studied his manicured nails with assumed nonchalance. 'I know everything about you, my dear Katie.'

'I'm not your dear, and how do you know?'

'A restaurateur learns a lot.'

'A restaur . . . oh, is it your place George speaks about, the place with the funny name . . . Leedinnie, isn't it?'

'He does come in to Le Denis for meals.'

'How did you know he was married to me?'

'That would be telling, but don't worry, I haven't said a word to him about our previous . . . entanglement.'

'Thank God.'

'So you didn't tell him yourself? That's good news.'

'I don't understand.'

'You will, Katie. Why don't we sit down and have a chat?'

She knew that he was up to something, and perched uneasily on the edge of a chair. 'We've nothing to chat about.'

'Oh, but we have. Let me bring you up to date. I married money, which is why I now run my own restaurant, and I've been living the good life, but, unfortunately, my wife is clamping down on me. She disapproves of my gambling.'

'And your women, I suppose?' Katie interrupted, bitterly.

'That, too. Anyway, she's refusing to pay my debts, and to be frank, Katie, I'm desperate for cash.'

The penny dropped. 'If you think you'll get money out of me, you've another think coming.'

'I don't *think*, Mrs Buchan, I know I will.'

'You won't, for I've none to give you.'

'Come, come, Katie. I believe your grandmother left you very well provided for.'

'She left me quite a lot, but I paid her funeral out of it, and I gave George the rest to buy his boat.'

'Oh.' This had not occurred to him. 'But he's a prosperous skipper, so there must always be plenty coming in.'

'We're saving to buy a better house.' Katie bit her lip in anger at herself for letting him know they had any savings.

'We . . . ? A joint account, I hope?'

'Yes, but . . .'

'There's no problem, then, is there? I'm not greedy. Fifty pounds, that's all I want.'

'Fifty pounds? You must be mad!'

'Never been saner, my dear Katie. Fifty pounds, or I'll tell your darling hubby all about us.'

Recalling how jealous George had been about Sammy, Katie was afraid to take any chances. She could put £50 back bit by bit from the house-keeping money and he would never know. 'I'll have to take it out of the bank.'

Beaming with satisfaction, Dennis leaned back and watched her taking the passbook out of the dresser drawer. 'No need to hurry, Katie, I can wait.'

Sweat dripping from his brow, Angus Gunn let the whip fall to the floor, his brain clearer than it had been for many months. There was no one there! He had been lashing an empty bed and the screams had only been inside his head. But why on earth had he been doing it? Was he going insane?

He sat down on the chair and took great gulps of air into

his lungs, waiting until his overstrained heart stilled and his stomach muscles untensed. He must stop this nonsense. It *was* nonsense. Catching sight of the sticks ranged against the wall and the ropes lying on the floor, he had a moment's panic. What would Betty think if she saw them? He would have to hide them somewhere.

Two hours later, sitting sedately in the kitchen, he turned to smile at his wife when she came in. 'Have you been busy today, my dear?'

She thumped down on a seat. 'Rushed off our feet.'

'Your assistant is coping, I hope?'

'Henry's very good, a natural salesman.'

Angus was surprised at the little thread of jealousy that looped round his heart at the softness of her eyes when she spoke of this other man. 'You think a lot of him?'

'I couldn't think any more of him.' Having been caught off guard, Betty added quickly, 'As an employee, not a person.'

The afterthought was obviously to put him off the scent, Angus guessed, and wondered if he ought to go back to the shop himself to get rid of his rival. But he couldn't bear to stand all day again, and besides, he was not sure if he was mentally capable of coping with the pressures. 'Have you noticed anything odd about me recently, Betty?'

'What do you mean, odd?'

'Unnatural behaviour. I sometimes wonder if my mind is . . .'

'If you've been speaking to yourself again, it's nothing. It's because you're on your own so much.'

'I found myself actually *doing* something today – I cannot tell you what, it was so foolish – and I was not conscious of doing it until I caught myself with the . . .' He halted, confused.

'I haven't noticed anything,' she soothed. 'Your memory maybe slipped a bit. It happens when we grow older. I often can't remember why I've opened a cupboard, or why I've gone upstairs.'

He was relieved that his wife did not consider that his brain was disintegrating. She would tell him if she thought it was. But who had he thought he was whipping?

Each time Dennis returned, his demands grew, and with having to buy new oilskins for George, sea-boot stockings and thin underclothes for the summer, Katie had watched their bank balance sink lower and lower. The *Mary Ann* had hit a bad patch, never finding the best shoals of fish, and after George had paid his crew – he didn't make them suffer for his ill fortune – he hadn't much left to hand over to her.

'You'll have to take something out of the bank to keep you going,' he had told her after the first poor trip. 'It's a good thing we'd something at our back, and we can make it up when my luck turns.'

When he was at sea, she lived on bread and margarine, and burned sticks from the shore to save coal, even going whole days without a fire, she was so determined not to take more out of their account, and always at the back of her mind was the fear that he would find out how low their bank balance was. But over-riding that was the fear of what Dennis would do when she told him she had nothing left.

She knew when to expect him – he always turned up the day after George sailed, so he must watch for the *Mary Ann* going out – and when he arrived, she took out the bankbook and showed it to him. 'That's all there is.'

'Only ten pounds? That's a fleabite, but I'll take it for now. I expect you to get some from somewhere before I come back, though. It shouldn't be hard for a lovely young woman with a body like yours to earn some – there's always plenty of men ready to pay for a quick thrill.'

'Damn you, Dennis!' she cried. 'You needn't bother coming back, for I'll have no money – not even to buy food!'

His sneering eyes hardened. 'I warn you, Katie, if you don't give me something, I'll put your husband off his food next time he comes in for a meal, though he hasn't been in for a while. I'll tell him what we used to get up to, and I won't water it down.'

Katie ran to the bank, and after he charged out with two five-pound notes in his hand she wondered, hopelessly, what she should do. Blackmail was a criminal offence, but if she reported him to the police, she would have to tell them why he was blackmailing her, and George would find out anyway. The sensible thing would be to tell him herself, but how could she, when she knew how he would react?

When George came home that weekend, his face was grim. 'It never rains but it pours. Another poor catch, poor prices for what we did get, and to crown all, my mind wasn't on what I was doing, and I rammed the boat against the harbour wall when I was taking her in. The *Mary Ann*'s got a bloody big hole in her, and I'd better take a hundred out of the bank in case the shipyard asks for something in advance. I only hope the repair doesn't clear us right out.'

Without a word, she opened the drawer and handed him the passbook, bracing herself for the explanation she would have to give.

He turned the pages with satisfaction. 'It soon mounts up when you're putting in regularly. It's a shame we'll have to use it, but we can start saving again once . . .' He broke off as he turned the next page. 'What the hell – balance nil? And why have you made all these withdrawals? You couldn't have needed all that for housekeeping. What's been going on, Katie?'

'You'd better sit down,' she whispered, tearfully, 'but I wish I'd told you months ago.'

When she came to a trembling halt, George roared, 'So your fancy man was blackmailing you? You must have been laughing up your sleeve when I was jealous of that half-wit, when it was another man you'd been carrying on with.'

Her heart battering against her ribs, her insides heaving,

she cried, 'I was frightened to tell you. You left me when I told you about Sammy, remember?'

'I should never have come back to you, but I'll not be so stupid this time.'

'Oh, George,' she sobbed, 'it was years ago, before I was in love with you. Please, please, don't leave me.'

'You'll not get round me again, you and your lies! You swore you'd never been with a man, but you weren't a virgin. I thought it was Sammy, but why didn't you tell me about this one? Who is he? I'll knock the truth out of him.'

Thankful that she hadn't named Dennis, or said that he ran George's favourite restaurant in Peterhead, Katie told a further lie. 'I don't know where he lives now, or where he works. He just turns up.'

'It doesn't matter. I know enough to see you're not the kind of girl I should have taken as a wife.'

She followed him into the bedroom, tears still streaming down her cheeks. 'What are you going to do?'

'It's a good thing I didn't empty out my things. I'm going to my mother, then I'll likely go to Buckie, to Lizann. At least I know I was first with her. One of my crew happened to mention that he came from the Yardie the same as her, and when I asked him how she was liking married life he said she didn't marry her lad after all.' Swinging his seabag over his shoulder, he stared at Katie coldly. 'The next time you hear from me'll be through a solicitor!'

'George!' she pleaded. 'You can't end our marriage because of something I did years ago.'

'God Almighty, woman! You can't expect me to forget about this? You've cut the feet from under me, you're depriving me of my livelihood . . .'

'No, George, the *Mary Ann*'s yours! I gave her to you as a present.'

'I can't afford to have her repaired, and I want nothing to remind me what a bloody fool I was.' He lifted his reefer jacket and cap and charged out.

Left standing in the middle of the floor, Katie turned her eyes slowly to the slippers she had laid out to heat for him at the fireside. The intimacy of it raised a small glimmer of hope in her frozen heart. He had come back once before after they quarrelled, and he would come back this time, and all, once he cooled down. She would just have to be patient, and she had nothing to fear from Dennis, now George knew all about him. Everything would work out come time – it must!

Chapter Twenty-nine

Looking at Henry Ferguson as he was serving, Betty Gunn knew that she had never loved Angus. She had been drawn to him originally – had been mesmerized by him – because he was so different from any man she had ever met, like a brooding Rochester to her Jane Eyre, with the promise of great depths of passion in his mysterious dark eyes. The reality had not matched her expectations. The passion had been there for only a short time, slowly deteriorating to a desire for self-fulfilment, and she had long been aware that she was just a substitute in his twisted mind for the girl Katie, and sometimes, even for his first wife. It was inevitable, really, that she would fall in love with Henry . . . and, miraculously, he had admitted to loving her.

He was everything that Angus was not, a gentleman in the true sense of the word. In direct contrast to her husband's overpowering darkness, Henry was fresh-complexioned, fair-haired and only a little taller than herself. His soft blue eyes could hold her spellbound, and she sometimes felt like rushing up to him and kissing him in front of anyone who happened to be in the shop. He had nothing to lose if their love was uncovered, yet it was he who was careful. He had only agreed reluctantly when she suggested that they steal an hour once a week to be alone together.

So now, every Monday – the day they were never busy – they locked the shop at five and pulled down the blinds to save anyone seeing in. 'To safeguard your reputation,' Henry had said. He made her feel special, like a delicate flower that needed nurturing to bloom properly.

When his customer went out, Henry regarded her earnestly.

'We can't go on the way we've been doing, Betty. I thought
my life was over when I lost Edna, but you've given me . . .'
He paused briefly, and then said, sounding a little defiant
about it, 'We must stop all the secrecy, I don't want to degrade
our love by having a sordid little affair. I want to marry you,
and you had better tell your husband about us soon.'

She ought to have expected this, but it came as a complete
surprise, although she could see that it was the right thing,
the decent thing, to do. 'I'll have to choose the right time.'

'That doesn't sound as if you want to tell him.'

'You don't know Angus, Henry. He's so unbalanced . . .'

'If you're afraid he'll get violent, why don't we tell him
together? I can't bear the thought of you sleeping with him
again, so I'll come home with you tonight, and you . . .'

Her mouth went dry. 'Tonight?'

'We may as well. You can pack what you need while I tell
him, and then I'll take you away with me.'

Henry had to shift his attention to a man who walked in
at that moment, which gave Betty time to think. Why
shouldn't she grab at happiness when it was offered? Angus
would likely make them leave the shop, but after the scandal
broke there would be no customers, anyway. They'd be better
going somewhere else to start their life together.

Henry being free again, she murmured, 'All right, tonight,
though it seems awful to be doing something like this when
we're both in our forties.'

He grinned. 'The prime of our lives, my dear.'

It wasn't only their age that worried her, however. For the
rest of the afternoon, all she could think of was how Angus
would react.

George had not come back, and Katie had lost interest in
everything. She couldn't believe that he would condemn her
for what had happened before they were courting, and a faint
hope persisted that he would change his mind once he'd had

time to think things through properly. She didn't know if he had signed on someone else's boat or if he was still with his mother – she couldn't bear to think that he was living in Buckie with Lizann – so when someone knocked at the door, she ran to answer it, believing it was George and ready to welcome him home. Her heart sank when she saw who it was. 'Oh, it's you, Dennis.'

He laughed as he walked past her. 'You sound disappointed. Who were you expecting? Another lover? You must have learned a lot more about pleasing a man by this time. You know, when I'm in Queen Street in bed with my wife, I sometimes compare you with her and laugh at how innocent you were.'

Alarmed at the trend his thoughts were taking, and hoping it would stop him pestering her, Katie said, 'George found out our savings were all gone, and I'd to tell him why. You may as well leave, for there's nothing you can do to me now. He knows everything.'

'Everything? Are you sure? Does he know what you and Sammy got up to? You said he raped you, but my guess is you and him had been at it for years.'

'He did rape me!' Katie shouted, forgetting all caution in her anger at Dennis. 'It was all your fault . . . and I didn't know if it was his baby or . . .'

His eyes glittered at her abrupt, horrified stop. 'Now it all comes out,' he gloated. 'He put you up the spout? That's why you wouldn't let me touch you? Well, well!'

'It could have been yours,' she muttered.

'But you weren't sure. What did you do? Get rid of it?'

Realizing that she had placed an inescapable noose around her own neck, she nodded miserably.

'Better and better! Naughty, naughty Katie! I'm sure you don't want hubby to know that, though he'll be glad Sammy's dead and can't rape you again.'

Her heart cramping, she whispered, 'How did you know Sammy was dead?'

'A letter from Ladysbridge that Ella Brodie gave me to send on to you. I read it and burned it. Why should I pay a stamp for . . . ?'

'So that's why I never got it!' Katie cried. 'I thought the superintendent just made up an excuse for not notifying me. It was awful going to see him and finding out he'd died more than a year before. Oh, God! I hate you, Dennis McKay!' Her voice rose to a scream. 'I hate you! I hate you! Get out of my house!'

'Not so fast. Aren't you forgetting one little thing? If you don't cough up some cash, I'll tell Georgie boy you had to get rid of Sammy's baby.'

Beyond reason now, Katie yelled, 'I can't get any more and I wouldn't give it to you supposing I could! I'm going to do what I should have done the first time you showed your face here. I'm going to write to your wife!'

'She wouldn't believe you.'

Katie could detect a shade of doubt in his voice. 'I'll make sure she will. I'll tell her everything.'

This deflated him completely. 'You wouldn't?'

'I will! A man like you shouldn't be allowed to walk the streets.'

'Don't tell her, please, Katie?' He was begging now. 'You don't know what . . . she'll likely toss me out and I'll have nothing – no home, no job, no . . .'

'No wife, like I have no husband, for George walked out on me.' Katie strode over to the door and held it open. 'Go on! Get out of my sight!'

He made one last, feeble plea as he slunk past her. 'Oh, Katie, please? Don't write to my wife.'

She banged the door behind him then went over to take her writing pad and envelopes out of the dresser drawer.

Angus was about to carve the joint he had roasted when he heard the car door slam, and when he heard a second slam a moment later, he wondered if his ears had started to play tricks on him, as well as his brain. Then he laughed at his fears. Betty must have opened the door again to take out something she had forgotten. He lifted his head when his wife came in, his smile changing to a puzzled frown when he saw the man behind her. Their wary expressions warned him that he was in for a surprise – a very nasty surprise by the look of it.

'This is Henry Ferguson, Angus,' Betty said, a little too brightly, and when neither man made any acknowledgement of the introduction, she went on, less confidently, 'We thought . . . it would be best . . . to tell you together.'

His fingers closing more tightly around the knife, Angus snapped, 'Tell me what?'

Henry came forward now. 'I know this will come as a shock, Mr Gunn, and there is no easy way to say it. You see, Betty and I . . . well, we love each other, and we . . .'

'Love?' Angus shrieked, taking a menacing step towards him. 'You have the audacity to come into my house and tell me that you love my wife?'

'We couldn't help ourselves,' Betty cried.

His rough push sent her crashing against the table, and Henry, smaller though he was, grabbed him angrily by the shoulders. 'There was no need for that, Mr Gunn. We've been open about it, when we could easily have run off together without telling you . . .'

'Take your hands off me!' Trying feverishly to think what to do, Angus glowered at the interloper. If only his head would stop spinning, his ears stop buzzing, the red lights stop flashing behind his eyes . . .

What happened then was not clear to him. He did not know why the carving knife suddenly felt much heavier, as if some weighty object was attached to it, doing its best to drag him down. But he did not mean to let it. All he had to do was release his grip. Opening his hand, he felt the burden, whatever it was, sliding down his leg to the floor. Then his ears were assaulted by eerie screams and he put his hands over them to shut out the noise.

It was no use, he could still hear it. Dropping his arms, he saw that it was coming from his wife and he wondered why she was kicking up such a din. She was kneeling on the floor beside a strange man, who was lying flat on his back with something sticking out of his chest. Her fiendish screams tailing off, she turned her head. 'You've killed him,' she moaned. 'You've killed Henry.'

Angus bent over calmly and pulled the handle, wincing when he saw blood dripping from the blade down on to his clothes. Revolted, he raised his arm to fling it from him, but before he could, Betty began to scream again.

Chapter Thirty

✤✤

Dennis had meant to be up in time to destroy Katie's letter before his wife saw it, but he had been so frantic with worry that he had not fallen asleep until the early hours. When he did wake up, it was too late, for Beth had already gone downstairs.

She greeted him with the usual kiss when he went into the kitchen. 'How do you feel this morning, Dennis?' she asked. solicitously.

'I'm a lot better.' He had relaxed a little at her easy manner, and tried to sound offhand as he said, 'Was there any mail today?'

'Nothing important.'

His spirits soared. That was all he needed to know, Katie had been bluffing. 'It's funny what a good night's rest can do,' he laughed, putting his arm round his wife's waist. 'I feel on top of the world. I even feel like taking you back to bed and . . .'

'Now, now,' Beth smiled, turning back to the cooker. 'Sit down and eat your breakfast. We can go to bed early tonight . . . if you still feel up to it.'

Having breakfast in the kitchen, Angus knew that there was something he should remember, if only his mind was clearer. He could not think where Marguerite was, but he had a vague feeling that she had gone off with another man, which should have distressed him since she had been frigid with him for most of their married life, but, strangely, did not upset him in the slightest. He had slept much later than usual, and whilst

342

shaving he had noticed that his old scar looked red and angry – he had become so used to it that he scarcely noticed it any more and could not think how he came by it.

Laying another slice of toast on his side plate, he looked at the pearl handle of the small knife already there. It was all wrong. It should have a bone handle and a much longer blade … He gave his head an irritated shake. Why on earth had that come into his mind? He tried to figure it out, but all he could think of was his breakfast. After spreading his toast lavishly with butter, he was biting into it when the image of a small pair of scissors lying against a skirting board swam into his consciousness.

The picture worried him, but no matter how hard he tried, he could not rid himself of it, and gradually other details came back to him. He had spotted the scissors one day months ago in one of the garrets. He could recall picking them up and burying them in the garden, but whose had they been? He was so bewildered that the answer eluded him, and he allowed the scene to unfold in his memory. He had returned to the garret and rifled through the chest of drawers, where he had unearthed some items of underwear – ladies' underwear – and, under the lining paper, a small amount of money which he had left untouched.

He had totally forgotten the incident until now, and was at a loss to think who had been the owner of the items. It must have been some woman – or a girl? A girl! Angus almost choked as the solution hit him with the impact of a sledge-hammer. Katie Mair! She had used the nail scissors to score his face! That was why he had the scar!

Unable to eat another mouthful, he leaned back in his chair, his innards bubbling as if they were fermenting in yeast. How could he have forgotten? It was his need to take retribution on her that had made him concentrate all his activities in the garret where she used to sleep. This was what he had been trying to remember – the reason for the ropes, the sticks, the whip! He had sometimes thought that it was Marguerite he was meaning to punish for the years she had withheld her favours, but it wasn't Marguerite at all, it was that flippertygibbet, Katie. He took a deep breath and was relieved that everything remained as clear to him as before. All he had to do was to bring Katie Mair to Fenty, and he was almost sure that he knew where to find her! It was all to the good that Betty was not here to stop him.

'Where did she put the car keys?' he muttered, when he stood up. 'They are usually lying on . . . yes, here they are.'

When he went outside, a strange car was sitting behind his, but he had something far more important on his mind than to fret about a trifle like that. When he opened the driver's door, his arm ached as if he had been overworking it, but so many unexplained things had been happening to him lately that he thought nothing of it. He was on his way to bring about the culmination of the hatred he had nursed for many years until his mind had betrayed him – and nothing else was of any consequence.

The letter would have been delivered this morning, Katie reflected – there could only be one Mrs Dennis McKay in Queen Street, Peterhead. Would she show it to Dennis and believe his lies when he denied everything? Or did she know he wasn't to be trusted?

Lifting the letter she herself had received, Katie read it again and was surprised that it didn't upset her as much as it had when she read it first. George had said the next time she heard from him would be through a solicitor, and he had meant it. He had a nerve, though, expecting her to divorce him so he could marry that Lizann he was living with – it just showed he had double standards. He had condemned her for sleeping with somebody she wasn't married to, but it was all right for him. She'd a good mind not to release him from the vows he had made on the day of their wedding, but what was the point? He would never come back to her.

Determined to submerge herself no longer in useless self-pity, Katie stood up to start on the housework she had neglected since her husband walked out, and the kitchen was shining spotlessly when someone knocked at the door two hours later. She contemplated not answering – it certainly wouldn't be George – but curiosity got the better of her. 'Mr Gunn!' she exclaimed, stepping back in alarm.

'You seem surprised to see me, Katie,' he smiled.

He looked much older, his face grey as if he had been ill, and there was something about his eyes that alerted her to danger and made her keep a firm grip on the half-open door. 'What do you want?'

'I came to . . . ask how Sammy is.'

Gathering that he didn't know his son was dead, she couldn't help being sorry for him and impetuously opened the door a bit farther. 'You'd better come in. I'll light the fire and put the kettle on for a cup of tea.'

He followed her inside. 'Do not bother. I mean to leave as soon as you tell me about my son.'

'Sammy died a long time ago, Mr Gunn,' she said, quietly. 'I thought they would have told you.'

'I was notified by the police when he was committed to Ladysbridge but I had no communication from the institution itself, not at that time nor at any later date.' A sly smile stole over his face. 'Nevertheless, I did know that he was dead. Your young man told me, and although he swore that he did not know where you were, I guessed that you must have come back to Cullen.'

A muscle jumped in his cheek as he stared over the table at the unlit fire – set with sticks she had gathered from the shore some days before and had stacked in the yard to dry – then he said, 'I did not come to ask about Sammy.'

She could feel the hairs on the back of her neck standing up in fear, his eyes were so glazed. 'Why did you come?'

'The reason escapes me for the moment. My mind is not clear about many things that have happened to me lately, so

345

if you let me talk until I can organize my thoughts, I shall probably remember what brought me here.'

She was about to ask him to sit down, but he carried on, 'I had a housekeeper, I can recall that ... but for some time now I have been looking after the house myself. My wife ...' He stopped, his nose wrinkling and his eyes turning up to the ceiling. 'I cannot seem to .. . not Marguerite ... another woman ... Betty!' He focused on Katie again. 'Betty has been running the shop for me.' He ran his long fingers through his greying hair. 'There was a man ... he wanted to take her away from me ... I could not let him get away with that, so I ... I ...' He broke off again, shaking his head in agitation.

It passed through Katie's mind that Sammy had inherited his mental instability from his father, for Mr Gunn's brain had obviously snapped, and she felt it would be better not to interrupt his train of thought, confused though it was, so she waited for him to continue.

Frowning deeply, he said, as if he were outraged by it, 'Blood was dripping from the knife on to my trousers.'

Her own blood running cold at this, Katie steadied herself against the table and wondered if she should make a dive for the door. Unfortunately, he was nearer to it than she was, and he might ...

'He was dead. Yes, I remember that clearly. Henry Ferguson was dead ... and no one will ever find his body.' He smiled at her unexpectedly, a smile which sent shivers of ice shooting down her spine. 'I do not know if you are aware that Sammy used to hide in a tree?'

'I knew he'd a secret place,' she began, then decided it would be safer to deny any knowledge of its whereabouts. 'He never showed me where it was.'

'Good. Was it not strange that my half-witted son provided me with the means of disposing of my wife's lover?' He did not wait for her to reply and went on, 'Betty helped me to hide his body, you know.'

'Is your wife . . . still alive?' Katie had to find out – he was capable of anything in his present state.

His eyes clouded again. 'Marguerite is dead.'

'No, I meant your second wife.'

'Betty? I cannot remember . . . there is a long blank. She was not in bed with me when I woke up, that is all I can tell you, and I do not know where she is. Perhaps she went off with that Henry fellow, after all.'

Katie had just time to think that his wife could not have gone off with the other man if he were dead, and she could not have escaped, either – otherwise she would have gone to the police and he would have been arrested – when he looked at her accusingly. 'Why did you let Sammy make love to you and refuse me? I never understood.'

She felt as though she were being entangled in a net from which there was no escape. 'I didn't. I was never anything more than a friend to him.'

'You took him into your bed.'

'I was comforting him . . . he was scared of the thunder.'

'Comforting?' The word came out with a horribly sarcastic smirk. 'That is a peculiar way to describe what you did, but perhaps you are right, it probably did comfort him. Yet you would not comfort me when I came to you the next night.'

Conscious that she was on thorny ground, and that he was ready to misconstrue anything she said, Katie murmured, 'I was scared of you.'

'Scared? Of me?'

'I thought . . . I thought you were going to . . . kill me.'

He looked at her for a moment letting this new concept run through his mind. 'Why should you have thought that?'

Katie tried to think of an explanation and decided to tell the truth. 'I was only sixteen, remember, and I'd seen you hitting Sammy, and Mrs Gunn had bruises . . .' She broke off knowing that she had made a mistake, because his brows had shot down and he was glowering at her furiously. She waited fearfully, watching in astonishment as the anger in his eyes was slowly replaced by puzzlement.

'Betty was not at Fenty when you were there,' he said, at last, adding uncertainly, 'At least, I do not think so.'

Even knowing that she was dealing with a maniac, Katie was still startled when he said, angrily, 'You always put Sammy first, but you will be putting my wishes first from now on.'

Feeling desperate, Katie said, 'Doesn't your wife put your wishes first?'

'Marguerite does not care about my wishes!'

'Betty?' she ventured. 'You'd better go home, for she'll be wondering where you are.'

A sadness crossed his face. 'You are always so calm, but you are right, and I should go home to her.'

Believing that she had pacified him, Katie expected him to go, but he made a lunge at her, his fingers gripping both her arms so tightly that she could feel his nails through her blouse and cardigan. 'Betty knows what you did to me,' he whispered.

His feet were on either side of her, his legs locking hers together so that she couldn't move them. 'I am taking you captive, and I will keep you locked in the garret. Do not look at me like that, Katie. I promise you will like the treats I have planned for you.'

His lips drew back into a hideous grin, his hands moved up to her neck, his elbows kept her arms imprisoned, although she was powerless against him anyway, for his eyes held her hypnotized. She was beginning to feel her senses slipping away when he gave a peculiar grunt and fell to the floor.

The spell broken, Katie gazed down at him for only a second before her knees buckled and she knew no more.

Beth had waited until Dennis went to work before she set off in her car, and as she drove along the coast, she thought of the letter she had received that morning. She still hadn't got

348

over the shock. She gave a rueful sigh. She must be a masochist, wanting to have her heart ripped apart by hearing of her husband's infidelity when all along he had been swearing that she was the only woman in his life. Or was there a tiny grain of doubt in her mind? Did she hope, in spite of all evidence to the contrary, that Dennis was not a philanderer nor a blackmailer? But how had he come in contact with Katie Buchan? God, she had almost forgotten! Katie was the name of the girl Dennis had lodged with – slept with – at one time. Was this the same girl? He had probably come from Katie's bed to hers, and she, a conceited fool for all her mature years, had believed that he loved her for herself, not for her money. Beth felt a sudden spurt of anger – not at Dennis nor at Katie Buchan, only at herself for being so gullible.

When she arrived in Cullen, Beth's stomach began to churn. She had only been in the place three times before, and none of the occasions had been happy. This fourth visit also had every indication of being an ordeal, but she had better go through with it. She drove resolutely under the arch and carried on into Seatown, then, leaving the car on the main road, she walked through the huddle of familiar fisher-type houses until she came to the right one, Heart hammering, she hesitated outside. Was she a fool to stir things up? Maybe she should wait and have it out with Dennis when he came home at night ... but she was may as well speak to the girl now she was here.

Lifting her hand to knock, she noticed that the door was off the latch and only needed a feather-light touch of her finger to make it swing open. She was aghast at the tableau that met her eyes, but her reaction was swift. Grasping her handbag with both hands, she took three steps forward and brought it down with full force. She had intended only to stop the man from murdering the young woman, but instead of turning round angrily, he dropped like a stone, and a second later, the girl collapsed almost on top of him.

There was no sink to be seen, but noticing that the fire

wasn't lit, Beth lifted the cold kettle from the hob, tilted it to the girl's pale lips and forced a little water through her clenched teeth. Spluttering, she came round and looked up blankly. 'Who. . . ?'

'Never mind that,' Beth said, firmly. 'Tell me what was going on.'

Katie's broken explanations were almost incoherent, but Beth managed to pull one fact out. 'So he wasn't trying to strangle you?'

Katie rose unsteadily to her feet and sat down in one of the armchairs. 'He was going to take me home with him and lock me up and . . .'

Her violent shaking made Beth murmur, 'Tell me the rest when you've got over it. I'd better see to him now.'

Despite all her efforts, Angus did not come round, and she gazed at Katie helplessly. 'I think he's dead.'

'He can't be!' Katie gasped. 'I saw him lying like that once before, and I thought he was dead but he wasn't.'

Beth asked no questions about this. 'I'm nearly sure he's dead now, but I'd better get a doctor in case he's not.'

'Don't leave me here with him,' Katie pleaded, her eyes wide with terror.

'No, no, I'll take you with me.'

Half an hour later, Dr Fleming pronounced life extinct in the man he had been called to see, and as he fastened his bag, Beth said, 'I didn't mean to kill him. I only hit him with my handbag because . . .'

Lifting the weapon she indicated and hefting it in his hands, the doctor gave a reassuring smile. 'This isn't heavy enough to do any damage.'

'How did he die, then?'

'It would appear to be a heart attack. Do you know if he had any history of heart trouble?'

Beth looked at Katie, who lifted her shoulders, and the doctor said, briskly, 'I'll have to notify the police since it's a sudden death. They'll come and ask questions, but you've nothing to worry about. They just have to make sure that there had been no funny business going on.'

Beth had to smother a hysterical laugh at the irony of it. There had definitely been some funny business, but perhaps not enough to make the police take action.

When the doctor left, Katie was still trembling from her ordeal, her face ashen, and Beth put a match to the paper under the sticks in the fireplace to boil the kettle.

'How did you know my name?' Katie whispered, suddenly. 'I don't know who you are.'

'Just call me Beth. Now, where do I get water, and cups . . . and sugar and milk?'

Katie told her, then sat silently until she was handed a cup of tea, which did help her a little, and by the time the police arrived she was able to answer all their questions lucidly, and to explain why the dead man had been there. The sergeant – Johnny Martin promoted from constable – already knew of her connection with the Gunns, but other details had to be filled in before he was satisfied that Angus had not been in his right mind at the time of his death. At last, he said, 'Well, Katie, he'll never bother you again.'

He turned away to talk to Beth, but Katie couldn't stop thinking about what had happened, the scene replaying over and over in her head, the way he had spoken in disjointed phrases, and Martin was on his way out when she said, with a deep shudder, 'He said he'd killed somebody.'

The sergeant frowned. 'Was that the truth, do you think? Or would you say he was that mad he could have imagined it?'

'He *was* mad, but I think it was the truth.'

From being a routine, if particularly unusual, inquiry into a sudden death, it had developed into an investigation of murder, the first ever for Sergeant Martin. Without further ado, the two women were driven to the police station where he subjected Katie to such a barrage of questions that she hardly knew what she was being asked or what she was answering. After some time, he ran out of ideas, and while he considered what to do now, she had peace to think.

'He said his wife helped him to ... bury the body,' she quavered in a few moments, having only just recalled it, 'but his mind had gone blank after that so he didn't know where she was. Maybe he killed her, and all.'

Martin pounced on this new information. 'Did he tell you where he'd put the body?'

'In the woods ... at the ... Howe of Fenty.'

'He didn't say where in the woods?'

'Sammy's special place.' Katie forestalled his next question. 'I know where it is, he took me to it once.'

With a look of grim satisfaction, the sergeant got to his feet. 'I'd better phone the Huntly police and tell them to meet us at the Gunns' house in ... three-quarters of an hour. You'll have to show us where to find the ...'

'You're not making her go right now?' Beth asked, her body rigid with indignation. 'Can't you see she's had enough for one day? Leave it till tomorrow – she'll be better able to cope with things after a night's rest.'

'I can't leave it. We're not sure Mr Gunn did kill his wife, though from what Katie said, he might have attempted it and she could be lying somewhere badly injured. We have to find her as soon as possible.'

Understanding now the reason for his urgency, Beth said, 'Can I come with you? Katie would likely be glad to have another woman there.'

Receiving his permission, she linked arms with Katie and they followed Martin out to the police van.

Chapter Thirty-one

As they walked into the wood, Katie was shaking so much, and her breathing was so juddery, that Beth gave her arm a firm squeeze. 'Don't let go now, it'll all be over soon.'

'It's a long time since Sammy showed me his secret place,' Katie whimpered. 'Maybe I won't be able to find it.'

'You'll have to keep trying.'

Katie *was* trying, very hard, but she kept seeing Sammy popping out, beckoning to her with his old shy smile, and each step was more of an effort for her than the last. It was still early afternoon, but the density of the trees made the place dark and gloomy, and the police torches cast eerie shadows that terrified her. Not only that, she was beginning to wonder if she was going in the right direction.

'Are we anywhere near yet?' asked Sergeant Martin. 'We've come a good bit in.'

'It *was* a good bit in,' she muttered. 'I'm looking for something to remind me, but I can't see . . .'

She plodded forward, but the knowledge that everyone was depending on her made her even more nervous, until she felt certain that she was in the wrong area, and was about to say so when one of the wavering beams illuminated, for a split second, a familiar gnarled shape. 'Wait,' she cried. 'Will somebody shine a torch over there again?'

Following her hesitant instructions, all torches were soon focussed on the chestnut tree surrounded by thick clumps of holly. 'That's it,' she whispered, gripping Beth's hand so tightly that the woman winced in spite of herself.

Johnny Martin looked at her with his lips puckered, then said, 'You're sure, Katie?'

'Yes, that's it. There's a hole between the roots of that tree. That's where Sammy used to go.'

Although she was afraid of what they would find, her eyes remained glued to the policemen thrusting their way through the undergrowth, hacking away obstructing branches, until one of them shouted, 'There's something here!'

'I didn't really believe him when he said he'd killed a man,' she sobbed, turning her face away as Henry Ferguson's twisted body was taken out of its resting place. 'I thought he made it up to scare me.'

'You said you believed him,' Sergeant Martin said, quite sharply, but a stray beam of light playing over her swollen eyes and pinched cheeks made him relent. 'It's a good thing you did, though, or we'd never have started looking. Well, lads, that's one, but there's still Mrs Gunn to find.'

After the men from Huntly had been detailed to search the area surrounding the chestnut tree, and to keep widening the circle if necessary, Katie and Beth were taken to the Gunns' house, where Martin instructed Murdoch, his young constable, to make a pot of tea in the kitchen. 'I'll go and take a look through the other rooms,' he added.

It wasn't long before he returned. 'There's no sign of the woman downstairs, or in the two bedrooms on the first floor, but what's up that second flight of stairs?'

'Just garrets,' Katie whispered, her hands covering her mouth for a moment. 'That's where he said he was going to lock me up.'

The sergeant looked at Murdoch. 'You'd better come with me, Tim. God knows what we'll find up there.'

What they found was a semi-conscious naked woman tied to the bed, her body a mass of angry blood-red welts. 'Christ!' Martin exclaimed, his trained eye taking in the whip and heavy sticks lying on the floor. 'What a bloody monster, and it's a good thing for him he's dead, or I'd have choked the life out of him myself.'

Gulping in air to stop him being sick, Tim Murdoch said, 'Will I go down and phone for an ambulance?'

'Aye, if there's a phone, and I'll come down with you.'

Betty having had the telephone installed after Angus had the heart attack, the constable was able to make the call while the sergeant went into the kitchen. 'We've found her,' he announced, grimly, 'and she's still alive.'

'That's a relief,' Beth breathed, releasing her grip on Katie's wrists.

'I think you two ladies should go up to her, for she's in a pretty bad way. Oh, and take a knife or something, you'll have to cut her free.'

They took a pair of scissors, and even though they thought they were prepared for anything, Betty cried, 'Oh, my God!' when she saw Mrs Gunn, and Katie had to hold on to the jamb of the door.

'Get a blanket to put round her,' Beth ordered, 'and I'll cut the ropes.' She went over to the bed as Katie went out. 'You're all right now, Mrs Gunn,' she soothed. 'You'll soon be free. Don't say anything till you feel up to it.'

Luckily, the scissors had recently been sharpened, and the bonds were soon cut, but the woman seemed unable to speak and it was not until Katie came back that she whispered, with an obvious effort, 'Angus?'

'He's dead,' Beth assured her, laying the blanket gently over the lacerated flesh. 'Is that any better, Mrs Gunn. You were as cold as ice.'

'He killed Henry.'

'Yes, the police found the body.' Beth made sure that the woman was suitably covered from neck to toes.

'How did they . . . know where to . . . ?'

'He told Katie where it was.'

Betty shifted her tortured eyes to the young woman. 'So you're Katie? He found you again?' Her voice strengthened. 'He was raving mad at the end. Stark, staring, raving mad.'

Katie nodded. 'I know that, and from what he said, I think

he was going to take me here and whip me, and all. I could see he still had the mark where I stabbed him.'

'I think he'd forgotten about you. He's been going queer for a long time, and it came to a head last night when . . .' Her eyes filling with tears, she told them, in spurts with long pauses in between, what had led up to Henry Ferguson's murder, and then went on, her voice breathy and high, 'He made me help him to carry . . . the body . . . and I was sure he would kill me, too, and put me in beside Henry . . . but . . .'

'It's all right,' Beth soothed. 'Don't speak about it.'

But Betty clearly had to tell somebody. 'Once he collected the . . . whip and things . . . he took me up here and stripped me, and tied me to the bed . . . and when he lifted the whip, he held it over me for a long time . . . and then he yelled, "This is for being such a cold bitch to me, Marguerite!" Then he took it down, over and over . . .' She stopped, shuddering.

'We've heard enough,' Beth told her. 'Just rest now.'

'I can't understand it,' Katie gulped, flopping down on the chair at the side of the bed. 'He knew his first wife was dead. And if he'd forgotten about me, why did he come to Cullen?'

Beth snorted. 'You can't fathom what goes on in a deranged man's brain, but he's dead now and you should both put him out of your heads altogether.'

Betty looked at her doubtfully. 'Are you sure he's dead?'

'Oh, there's no doubt about that! The doctor said it was a heart attack, and asked if he'd a history of heart trouble, but Katie couldn't tell him.'

'Yes, he's had several heart attacks – one quite bad, when I thought he was a goner.'

The arrival of the ambulance stopped the discussion, and Betty was laid on a stretcher and carried out, protesting that she would rather they shifted her to her own bed.

'She was lucky he didn't kill her,' Beth observed, when the vehicle drew away, 'but it'll be a while before all the cuts heal up. There's one good thing, though, she'll get the house and all his money . . .'

'And the shop,' Katie said, thoughtfully, 'but she's paid an awful price for them.'

The commotion over, the police van took the two women back to Katie's house, and even though the body had been removed, she burst into tears of hysteria. Beth let her sob for some time, then said gently, 'I'd better stay with you tonight.'

'Oh, would you?' Katie regarded her gratefully. 'There's only my bed made up, but it won't take me long to make up the one in the other room.'

'Don't bother, I can sleep with you, but I'd better tell you first . . . I'm Beth McKay.'

She had expected a violent reaction, but Katie's eyes remained dull. She was obviously still too deeply shocked by what had happened to make any connection. 'Dennis's wife,' Beth explained, softly.

'Dennis's wife?' Katie regarded her blankly.

'We'll forget about that just now. Do you still want my company, or would you rather I left?'

'Don't go!' There was panic in Katie's voice. 'I'm scared to be on my own.'

Standing up, Beth pulled her to her feet. 'Come on, then. It's time we got our heads down.'

Before she fell asleep, it crossed Beth's mind that she was sharing a bed with her husband's ex-lover, but at least Katie herself had not realized that. She was in no fit state to discuss Dennis or anything else, she'd had more than enough for one day.

His guilty conscience having made him hurry home as soon as the restaurant closed, Dennis was quite put out that Beth's car was gone, and as time passed with no sign of her, his annoyance changed to fear for her, quickly followed by fear for himself. She had said nothing important came with the morning post, and he had believed Katie hadn't carried out her threat, but her letter might have come by the second delivery. Had Beth gone to tell her man of business to cut him out of her will? She always stayed overnight when she went to Glasgow ... but he didn't even know if he was in her will. He had assumed that as her husband he would inherit everything, but if she had learned what he'd done, he might not be her husband for much longer.

This was too awful to contemplate, and he turned his mind to Beth herself. It was after one in the morning, so where the devil could she be? Remembering that she always went to Glasgow by train, he felt some degree of relief. She hadn't gone to see her solicitor, thank God, but she should have left word to let him know where she had gone. Maybe she'd had an accident? For all he knew, he could now be the owner of all her worldly goods.

He savoured this lovely thought for some time, then common sense prevailed. If she had been in an accident, the police would have come and told him. This led to a more disturbing thought. Any normal husband would have reported his wife's unexplained absence, but he wasn't any normal husband – he was a blackmailer and a thief, and the last thing he wanted was bobbies sniffing around.

Then it crossed his mind that there was quite a bit of cash in the safe at Le Denis. He could help himself to the lot and scarper. He would have enough to get him anywhere in Europe, maybe even farther, and there were hundreds of rich widows in the world just waiting to be fleeced. He could assume a new identity, and begin a new life.

For some time, he pictured himself surrounded by admiring females, then his castle-in-the-air disintegrated abruptly. Beth would never let him get away with it, and he'd be as well going to bed and waiting for further developments.

Emerging from the deep sleep of exhaustion and finding that she was not alone in bed, Katie thought for one delicious moment that George had come back, then the events of the previous day bulldozed into her consciousness. Her elation vanished as she remembered that her bedfellow was Beth, who had seen her through the whole horrific business.

The woman at her side stirring, Katie said, shyly, 'I'll get up and light the fire to make some tea.'

Beth rolled over and smiled. 'That's a good idea. I don't know about you, but I'm famished.'

There was a moment's silence, then Katie murmured, 'I'm sorry, but there's nothing in the house. You see . . .' She tailed off, her cheeks reddening with embarrassment.

Guessing, correctly, that she had no money, Beth smiled, 'It's all right, I'll dress and go and buy something.'

Neither of them having had anything to eat for nearly twenty-four hours, they made short work of the bacon and eggs Beth brought back, and demolished six slices of toast between them, then she leaned back with a satisfied sigh. 'The time has come, the walrus said . . .'

'I haven't thanked you for all you did,' Katie murmured. 'I'd never have survived yesterday if you hadn't been here.'

'All part of the service,' Beth laughed.

Katie looked suddenly puzzled. 'Beth, did I dream it, or did you really tell me last night you were Dennis's wife?'

'I did and I am. I got your letter and I came here to find out exactly what my dear husband had been up to . . . but things took it out of my head.'

'Yes, things took everything out of my head, and all. I'm sorry if my letter upset you, but I was mad at Dennis . . .'

'It didn't upset me. It just proved he's the stinker I suspected he was, but I . . . well, I loved him. Not any longer, though! You said he'd been blackmailing you for months, so what finally drove you to write? Or would it help if you started from when and how you met him? I'm a good listener.'

Katie began even further back, at the time she went to the Howe of Fenty, to explain where Mr Gunn fitted in, and why she had eventually ended up in Peterhead. There was no bitterness as she described how Dennis had treated her, but her eyes darkened when she came to what had finally made her crack. 'I felt awful when I discovered Sammy had died, and I often wondered why I hadn't been told, so you can understand why I saw red when Dennis said he had destroyed the letter the superintendent sent me. He actually sneered about it, and the only way I could get back at him was to write to his wife. I didn't stop to think how you would feel.'

'I'm glad you wrote, it helped me to make up my mind. He's an out-and-out waster, and I'm going to divorce him.'

Katie heaved a deep sigh. 'George wants me to divorce him, and all. He's living with a girl in Buckie, so I do have grounds, but I don't want a scandal.'

'But the scandal won't be about you, it's not your fault. Be sensible, Katie. Why should you keep yourself tied to a man who doesn't want you?'

'You think I should go ahead, then?'

'Yes, I do. Cut yourself completely off from the past and learn to live freely again.' Beth stopped, pursed her mouth for a moment, then said, 'I'm in no hurry home, not to that twister, so do you feel like taking a walk? The fresh air would do us both good, then I'll treat you to lunch in the Seafield Arms.'

There was an underlying motive behind this proposal. Beth still had something to find out, and she needed time to work out the delicate questions she would need to ask.

Chapter Thirty-two

❖

When Katie came in from the coalshed, Beth noticed that the scuttle was less than half full – mostly just dross – and she made a mental note to do something about it . . . after she had cleared up the other matter.

'I really enjoyed that,' Katie smiled. 'I've never had a meal in a hotel before, though I served plenty in my time.'

Beth's laugh was a little edgy, because she knew she could procrastinate no longer; it had been niggling at her, eating at her very core, ever since she opened Katie's letter. 'I don't suppose you know who lived in this house before you, do you?' She tried to sound nonchalant, though her nerve ends were raw with apprehension, and she wasn't sure that she wanted to know, after all.

The question was so unexpected that Katie looked at her in amazement. 'I've no idea who was here before us.'

'Oh, well, it doesn't matter.'

Katie wouldn't let it rest. 'Why did you ask that?'

'I said it doesn't matter,' Beth said, her disappointment making her tetchy. 'I thought this was where . . . somebody I knew used to live, but maybe it's not the right house.' It was the same house, she was sure of that, but she added, 'I must have made a mistake. It was a long time ago.'

'In that case, I can't help you. If my Grandma had still been alive, she'd have been able to tell you where to go. She knew everybody in Seatown, for she came to this house when she married Granda.'

The blood drained from Beth's face, and she could feel the pulsing of her heartbeats in her ears and throat. She had not expected this, never had the slightest suspicion. 'What was their name?' she whispered.

'Mair. Mary Ann and William John Mair.'

'Ah!' It came out in a long breath as Beth struggled to come to terms with what this information meant.

Wondering why she looked utterly thunderstruck, Katie said, 'Did you know my Granda and Grandma?'

'Yes, I knew them.'

She had closed her eyes, and her voice was so strange that Katie waited in suspense for her to speak again.

'Katie, would you mind telling me when you were born?'

Mystified as to where these questions were leading, Katie replied, 'The fourth of June, nineteen hundred and seven.'

Beth took a handkerchief from her sleeve to wipe her eyes, then said, unsteadily, 'I never dreamt . . . when I read your letter . . . the name Katie didn't mean anything to me except the girl Dennis had . . .' She stopped and swallowed. 'I had you christened June, you see, after your birth month.'

'*You* had me christened?' Katie's mouth dropped open in astonishment. 'You're my mother?' Her initial joy changed to resentment that this woman – who, for most of her life, she believed had died giving her birth – had stayed away for so long after abandoning her. 'Grandma thought June was too fancy,' she said, stiffly, 'and she called me Katie, after her own grandmother.'

Aware that Katie's emotions were acutely fragile, Beth blew her nose. 'I'd better tell you everything, so you can understand why I did what I did.'

Katie listened with an expression of resignation as she learned that Lizzie Baxter, as Beth had been then, had met the young William John Mair in Portknockie when he had been visiting one of his shipmates. 'It was love at first sight,' Beth went on, 'for me, anyway, and after we'd kept company for a good few weeks, William John took me to Cullen to meet his folks. His father made me very welcome, but it was like his mother couldn't bear the sight of me, I don't know why.'

'I know,' Katie said, quietly. 'You're the daughter of the man that jilted her when she was young. It was in the letter she left, and she said she never forgave him.'

'So that's it!' Beth cried. 'I wish I'd known at the time, I wouldn't have felt so hurt.' Wondering if the brutal truth would be too much for Katie, if she should water it down, she decided against it. 'Your father always wanted something better than he had, and when somebody told him there were fortunes to be made in America, he was determined to go over there and get rich. I knew he resented you from the minute you were born – he was jealous of the love I gave you – but I couldn't believe it when he said you were the only thing holding him back. I thought at first it was an excuse for him not going, that he'd got cold feet, but he came home one night, half drunk . . .'

Her abrupt stop made Katie say, 'Go on. What happened?'

'He said we were leaving Portknockie in the morning to get the boat from Greenock, and I'd have to leave the bairn with his mother, and when I told him I'd never do that, he said he would smother you. Well, I pleaded and pleaded with him for ages, but it ended up with him saying he would go by himself if I hadn't got rid of you by the time he came back, and then he went out. I was nearly demented, for I was very young, not long seventeen, and I loved him in spite of the other girls he took up with, in spite of knowing he was capable of killing his child to get his own way. And so . . . there was only one thing I could do. Oh, Katie, you can't imagine the agony it was, but I bundled you into a basket and pinned a note to your shawl . . .'

'I know, I found it among Grandma's things.'

'It was the middle of the night, and his mother had been so nasty to me I just left you on the doorstep.' There was another silence as Beth recalled the heartbreak of her walk along the coast road on that July night nearly twenty-five years before.

In a strained voice, Katie said, 'Why did you come back from America? And what happened to . . . my father.'

Beth sighed deeply. 'He caught a fever just weeks after we went to Detroit, and I nursed him till he died. I was left penniless, so I took a job in Morton's factory, and . . . well, to cut a long story short, I married the boss three months later. I didn't love Tom at first, but he was a good man and I had twelve very happy years with him before he was killed in an accident.'

'I'm glad you were happy.' Katie pointedly stressed the word 'you'.

Caught up in her memories, Beth did not recognize the sarcasm. 'I was a widow again, but not destitute this time. The factory had been converted into an automobile plant, and I'd more money than I knew what to do with. All the fortune hunters of the day swarmed round me, and I got so sick of it I rented out Tom's house and booked a passage to Scotland. I came straight to Cullen after I landed.'

'But you didn't think of coming to see me?' It was clearly an accusation.

'Katie, I was aching to see you, to know how you'd grown up. I wanted to take you away with me, but I wasn't sure if you'd want to come. You'd have been thirteen, old enough to be angry at me for deserting you.'

'I didn't know you deserted me, for my Grandma told me you died when I was born.'

'So that was how she explained it?' Beth shook her head at Mary Ann's cruel invention. 'I was terrified of her, Katie, after the way she treated me the only time I met her, and even though I was a lot older when I came back, my stomach was in knots when I was walking down from the station. Then I spotted her coming out of the butcher's, and I couldn't face being humiliated in the street, so I turned and took the next train out. The only way I could bear to leave you again was telling myself your grandmother would be looking after you properly.'

Katie sighed. 'I suppose she did look after me properly . . . but I always thought she didn't even like me, till I found her letter telling me everything.'

'If I'd known you weren't happy, I'd have confronted her that day, but . . . oh, what's the good of crying over spilt milk? Anyway, I started looking for somewhere to settle, and I chose Peterhead because I fell in love with Dennis.' Beth gave a wry smile. 'I couldn't have done much worse, could I? He really took me in.'

'Me, too,' Katie said. Knowing that her mother had made an effort of some kind to come and see her, she felt slightly warmer towards her.

'After a while, though,' Beth continued, 'I could see the kind of man he was, but I let things drift because I still loved him.' She pulled a face and added, 'I'd like to wring his blasted neck now.'

The ghost of a smile touched Katie's lips, and Beth went on, 'I was knocked sideways when I got a letter from the very house where I'd left my baby. I thought a family called Buchan had moved in when the Mairs died, and I really came to find out if any of them knew what had happened to my daughter. I'd no idea Katie Buchan was really June Mair.'

'I've never been June,' Katie burst out, defiantly, 'and I don't feel like a June, so I'm going to keep on being Katie, whatever you think.'

Beth realized that the barrier Katie had erected between them would take a long time to breach. 'I don't mind. I stopped being Lizzie when Tom called me Beth, and I thought it sounded nicer. Katie's a lovely name, and I couldn't wish for my daughter to have turned out any better.'

Katie looked at her doubtfully. 'I still can't think of you as my mother.'

A great sadness swept over Beth, and she wondered if the barrier was too great to be broken, after all. 'That's not surprising, since I was only a mother to you for the first month of your life.'

Hearing the pain behind the words, Katie said, 'I'm sorry. I know it wasn't really your fault, but I can't . . .'

Beth was unable to keep back the tears which spilled out, and the sight of them coursing down her cheeks made Katie move over to kneel beside her. As she hesitated, wondering if she should say something or just leave her to cry, Beth turned with a hoarse sob and held out her arms. In the next instant, they were holding each other tightly, Katie's eyes overflowing, too, and for the very first time, she knew the comfort of a mother's arms.

Beth was weeping for the infant she had abandoned, for the years of childish development and growth she had missed, and with joy at having found her daughter again. Katie, on the other hand, was weeping for the grandfather who had loved her, for the simple-minded youth who had set himself up as her protector, for the grandmother who had hidden her love until it was too late. Then, and only then, did she spare a few tears for the woman who had borne her, the woman who had been forced to leave someone else to bring her up.

'Oh, Katie,' Beth said at last, with a catch in her voice, 'I knew you'd come round.'

Drawing in her breath, Katie pulled away, scrubbing her eyes with the cuff of her sleeve. 'I don't know . . . give me more time, Beth. It's been an awful shock, coming on top of . . . everything else. Once I get over that, maybe I'll . . .'

'Yes, I guess I'm rushing you. I should let things take their own course.' Beth took out her handkerchief to dry her tears. 'Now, I think we need a cup of tea.'

After the refreshment, Beth got to her feet and picked up her handbag. 'Katie, don't go flying up in the air at me, but I know you're short of money, so . . .'

Katie's face turned scarlet. 'I won't take anything!'

'You never had anything from me in all those years, and

I'll be cut to the quick if you refuse. I've got plenty. I took quite a lot out of the bank the other day, and I never leave anything in the house in case Dennis finds it.' She took out a roll of notes, peeled off some and laid them down on the table. 'I can't have my new-found daughter starving herself to death. Pocket your pride, Katie, it'll get you nowhere. Buy coal and whatever else you need.'

At the door, she turned with a grin. 'Dennis is in for the shock of his life tonight. Doesn't that make you feel good?' She left without waiting for a reply.

Even the thought of Dennis reaping a fitting harvest from all his treachery didn't matter to Katie at that moment, and sitting down in the armchair which had once been her beloved grandfather's – where he had so often taken her on his knee and made her feel the most important person in the world – she drew her legs up under her and curled into a tight ball. If Beth had claimed her when she was thirteen, she thought miserably, she would have been saved all the anguish she had gone through in later years. That would always rankle in her mind, keep her from being a loving daughter. She gave a low groan. 'Oh, Granda, I'd give anything to have you here now to tell me what I should do about Beth.'

All day, Dennis had the feeling that the sword of Damocles was about to fall on him. It grew so strong that he wondered if he should go home to pack and make himself scarce before his wife turned up, then he laughed at himself for worrying. Even if Katie had written and Beth had gone to see her, he would deny everything, and she loved him so much she would believe him. As the old saying went, 'There's none so blind as them that don't want to see.' Or something like that.

When his staff left, he transferred all the money in the cash register to the safe, for it wouldn't do to be found helping himself at a time like this. Putting on his trilby, he locked up and set off for Queen Street. His step faltered when he saw the car outside the door, then he strode inside, bracing himself for the attack, not the defence.

'Where the hell have you been?' he demanded, angrily.

Beth raised her eyebrows. 'Doing a good turn to a friend.'

This took the wind out of his sails. He had meant to make the accusations and to soothe Beth's ruffled feathers if she threw any at him, but Katie couldn't have written, and he didn't want to aggravate his wife if it wasn't necessary. 'What friend?' he asked, less aggressively.

Beth smiled mysteriously. 'More than a friend, really.'

'Another man?' This had never crossed his mind. 'So you've been whoring around when I was slaving my guts out? You're not getting away with that.'

'No?'

He was rattled by the peculiar way she was looking at him. 'Who is he?'

'It wasn't a he, it was my daughter.'

'Daughter?' He sat down heavily on the sofa. 'You never told me you'd a daughter.'

'There's a lot of things you didn't tell me.'

'Such as?' He felt better now. If she'd been seeing her daughter, she hadn't been to Cullen. 'Get on with it,' he snarled, 'you've a lot of explaining to do.'

Beth glared back at him with deep contempt. 'I don't have to explain anything to you, Dennis, but I will, and it might surprise you to know it's through you I found Katie again.'

'Katie?' he gasped. 'Katie's your daughter?'

He listened with his mouth agape while she told him of her earlier life, but when she accused him outright of marrying her for her money, he hastened to sidetrack her. 'You said you'd done a friend a good turn,' he began, sarcastically, 'then you said it was Katie. What did you do for her?'

She described the disastrous consequences of Angus Gunn's visit, and ended, caustically, 'He's another slimy creep who got what he deserved.'

'An-another c-creep?' Dennis stammered.

Beth stood up. 'I've packed all your belongings and I want you out of my house right now.'

He stared at her incredulously. 'You surely didn't believe what Katie said about me . . . ?' Her cold eyes told him that it was useless, and his tone changed. 'Where can I go at this time of night?'

'I'm sure there's dozens of women falling over themselves to get you in their beds.'

'You can't do this to me, Beth. You said you weren't going to pay off any more of my gambling debts, and I asked Katie for some cash. I swear that's the only reason I went to her. It's you I love.'

'Love? The only person you've ever loved, Dennis McKay, is yourself. Now hand over all the keys and get out. I packed all your things into a suitcase and left it in the hall, so don't forget to take it with you.'

'Beth, please?'

'I'm selling up and divorcing you. I've put one hundred pounds in the case to keep you till you find another job – and before you get your hopes up, you won't get a penny more from me.'

He sprang to his feet and grabbed her hands. 'You can't throw me out. You said you loved me.'

Furious, she struggled free. 'I loved the man I kidded myself you were, but I've seen the light. You're a liar, a cheat, a thief and a blackmailer – a big round O, that's what you are, and you'll never amount to anything. You should be behind bars, and you'd better go before I change my mind and hand you over to the police. Oh, and you may as well know, I'm going back to America once I've settled all my affairs, and I'm going to ask Katie to go with me.'

'You're a bit late with the mother-hen act,' he sneered.

He jumped back as the palm of her hand connected with his cheek. 'Give me the keys,' she hissed, 'and get out.'

He threw his key-ring on the floor, but couldn't help a parting shot as he went to the door. 'Did your precious daughter tell you she'd to get rid of Sammy Gunn's baby?'

The vase missed him by a fraction of an inch, and Beth's voice followed him into the hall. 'Yes, she did, and that was all your fault, too, you . . . you . . .'

Not waiting until she found an appropriate word, he lifted the suitcase and slammed the front door behind him.

Katie rose next morning feeling less confused than when she went to bed. At least she knew now that her father and mother had been married, which would be a slap in the face to Ina Green for casting aspersions on her legitimacy; she had seen George for the narrow-minded bigot he was . . . and Dennis would have got his come-uppance by now. Beth wouldn't have let him get round her this time.

She made herself ready to go out, her hand hovering over the notes on the table before she picked them up and put them in her purse. There would be no more scavenging on the beach for sticks nor living on bread and margarine, whatever happened . . . not for a while, at any rate.

After ordering coal and buying as many provisions as she could carry, she returned home and was laying her basket on her table when Beth arrived. 'You look much better today,' she smiled, 'and I'm glad to see you took my advice and did some shopping. I just wish you could have seen Dennis's face last night, though, when I told him you were my daughter. He looked as if he'd swallowed something that didn't agree with him – you know, green about the gills. He tried to bluff his way out of everything, and when I said I was divorcing him and told him to get out, he was nearly down on his knees begging me to let me stay.'

Katie couldn't help murmuring, 'Poor Dennis.'

'Poor Dennis, my foot! He deserved what he got, and I hope it teaches him a lesson.' Beth paused, then said, gently, 'I've something to say, Katie, but first I want to know how you feel about me now?'

'Well, I don't condemn you any more for leaving me. I did yesterday, but now I've had time to think, I know you didn't have any choice. It still feels funny being able to put a face to the mother I thought I would never see, but I do like you, and that's half the battle, isn't it?'

'It sure is!' Beth beamed. 'It's just a small step from liking to loving. Now to what I wanted to say. I've decided to sell up and go back to America, and I . . .'

Katie was aghast at this. 'You're not going to leave me again, are you?'

'I thought . . . I want you to come with me.'

'To America? Oh, I couldn't!'

'What is there to keep you here? A tumble-down old house, where you were never really happy?'

'That's true enough, but still . . .'

'By the time everything's settled, we'll likely both be free. You might find a rich husband over there, like I did.'

'I don't want . . .'

'You think you can't trust men again? I know, I've been through it . . . twice, but I did have one good man. You've been unlucky so far, Katie, but somewhere, maybe in Detroit, the right man's waiting for you. All that aside, we have to give it a try, just you and me, a mother and daughter getting to know each other, doing things for each other . . .'

Katie felt a surge of excitement. 'Yes, Beth, I'd like that.' Her happy smile faded. 'I'm sorry, but I can't help calling you Beth . . .'

'Beth, Mother, Hey You, I don't care what you call me, as long as we're together. So now that's settled, I'll have to see my solicitor and I'll ask him to start proceedings for divorce, and I'll get him to put the house and restaurant up for sale, as well. We can ask him to handle your divorce and sell your house, if you like, or would you rather have a solicitor nearer

Cullen? Whatever you decide, we've a lot of work ahead of us, before we cross the Atlantic to start our new life.'

'Oh, Beth,' Katie laughed, 'I've never met anybody like you before, and I think I'm beginning to love you already.'

'Good. It *will* work out, I've no doubt about it now.'

After Beth left, Katie was so happy that she wished she had a friend to tell about having a mother, a mother who could make lightning decisions, a mother who must surely be the most lovable woman in the world, then she remembered that she was not entirely friendless. Jumping up, she put on her coat and headed for the shore.